THE
HUNT

Faye Kellerman is the author of thirty-four novels, including twenty-six books in the bestselling mystery series featuring the husband-and-wife team of Peter Decker and Rina Lazarus. She has also penned two bestselling short novels with her husband, *New York Times* bestselling author Jonathan Kellerman and teamed up with her daughter Aliza to co-write a young adult novel, *Prism*. She lives with her husband in Los Angeles, California, and Santa Fe, New Mexico.

Also by Faye Kellerman

Peter Decker/Rina Lazarus series
The Lost Boys
Walking Shadows
Bone Box
The Theory of Death
Murder 101
Predator
Blood Games
Hangman
Blindman's Bluff
Cold Case
The Burnt House
Street Dreams
Stone Kiss
The Forgotten
Stalker
Jupiter's Bones
Serpent's Tooth
Prayers for the Dead
Justice
Sanctuary
Grievous Sin
False Prophet
Day of Atonement
Milk and Honey
Sacred and Profane
The Ritual Bath

Standalone books
Killing Season
Moon Music
The Garden of Eden and Other Criminal Delights: A Book of Short Stories
Straight into Darkness
The Quality of Mercy

With Jonathan Kellerman
Capital Crimes
Double Homicide

With Aliza Kellerman
Prism

FAYE KELLERMAN

THE
HUNT

HarperCollins*Publishers*

HarperCollins*Publishers* Ltd
1 London Bridge Street,
London SE1 9GF

www.harpercollins.co.uk

HarperCollins*Publishers*
1st Floor, Watermarque Building, Ringsend Road
Dublin 4, Ireland

This edition published by HarperCollins*Publishers* 2022
1

First published in the USA in 2022 by
William Morrow, an imprint of HarperCollins*Publishers*

Faye Kellerman asserts the moral right to
be identified as the author of this work

A catalogue record for this book is available from the British Library

ISBN: 978-0-00-832753-8

This novel is entirely a work of fiction.
The names, characters and incidents portrayed in it are
the work of the author's imagination. Any resemblance to
actual persons, living or dead, events or localities is
entirely coincidental.

Set in Stempel Garamond

Printed and Bound in the UK using 100% Renewable Electricity
at CPI Group (UK) Ltd

To Jonathan, who has continually supported me in every aspect of my life,
I love you and I thank you.

To my children and grandchildren,
I love you so much.

To all the people in the publishing industry who have helped
me throughout the years, including the Karpfinger Agency and
my longtime publisher, William Morrow, and the crew over
there. A special thanks to Carrie Feron, my editor supreme,
my occasional therapist, and my wonderful friend.

And finally, to all my fans who have supported my books and me,
I dedicate the final Peter Decker and Rina Lazarus novel
to you. I could not have done this without you.
Thank you, thank you, thank you.

PROLOGUE

I T TOOK ABOUT fifty phone calls, but the family finally decided on a place to eat dinner before Decker and Rina took off for Israel from Kennedy. Decker looked around the table at their truly blended family: Rina's two grown sons, Jacob and Sammy; his adult daughter, Cindy; their baby daughter, Hannah, who now had a baby of her own; and their foster son, Gabe. There were also three spouses, two fiancées, and five grandchildren. He and Rina had done well. Even if he died tomorrow, Decker would go out a winner.

As usual, the conversation turned lively, then loud. Adults shouting, children interrupting, along with the usual spillages and meltdowns. Right before the entrées arrived, the server came over with two big bottles of rosé champagne and flutes.

"Who ordered this?" Rina asked. "Not that I'm complaining."

"Group effort." Jacob stood up and gently tinkled the glass with a fork. "Now that we're all here, I propose a toast to the happy couple. May they find peace and solitude on this trip to the Holy Land, and may their construction plans go easily. *L'chaim.*"

"*L'chaim*," everyone echoed.

"One more thing." Jacob held out two envelopes to his stepfather. "For you two. A small gift for all your long sufferings with the clan."

"This better not be money," Rina said.

"It's not money." Cindy smiled. "Open it."

Decker complied and pulled out two business-class tickets to Israel, then showed them to Rina.

Rina said, "What did you guys do?"

"Go in peace and go in style," Sammy said.

"This must have cost a fortune."

"Not so bad between all of us. We just upgraded your original tickets."

"Unfortunately, we couldn't get seats together for the outbound at this late date," Hannah said, "but you're together for the return flight."

"Wow, thank you, children. It makes the trip even more exciting." Decker held up his champagne flute. "A toast to all of you."

Just then Gabe's phone rang. He looked at the screen. The number was blocked. No doubt it was his father. Chris often used burner phones, although he had a regular phone with both burner and hush features. But that was just Chris. Nothing with him was ever consistent.

"*L'chaim*," Gabe said. "I've got to take this." He stood up and walked out of the restaurant. The street noise wasn't much quieter, but at least his ears weren't ringing from little kids screaming. "Hey."

Breathing on the other end. Gabe almost hung up, except it wasn't perverted breathing. It was labored. "Hello?"

"You've gotta . . . get me."

A woman struggling to talk. Confusion and then the lightbulb. Gabe's heart started racing. "*Mom?*" No response. "Are you okay?"

"No."

"Are you hurt?"

"Yes." She was crying. "They took Sanjay . . . Juleen . . . They're gone. I'm . . . dying."

"Mom, where are you?"

"L.A."

"Where in Los Angeles?"

"Valley."

"Mom, call 911."

"*No!*"

"You have to—"

"*No!*"

"You have to call the police, Mom."

"They'll arrest me." A long pause. "You need to come get me."

"Mom, I'm three thousand miles away. If you're hurt, you need to go to a hospital. *Call 911.*" There was no response. "Mom, are you still there?" She didn't answer, but Gabe could hear her breathing. "Mom, I love you. Please call for help!"

"Hold on . . . Oh God, I think that's Juleen!"

"Mom?" But she had hung up. With shaking hands, he dialed her number, but it went straight to voice mail. "Why do you *do* this to me!"

He called again. And again. And again and again and again.

He texted her: *CALL ME!*

Decker had stepped outside, saw his foster son pacing. "Everything okay?"

"No," Gabe told him. "My mother just called me. From what I could gather, someone kidnapped my brother and maybe my sister. My mom's hurt."

"Where is she?"

"Los Angeles. The Valley, I think."

"Her old stomping ground. *My* old stomping ground. What's her number? I'll see if I can't get someone to send a uniform to look for her."

"She doesn't want the police involved, Peter. Besides, she called on a blocked number. My calls go straight to voice mail." Gabe paused. "She took her kids out of India. I suspect she had a court order not to leave the country with them. You know she's divorcing her husband. There's probably a custody dispute."

"She's a fugitive?"

"Possibly."

"Maybe her husband kidnapped them back."

"Possibly . . ." Gabe continued pacing. "Honestly, at this moment I'm less worried about the kids than I am about her. She sounded horrible."

"Gabe, let me call up my old station. I still know lots of people. Maybe they can ping a location off her phone."

"She said no police."

"If she's really hurt, do you think you should listen to her?"

"No, you're right. But I don't think that will get you anywhere, Peter. I think she turned off her phone."

"Then I'm out of ideas," Decker said. "You're three thousand miles away and probably can't get there until tomorrow . . . which may be too late."

Gabe's eyes turned moist. "I love her dearly. But my mom's a disaster! We know her current husband owes money to bad people, so it could be something to do with that. She sure can pick them. I do think that Devek is even worse than my father."

Decker raised his eyebrows. He held a finger up in the air. "Gabe, call your dad."

"What?"

"Call your dad. Nevada is in the same time zone, and he has a private jet. He can probably get there in a couple of hours. Plus, he knows the Valley as well as I do. That's where he and your mom met. And if she's running from bad people, he can protect her better than anyone. Call your dad."

"He's not going to help. He's been waiting years for her to crash and burn. I think that's what's kept him alive all this time. Revenge."

"At least try." No answer. Decker shrugged. "Do you have any better ideas?" Silence. "Do you want me to call him?"

"No, absolutely not!" Gabe shook his head. "Go back to dinner, Peter. I'm twenty-four. I can handle this."

"No shame in asking for help."

"I don't need help." *Even though he did.* "Please go back before everyone realizes there's a problem."

"Are you sure?"

"I am."

Gabe watched his foster dad go back into the restaurant. Then, with shaking hands, he tried to punch in the numbers he knew by heart, but he kept making mistakes. Finally, he looked it up in his contact list under *Dad.* His heart was banging out of his chest.

A lot of times, Chris turned his phone off. Even when it was on, he didn't bother to answer most of the time. Christopher Donatti was a very busy man. He didn't like phone calls. He *especially* didn't like phone calls from his son, who was always managing to interrupt some important business his father was doing.

His oft-repeated line: *You're losing me money. This better be good.*

The phone rang, which meant the current number was still active. A moment later, he heard the line kick in.

"*What!*"

Thank you, God. "Dad, you've got to help me. Mom called. She's in California. The Valley, I think, but I don't know. She's badly hurt but she won't call 911 or go to a hospital—"

"Hold on. Let me go somewhere private." A moment later Donatti was back on the line. "Your mother is on the West Coast?"

"Yes."

"Where are her kids?"

"She had them, but now they're gone. She's in the middle of a messy divorce. She might have taken them out of India without permission."

"Ah." A pause. "Someone took them back."

"I think so." Gabe was breathing hard. "Chris, I know she wouldn't let them go without a fight, and I think she got a bad one. She sounded in real trouble. She wants me to come and get her, but I'm in New York. Furthermore, she called me on a blocked number, so I can't call her back. I think her phone is off." Gabe paused, but his father didn't talk. "I'm hoping she'll call me back. As soon as she does, I'll get more details. But in the meantime, you're a lot closer to L.A. than I am. And you're good at finding people."

Another pause. His dad was waiting . . .

Gabe said, "Look, I know you parted on bad terms—"

"She had an affair, got knocked up by the motherfucker, had a bastard child while still married to me, and then dumped me unceremoniously. Yeah, I'd call that *bad terms*."

"I've had issues with her as well. I've forgiven her."

"That is certainly your prerogative."

"She's my *mother*, Chris!" Silence. "You know what it's like to lose a mother."

"I'm not moved. Try a different tactic."

"You loved her once."

There was a long pause. Gabe thought he might have hung up. But then Donatti said, "Who says I don't love her still?"

Gabe took in a deep breath and then let it out. This was a battle that he knew he was going to win. "Will you help her out? Yes or no?"

"Yes, I'll go." No hesitation. "I'm entertaining about a dozen people in my outer office right now. Give me a half hour to get rid of them, gas up the jet, and get a flight plan. If she calls you, get a phone number. And give her my number."

"As soon as I know something, I'll call you."

"And I'll tell you this, Gabe. She'd better want my help. I don't have a good track record with your mother. If I don't hear from her by the time I get to Los Angeles, I'm turning around, and she'll be your problem forever."

"Agreed. Let me give you Mom's number."

"I have it."

"It's going to voice mail."

"If she took the kids out without permission from the courts, she probably doesn't want to be tracked. I'll figure something out."

"Thank you, thank you, thank you—"

"Yeah, fine. Let me get going on this." Donatti cut the line and pocketed his cell, running his fingers through his shoulder-length white hair, letting his conflicting emotions battle it out, not knowing what to feel now that the moment was actually here.

For over a decade, he had been formulating his delicious slap of vengeance . . . a righteous justice in his mind. He had planted it, nursed it, fed it, watered it, sheltered it from the cold, and given it relief from the heat. He had watched it grow and blossom into something mean and unstoppable. It had consumed his thoughts. How he'd make her *pay* for what she had done. And now that his chance for retribution was so close—so, so very close—all he could feel was the rapid beating of his heart, pounding not with revenge but with excitement.

He really, really wanted her back!

The thought of sex with her even after all these years was making him pant like a dog. He had at least a thousand fantasies about it—some benign, some dark and cruel—all of them HD vivid in his brain. To see her face again . . . to feel her body. To hear her *voice*. It was her voice that had haunted him the most. Her voice that had kept him awake at nights and dreaming through the days. Sometimes she'd talk to him so clearly, he'd turn around only to find empty space.

After she left him for the third time over a decade ago, it had taken him years to recover. But he had finally, *finally* gotten his shit together. He had gotten off heroin, had weaned himself from cigarettes, and had significantly cut down on the booze. Now he exercised regularly. He ate a healthy diet. He had reformed while slaving away at his business—a multimillion-dollar playground for rich men of any sexual persuasion. He had spent years building his own little fiefdom. Lord of the manor, where no one dared to get in his way. He had tons of money, he had loads of sex, and he had *respect*. Most important, he had control over *everything* in his life.

Now that same *everything* was about to blow up in his face.

And even though he just knew it would end in disaster—like it had three times before—he also knew that he'd take the plunge into the deep end without a second thought, idiot that he was.

Fool me once, shame on you.

Fool me twice, shame on me.

Fool me three times, and someone's a moronic dumbass.

He flipped hair out of his eyes, then walked out of his inner office into the fray he was hosting, thinking:

Here we go again.

Here we fucking go again.

AT SIX FEET four—well, maybe six three and a half now, allowing for shrinkage—Decker had always dreaded flying, cramming his oversize body into seats unfit for someone as tall as he was. The flight to Israel was long, and each time after he arrived, it took him hours to unfold. This time maybe it would be different.

He beamed as he thought of his children, chipping in money to buy Rina and him business-class tickets. Such a lucky man. He slid into a chair with a footrest. He had a bigger pillow and a thicker blanket than usual. He had his own TV, with flight attendants offering him juice, water, or champagne before the takeoff.

He could get used to this.

Rina came over. She was seated three rows behind him. "Pretty luxurious."

"Unbelievable," Decker said. "Nice surprise."

"We did well," Rina told him. "Any word from Gabe?"

"I know he got hold of his father and that Chris agreed to help."

"Nice, if he doesn't kill Terry first," Rina said.

"It's been over ten years."

"Why do I feel Chris is the type of person to carry a grudge?"

Peter's phone buzzed.

Rina said, "Turn that off. We're on vacation."

Decker looked at the screen. "It's Tyler."

"It's eleven-thirty at night. He can't miss you that much."

"Yeah, this isn't good." Decker clicked in the call. "What's going on?"

His partner said, "Someone found a body earlier in the evening. In the woods about three miles from the diner where Bertram Lanz disappeared."

Decker's heart sank. He and the entire Greenbury police force had been looking for the disabled man for weeks. He had hoped that Lanz was safe with his parents in Germany. But maybe that wasn't the situation. The incompletion of his case was a weight on Decker's shoulders. He knew he shouldn't have taken time off without the solve. "Where are you now?"

"I just left the scene to call you. No bars up there. I'm going back as soon as I hang up."

"Do you need me to come back, McAdams?"

"Peter!" Rina said.

"No, no. We're fine, boss. Coroner should be here soon. Kevin cordoned off the area. I'll keep you posted. I just wanted to let you know."

The flight attendant started making announcements. Rina said, "If you're going to be intransigent, I'm going back to my seat."

Decker barely heard her. He stuck his finger in his ear. "You're sure that you're okay?"

"We're great, boss. Don't worry. Enjoy your time overseas."

Decker said, "Before you go, any thoughts about the body?"

"Rigor's come and gone, bloat has come and gone."

"Then the corpse is weeks old?"

"Possibly. There's decomposition."

Decker asked, "Insect activity?"

"Some in the orifices—nostrils, eyes, and mouth."

"Then part of the face was exposed to the air, so the flies could lay their eggs."

"Yeah, we found the body partially buried."

"Animal activity could have disturbed it."

"Nothing we can see," McAdams answered. "But that may change once the autopsy is done."

"Any idea if the corpse is male or female?"

"Probably female, from the size. The face is messed up, and we can't move anything else until the coroner comes."

"Is the body nude or is there clothing?"

"Some rotting clothing. Looks like jeans, plaid shirt, sneakers."

A flight attendant named Nurit came over. "Everything okay, sir?"

Decker looked up at her. "Yes, thank you."

Nurit swallowed. "The woman across the aisle overheard you talk about corpses. I think it's upsetting her."

"Oh, sorry."

"Sorry for what?" Tyler asked.

"No, not you." Decker smiled at the flight attendant. "I'm a police detective. I'll finish up the conversation." To McAdams: "I have to go."

"Don't worry, boss, I have it covered."

Decker hung up. Rina had rematerialized. She was standing over him. "You are *not* going back."

"No, I'm not going back," Decker said.

"I hope this won't ruin our vacation."

"When we land, I'll give you my laptop and phone. How's that for commitment?"

"I'll take you up on that," Rina said. More announcements. "I have to sit down." She kissed the top of Peter's head. "And remember to take your Ambien as soon as we're in the air. It'll help with jet lag. I'll see you in the Holy Land."

"A new adventure," Decker said.

"A new adventure." Rina mussed his hair and left.

Three hours later, Rina was sound asleep. Decker, on the other hand, was stretched out with his eyes wide open, with a ton of thoughts whirling around in his brain. He probably would have been sleeping if he had taken the pill, but he had chosen not to.

You can take the man out of the investigation, but you can't take the investigation out of the man.

He had promised Rina to unplug from work when they landed. She deserved that. But why toss and turn for hours when the solution to his insomnia was at hand? Quietly, he stood and took down his laptop from the overhead compartment. After booting up, he looked at his options for buying the plane's internet. He thought about the thirty-minute plan. Just a few quick questions and then he'd turn off the noise. But an unknown force led his fingers to choose the two-hour plan. He typed in Tyler's email address.

He wrote:

I'm signing off on all my electronics when we land.

But for now, I'm up and I can't sleep.

Tell me everything that's going on.

CHAPTER 1

THIS WAS HOW I remembered it, after gaining consciousness, lying on the floor, bloodied and battered.

I was sitting on the couch, going over my legal options for what was going to be a protracted and nasty divorce, trying to figure out how to make this happen with no money and working with a legal system over seven thousand miles away. My five-year-old son was sitting beside me, playing a video game. My eleven-year-old daughter was in her bedroom, door locked, doing whatever she did in the privacy of her own space. Juleen was hyper-adult, and one of the things I did when I rented this apartment was ensure she had her own space. It was a two-bedroom place and Sanjay slept in the smaller of the two rooms. Juleen had the master, and I slept in the living room on the couch.

I was so lost in thought that I didn't hear the footsteps outside the door. The building was exposed, and usually I heard people walking up and down the steps. Not this time. Had I been more alert, all this may not have happened.

It was only after the door flew open and I screamed "Run!" that everything kicked into high gear. Two Indian men: one immediately grabbed Sanjay, while the other said something about finding the girl. My son was kicking and screaming as I gripped his legs, pulling him toward me with my opponent pulling in the opposite direction: a mortal tug-of-war. The man had covered Sanjay's mouth, and I remembered telling my son to bite his hand as I scratched the intruder's arm and yanked Sanjay furiously. But the man was taller and bigger than I was and held on fast even with one hand over my son's mouth and nose. I kept at it until the second man returned, asking where the girl was.

When I didn't answer, he whacked me across the face—once to the right, once to the left, and another time to the right. Then he took my hair, wrapped it around his hand, and yanked so hard a clump came out. Sheer willpower was preventing me from letting go of my son's legs. Then he hit me again on the right side of my cheek, this time with a closed fist. My vision sparkled and danced as I began to reel. As I was going down, he kicked me in the head and then twice on my right side in the ribs. I felt the crack. For good measure, he gave two final kicks—one in the stomach and one in the back. Still, I was clinging on to my son's feet. It wasn't until the siren came into earshot that the men panicked, saying something about a neighbor hearing the noise and calling the police. One final twist and then a hard jerk that brought an electric wave of pain through both arms, and my baby was gone, leaving me empty except for his small polka-dot Vans still in my hand. I brought it up to my face, balled myself up into a fetal position, and then things went quiet, then dark.

When I awoke, I hadn't any idea of how long I'd been out. Only that things were silent and I was in excruciating pain. My right arm was dangling uselessly by my side, my jaw was throbbing, my head was ringing and pounding, and my face was on fire. I tried to stand, but as soon as I moved, my sides caved in and a new wave of pain and nausea coursed through my body. My nose felt clogged and runny at the same time, and as I wiped it with my left hand, I saw blood.

The siren that I had heard must have been from an ambulance or a police car passing by, because no one had come to save me. Since it was summer, it was still light outside, with the sun filtering in through the top of the curtain. I always kept them closed, but the gap at the top allowed me to see if it was day or night.

I lifted my head, and through swollen lids, I could make out my purse. I inched over, doing a soldier's crawl to a side table next to the couch, and yanked it down with my left hand. The contents spilled out, including three phones: my personal cell and two pay-as-you-go burners that I picked up a few days ago from Walmart. I retrieved one of the burners and called my son in New York. Gabe answered after the third ring, thinking it was his father, but then he heard my voice and asked what was wrong.

I told him I was in trouble. I told him he had to come to L.A. and pick me up and that I was seriously hurt. All he kept saying to me was "Call 911."

I couldn't call 911. I couldn't go to the police or to a hospital. They'd ask questions. They'd learn that I took my kids out of India without permission from the courts. I'd lose them.

I was still under the delusion that I hadn't lost them already.

My personal phone sprang to life, Juleen's name on the screen. Abruptly, I hung up on my son and took her call, but I didn't speak right away because it could have been the goons on the other end of the line. But then she said, "Mommy, are you okay?"

Stinging tears leaked from my inflamed eyes and ran down my bruised and cut cheeks. "Juleen, where are you?" My voice came out muffled and garbled. I could barely move my jaw.

"Mommy?"

This time, I spoke slower and as clearly as I could. "Where . . . are . . . you?"

Probably not the brightest question to ask. I had no idea if my phone was being bugged and tracked.

"Hiding—"

"Quiet!" I said. "Remember where we ate dinner last night?" It took me several attempts to make myself understood. Every time I spoke, electric shocks ran through my jaw.

Finally, she said, "Yes, I remember."

"Can . . . you . . . get there . . . by yourself?"

"Yes."

Ms. Hyper-Adult.

"Turn . . . off . . . your phone. Look around. Wait near . . . door. I'll . . ." It was getting harder to talk and harder to breathe. "I'll . . . meet you."

I hung up. I regathered all the contents of my purse while still lying on the floor. Then I managed to sit up, then stand. Immediately, I was light-headed and nauseated.

I threw up.

It was good that I gave the manager of the apartment a big cleaning deposit.

I was holding on to the back of the couch, telling myself to move slowly—as if I had a choice. Clutching on to furniture and then the wall, I made my way into the kitchen and retrieved two plastic garbage bags. I groped my way into Juleen's bedroom using the hallway for support. We shared a closet, although neither one of us had much in the way of clothing. I began to throw dresses, pants and shirts, shoes, socks, and underwear into the sacks: enough to get us through three or four days without doing a wash, but still light enough to carry.

I didn't bother with my son's things.

More tears.

Not now, Terry, not now.

I was holding everything in my left hand because my right arm was in searing pain. Before I inched my way out of Juleen's room, I noticed her violin case. I bent down in a squat—easier than bending at the waist—and picked it up. The extra weight was hitting me in waves of pain, but I couldn't leave without it. Although she wasn't anywhere close to the prodigy that Gabe was, she loved that violin.

I knew I couldn't go out the front door. They might still be out there, waiting for me. I had to follow the plan I had formulated with Juleen should a break-in like this happen in this apartment.

Lock your door, jump out the window, and run like hell.

And she had executed it perfectly. The back window was still halfway open. I couldn't lift it any higher. Too much pain and too little strength. Luckily, I was small in stature—not like Juleen, but I could squeeze through. I pitched the bags out the window along with my purse. I took the violin case in my left hand, held it close to my body, and hoped for the best. When I landed, I nearly passed out as agony ripped through my right side. But I got to my feet, gripped the bags and my purse, and started the block walk to my car.

I realized my face was probably a mess. One eye was shut closed; the other was bloated, but at least I could see out of it if I squinted. I probably would have looked like a homeless lady to anyone still out on the streets. But this was Los Angeles. No one walked. And even if there had been someone, one look at me and eyes would have been averted. No one wanted to see ugliness. Furthermore, no one cared.

I never parked in front of my apartment, but Devek had caught up with me anyway. Normally my husband was mild-mannered and even wimpy. But his gambling over the last three years had put him on edge. He had tried desperate measures to get money, and in his last couple of ventures, he had crossed the line. I had to leave.

I *had* to leave.

I was constantly on high alert, but that didn't mean I wasn't praying. Gabe had converted to Judaism, and my two younger children were Hindu. I was born Catholic. I wasn't choosy about who was up there as long as God was listening. And as soon as I managed to fish out my car's fob and unlock the door, I said my thanks. I opened the back door and stuffed my belongings inside. Once behind the wheel, I locked the door and took a deep breath.

Sitting on my butt hurt more than standing on my feet, but I had no choice. I pressed the ignition button with my left hand, looked around several times, taking into consideration that I could barely see, and pulled out from the curb. It took me five minutes in a car to get to the restaurant. Juleen was sitting on the bench by the door, phone and laptop in hand. I pulled up and she got up. I noticed that she was hobbling as she walked toward me. She opened the front passenger door and slid in. It was closing in on seven p.m. She saw my face and gasped.

"I'm fine." Clearly, I wasn't. I left the parking lot and pulled into traffic. "I'm okay."

Tears were running from her eyes. She took my useless right arm and I cried out in pain. Immediately, she dropped it.

"It's . . . a little sore."

"Mommy, I'm calling 911—"

"No!"

"You've got to go to a hospital!"

"They'll take you away . . . send you back to India. Is that what you want?"

I couldn't tell how much of my muffled speech she understood, but she must have gotten the gist of what I said. She shook her head and said no.

"I'm fine." I stopped at a long red light. I had no idea where I was going or what I was going to do. Then I remembered. "Gabe. Call him." When she picked up her phone, I said, "Use a burner . . . my purse."

"Right."

She fished out a burner and called up her brother, knowing his phone number by heart.

Hyper-adult.

Over the phone line, I heard my son's exasperated voice. "Finally! Where are you?!"

I told my daughter to put it on speaker. Juleen said, "Gabe, you've got to come. Mommy is hurt!"

"Badly?"

"Badly."

"What happened?"

Juleen sidestepped the question. "You've got to come get us. I don't know what to do."

"Where's Sanjay?"

Tears overflowing from my eyes, I whispered, "Gone."

"What happened?" A pause. "Mom?"

Juleen said, "Someone busted into the apartment. That's all I know. Mommy told me to run and I did."

"They took Sanjay?" he asked.

I nodded, then realized he couldn't see me. "Yes."

"And beat you up?"

"Yes."

"Where are you now?"

Juleen said, "We're in the car."

"She's *driving*?"

"Stopped. You're on speaker, Gabe. She can hear everything. But she can't talk well. They hurt her face."

"Oh God," Gabe said. "I don't know this phone number. Are you on a burner?"

"Yes," I whispered.

"Can you give me the phone number? It's coming up blocked. If it's like an iPhone, it should be at the top of your contacts list."

"Let me look," Juleen said. "Okay . . . got it. Here it is."

"Great! Thank you, Jules." A pause. "That's a start. Mom, listen to me and listen carefully. I can't get there until tomorrow afternoon at the earliest. You're hurt. You need to go to the hospital—"

"No!"

"She won't go," Juleen told him. "She says they'll ask questions and then take me away."

"I thought that might be the situation." Another pause. "So, this is plan B. Mom, are you listening?"

"Yes."

A sigh over the phone. "When I talked to you the first time, it sounded like you needed immediate help."

"She does," Juleen said.

"Mom, I asked Chris to help. He's much closer to you and he knows L.A. as well as I do. He has a jet. He can get down there in a couple of hours. As a matter of fact, he could be on his way now. If you need protection, and it sounds like you do, there's no one better who can help you."

I closed my one good eye. Chris. From the frying pan . . . My life was a complete and utter mess!

"Mom, are you there?"

"I'm here."

"Mom, he'll only help you if you ask for help. I know this is a deal with the devil, but you've got to call him. This is not just about you, it's also about Juleen."

I didn't answer, but I knew he was right.

Juleen said, "Give me the number and I'll call him."

Gabe said, "He won't help you, Jules. Only Mom. *She's* got to make contact."

I said, "Give me the number."

"What did she say?" Gabe asked.

"She said to give her the number," Juleen said. "I'll write it down for her."

"Jules, call me back as soon as Mom has spoken to my dad, okay?"

"Okay."

"Jules, my dad can be super abrupt and mean. When you meet

him, no matter what he says or how he acts, just be calm and super polite."

"Okay."

"I'm really giving you the benefit of my wisdom. Please listen."

"Okay. Let me get off the phone so Mommy can speak to him."

Hyper-adult.

"I love you, Mom."

I couldn't answer. It was getting harder and harder to speak. I could barely stay awake. Juleen hung up and called my ex's number. It rang three times and then went to voice mail.

Juleen said, "Mr. Whitman, this is Teresa McLaughlin's daughter, Juleen. My brother Gabe said to call you. My mother is hurt and can't talk very well, but she will talk to you when you call back. I'll give you the number of this phone. Please, please call back. Thank you very much, sir."

I gave my daughter the thumbs-up.

"Now what?" she asked. When I didn't answer, Juleen said, "Mommy, we can't stay here. They might come back."

I nodded and pulled into traffic.

"Where are we going?"

"I don't . . . know."

"You can't just drive around."

She was right. I thought for a moment. "My . . . house."

"What house?"

I waved her off.

"What house?"

"Where I grew up."

"You grew up here?"

I nodded.

"Does Mr. Whitman know it?"

"Donatti," I told her. "Mr. Donatti."

The burner rang. Juleen put the cell on speaker and answered the phone. "Hello?"

I heard my ex's voice. "Terry?"

It wasn't the first time Juleen and I had been mistaken for each other over the phone. Our voices sounded alike. "I'm . . . here," I whispered.

Chris said, "What's going on?"

I started to cry and so did Juleen. She said, "They beat her up."

"Where are you?"

"Valley," I answered.

"*Where* in the Valley?"

"She's driving to her house where she grew up," Juleen answered.

"She's *driving*?"

"Do you know where her old house is?"

"Yes, I know where it is. Don't go there—"

His phone cut out. Juleen called him back, but it went to voice mail.

The sun was beginning to go down, and soon we'd be under the cover of darkness. We were about a mile away from the apartment we were renting but four miles away from my old house. My one good eye was starting to close up. I knew if I didn't get there soon, I wouldn't be able to drive at all. My head was exploding with pain, and I was getting very sleepy. I decided to head in the direction of my old high school—a common landmark for Chris and me. I kept shaking my head to stay awake. Each time I did that, bolts of lightning and thunder clapped inside my brain.

The burner sprang to life. Juleen answered. "We're on speaker, Mr. Donatti."

"Terry, are you there?"

"Hi, Chris."

"Terry, listen to me. Are you physically able to drive?"

I didn't answer.

"Terry?"

"Yes." *For the moment.*

"Don't go to your old house, babe. If I were looking for you, that's one of the places where I'd camp out. Do you remember where I used to live?"

"Yes."

"Go there. It's on Jasper—8246 . . . no, 8446 . . ."

"8226," I told him.

"Your beat-up brain is working better than mine. Can you make it there?"

"Yes."

"Okay, good. I'll meet you in a couple of hours. Probably less. I'll blink the headlights twice, then pause and blink them twice again, so you'll know it's me. You blink back. Do *not* leave the car for any reason. I'll come to you."

"Okay."

"Juleen, do *not* let her fall asleep under any circumstances. Can I trust you to do that?"

"Yes, sir."

"Good. I'll see you later."

After he hung up, Juleen said, "Can you drive, Mommy?"

"Yes." *Sort of.* "I'm . . . okay."

It took me about a half hour to go four miles on empty streets. I arrived on Jasper just as the last bit of daylight was fading from the horizon. The last time I had been at this apartment, I had been sixteen years old, in deep love with the most gorgeous guy in high school. I had tutored Chris at his apartment and at my house for about three months until the relationship turned odd and weird and was too much for me to handle. Inside, I knew he was bad news, but I kept going back. The last time I was here, we had spent the night together. It had been sexual but not sex. That happened in a prison somewhere in the Mojave Desert. By the time I had decided to cut bait, it was too late. But it all worked out. I couldn't imagine a world bereft of Gabriel. I closed my eyes, hoping for numbness.

Juleen suddenly blasted the radio.

"Turn . . . that off!"

"He told me not to let you fall asleep."

"Who?"

"Mr. Whit— Mr. Donatti. You know, Gabe's father."

I reached over and turned the knob to off. "I'm fine." A minute later, my eyes started to close. Juleen shook me. I said, "Leave me alone."

"You can't fall asleep."

I barely heard her words. I was fading away. She kept shaking me awake. She turned on the radio again. I turned it off. When she went for the knob again, I hit her hand. She didn't care. She kept shaking me, screaming at me, clapping her hands in front of my face. I became too tired to even yell at her. Then I began to cry in earnest. I was crying because I had made a mess of my life. I was crying because I was in terrible pain. Most of all, I was crying with heartbreak for my lost little boy.

He must be so scared!

"It'll be okay, Mommy," Juleen said. "It'll all be okay."

I couldn't answer her. I could barely breathe, and crying was only making it worse. Here I was, a forty-two-year-old woman, completely broke and utterly broken. I had made terrible choices in men. I had abandoned my older son and I couldn't save the younger one. I was a terrible role model for Juleen. She was comforting me instead of the other way around. What was wrong with me that I couldn't even provide the minimum of parenting?

I dried my eyes on my sleeve. My lids had swollen shut. If I picked one of them up, I could see. My head was throbbing, and I was dizzy and nauseated. On the plus side, I could still think, which meant I had a functioning brain. I also had my eyesight, one good arm, and two working legs. That was a lot of good stuff.

A text registered on the burner in Juleen's hands. She said, "It's Gabe. He's asking about us and his dad. What should I tell him?"

The lightbulb went off. I couldn't talk, but I could text with one hand. I took the phone and pecked out my sentences with my left index finger.

We made contact with Chris. He's on his way down.

Thank God! I'll come to see you. Probably tomorrow.

Don't worry. I'm fine.

How are you feeling?

Ok. Tired. TTYL.

And it was all true. I was exhausted. I gave the phone back to Juleen. She was texting him something. I put my head back, looking at the roof of the car as I drifted off to sleep. Juleen started shaking me after fifteen seconds of blissful nothingness. As soon as I awoke, the pain recurred in full force. The burner rang and Juleen put the cell to my ear. It was Gabe. "You're a doctor. You know better. Stay awake!"

"Yeah . . . yeah."

But as soon as he hung up, I started to fall asleep. Juleen snapped her fingers, clapped her hands, and pulled my hair, which really hurt. I thought about how that goon had ripped my hair from my head. I felt my scalp, and sure enough there was a small bald spot.

I just wanted to sleep, but Juleen wouldn't let me. I didn't know how long the clapping and snapping and shaking went on, but it seemed like forever. Eventually I heard a car motor. I lifted an eyelid and saw two blinks, a pause, two blinks.

That's him, I thought. I forgot to signal him back. Instead, I opened the door, started to stand, and immediately dropped to my knees and fell on my face. Nausea had overwhelmed me. I vomited again, hard and fast. So hard, I wet myself—something damp and metallic smelling spreading in the groin area of my jeans.

From ground level, I saw this very tall man with shoulder-length hair exiting the car and running toward me. In one giant swoop he picked me up without effort. Strong arms—his arms. His smell. I, on the other hand, was covered in barf and blood and stank like a public urinal. But he didn't say a word as we headed toward his car.

I picked up an eyelid and looked over my shoulder, at my daughter, who was carrying two trash bags, her violin case, her laptop, and my purse, hobbling furiously to catch up with me. Chris followed my eyes.

"Someone get the girl!"

Another man sprang into action and came to Juleen's aid.

Santa had come with his elves.

Chris propped me up in the middle backseat of a stretch limo and slid in beside me. I was still holding my eyelid up when he cupped my chin and examined my face. "Jesus fucking Christ!" He looked at my pants. "Terry, you need to go to a hospital."

"No . . ." I dropped my eyelid, leaving me in pain and darkness. If I couldn't see, maybe this would all go away.

"You're pissing blood!" To someone else, Chris said, "What's the closest hospital from here?"

He obviously wasn't listening to me, which was par for the course. I yelled out, "No!"

I heard Juleen's voice. "She won't go. She's afraid they'll take me away."

"Then they'll take you away," Chris said. "It's better than her dying."

Someone started the car. We rode a few minutes, and I began to get motion sickness. I gagged a few times.

Chris said, "Stop the car." I heard the car door open, and he held me as I threw up a third time, retching until I felt my stomach was coming up my throat. He said, "You're also vomiting blood."

I knew what that meant, but I didn't care. I'd rather go out fighting. I hit him. "No . . . hospital!"

Chris lifted up my eyelid. "Listen to me, Teresa. If you don't get help soon, you are going to *die*! You're a fucking doctor. You know better."

Gabe's words almost to a T. I hit him again. "No!"

"Stop hitting me. It's like an annoying gnat." He was still holding up my eyelid, a brilliantly blue iris staring back at me. Then he let my lid drop and I was encased in darkness.

"This is against my better judgment." He paused. "Okay, Terry, this is what I'm going to do. I'll take you two back with me. I co-own a twenty-four-hour emergency room. I'll take you there. I promise that no questions will be asked, okay?"

I nodded.

"We're not equipped to handle this kind of situation. Most of the time, we just give out antibiotics or pain medicine, or wrap a muscle strain. The most we ever do is stabilize heart attacks and send them off to a bigger hospital in Elko. But I'll call in and tell them what I'm dealing with. If the doc there tells me that you have to go to Elko, you're going to Elko. End of discussion. Okay?"

"Okay."

"Start the car," Chris said. "God help me if you die." He was silent for a few moments. "What the hell is wrong with your arm?" He lifted my right hand and I screamed in pain. "I think your shoulder's dislocated. Stop the car again."

The driver obeyed.

Chris said, "I can fix this. It'll probably take some pain away, but if your arm is broken it might make it worse."

"Tape . . ."

"What'd you say?"

I motioned to Juleen to give me the phone. I picked up an eyelid and managed to orient a finger on the phone's letters. I pecked out: *Tape the arm.*

Chris read it. He said, "Anyone have any tape?"

Someone from the front seat said, "I have electrical tape."

Serial killer, I thought.

"Give it to me," Chris said. "This is going to stick to her arm."

I made a motion with my left hand.

"I don't understand," Chris said.

"Flip . . . it."

"Flip . . . Oh, right." He took my right arm, and again, I screamed in pain as he started wrapping my forearm on the nonsticky side as tight as he could. It felt like a tourniquet. I was sobbing, it was so painful.

"Hold on, baby doll. Almost done." Finally, he said, "This is going to hurt—"

"Go . . ."

He took my wrist and pulled my arm forward and straight out from my body with some force, guiding the ball back into the socket. I shrieked in pain. Afterward, it still hurt, but I could wiggle my fingers.

I still couldn't move my arm without pain. "Better," I whispered. I pulled at the tape.

"You want me to take the tape off?" Chris asked.

I nodded.

"Hold still." A moment later, something cool touched my skin as it ran the length of the electrical tape up my arm. A knife, I presumed. Chris always carried weapons. Even lying next to him, against his chest, I could feel his gun in its shoulder holster.

He said, "Don't you dare fall asleep." I was too tired to answer him. Still, he kept talking . . . to keep me awake. "We had problems, I know, but we also had a lot of good times too. Like . . . like remember in Vegas . . . I took you there for our five-year anniversary. And we both got so plastered that as soon as we entered the hotel room, we fell down onto the floor." A pause. "And we laughed and laughed and laughed. And we made love all night. And . . ." Another pause. "And then we left for breakfast . . . after having been up all night. We both looked a mess—well, I did, not you. You always looked good, Terry, no matter what."

Uh, I beg to differ.

"Anyway, we went down to the casino. And there was the giant slot machine that only took ten-dollar tokens. And you wanted to play it, and I said gambling was flushing money down the toilet."

How true is that.

"But you insisted, so I bought you a token. And you pulled the lever. One time." He gave a laugh. "One pull and the bell went off. You won a couple of grand. It wasn't the big jackpot, but it was a good return on your investment."

His voice was far away, like the distant music of a parade.

"And you wanted to give it to me . . . the money. But I told you to keep it and spend it on whatever you wanted. After all, it was your money." A beat. "And you bought me a gun with it—an antique Belgian Mauser Model 1893 rifle. I mean, what the hell was I going to do with an antique rifle? But you were so happy to buy it for me. The smile on your face . . . pure joy. I still have it, you know. The rifle. I've bought and sold lots of guns over the years, but I'll never give that one away."

He stopped talking for a moment.

"And remember when you used to bake me these fancy cakes for my birthday? I think the first one . . . I think it was a cake in the shape of a cello." A moment passed. "And then there was one that looked like an artist's palette. And another one that was in the shape of a gun. But the best one . . . the one I remember the best was when I was on trial for racketeering and jury tampering with my uncle. You baked me a 'get out of jail free' cake. God, I laughed my ass off. It was such a tense period of time and that just . . . I don't know. It just cut through . . ." Chris said, "How much longer?"

From the front seat, a man said, "Two minutes, sir. They've just finished gassing up the plane."

"Get a route from the FBO. Once we get there, I want to move."
"Yes, sir."

A few minutes later, the car slowed and I heard a roaring engine. I opened an eyelid and saw that the limo had pulled up right next to a plane. With his long arms, Chris leaned over Juleen and opened the door. "Go ahead, up the steps." When I started to move, he said, "Not you. Your daughter. You just wait here."

As soon as he moved—taking away his shoulder for upright support—I slid until I was lying down. A moment later, Chris helped me out and then picked me up, taking me up the stairs and settling me into a chair. "Someone get me a wet washcloth and a couple of ice packs." A second later, he said, "This is cold. Put it in the microwave. And get me a towel. And where the fuck is the ice pack?"

I opened my eyelid and looked around for my daughter, but Chris was standing over me, blocking my vision. He said, "Close your eye. It might burn a little."

I cooperated. He began to clean up my face. It took a few minutes, and when he was done, he patted it dry. I still stank. He placed an ice pack into my left hand. "Hold this on your face for maybe a minute on and a minute off."

"Thanks." I paused. "Sorry."

"Shhh. None of that. I have to copilot the plane, baby. If you need anything, tell your daughter and she'll come get me."

I nodded. He stood up, and then I saw Juleen was sitting across the aisle from me. The plane was a six-seater, and four seats were taken up. Chris had brought two sidearms with him. The men weren't just men, they were also his weapons.

Chris put on my seat belt. "We're going over mountains. We're actually going into the mountains. It's going to be really bumpy, especially because it's summer and the heat rises after dark. It's normal. Don't be nervous." He stroked my arm. "It'll be okay, I promise you." To Juleen, he said, "If she starts to fall asleep, just put this ice pack on her face, okay?"

"Okay."

I held out my hand to my daughter and she took it. Within a minute, I was going under. And no amount of yelling, shaking, ice packs, and turbulence would disturb my rest. At one point, they thought I'd died.

Maybe I had.

CHAPTER 2

HE STANK OF vomit, blood, and his own sweat. As meticulous as he was, he tolerated the stench out of necessity. But as soon as she was wheeled into a treatment room hidden behind double doors, he had to change his clothes. He always kept spare duds in all his offices. And he had a *lot* of offices. The convenience factor was that he wore the same thing every day: black suit and a black T-shirt, either long- or short-sleeved, depending on the weather. His boots were the only item that showed creativity. He had hundreds of pairs in every possible color and animal skin available.

He leaned against the wall, trying to catch his breath. The place didn't have a waiting room. The men who came here were usually certain types: those who had purposely ditched hearth and home for a couple of nights of bacchanalian freedom, rich single men who wanted it done in a very specific way, and on-the-spectrum coders with no social skills and money to burn. The cash bought them good food, fine spirits, and copious amounts of sex with as many women—or men—as their wallets could afford. Who the hell would be pacing for them in a hospital waiting room? No wives, no girl-friends, no boyfriends, no friends at all.

Nope. No waiting rooms. Just a hallway with a few chairs. The girl was sitting in one of them, head down, with two trash bags, a purse, and a violin case at her feet.

Donatti said, "I'm going upstairs. I reek like a garbage dump. Landon, you watch the doors. Petry, you watch the girl. No one goes in those doors until I come back. And no one, and I mean no one, touches the girl without my say-so. Anyone disputes those orders, shoot first and ask questions later. I'll be back in ten minutes."

The girl raised her hand.

"What?" Donatti said.

"I have to use the toilet."

It probably had been eight hours since she'd taken a piss. He picked up Terry's purse. "C'mon . . . this way." He took her to the elevator, and they rode it up to the dark fourth floor. Donatti turned on the lights, then strode down the hall to his office door. He suddenly realized that the girl was twenty paces behind. He waited for her to catch up, and then he opened the door and turned on the lights. He pointed to a door. "In there."

She limped inside and shut the door. He looked around. This was one of his smaller offices. Desk, chair, and a closet. He kept very few files here—just on the men who had serious health conditions. He monitored them like he monitored everything. He certainly didn't want any of his clients dying on the premises.

Bad for business.

He put his ex-wife's purse on the desktop and took out a fresh ensemble, while waiting for the girl to get out so he could shower. He could hear her crying from behind the door.

The bastard child.

Despite himself, he felt bad for her.

The girl looked like Terry dipped in caramel. The same oval face, lovely cheekbones, and bee-stung lips. Her hair was long like Terry's but darker in color, as were her eyes. They also had similar voices. It made it easier for him to tolerate her. If he took his imagination to the limit, he could almost pretend she was his and her coloring came from a black Irish ancestor. Of course, she wasn't his. She had a father, and he had no desire to become a substitute. Although he'd protect Gabe with his life, one kid had always been one too many.

Finally, she came out, her face freshly washed. "Thank you."

"Wait here." Donatti took his change of clothes and went inside the bathroom. A quick shower and clean garments made him feel better. He came back into the office, sat at his desk, and fished through Terry's purse. He took out four phones—three burners, including a Xiaomi phone, whatever that was, and a Samsung. To the girl, who was still standing, he said, "Sit down. You're making me nervous."

She obeyed. "Sorry."

He began to scroll down one of the burners, kept the one that Terry had used most. "Is this your phone?" He showed her the Xiaomi.

"Yes."

"What's your code?"

"My birthday."

"That doesn't help me." She gave him the numbers. He said, "Want to tell me what happened?"

"I don't know what happened exactly."

"Then tell me what you know inexactly."

"I heard something loud in the living room. I heard Mommy shout 'Run!' I grabbed my phone and laptop and took off and jumped out the window. That's how I hurt my ankle. It was a second-story apartment."

He took out Terry's personal phone and turned it on. "You and your mother planned an escape route just in case?"

"Yes, sir."

Donatti looked up. "You can call me Chris."

"Yes, sir . . . Chris."

"Do you know your mother's phone code?"

"It's a bunch of numbers. I've got to think."

"Her birthday maybe?"

"Not her birthday or mine or Sanjay's. It's one-one-oh-five or oh-six—"

Donatti smiled. "Eleven-oh-five-seventy-six."

"Yeah . . . How'd you—?"

"It's my birthday." Once it was unlocked, Donatti started scrolling down the numbers in Terry's call history. Devek had called her sixteen times in the previous five days. Donatti looked up Terry's husband in the contacts and wrote down the number. "Is +91 the country code for India?"

"I think so."

"Do you know the state code?"

"No, sorry."

"I'll find out." Donatti wrote down some numbers and showed them to her. "Any of these look familiar?"

"No . . . sorry."

He pocketed the phones, picked up the purse, and stood up. Then he gathered his dirty clothing and cocked his head in her direction. "C'mon." As they walked to the elevator, he dumped his clothes in a hamper of dirty sheets.

The girl said, "Will she be okay?"

"I hope so." The elevator came. He turned off the hall lights and they went inside. Donatti pushed the down button. "I'll find someone to look at your ankle."

"I'm okay."

"I got eyes. You're not okay." She didn't answer. He said, "Gabe tell you I was an ogre?"

"No."

Her face was flat. Unlike her mother, he couldn't read her. "I am an ogre."

"You look like him . . . like Gabe."

"No, he looks like me."

Her skin darkened. "Yeah, I got the order a little mixed up." A pause. "He's tall, but not as tall as you."

"Few people are."

"And he has green eyes."

"Your mother has gold eyes. Yellow and blue make green."

"People say I look like Mommy."

"People are correct." The elevator doors opened. They walked over to the hallway chairs. She sat; he didn't. Donatti talked to his men. "Everything quiet?"

"Not a soul, sir."

Donatti checked his Rolex. "You two have been on shift for over ten hours. Go back and switch with Kent and Giraldi. Put in for overtime."

Landon said, "I can stay if you want, Mr. Donatti."

"No, no, I'm fine. Nothing to do except wait. Go."

The two men left. Donatti ran his fingers through his hair. He looked at the girl. "I'm sorry you're going through all this shit. It's a terrible thing when your parents are at war."

"All I care about is Mommy."

"True that," Donatti said. "Who do you think is after you and your brother?"

"I'm assuming it's my father."

"Is your father violent?"

"No, not at all."

"Someone beat up your mother."

"It *wasn't* my father." She crossed her arms.

"Just trying to figure out things. Don't get defensive."

"I'm just saying . . ."

"Okay. Let me put it this way. If your father did take your brother, would he hurt him?"

"No, of course not. He worships Sanjay."

"And you?"

Her eyes welled up. "My dad loves me."

"But . . ."

"Nothing. He loves me." A pause. "But Mommy loves me more."

"Don't take sides."

"It's true. She does love me more."

"Does your mom talk smack about him?"

"No. She never says anything mean about anyone."

"Including me?"

"Only that Gabe gets his talent from you."

"She forgot the good looks."

Juleen regarded his face: beautiful blue eyes and thick blond-streaked white hair that fell down to his shoulders. He was good-looking for an old guy. "My dad gambles."

"Some people do."

"Do you?"

"Nope. You always lose and I don't like losing money."

"Then why do people do it if it's so stupid?"

"Because people do stupid things." A pause. "Did your mom ever tell you I beat her up?" The girl looked at him with stunned eyes. "Not as bad as she is now, but I gave her bruises . . . a couple of black eyes. I scared her into not pressing charges. I didn't want to go to prison. It was cowardly—what I did and how I acted afterward. Like I said, people do stupid things. That was my stupidest."

She was silent.

"Don't be so hard on your father. People gamble because it's exciting . . . gives them a rush . . . like drugs." He turned to her. "Don't take drugs. Ever. It screws you up."

"I don't take drugs." A pause. "Do you take drugs?"

"Not anymore."

"But you did?"

"I was both an alcoholic and a drug addict."

"But not now?"

"For the most part, I'm sober. But it's always a battle. I've got an addictive personality. Don't even start."

"Why did you start?"

"I was depressed. I needed a rush."

"But you're not depressed now?"

"You ask a lot of questions."

"Sorry."

He sat back in his chair and observed the girl. She was squirming. "What?"

"Nothing."

"No, it's not nothing. What's on your mind?"

"I'm just thinking that if you don't gamble and you don't drink and you don't take drugs, like what gives you a rush if you have an addictive personality?"

"Sex." *With your mother.*

The girl's complexion darkened a couple of shades. Her embarrassment didn't bother him a whit. He was what he was.

Donatti felt his phone buzz in his coat pocket. He retrieved it and looked at the screen. "It's Gabe." He stood and walked away from her. "I have Mom. She's in my ER being treated."

"How is she?"

"Beaten up. She was semiconscious when we got here."

"I'll come out."

"Let me talk to the doctors first. What's your schedule?"

"It's whatever you want it to be."

"What's on your calendar?"

"I have a concert in Boston tomorrow—actually today, but I can call my agent. It's like five in the morning."

"Don't call anyone yet. What's after that?"

"Schedule-wise? The next day I've got a concert in the Berkshires, and then I'm free for ten days."

"Come out then. You know, maybe I can call Rina to come out . . . Help watch the girl."

"Rina and Peter are on a plane to Israel."

"*Israel?*"

"Yeah. They bought a place there."

Donatti was mystified. "*Why?*"

"It's the Jewish homeland. They're Jewish."

"Are they coming back?"

"Yeah, they'll be back in about two weeks."

"That may be good timing. She can come after you leave."

"Uh, you know Rina is religious. And you know you live in a brothel."

"I'm not pimping her out, Gabriel, I'm asking for help with your sister."

"Don't get mad, but I think we need someone to stay with Mom while she's in the hospital."

"Well, glory fuck, I never thought of that."

"I said don't get mad."

"I'm staying with her until she's out of the hospital, whenever that is. At some point, I'm going to have to settle your sister in your room, but that shouldn't take more than an hour or two. She'll be alone until I can arrange things, so it would be nice if you could spend some time with her while you're here."

"She'll want to stay at the hospital, Dad."

"I don't want her here. She talks too much."

"Juleen talks too much?"

"A regular chatterbox."

"Wow. News to me. She'll want to see her mother, Chris."

"Gabriel, stop *arguing* with me. I don't want her to see her mother laid up. You haven't seen her. I have. She looks horrible. Furthermore, I have no idea what shape she's in. The kid has enough worries. So just shut up and let me take care of this situation, okay?"

"Sorry." He meant it. "Whatever you think, Dad. Thank you for handling everything. I owe you one."

"You owe me more than one, Gabriel, but not for this. I'll call you as soon as I know more."

"Wait. Can I talk to Juleen?"

"Make it brief. Hold on." Donatti walked back to the girl. "It's your brother. Be quick."

"Yes, sir."

He walked away to give her a little privacy. A minute later, he saw Giraldi and Kent coming down the hallway. Donatti came back to the girl and took the phone from her hand. "I've got to go find someone to treat your sister."

"What's wrong?"

"She's limping. Maybe a twisted ankle. Bye." He pocketed his phone and talked to his men. "Keep a watch on the girl. No one comes near her."

They answered "Yes, sir" in unison.

"I've got to find someone to patch up her ankle. I'll be back in a few minutes." Donatti walked over to the double doors and pushed in the code. He found a nurse, Della Gratz. He knew all his employees, and between the restaurants, the shops, the casinos, and the brothels, there were more than a hundred of them on rotating shifts. Della was cleaning up a treatment cubicle, curtain wide open.

"How is she?"

She turned around. "I didn't hear you come in, Mr. Donatti. They took her to the OR."

"What's wrong?"

"I'm not sure. You probably should wait for a doctor, sir."

"I won't hold you to it, Della. Please."

The poor woman was wringing her hands. Everyone hated talking to the boss. "She needs dental work. They thought it would be easier to do it in the OR."

"Her jaw's busted?"

"It was dislocated. They fixed that, but she's got some loose teeth in the back. I think they're wiring her jaw, sir."

"What else?"

"I think they're going to x-ray her for broken bones."

"Fine. Is there someone who can look at her daughter's ankle? I think it's sprained or twisted. It probably should be taped."

"I can do that, Mr. Donatti." She stopped and started to wash her hands.

"Someone will bring her in, then. Thank you."

"You're very welcome."

He came back outside, summoned the girl. She limped over and he said, "I found a nurse who is going to look at your ankle."

"How's Mommy?"

"She's still with us. Let's go."

An hour later, she was taped and had a crutch. She started to sit, but Donatti shook his head. "I'm taking you to where I live. You'll stay in Gabe's room."

"I want to stay here."

"You can't stay here, Juleen."

Tears in her eyes. "I want to see Mommy."

"When it's appropriate." To his men. "I need the car keys."

"Do you want me to drive you, sir?"

"No, I'm fine. Just keep watch on the doors. I'll be back in about a half hour." He picked up the garbage bags and her violin case. "C'mon."

She followed him like a chastened dog. As they walked out, she said, "Why can't I stay with Mommy at the hospital?"

"Because you can't. The good news is Gabe will be here in a couple of days." He held up the violin case. "How long have you played?"

"Five years." A pause. "Gabe says you play the cello."

"I do." Silence. "That's how I met your mother. We were in orchestra together. She also played the violin."

"She told me she was terrible."

"She was." He let out a small laugh. "But her face more than made up for her lack of talent." He regarded the girl. "You'd better learn how to handle yourself with boys. They're all dogs. Don't trust any of them."

"I don't like boys."

"One day you will."

"No, I won't. I want to be a doctor like my mom. You have to study to do that. I don't have time for stupidity."

"Yeah, boys are very stupid. Stop walking. This is the car." Donatti opened the door and she slid in the passenger side. He started the engine and took off. "I have to go back to take care of your mother. You're going to be alone in the room until Gabe gets here. No one is allowed in there except Gabe and me."

"How do I get out?"

"You don't unless I say so. I'll bring you meals. I'm sorry, but after what happened to your younger brother, your protection is my responsibility, okay?"

She nodded. Her lip was trembling.

"I'll get you some teachers. Have you learned any languages other than English?"

"Hindi."

"I'll start you on Spanish and French. I'll also get you a violin teacher. That'll keep you busy. Are you hungry?" He checked his watch. It was three in the morning. "Want me to get you a hamburger or a pizza?"

"I'm vegan."

"*Vegan?*"

"I'm Hindu. I like rice and vegetable curry, if that's okay."

Donatti said, "You can't grow on shit like that."

She shrugged. "I'm growing, so I guess you can."

"Don't sass me *ever*," he growled out. "I don't like it."

She turned quiet.

Donatti said, "I'm not a nice man. But if you're respectful, we'll be okay."

"Yes, sir."

"I said you can call me Chris."

She didn't answer. A wave of fatigue suddenly overwhelmed him. He usually worked until four-thirty in the morning, but work wasn't stressful. This was way beyond stressful. "How about if I give you a pass because you had a hard day? You and me both."

He suddenly realized his jaw was aching. He'd been clenching it for the last ten hours. The lights of his kingdom were coming into view, and he took a hard left and parked in his reserved spot. He lived on the third floor of a four-story building. Offices took up the first two floors, and his son slept above him. After Terry had abandoned him, Gabe had lived with the Deckers for several years until he went off to Juilliard. But Donatti made sure that he'd spent a month each summer here when the weather was beautiful. His living quarters as well as Gabe's room were away from the main brothel. But Donatti never made any effort to hide what he did or what he was.

The place was over fifty acres of male sexual fantasy. Besides the main building filled with any kind of sex toy and fuck apparatus imaginable, the place had a boutique hotel for the clients after their encounters, two restaurants, a sports bar, a gentleman's club, a gym with trainers, two tennis courts, an Olympic-size swimming pool with six Jacuzzi hot tubs placed throughout the area, a two-story spa, and one casino. He also had built housing for the girls, a separate dorm for the boys, a big employee dining room, a staff lounge, a gym, a canteen, a small market, and a dry goods store. A little bit away from the action was a pawnshop and his private bank. The airstrip and hangar were about a block away from the bank. Convenience for his clients: pay your bills and go the fuck home.

He also owned the mountains that surrounded his erotic amusement park, pure wilderness where he had installed trails just for himself. He loved what he did, and he'd screw anything with a hole, but once in a while, he just had to get away.

He opened the car door. "This way."

The kid was even slower on a crutch. His patience was wafer thin, but it wasn't her fault. He waited, unlocked the building, and turned on the lights. She followed him to the elevator. Donatti inserted a key and looked into a metal square for pupil recognition. The doors opened. They both stepped inside. The girl began to shake. He said, "I'll take good care of your mom."

There were tears on her cheeks. She said, "Can I have my phone back?"

"Not yet. It may have a tracker on it. And I don't want you talking to your dad until I know what's going on."

"I promise I won't. Can I have a new one so I can talk to her?"

"Not right now. The truth is that your mom isn't going to be doing much talking for a while. And when she gets out of the hospital, she is going to need her rest."

The doors opened and Donatti, once again, went through the high-tech security. After he heard the clicks, he took out the key to his son's room and let them both inside. Gabe had set up his area as a suite. The Steinway sat in the living room, along with Donatti's cello, and there was a small sitting area with a TV. The bedroom held a king-size bed and not much else. But it did have a walk-in closet and an en suite bathroom.

Donatti dropped the bags on the floor. "I want to settle you here so everything will be ready when your mom gets out of the hospital. Tomorrow, when you're rested, separate out your mom's things from your things."

"Why? Won't Mommy be staying with me?"

"No, darling," Donatti said. "Mommy will be staying with me."

CHAPTER 3

ANYTHING?" DONATTI ASKED.

"No, sir," Giraldi said. "Everything's been quiet."

"That's good." He shook his head. "You two go back to my office. One of you watch the door, the other watch the elevator. You've been on since what? Ten?"

"Yes, sir."

"So, you're done at six. Do you mind doing overtime?"

"Not at all, sir."

"Who's on after you?"

"I think it's Bacon and Millard."

"Tell them to start at ten. I think you're going to have to do ten-hour shifts until I figure this out."

"It's fine."

"Good. I'll check in with you before ten." He took out the car keys and threw them to Giraldi. "Go."

The men got up and left, leaving him alone for the first time since this entire ordeal began. He sat down and threw his head back. Too wired to sleep, but too tired to do anything useful, he just sat and waited. Fifteen minutes later, the double doors opened. He stood up and then sat back down. It was the chief sheriff; the man also worked for him. Glorified security guard. Basically, his job was to calm down drunks and take ODs to the ER. Bill Saverhall was about six feet with a gut, but he had strong arms and was good with managing people without handcuffs. Anything really physical, Donatti and his men took care of themselves.

"Hey, Bill," Donatti said.

"Chris."

"What's going on? What are you doing here?"

"One of your clients might have overindulged. They're pumping his stomach."

"Do you have a name?"

"Richard Feller."

"He's been here before. He should know better. Thanks for letting me know."

Saverhall looked at the floor. "I understand you've got a team working on a female who was beat up." Donatti waited. "Relation to you or . . ."

"My wife . . . ex-wife."

"You were married?"

"I was."

"Does she live here?"

"No."

"How'd she get here?"

"I took the jet to Los Angeles and picked her up." A pause. "Where is this leading?"

"Chris, I'm sorry. You can fire me if you want, but I need to see your hands."

Donatti gave off a sour laugh. "You think I did it?"

"You go all the way to Los Angeles to pick up your ex-wife who was beaten badly? There are better hospitals in L.A. If you were me, what would you think?"

"Fair enough." Donatti held out his hands. He had had a manicure yesterday morning, so his nails were perfect.

"Flip them over." Saverhall nodded. "Thank you. I need to see your arms, sir." When Donatti stared at him, he said, "She had skin under her fingernails."

Off came the jacket, exposing his forearms and his piece in its shoulder harness. Donatti was surprised. For years, Saverhall had overlooked a variety of illegal drugs and all the weapons. Something about a beaten-up woman must have gotten to him. He raised his shirt, exposing his abdomen around his gun harness. "Satisfied?"

"One more thing. Your feet."

"This is getting to be a pain in the ass." Saverhall waited, and Donatti took off his boots and socks. Saverhall looked at his toes and nails and then nodded.

Donatti said, "You want my DNA while we're at it?"

"Chris, I'm sorry, but I'm only doing my job. I don't know how you feel about this woman, but she is your ex."

"She called our son. Our son called me. She wanted out of L.A. and I came for her."

"Nice of you to do that for your ex-wife."

Donatti smiled. "Never figured me for a nice guy, huh?"

"Sorry to inconvenience you."

Donatti waved him off. "We're square. Go home to your wife . . . Marquetta, right?" Just then, the double doors opened again and a doctor emerged, face mask dangling like a monk's collar. "I gotta go."

Drew Jamison had been an ER doc on staff for four years. Single guy and good-looking—dark and well built. He often took advantage of the employee discount. The girls and boys got paid the same whomever they serviced. Donatti made sure of that. It was good business and prevented sexual harassment lawsuits. He had drilled it into anyone who worked for him.

Never give it away for free—not even to the boss.

Donatti jogged over to him. "Tell me good news."

"There's a lot of good news," Jamison said. "First of all, her cranial pressure is normal. Her pupillary response appears fine. She was able to follow some simple instructions."

He exhaled. "That's good."

"Yes, it is, but brain swelling sometimes happens later. We'll have to watch her, but she's okay at this moment. Her jaw was dislocated and she has some loose teeth in back. We wired everything so her mouth is stable. That can probably be removed in three or four weeks. She isn't eating anyway."

"Anything else?"

"She has two broken bones in her right forearm. The radius has a hairline and the ulna has an incomplete fracture that was threatening a complete break. We put her arm in a cast to the elbow. She also has three broken right ribs, which will take time to heal too. She was vomiting a little blood, but that should be okay." A sigh. "The main problem is her kidneys. She's pissing blood, which is not good, but what I'm concerned about is a condition called rhabdomyolysis, which can be life-threatening. It happens when the kidneys are damaged. She has to be watched."

"But she'll be okay."

"She has to be watched, Chris. If her kidneys start failing, that's bad. This hospital is small. You know that. She should be somewhere bigger with more services. But since she is here, I suggest you get someone to watch her twenty-four seven. We're busy and it would be terrible if something got overlooked."

"I'll watch her."

"You don't want to camp out here. The rooms are small, Chris. You can barely fit a chair in there."

"Put her in a double room with two beds. I'll watch her. Discussion done, Drew. When can I see her?"

"In about an hour. She's out of it. When she wakes up, she's going to be in pain. I'll have to see what we can give her that doesn't affect her kidneys. Problem is almost everything affects the kidneys. But I'll do what I can."

"Thank you."

"No problem. Can't mess up with the boss." Jamison bit his bottom lip. "It's nice that you're such good friends with your ex."

"We're not friends. Straight men can't be friends with women. At some point, we all want more even if it didn't start out that way. We're always thinking, *I wonder what she looks like naked.* And if you don't want to fuck her, she certainly isn't your friend."

The doc raised his eyebrows. "I don't think she's going to be interested in sex for a while."

"I'm aware of that."

"Have you seen what she looks like?"

"Of course I know what she looks like. I brought her in. She's a wreck. Hopefully she won't always be a wreck. But either way, she's still my baby. So in about an hour?"

"About."

"I'm going up to my office. Have someone buzz me when she's been transferred."

"No problem, sir."

"That's what I like to hear, Drew. No problem."

THE FIRST TIME I remember being awake, I saw snippets waltzing through my head like movie trailers. I heard noises, and then minutes later, it went dark.

The second time I was awake, I felt something itchy on my nose, and as I reached to scratch, something hard bonked my face. Immediately, my head started to throb. I attempted to open my eyes, but all I saw was darkness. I tried to talk, but I couldn't move my mouth. Panic set in as pain spread over my body. I supposed that I was making sounds, because a male voice shushed me, telling me it was okay.

"You're in a hospital." The voice was echoing. "Your eyes are swollen shut and your jaw is wired. Your right arm is in a cast. You have a few broken ribs. But you're safe and you'll be okay."

I didn't answer, breathing in shallow gulps.

"Are you in pain, angel?"

The voice was familiar, but I couldn't quite place it.

"Do you remember what happened?" he said.

Gabe's voice, but not exactly. And then it started coming back in detailed flashes. "Juleen!"

"She's safe. I have a guard on her."

Okay, now I knew who he was. And yes, I was in pain. Lots of it. I started to cry.

"I'll get the doctor."

I heard him leave. I tried to open my eyes again but couldn't. I raised my right arm and it felt incredibly heavy. Oh yeah, arm in cast. I raised by left arm and opened an eyelid. Light coursed through my pupil and I could make out a space with objects that began to spin around me. Nausea oozed from my pores. I began to cough and then gag.

"Sit up, sit up." Chris was holding me as I bent over and began to retch. He pulled back my hair as I vomited. "You're okay, baby. Doc is here."

I heard them talk to each other. The male voice said, "Not much blood here. That's good." To me: "Terry, can you hear me?"

I nodded.

"Do you know where you are?"

"Hospital." My voice was thick. My jaw was sore. I was talking strictly by moving my lips in front of my teeth and my tongue in back of my teeth. It was really weird.

"Are you in pain?"

"Yes." It came out as a hiss.

"I'm going to give you something to take the edge off, okay?"

I nodded. I felt my nose itch again and went to scratch it. Heavy arm—that one in a cast. The left arm went to my nose and something was stuck in my nostrils. I tried to pull it out, but someone stopped me. "That's your oxygen tube, angel. You have to leave that in."

Okay. So that's what was itching me.

I heard a panicked beeping. Chris said, "You have to keep your arm straight, Terry. Every time you move it, your IV crimps and the machine beeps."

I felt something alternately tightening and loosening around my legs.

Okay, I knew what that was. Intermittent pneumatic compression.

A moment later something tightened above the cubital fossa on my left arm. Beeps followed the release of the tension.

Blood pressure cuff—check.

IPC—check.

IV—check.

Oxygen tube—check.

Catheter? I felt something down there. Check again.

I could hear my heartbeat, slow . . . steady.

Heartbeat—check.

I didn't know what the doctor put in my IV, but within a minute, all went black.

The third time I roused, I still couldn't open my eyes. But I heard one voice in conversation with itself until I realized it was Gabe and Chris talking to each other. It was the first time in over a decade that the three of us had been in a room together.

And people say miracles are only in fables.

I was trying to eavesdrop, but I couldn't make out the words. The dialogue was on digital delay, a reverberation of each sentence that overlapped the next one, which made it virtually impossible to understand. I must have groaned, because the talking stopped.

"Mom?" I felt someone take my hand. "Mom, it's me, Gabriel. Can you hear me?"

I nodded. I tried out a smile but didn't quite get there. I squeezed his fingers. I think I must have asked about Juleen because of his answer.

"She's fine. Chris set her up with violin and Spanish lessons."

Okay, I thought. *Spanish is good.*

"She's doing okay. She asks about you, but we both don't think it's a good idea for her to see you until you're a little stronger."

The more awake I became, the more pain I felt.

Somebody, please knock me out.

I must have groaned, because Chris asked if I was in pain.

I nodded.

Doc came in a minute later, pain subsiding, lights out.

It was like that for a while. Each time I woke up, I could manage a little more time before things became overwhelming and I needed to sleep. Sometimes I heard people talking, not realizing that I was listening. Bits of speech here and there, some of it positive.

Good vitals.

Good bloods.

Swelling subsiding.

Kidney function improving.

Kidney function improving? What was wrong with my kidneys? No matter, because whatever was wrong, they were on the mend.

I had no idea how long I'd been hospitalized. It seemed like forever. This alternating pattern of wakefulness, nausea, pain, and slipping back into darkness. Sometimes the room was almost silent except for the clicking of a keyboard. Sometimes I could feel Chris's presence. Sometimes the room felt devoid of anything alive, including myself.

But I was getting better. I remember the turning point was waking up with the ability to open my eyelids without manual help. Slits of light came through, and I was actually able to recognize things without the room spinning. I could cock my head and see hospital monitors. I could turn my neck to see a body from the shoulders down, sitting on a chair with a laptop. If I craned upward, I could see a face in intense concentration, eyes behind wire-rimmed glasses fixed on the screen, hair playing peekaboo with high cheekbones. There was a wide mouth, a prominent chin, and thick light eyebrows arched over what I knew were brilliant blue eyes. White hair that still held streaks of the blond that once was.

He was as gorgeous as ever. Probably as charming as well. How else do you get women to whore for you? Once, I had been deeply in love with him, the only boy—well, man now—I had ever passionately loved. That had faded but wasn't completely gone. What hadn't faded were the memories of why I'd left him—twice. In today's vocabulary, he'd be designated as a toxic male, which really was a nothing label. It certainly didn't explain the scope of what Christopher Donatti was capable of doing. He was a violent man, abused as a child and abusive as an adult. I had stuck it out with him for a long time. Then a serene man and an unplanned pregnancy convinced me to make a hasty retreat. Devek had been kind, especially in the beginning, a quiet lover but not a particularly good one. I thought I had wanted calm and tranquility, but sometimes you needed a little wind to make the boat sail.

I wasn't sure what crises had turned Devek into a gambler once again. His family had told me that chapter had passed. It could have been pressure from his stressful job as a cardiac surgeon. It could have been his desire to keep up with his older brother, who controlled the family fortune. Or it could have been the addictive rush that was missing in his life. It played havoc on the family. He lost everything. He started to owe money. Lots of it.

He was looking for insane ways to get out of debt. Some of his half-baked ideas included me, others included Juleen. Of course I wouldn't agree to anything. So I left with my children.

I was sure that Devek had sent over the two goons to retrieve

Sanjay and Juleen and take them back to India. I didn't know if beating me up in the process was part of the plan. I couldn't picture him doing that to me. But I was very bad at reading men. I had made terrible choices. I could have blamed it on my father—my mother had died in childbirth—but the truth was I had a brain. I just didn't use it when faced with the Y chromosome.

Chris was still working on his laptop, oblivious to my awaking. When I said hey, he jerked his head up.

"Hey there." He took off his glasses and closed his laptop. "How are you?"

How was I? I wasn't sure.

"Are you in pain?"

"Little."

"I'll get the doctor."

"No." I shook my head. I was tired of being out of it. "No." I closed my eyes. It was a strain to keep them open. "How long have I been here?"

"Five days. Wow, you sound much better."

I did sound better. I could talk in full sentences. "Juleen is okay?"

"She's doing fine. She's safe. She's with Gabe. Do you remember Gabe visiting you?"

"No."

"He's going to Japan tomorrow. His agent got him an Asia tour. I told him to take it. I know he'll want to see you." A pause. "It's midnight."

"Don't wake him." I felt his hand on my cheek. His touch was delicate. "I'm tired."

"I'm happy to see you, Terry."

Tears in my eyes, I turned my head away from him.

"I'm going to get the doctor. I want him to see you awake, okay?"

"Okay."

He took his hand away and I heard him leave.

Awake, I could feel waves of pain—sometimes it was acute, sometimes it was a throbbing pulse. It didn't feel good, but it was tolerable. A minute later, I heard two men come in. I opened my eyes. The stranger introduced himself as Drew Jamison.

"How are you?"

"Passable." My speech was funny sounding but understandable. "What are my vitals?"

"Your vitals?"

"She's an ER doctor," Chris told him.

"Your vitals are fine. Your temperature is back to normal."

I had had an infection, then. Not surprising, considering what I went through.

He said, "Your creatinine levels are still high."

"Rhabdo."

"Yes, but they're starting to come down. I'm hoping to take the catheter out soon. Once you can drink and pee on your own, I can send you home in a day or two."

Home. Where exactly was home now?

"You know your jaw is wired."

"Yes."

"You can drink from a straw. I'll start you on liquids. But you're going to have to drink tons and tons of water to get rid of the excess protein in your urine."

"I know." I sighed. "I'm tired."

"I understand. I'll set up to remove the catheter. Once that's gone, you should try to walk. I can order a physical ther—"

"I'll help her," Chris said. "I'll have to do it when I get her home anyway."

I guess home for the time being was with him.

"It might be good to have a physical therapist just to see how it's done, sir."

"Whatever."

I recognized the annoyed sound in his voice. Chris did not like help.

The doctor said, "I'll order that for tomorrow. I guess tomorrow is today."

Chris said, "Anything else you need, baby?"

I said, "I'm in some pain."

"As you probably know, most of the regular painkillers are renal toxic," the doctor said. "How about tramadol?"

"Low dose."

"You get sick from it?"

"A little. Thank you."

"You're very welcome. Good to see you talking, Doctor. Take care."

"Sure." I let out a big sigh. It hurt my ribs. I opened my eyes and strained to look at my ex-husband. "Sorry."

"Don't be silly." Chris took my right hand and kissed my fingers. "Can I sign your cast?"

"Draw a picture."

"I can do that." A megawatt smile. "What do you want?"

"You choose—G-rated, please."

"Spoilsport." He took out a pen from his jacket pocket. "How about a unicorn?"

"Unicorn?"

"Yeah, don't girls like unicorns?"

"I'm a woman."

"Women like money. Want me to draw a wad of cash?"

I felt myself smile. "Unicorn."

"I thought so." He gently stretched my right arm and started sketching. I couldn't see what he was drawing, so I closed my eyes again.

He went silent. Then he said, "Do you remember what happened?"

"Dribs and drabs."

"Any idea who did it?"

I could feel emotion get stuck in my throat as I thought of my son. "Probably Devek." I paused to find my voice. "He wasn't there when it happened."

"How do you know?"

"I didn't . . . sense him."

"Did you recognize who was there?"

"No." Again the tears. "Does it matter? My son is gone."

We didn't talk. Chris kept drawing. I could feel scratches on the cast. About two minutes later, he let go of my arm. "What do you think?"

I labored to open my wet eyes. It was a very cute unicorn with a big smile on his face. "Nice."

"I was thinking of giving him a cute little hard-on—"

"Stop it—"

"That's why he's smiling."

"Same Chris."

"Yeah, I haven't changed." He stroked my upper arm. "I'm still compulsive, aggressive, dominant, controlling, and addicted to sex. I hate to be told no, and because of what I built I don't hear it very often."

"I'm happy for you."

"Are you?"

I closed my eyes. "Yes. Truly."

He said, "I haven't changed . . . but I am older. At forty-four, I try to think before I react. Being sober helps."

"I'm proud of you."

"Thank you." A pause. "What about you? Have you changed?"

"I don't know." I was completely demoralized. "I don't know."

"You don't need to change," he told me. "In my eyes, you were always perfect."

"Thanks, but we both know that's not true."

Please make him stop. I can't go into this now.

"You look tired, baby."

"A little."

"Go to sleep. I'll be here when you wake up." A pause. "Your worst nightmare, huh?"

"Not at all." I had already gone through my worst nightmare. Even dealing with Chris was a cakewalk in comparison. My eyes turned wet once again. "Not at all."

He dabbed my puffy cheeks with a tissue. "I'll keep you safe, angel. You and your daughter. I promise."

"Thank you."

"Heal up and get some sleep."

I didn't argue. Even if I wanted to, arguing with him was fruitless. His MO. He could be utterly beguiling, then turn fierce in a toe tap. And he would turn: a matter of when, not if. I had left him for another man. The reality of it was I hadn't left him for another man. I had left him for the baby who just happened to be fathered by another man. Chris might overlook some things, but not that.

No, not that.

CHAPTER 4

I T WAS PENDERGAST who got the buzz to come to the hospital. He was older than most of the bodyguards and a crack shot; Donatti had employed him from the beginning, almost ten years ago. As he waited for the man to show, Donatti took out the two foreign phones he'd confiscated from Terry and the girl five days ago. He had the chargers—he was smart enough to bring those—but he didn't have the adapters from the Indian plugs to American electrical sockets. Terry probably had one in her purse, but the purse was in his room, and he was the only one who had access to his personal space. No one could break into the room even if they wanted to. It was built like a bank vault. Donatti even had a bank vault inside. A bank vault in a bank vault. Terry would be the exception. He'd keep her there because it was secure, and he needed her safe when he wasn't with her. And it was the one place where he could be completely alone with her.

The phones had been off all this time. Maybe they still had some juice. While he waited for backup, he thought about a lot of things, his opposite emotions waging war. On one hand, he was deliriously overjoyed to have her back in his possession. On the other hand, he was still enraged at her.

At forty-four, I try to think before I react.

His phone buzzed. Donatti pushed the button. A voice said, "I'm here, boss."

"I'll come get you."

He walked out of Terry's hospital room—there were only ten beds—past the treatment room, and out the double doors into the hallway. Pendergast was about six even with a stocky build and big arms. Donatti often saw him reading in the staff dining hall on his off-hours, sipping coffee and engaged in the classics. He motioned to him with a crooked finger, took him through the medical maze until they reached Terry's room.

"I'll be in my office upstairs. If something comes up, call me. I'll be down in thirty seconds. Stay outside her room. No one goes in. Not even the doc."

"Got it."

"You want a chair?"

"Been sitting all night, boss. I'm fine."

"Good man." Donatti turned and went up to his office.

Sitting at his desk, he turned on the phones and both of them had about 20 percent power left, which was enough for his purposes. He went on Terry's phone app first and took several snapshots of every single call that had been placed to her in the last five days. Did the same with texts. He repeated the procedure with Juleen's phone. Then he turned them both off.

On the first day, the call list showed Gabe's number, his number, and Juleen's number. Then it went dark for thirty-six hours until there was a series of calls from just a name.

Devek
Devek

Devek
Devek

Must have been over two dozen calls.

The texts were equally frantic.

Where are you. Call me! It's urgent.

Call me, Terry. It's very urgent.

Emergency. Call me.

About twenty texts, all of them displaying panic.

Time to find out what that was all about. The difference between India and Nevada was thirteen and a half hours, which would make it about two-thirty in the afternoon there. He turned on Terry's phone, pressed the call button, and waited. It was picked up on the second ring. Donatti waited.

"Terry?" A male voice. "Where *are* you? I've been trying to reach you for three days. Is Juleen with you? Is she okay? Are you all right?"

Donatti said, "It isn't Terry."

"Oh, dear God, please don't hurt her. Please don't hurt my daughter. Please, please. I will get the money. It will take a little time, but I swear to you I will get all the money. I will give you one hundred thousand USD as a show of good faith, but please don't hurt—"

"It's Christopher Donatti, Devek. I have them. They're safe."

There was a pause over the line. "Terry is with you?"

"Yes."

"And Juleen too?"

"Juleen, yes, but not Sanjay. He was taken from Terry, and, as a parting gift, they beat the shit out of her."

"Oh, dear God! Is Terry all right?"

"No, she's not all right. She's in the hospital."

"How bad?"

"Bad, but she should recover."

"This is all my fault."

"I'm sure that's true. Confession may be good for the soul, but it won't help your situation. How much do they want for the boy? I'm sure they've contacted you about him."

There was a protracted silence. "It's a long story. You see, I have some gambling debts—"

"I'm up to speed, Devek. How much do they want for your son?"

"They want what I owe them."

"And how much do you owe them?"

"A lot."

"How much?"

"More than I have—"

"Devek, do you want my fucking help or not?"

"Two and a half million."

Donatti's heart skipped. He often worked with women—and men—who had racked up gambling debts. Casinos would call him and he'd pay off the debt at a discount, then the debtors would work off what they owed him by whoring. But even as someone who had done this for a while, Donatti was staggered: $2.5 million was a huge amount of debt.

Devek added, "That includes the interest."

"That's a shitload of money," Donatti said. "How the fuck did they let you go so far?"

"No one was paying attention until it was too late."

"Stop spinning me bullshit, okay? I don't like it, I don't like you, and I'm a millisecond away from hanging up. I have worked with casinos for over a decade. I own a casino. You are *always* paying attention. Why did they give you so much credit?"

"I come from a wealthy family."

"Very wealthy, right?"

"Yes."

"And they're not helping you out?"

"My father is ill. He assigned my older brother executorship of all our holdings. He pulls the purse strings. And he's angry at me right now."

"He's angry enough to let his nephew die for your sins?"

"He says he'll give me a little to stall them. But he's very, very angry. He has helped me out before, and I swore I would give it up. And I did give it up. But then things . . . spiraled. My fault, yes. The problem is now he doesn't trust me."

For good reason. Donatti thought a moment. "Why don't you sign a promissory note to him?"

"I offered. He won't take it."

"Okay. I'm doing this for Terry, not for you, okay?"

"Yes, okay."

"How about this? I'll call him up and act as guarantor of the note. Anything goes wrong, you'll have two people riding your ass."

"He won't do it."

"Why not?"

"Because he's too angry."

Had to be more to the story than what he was letting on. "What did you do to make him so angry?"

"I told you. I broke my promise about gambling."

"What did I say about spinning bullshit? What did you do to piss him off?"

"I'd rather not say."

"You're in no position to make the conditions. What did you do?"

"I made him a promise in exchange for my debt." A long pause. "I couldn't deliver."

"Stop being evasive. What did you promise him?"

"I can't say . . . I'm too ashamed."

"Ah." Donatti let out a small laugh. Sick bastard. "You promised him your daughter, didn't you?"

"That would not have been a problem." A long pause. "Juleen wasn't who he wanted."

And then it dawned on him. "Terry."

"He had always liked her."

"You pimped your wife."

"Please don't—"

"Hey, I'm no citizen myself. I don't judge. But I imagine she judged plenty. That's why she left?"

"She said she needed time to think about it. And then I didn't hear from her." He was breathing hard over the phone. "You must understand. They were going to kill me."

"They should have. Would have done everyone a big favor." The line went silent. Donatti said, "How much is your brother kicking in? One hundred thousand?"

"Yes, but I think I can get more."

"How much more?"

"Maybe I can squeeze a half million. But I really don't know. Even my brother doesn't have that much cash. Can you help me? I'll pay every cent back. It may take me time, but I have a good job. I'm a surgeon. I swear I'll pay you back every penny."

"Devek, I don't take layaway plans."

"I don't know what that is."

If Donatti could have strangled him over the line, he would have. He said, "How long did they give you to raise the money for your son?"

"Two weeks."

"Starting when?"

"Three days ago." When Donatti didn't answer, Devek said, "Hello?"

"I'm thinking. Give me a moment." A minute passed. "Okay, the next time your son's kidnappers call you, give them my number. Do you have a pencil?"

"Yes, hold . . . yes, yes. I have a pencil and paper."

Donatti gave him the number. "Recite it back to me." Devek repeated the numbers. "Good. Have them call me. Tell them you don't have the money, but I do. Tell them I'm a businessman just like them, and if they don't believe you, tell them to look me up. I've got an illustrious history."

"I'm aware of that."

"Good. You should be."

"Can I talk to Terry? I want to tell her I love her and that I'm so sorry."

"No, you can't talk to her, but I'll pass the message along."

"Can I please talk to my daughter? You have a child. You must know how I feel."

"I don't care how you feel, Devek. Besides, it's one in the morning. But even if it was one in the afternoon, I'd say no. And I'll tell you this much. I'm a lot nicer to your daughter than you ever were to my son."

Silence. "I sincerely apologize—to both of you."

"Yeah, too little and way too late, but it doesn't matter now. Give the goons my number, and we'll go from there."

"Chris, I don't know how to thank you—"

"It's Mr. Donatti to you, and don't bother thanking me because I'm not doing you a favor. You're going to owe me, big time."

"I already told you I'll pay you back every cent—plus interest."

"Nuh-uh. I don't need your money. I've got plenty of cash that's already gathering dust. Listen carefully, motherfucker, because this is the deal. You took my wife. I want her back."

WHEN CHRIS WHEELED me out of the hospital, I could open my eyes, although I had blood-filled black bags under my orbs and deep purple eyelids on top. My face was a Pollock painting in mixed berry colors. The good news was that the green was starting to come in, and as ugly as it was, it indicated healing. My ribs didn't hurt as much anymore, and I could breathe better now. That wouldn't be an issue going forward. My arm was in a cast, and I had the option of a sling should the plaster prove to be too onerous. I could walk, but at the pace of a turtle. My back still hurt, and although my creatinine levels were back down, I wasn't completely out of danger.

I wanted to see Juleen, but she was in the middle of lessons, and part of me agreed with Chris and Gabe—that perhaps it was wiser to wait until I looked better and was a bit stronger. The one thing I didn't want was her mothering me. A few more days wouldn't make a difference. She was being looked after and she was safe. That was all that mattered.

Chris seated me in the back of a stretch limo, and he came around and sat behind the driver. I struggled to put my seat belt on. He watched me, knowing I didn't want help. When I finally clasped the buckle, he told the driver to go.

He said, "You doing all right?"

I looked out the window: it was all greenery and mountains. "Disoriented."

"You'll get the lay of the land."

"Do you own all this?"

"I do."

"Lots of acreage."

"Lots and lots. I have my own town—my own police and fire and my own zip code."

"What's the town called?"

"Mountain Pass. Not very original, but it's neutral."

"Do you have your own laws?"

"No. We're subject to the laws of the state and, of course, federal law. Recreational marijuana is legal here. I own a dispensary." A pause. "I say own, but it's all in Gabe's name under shell corporations. He doesn't want to be associated with brothels. He thinks it's bad for his image."

I nodded. A minute later, buildings came into view. The closest one was a four-story square of brick and glass that sat isolated in its own space. The others looked to be about a quarter mile away.

We passed a front entrance, and the driver pulled around the back, which I suppose was mutually beneficial. I didn't want to see any-one, and I was sure that Chris didn't want anyone to see me. Once the driver turned off the motor, he hustled to get the wheelchair out. I said, "I'd rather walk."

"Whatever you want." Chris turned to the driver. "You can fold that up."

"Of course," the driver said. "Anything else, sir?"

"No, we're fine."

Chris punched in numbers on a call box. The first door led us to a sally port. The second door could be accessed only with two keys after an iris or retinal eye-recognition-system scan. After it clicked, Chris opened the door and let me go through. We walked a few paces until we hit an elevator. That too required keys and eye recog-nition. Once inside, we rode the elevator to the third floor, and the door wouldn't open until Chris punched in more numbers.

Finally, we were in a small anteroom with two doors. Chris said, "This one leads to a staircase that goes to Gabe's room. It's where your daughter is. I've got a guard outside her door and one inside while she has her lessons. It would take an army to get through to her."

"Thank you so much for keeping her safe."

"No problem. This door leads to my lair. No one goes in there ever. Well, Gabe was in there once or maybe twice while we were waiting for a doctor. But I took him downstairs to be treated. You are an exception."

"I can stay with Juleen if you'd prefer."

"I don't prefer." He punched in numbers on a keypad and looked at a camera. "Your god is a very jealous god." He regarded me with flat eyes. "Besides, you need someone to tend to you. That's not your daughter's job."

"Agreed. I just hate to invade your private space."

"You're not invading anything. I want you near me." More keys, more biometrics, more punch panels. Security on security. This one used a thumb and eye system. Finally, a door as thick as a bank vault opened. He turned on overhead lights even though there was daylight inside.

I stepped over the threshold.

I was gobsmacked.

It was something in between the NASA mission control center and a medieval torture chamber. All the walls were bare. Some were painted black, and some were painted bright white. The floors were deep black marble without a hint of veining. Directly to the right was a cube-shaped area consisting of a black desk with a black leather chair and a black set of filing cabinets. Across from the desk were black shelves that held a microwave and a coffeepot. Next to the shelves was a black refrigerator, and next to the refrigerator was a partially opened door that looked like it led to a bathroom.

I stepped forward and saw straight ahead a bank of monitors—about a dozen stacked screens along with a control panel with dials and buttons and several keyboards. There were gadgets and gizmos that looked very important, but I had no idea what they were. Behind the controls was a captain's chair—in black leather, of course—on a raised platform. This was no doubt where he ran the entire system, whatever it was.

Next to mission control was a nine- or ten-foot extra-wide black leather couch. I don't know why he bothered with the couch in a place where no one ever came up. It certainly didn't make the place look homey.

I glanced to my left and saw that the floor had been covered with black mats. There were weight racks, each one holding numerous barbells on either side stacked like a wedding cake. There were also racks with multiple dumbbells. On the floor were kettlebells of different sizes. Hanging from a long black pole that stretched across the weights were straps and chains and other accoutrements that I couldn't name. There was also a stationary bike, a treadmill, and an elliptical machine.

Like Chris, everything was meticulously organized.

I said, "Your torture chamber?"

"Except the only one I'm torturing is myself."

"What are all the straps for?"

"Weight belts."

"The chains?"

"Strength exercises."

"If you say so." I shook my head. "You've heard of *Fifty Shades of Grey*. This is *One Shade of Black*."

"I like to keep things simple."

The surroundings were so dreary, especially after the vibrancy of India. "You're an artist, Chris. Where is the color?"

He lifted up a pants leg and showed me a royal-purple lizard-skin boot. That's right. He loved boots, especially those with heels that gave him even more height. All coming back to me.

He said, "You know that I work primarily in pencil, charcoals, and pen and ink."

He was correct. "I suppose you don't have much need for a woman's touch."

"No women in my life."

"What about your secretary? What's her name?"

"Talia. For a while, she was a convenience. Then times changed, and I thought it was best to cut out anything that smacks of sexual harassment. Now she's just an employee. A good one, but that's all."

"How did she feel about the change?"

"Probably she didn't like it. I don't really care. Business first."

"What about your prostitutes?"

"We call them 'sex workers.' I pay for everything."

"You pay for your own women?"

"Yep. I technically pay myself, but the workers also get their cut and their tips. Are you hungry? I've got stacks of protein shakes in the fridge."

"Thank you. I'm okay for right now."

"I hope you're not a vegan like your daughter."

"Vegetarian. What's wrong with being a vegan?"

"It's a pain in the ass. I finally found someone who can cook Indian."

"Who's that?"

"One of my sex workers."

"You have a *prostitute* cooking for my daughter?"

His eyes narrowed. "Stop being so damn judgmental. You were down-and-out once. Have a little compassion."

I sighed. In reality, I was once nothing more than a prostitute, except it was to just one man. When I graduated medical school, I put all the dependence behind me—or so I thought. Here I was, once again, in the same situation I had been in twenty-two years ago. "You're absolutely right. I'm sure she's a good cook."

He said, "Your daughter says she makes great samosas and curries."

"Great," I said. "She can cook for me as well once I can open my mouth."

"You're going to need meat to get your weight and strength back."

"It's a moot point. Unless you're planning on giving me a meat shake."

"Yum." He smiled. "C'mon. You need your rest."

As he led me through his space, I notice a steel door that looked like it belonged in a bank. "What's this?"

"My vault." A pause. "Want to see it?"

"Another time."

"Tired?"

"A little. It's freezing in here."

"I work at night. The temperature keeps me from falling asleep. C'mon, let's get you some rest."

His bedroom was enormous. The plus was that it had natural

light coming in through a window that framed the mountainside. I could tell the glass was bulletproof because the thickness made the outside look a little smeary. The walls were painted bright white and were bare except for a drawing hanging over a chest of drawers opposite the bed. The serene look on my face spoke to happier times.

"When did you do that?" I whispered.

"Right after you left me. Notice it's pen and ink."

"Right. I'm surprised you didn't throw darts at it."

"Why ruin a perfect drawing?"

I sighed. "It's lovely."

"Like the subject."

Saith the prince of darkness. "Thank you. It's better looking at that than looking in the mirror."

He studied my face. "You'll heal. But you'll need to take it easy."

The bed was as oversize as he was, with a black comforter that was obviously custom made and black pillowcases. The mattress was high off the floor. He pulled back the covers and helped me get into the bed. Once I was adequately propped up, he pulled the comforter back onto my lap.

"I think I need a nap," I told him.

"I'm not surprised. Want me to pull the shades over the window?"

"No, I actually like seeing the mountain. Something so majestic. It makes you feel small, and that's . . . comforting."

"I'm glad you like it. I framed the window around it. By the way, I laundered all your clothing. The long stuff is hanging in the closet. All the rest is in drawers. Do you want pajamas?"

I was wearing a loose, long dress. "The elastic on the waistband still hurts my ribs. I'm okay."

"Bathroom's over there, but don't get out of bed unless I'm around. I've got a thick, high mattress and don't want you falling."

"Right." I waited a second before I spoke. "Don't you have a bathroom next to your refrigerator?"

"I do."

"Why do you have two bathrooms?"

"Because I can. And aren't you glad that's the case now that you're here?"

I laughed. "Who cleans everything?"

"Well, since there are no such things as housekeeping fairies and I'm the only one who steps foot into this room, it means I clean everything."

"I'll do it for you," I blurted out. "After all, I know how you like it."

He sat down next to me. "I don't need a maid, Teresa. I need for you to get better." He touched my cheek. "God, you are lovely! Even in this state it's easy to see how gorgeous you are."

"Right!"

"You never really got it . . . how the boys slavered over you in high school. The way men looked at you when you got older . . ." He raised his white eyebrows. "Get some rest." He went to the closet and took down a blanket and pillow from the top shelf. "I'll sleep on the couch."

"Why don't you let me sleep there?"

"Because I work all night. Sometimes I don't even bother to use the bed. I'm very comfortable on it. It was custom built to my size." He smiled. "There are things I have to take care of now that I'm back. You're okay being here alone?"

"I'm fine."

"If I leave you alone for a couple of hours, don't get ambitious, please. I know you. You don't like help, but you need it. Just wait until I come back. Promise?"

"I promise." I smiled as best I could. "Thank you, Christopher. Thank you, thank you. Talk about down-and-out. I'd be lost without you . . . again."

"Stop talking nonsense. You're a doctor. You've got options." He grinned. "You can always work for me. I pay very well."

"I may take you up on that."

"Actually, that would be a terrible idea."

"Why? I'm a very good ER doctor."

"I know that. Competence is not the issue. Once you become my employee, you're off-limits." He winked at me. "Can't let that happen." He kissed his fingers and put them on my lips. "Sweet dreams, angel."

After he left, I stared at the mountains, wondering if somewhere within the depths of the earth, there was a creature eagerly waiting to devour anyone who trod upon its path. Of course, I knew there were no creatures like that down under, only those living on the surface of this planet who devoured with equal alacrity.

CHAPTER 5

A S THE PLANE began its descent into Miami International, Decker and Rina placed bets on who would have the most emails and who would have the most texts. They had turned off all U.S. electronic equipment upon arriving in Tel Aviv nearly two weeks ago and had rented a simple flip phone for Israel—a primitive mode of communication, but it worked.

"You're going to win, hands down." While seated, stretched out on the leg rest, Rina began to fold her blanket. "When you left, there was an unidentified body in the woods. I'm betting that the department texted you every few minutes with updates even if you didn't respond."

"The body is female," Decker answered.

"Aha!" Rina wagged a finger. "You did check your phone, you rat fink."

"Only on the way over." Decker paused. "I couldn't sleep."

"Because you didn't take Ambien. And you didn't take the pill because you wanted to be up and ask about the case."

"I just asked Tyler if the coroner had anything to say about how she died."

"And?"

"Well, she sustained stab wounds," Decker said. "Don't know how many and what was lethal."

"Something was lethal. She was buried."

Good point. "How long are we scheduled to visit our respective moms?"

"Two days with yours and two days with mine. Your mom's visit is first. If you have to get back to Greenbury PD, I can see my mom by myself. I might stay a little longer if you're busy."

"Whatever you want, darlin'." A smile. "Even with the body in the woods, I think you're going to win the text-and-email competition. There's always a kid calling you every three minutes."

"Why would one of the children call me when he or she knows I'm not going to answer?"

"Force of habit. Or just to vent about something. When they vent, they don't even care if we respond. As a matter of fact, they prefer it if we don't say anything."

Rina laughed. It was true. "No, you're going to win. Not only do you have the female body in the woods, you also have Gabe, who will probably want to update you on his mother and what happened to her."

"Yeah, but Donatti will tip the scales on your side."

"Why would Chris call me?"

"Because he's always calling you."

"He doesn't call me that often. Besides, now he's busy with Terry. I wonder what happened to her?"

"I'm sure we'll find out." A pause. "Are we still on vacation with our moms?"

Rina said, "What do you mean?"

"Does the unplugging extend to Florida?"

"What do you think?"

Decker said, "I vote we can plug back in."

"I vote yes as well. We're in America. It's back to the grind. But it's a nice grind."

"It is. But I'm already missing Israel. I can't wait to get started on the remodel." Decker smiled. "The place is perfect."

"The house is nicer and bigger than I remembered. I love the arched windows. And the old Moroccan tiles on the living room floor. I didn't remember that either."

"Neither did I," Decker said. "And the location. You can't beat the location."

"The location is great."

"I saw you eyeing the front yard. What do you have in mind?"

"The usual. Flowers and some nice greenery. Also, fruit trees. It would be nice to have fresh oranges and lemons instead of buying them in the supermarket." She smiled. "I suppose we should close the deal before we start fantasizing."

"It's going to happen," Decker said. "Besides, fantasizing is so much fun."

"Better than reality, with all those sticky details."

"Ach." Decker waved a dismissive hand. "We're not in a hurry. It'll be fun."

The seat belt light came on. Seats upright, tray tables and footrests stowed in the landing position, and carry-ons back in the overheads.

"Never ate so much good street food in my life."

The plane broke through the clouds, gliding over the Atlantic until a city of high-rises gave way to green land and intercoastal waterways.

"Here we go," Decker said.

"How are your legs?"

"A little cramped, but *waaaay* better than coach. This is going to spoil me."

Rina said, "Maybe we can tell the kids how much we truly appreciated the gift and how comfortable we felt for the first time, and it was really, really a treat and it would be really nice if we could do it again sometime in the future. Because after all, you only have one mother."

"That's called a guilt trip."

"Like they haven't guilt-tripped *me* before? Don't you know, darling? Guilt is a two-way street."

DECKER WON THE email-and-text bet, but Rina wasn't far behind. The ride to Ida Decker's house was silent except for the constant tapping noise elicited from the phones as they pecked at the keyboards. It was a pleasure to be chauffeured by a car service rather than rent a vehicle. Decker could relax instead of battling traffic.

Rina said, "Oh my Lord!"

"You're reading Gabe's emails?"

"I am. Poor Terry." Rina shook her head. "Her daughter is with her, but her son is gone. Gabe thinks that Devek kidnapped him."

"Why just his son and not his daughter?"

"It sounds like Juleen escaped when they broke into her apartment."

Decker shook his head. "Jeez. Someone really did a number on Terry."

"Shocking."

"I still think of her as an innocent little sixteen-year-old girl. She was so pretty and so bright back then!"

"When I saw her three weeks ago, she was gorgeous and bright. Just dumb when it comes to men."

"Looks like Donatti got his claws back into her. Can you call Gabe? I've got a bunch of stuff from Tyler to go through." Then Decker said, "It's Pauline Corbett."

Rina looked up from her phone. "The body in the woods is Pauline?"

"Yes."

"How was she identified?"

"I think a sister identified her remotely from a tattoo. I'll check that out. Tyler said that Forensics took her DNA to the lab, and they should have confirmation in a couple of weeks. Since the email was written ten days ago, the results should be in very soon."

"One mystery solved," Rina said.

"It only brings about more questions." Decker thought about his latest victim and how she was related to his unsolved Missing Persons case.

The events started months ago, when Bertram Lanz had disappeared from a field trip in the woods. He had gotten separated from his fellow residents from his board and care facility, Loving Care. Lanz came from a rich family in Germany, and a kidnapping for ransom had been tossed around as a possibility. But when no note was forthcoming and Bertram's parents never called back, the kidnapping scenario seemed remote.

Then clues popped up, namely a vanishing act by a former nurse named Elsie Schulung, who had worked at Loving Care. Everyone at the facility said Elsie and Lanz were close. Elsie and Pauline Corbett had been lovers. Now Corbett was dead, Schulung was missing, and Lanz had yet to be located. The general thought was that Schulung and Lanz, along with Bertram's girlfriend, Kathrine, had defected to Lanz's hometown in Germany.

But now, who knew?

"I've got calls in to the station, but no one has returned my messages," Decker said. "I don't know whether that's a good or bad sign."

"Have they connected with Lanz's family in Germany?"

"If they have, no one's told me." A sigh. "If only."

"We've been back a couple of hours and you already sound frustrated."

"I'm okay. At least the latest victim is in our jurisdiction."

"And since the body is Pauline, you're certainly not starting from scratch."

"Yes, we've got suspects. First thing we need is Corbett's crime scene. She wasn't killed where she was buried."

"Pauline's blood was in Elsie Schulung's house."

"Yes, but I'm still bothered by the scant amount. It's not enough."

"It's a start," Rina said.

"Well, yes and no," Decker said. "She and Elsie lived there. Pauline's blood could be old. She might have had a bad accident once."

"Well, someone buried her."

He shook his head. "Maybe there are forensics at the scene."

"It's still early days, Peter. I'm sure you'll be right on it once you're back home. In the meantime, we've still got our mothers to deal with. One issue at a time."

Decker laughed. "Right you are."

"You're right about one thing," Rina said. "Chris did call me. Three times. It was almost two weeks ago. I wonder what he wanted."

"We are *not* taking Juleen."

"Yeah, that could be what he wants," Rina said.

"I'll call Gabe. Maybe he knows what's up. At the very least, I'll get an update on Terry."

Gabe answered after three rings. "Rina?"

"Hi, honey. How are you?"

"I'm fine. I'm just about to go into rehearsal. Are you back?"

"Yes, we're in Miami. How's your mom?"

"Thank God she's much better. She left the hospital last week."

"What happened?"

"A couple of men broke into her apartment. They took Sanjay, but Juleen escaped. Mom was beaten up pretty badly—broken bones, black eyes—her jaw's wired. She got kicked in the kidneys."

"Oh, that's so awful!"

"Yes, she looked awful. But thank God she's healing."

"And Juleen?"

"She's fine except for a twisted ankle. They're both at my dad's place. I was with them for a few days. Then this tour suddenly came up. Chris told me to go. I had reservations about leaving Mom, but Chris seems to be taking good care of her."

"Do you know what happened to Sanjay?"

"We suspect that he's with his father, but we don't know. We haven't heard from Devek. Or maybe they have but they're not telling me. Pray for him."

"I will, sweetheart," Rina said. "Chris called me about two weeks ago. Any idea what that was about?"

"Yeah, actually. I think he wanted you to stay with Juleen while Mom was in the hospital. But it's a moot point now. She's out."

Rina paused. "And Chris is okay with Juleen being there—with Terry?"

"I think so. No one has complained to me. Poor kid. I feel so bad for her. I wish I could take her with me, but Mom wouldn't allow it and that would be unfair to Yasmine. It's all she can do to cope with medical school."

"Both of you are busy people. Juleen will be fine as long as she has her mother."

"Juleen is resilient. Even more than Mom." A pause. "Rina, I'm sorry, but I have to go. I'm already late. Can I call you later?"

"Sure. Where are you?"

"Japan. How was Israel, by the way?"

"Fabulous."

"Good. Both Peter and you deserve a little fabulous."

THE FIRST FOUR days, I barely remember anything, sleeping most of the time, occasionally waking up for a protein shake, then going back to sleep. It took about five days to wake up and stay up. The door to the bedroom was partially open and I didn't hear any signs of life. Whatever I felt about Chris personally, I had interrupted the man's life. An enterprise of this magnitude did not run itself, and for the last couple of weeks, he had focused on me. I'm sure he was playing catch-up with everything in his business. I assumed I was alone, trapped in his vault of a bedroom like some modern-day Rapunzel. I had the long hair as a go-with. Living in Mumbai for the past decade, I hadn't cut it at all, as is the style of a lot of Indian women.

I didn't mind being alone. In Mumbai, solitude was a concept encountered solely in ashrams, certainly not in the streets that teemed with people regardless of the hour. On the rare opportunities that solitude presented itself at home, I breathed easier, unencumbered by children or husbands who kept an eye out. Devek was always sneaky about it; Chris was blatant. Whenever we were among people, his eyes were always focused on me even when he was working the crowd. Chris was jealous, but since I wasn't a flirt, he never had cause to accuse me of anything. The affair truly caught him by surprise. I know it gutted him. Not that being faithful was ever high on *his* list, but I had been his property, and someone else had stolen it. I was shocked that he didn't come after me. I thought I had finally dodged the bullet.

And here I was in the same situation as I had been over two decades ago.

It was eleven-thirty in the morning. I had slept for almost twenty-four hours. I should have been ravenous. Instead, I was sick to my stomach. There was a water bottle on my nightstand. I opened it and drained it and waited for the nausea to pass. About ten minutes later, I felt better. But I was sticky and dirty, and my mouth, shut tight with wires and braces, felt like glue.

I sat up in the bed. Then I slid my feet over the side and tried to stand. Shaky, but not as weak as I thought I'd be. After a few minutes, I felt that I could support my weight, and I slowly made my way to the bathroom. After using the facilities, I noticed that a new toothbrush, toothpaste, a washcloth, liquid soap, and body wash had been laid out on the counter. There were two white towels folded in a cubby. I wasn't sure if all this was his or mine, but I hoped he didn't mind sharing. My bandages had been removed, but I wasn't quite sure what to do about the cast on my arm. I knew I shouldn't get it wet, so I wrapped it in a towel.

Chris's shower was enormous, befitting a man of his size. I could barely reach the controls from the outside of the shower door. It was set on hot, which was fine with me, and steamed up the glass almost instantly. Stepping inside, I luxuriated in water washing over me like a baptism, hot needles running down my back. I dumped a handful of body wash on my hair and brought the liquid to a helmet of lather. I was going to sit down on the shower bench, but then I realized I wasn't going anywhere. My eyes saw pinpoints of light as my knees buckled until I was sprawled out on the floor, breathing fast and shallow. I tried to lift my head, but that only made me dizzier.

I called out for Chris, but of course no one answered me. Okay, so I'd just lie here until I could gather up my strength. Unless the drain clogged, I wouldn't drown. The problem was every time I moved my head, things spun around me.

A moment later, I heard him enter the bathroom. He opened the door and I smiled.

"I could use some help, please."

"What the fuck are you doing! I told you not to try to do this by yourself." A sigh. "Hold on." He took off his black jacket and his T-shirt and turned off the water. He knelt down. "Grab my hand."

"I can't move."

"Fuck." He stripped naked and stepped inside, water dripping on his head from the leaky nozzle. He knelt down and looped his arm around me, pulling me up like a rag doll. Soap spread all over his chest. "C'mon."

"I have to rinse my hair."

"You're impossible." He sat me on the bench, and instinctively, I crossed my arms over my chest. He looked at me covering myself and laughed. "Nothing I haven't seen before." He turned the handheld showerhead on. "I told you not to do this without me."

"Yeah, you already said that. I felt yucky."

"Stop squirming." He was trying to rinse my hair, but because I was sitting next to him, the water kept splashing back in his face. "Fuck it." He lifted me onto his lap, pulled my arms away from my breasts, and we sat chest to chest. "Bend your head down. Hold still."

Water rained down on my scalp. He was massively aroused. Even if I hadn't felt him underneath, which was impossible, I could have sensed it by the change in his breathing alone. I had been there a thousand times before. He wasn't even trying to ignore it, to pretend it wasn't happening. I tried to avoid his eyes, but he pulled my chin upward and gave me *that* look.

Oh *God*! I should have expected it, but it still came as a shock. You'd think that surrounded by bevies of beauties, he'd find something other than a forty-two-year-old woman with a purple face from black eyes, a wired jaw, a broken arm, and bruises to stir him up.

I thought, *Nothing I haven't done before.*

I gave him the nod.

It took all of thirty seconds.

Immediately, he shut off the water and lifted me up as I wrapped my legs around his waist. He brought me to the bed. "Turn around."

"Chris—"

"*Turn around.*"

"Chris, please—"

"Turn the fuck around!"

He flipped me over and entered me from the back, pushing in as roughly as he could. "Stop, you're hurting me!" Deaf ears. "You're hurting me!" Instead he jammed my head against the pillow and kept at it, harder and harder until I began to cramp. Tears formed in my eyes. "Please, stop it . . . stop." A pause. "Please."

Eventually, I grew quiet. I don't know how long it took, but it seemed like forever until finally he gave a massive shove. When he pulled out, I curled up in a ball, trying to stem the horrible spasms from my insides. He wouldn't even let me do that in peace. He rolled me on my back, his knees on either side of my hips. He pinned my arms down. Staring at me, his face was a mask of fury. He was still naked, dripping with water and probably sweat.

"How long?" he whispered.

I was completely confused. "Wha . . ."

"*How! Long!*" A pause. "Six months? A year?"

Ah. The affair. My head was reeling. I felt sick to my stomach. "Two—"

"*Two years?*"

"Two months."

"Two *months*?"

I was struggling futilely in his grip. When he finally let go of my hands, I pushed him away, curling back into the fetal position, trying to pull the bedcovers over my body. But they wouldn't budge because he was on top of them. I started shivering like a wet newborn pup.

"He knocked you up after *two* months?" He rolled me on my back again, staring at me. "How many times did you fuck him?"

"I don't know . . ." I was so cold. "Four times—"

"He knocked you up after *four* times?"

"Maybe it was six."

"Six times in *two* months?" I didn't answer. He said, "Didn't you use protection?"

"Of course we used protection. I'm not an idiot." A cramp seized my guts. I turned to my side and balled my body up. "It must have ripped."

"We were having sex all the time without protection. How did you know it was his?"

"I didn't know." I turned over so as not to look at him. "I made him do a paternity test."

"Why did you even bother with the test when he was wearing protection and I wasn't?"

I was silent. My unspoken words cut to the heart of the problem.

Chris had been beaten as a child, once so severely that he had lost a testicle when he was around nine. Although he wasn't sterile—our son proved that—it had never happened again. He refused to take tests, but we both knew what was flying. The fact that I got pregnant after two months with a stranger must have torn away whatever shield Chris had constructed to protect his male pride.

He finally said, "Why didn't you have an *abortion*? I already thought you had one. I beat the crap out of you because of it. I wouldn't have known the difference." When I didn't answer, he said, "Did you love him that much?"

"I didn't love him at all. I was going to end it—"

"Then why did you *run away* with him?"

"I was *pregnant*!"

"Why didn't you just get *rid* of it?"

"I'm Catholic—"

"Don't hand me that utter *bullshit*, Teresa. You're about as Catholic as I am. When you found out it wasn't mine, why didn't you *do* something about it?"

No answer for that one either.

He waited for a minute for me to say something.

A minute was a long time not to speak.

"Ah." He got up from the bed. "I get it." He ripped away the towel that had been wrapped around my cast and dried himself off, then threw it at my face. He started to dress. "You wanted a *baby* more than you wanted *me*."

When he was fully clothed, he rolled me on my back once again. We were face-to-face, nose-to-nose. His eyes told me, in those few moments, that he was reliving all the humiliation I had put him through. I always could tell when he was a finger's snap away from losing it. Instead he stood up and clenched his fists. He said, "You're lucky someone got to you before I did. Otherwise there wouldn't be a whole bone left in your body."

He turned around and left, slamming the door behind him.

HE SHOULD HAVE felt great.

Instead, he felt lousy.

Like always, she had managed to turn triumph into misery.

Fucking bitch!

He came down to the public office—an enormous space that included an entertaining area made up of brown, instead of black, leather couches, tables, TVs, a gaming system, and a professional built-in wet bar. There was a wall facing a view of the mountains. A door led to a private business office. His secretary worked in the main area in an open-plan design. Talia was in her mid-thirties: nice-looking with blond curls that trailed down her back, round brown eyes, and a slim figure, as well as big boobs and a fine ass. She had been adequate as an intimate companion, but when he decided to break it off for business reasons, it was as if it never happened for him. For her, who knew? Who cared?

She was working at her desk and smiled when she saw him.

He didn't smile back. "Coffee, please. Then come into my office and we'll go over scheduling."

Talia stood up. "Right away."

Sitting at his desk, the door ajar, he dropped his head in his hands.

Terry had cheated on him. Big deal. He had dozens upon dozens of women—and men—while they were married. He could have for-given that. He had been a shitty husband. She was entitled.

But to get knocked up after two months?

Six times?

Humiliation coursed through his veins. All his conquests, and he couldn't even manage the most basic of male functions with his own wife.

Talia came in and laid the coffee mug on his desk. "I brought you a biscotti."

"Thank you." He exhaled forcibly and shook his head. "It's been a while. What's on the agenda?"

"You have that bankers meeting at three. You know that, right?"

"No, I don't know a thing. Are we meeting here?"

"Yes."

"How many people are we talking about?"

"Three—Northwest, Central Nevada, and Silver."

"Okay. What else?"

"Pearson and Groger called. They want to know whether to continue the ad campaign."

"What's our capacity?"

"I think over ninety percent. I'll talk to Ann and get you the exact figures for the month."

"That would be helpful. Over ninety is pretty good for summer. I'll call Barry and see where we're at pricewise with them. Pearson is good, but expensive."

"Speaking of Barry, he called. He wants to set up something."

His accountant kept good tabs on what was going on. Donatti said, "Give me some dates. Anything else?"

"Gambling commissioner for the county . . . you said you wanted to set something up with him? When should I do that?"

"Any time."

"You haven't been around much. Is one time better than another?"

"Talia, just set something up and I'll work around it. Jesus!"

She stared at him. Then she said, "She's been in your life less than a month and already you're miserable."

Donatti jerked his head up. "*She* . . . is none of your fucking business."

"It's just because I care—"

"You're skating on very thin ice. I'm about thirty seconds away from blowing." Talia was silent. Donatti said, "Anything else that needs my immediate attention?"

"At some point, we should go over the employee list and payroll. It's been over two weeks."

"Give me about an hour and we'll do that."

"Okay." Talia paused, brushed blond curls from her eyes. Calmly, she said, "Are you going to fire me?"

Donatti stared at her. "What?"

"Is she going to take my place?"

"Terry's a doctor, not a secretary. Last thing she'd want to do is work for me. At the moment, she doesn't even like me." He exhaled again. "But she'll get over it. She always does." He shook his head. "What else?"

"Nothing for now," Talia said. "I'll set up those appointments."

When she started to leave, Donatti said, "Talia?" The woman turned around and he pointed to the chair in front of his desk.

She sat.

Donatti said, "I have no intention of firing you. You're good at what you do and this is your job for as long as you want, okay?"

"Thank you." A small smile. "I appreciate it."

"But . . ." Donatti ran his fingers through his hair. "She isn't going away. She's my wife—"

"Ex-wife—"

"We're Catholic. We got married in a church, and before the eyes of God, she still is my *wife*. More important than God, before my eyes, she's still my *wife*. She will always be my *wife*. You've got to be able to handle that."

She slowly nodded. "No problem."

"Anything she wants, you do with a smile on your face."

"Of course." Talia looked at him. "Is she demanding or something?"

"Terry?" He shook his head. "I don't think she ever asked me for a penny beyond what I gave her. Once she started working, she only used my money for Gabe. Even during the divorce, she didn't ask for anything other than her freedom. She's a good girl." He looked at his secretary. "I'm just saying there's a pecking order and she's at the top. If I tell you something and she tells you something different, you listen to her, not me. We'll sort it out later."

"Understood." A forced smile. "Anything she wants."

Donatti's phone rang. Blocked number. "I've got to take this. Close the door on your way out."

"Of course." She got up and shut the door as she left.

He slid the green icon and said, "I think you have something that I want."

"That could be." A gruff voice crackled over static.

"I need to know what I'm buying."

"I need to know what you're paying."

"I'm not making any offers without seeing the merchandise."

"I'm not showing you anything until I know what you're paying."

"Look," Donatti said. "You're a businessman, I'm a businessman. Everything starts by negotiation. You're not willing to do that, go find your money elsewhere. I'm not even interested in what I'm purchasing. I'm doing a favor for a friend."

"A very close friend," the voice said. When Donatti didn't answer, he said, "You can tell your friend that it's going to cost dearly. And if someone doesn't buy it, I'll have no choice but to destroy unclaimed property."

"If you're not going to negotiate, do whatever you want," Donatti said. "And take out the old man while you're at it. You'd be doing us both a big favor." A pause. "You know, I deal with these kinds of situations all the time: people who don't know how to stop and end up owing a lot of money to the wrong type of men. This is my bread and butter. If you're going to demand full price, I'm out. Like I said, I'm just doing a favor."

There was no response.

Donatti said, "I'm counting to three, then I'm hanging up. One . . ."

"What will you pay?" the voice said.

"We're not even close to that. I need to see the goods."

"I don't have the goods with me right now."

"Then call me back when you do."

"I need a guarantee before I show you anything." A pause. "Something that shows me you are acting in good faith."

"Okay." Donatti exhaled. "I can deal with that. Give me the account numbers and something will be there tomorrow."

"How much?"

"Why don't you wait and see?"

"Do you know how much he owes?"

"Yep. It's still not going to happen. I'm not saying this is the end point. But that's all you're getting at this stage. I give you earnest money, you show me the goods, and we go from there. Yes or no?"

"How much?" he asked again.

"I haven't decided. Whatever it is, it's found money. But I do expect negotiations once you take anything from me. Otherwise, I'll be pissed. You don't want to get me pissed."

The voice paused. "How do I know you aren't working with the police?"

Donatti laughed. "Do you know a fucking thing about me?"

No answer.

"I know you've looked me up. Account numbers? Yes or no?"

"I have to think about it."

"Take your time. I'm not going anywhere."

Donatti hung up. He exhaled again and shook his head. She was positively the most expensive whore he had ever owned.

CHAPTER 6

"WHEN WILL YOU be back?" McAdams was talking over the station house phone.

Decker checked his watch. It was almost seven in the evening, but there was still plenty of daylight. At least he and his partner were in the same time zone. "Probably three days. I'm itching to come home, but I can't skip out on my mother."

"How old is she?"

"Ninety-seven."

"No, you can't get out of that one. We'll hold the fort. Nothing's urgent."

"You must have the coroner's report by now."

"It came in a week ago. She sustained around three stab wounds. None of them got a major vessel but they were deep. She probably bled out."

"Any evidence at the grave site?"

"No knife, if that's what you're asking. This area is filled with rivers and woodlands and creeks. Plenty of places to jettison the knife. We're going to Corbett's place tomorrow. We'll see if we can find anything incriminating. Maybe evidence of animosity or a fight between Corbett and Schulung. Something that would give us a motive for Elsie wanting Pauline dead. We're also back to looking at CCTV for Pauline's car. Anything else we should be looking at?"

"Tyler, do we have *any* evidence that Lanz is back in Germany?"

"No. We could send someone over to see if we can get visual contact."

"We might have to do that," Decker said. "It would help if you had something to justify the trip—like an airline reservation."

"We're attempting to find airline tickets. The most direct route for them is JFK to Frankfurt nonstop. But if you want to cover your tracks, maybe you'd fly to some other airport in Europe and go home by car or train. It's going to take a while."

"Keep at it. Thanks for taking this on while I'm away."

"No problem, boss. Just invite me over to dinner when you get back. I haven't eaten a decent meal in two weeks."

CHRIS HAD CONFISCATED my phone, so I had no way to communicate with my daughter. He had taken my purse and, with that, any money that I had accumulated, but he did leave a digital clock on the nightstand so I didn't lose all sense of reality. It was around four-thirty in the afternoon, still light outside with a strong mountain sun shining in through the bedroom window. He'd been gone about five hours. In that time, I managed to find several towels to dry my body and my hair as best I could. I got dressed in one of the three or four loose-fitting dresses I had packed. They were all short-sleeved, and if I forced the issue, I could accommodate my cast through the armhole. After that, I was exhausted. I napped for a few hours, and when I woke up, I woke up with resolve. I had made a total mess of my life. It seemed at every turn, I had chosen the road less traveled and had wound up lost. But while I was still breathing, I cracked on.

I removed my clothes from the closet and the drawers. I tried to be neat about it. He came in right when I started folding my dresses. He was saying something, but I couldn't make out the words. As soon as he reached the bedroom, he stopped talking. I glanced at him. He was leaning against the doorjamb, staring at me.

"What are you doing?"

Another quick glance. His face, as expected, was angry. I said, "I'm not anyone's whipping boy."

"Whipping boy?" His eyes narrowed. "What are you talking about? I didn't beat you. We had sex."

"You *raped* me."

"I didn't rape you—"

"Yes, you did rape me." I paused for a breath. "I told you to stop. You just ignored me."

"Aw, *c'mon*!"

"You *hurt* me, Christopher. As if I wasn't in enough pain."

"Jesus!" He came over to me, put his hand on my shoulder. "I'm sorry, okay?"

"No, it's not okay. I'm out of here." I shook his hand off.

He didn't speak, but I could sense that he was close. Then he spoke in a low, menacing voice that I knew usually preceded something violent.

He said, "You have an affair, you get pregnant by some ... motherfucker you've known for two months and run off with him. And then after a decade plus—after you refused to even have the *decency* to answer my calls and at least speak to me—Gabe calls me out of the blue and tells me you're in trouble. And I stop my entire life to rescue you and nurse you back to the living. And you have the fucking nerve to bail on me because the sex got a little rough?"

"I'm not your punching bag!"

"It was just fucking *sex*!" he yelled.

"Do you have a suitcase?" I asked.

He was momentarily perplexed. "What?"

"A suitcase. Something small. I don't have hardly anything to pack." I continued folding clothing. "I would use a garbage bag, but I really don't want to appear in public like a homeless woman."

"Why not?" he said. "It's what you are."

I ignored him and kept folding.

He reached toward the top of his closet, opened a cabinet door, pulled down a valise, and shoved it into my chest. "Take it."

I winced with pain as it hit my broken ribs. It was a beautiful, burnished leather case with his initials in gold. "This looks nice," I told him. "I don't want to ruin it. Do you have anything cheaper?"

"I don't do cheap . . . only in wives."

Again, I ignored him. "I'll send it back when I get to where I'm going. Thank you."

He said, "And where are you headed?"

Sarcastic tone. "Well . . ." I stopped for a moment. "I can't go back to L.A. And I can't go to New York because Devek knows the city. I figured I'd try Chicago since I went to school there—"

"Which I paid for."

"You did. Thank you." I resumed my packing.

"Terry, this is ridiculous," he said. "C'mon. I know things got a little out of hand—"

"You *raped* me, Chris." I looked into his eyes. "Then you threatened to *beat* me."

"Terry, you know how I am when I'm mad. I was blowing off hot air."

"And sometimes you do more than just blow hot air."

"I told you it will never happen again!" He was breathing hard. "You're not even well enough to take a shower by yourself, let alone settle yourself and your daughter into a new city."

"I was hoping to leave Juleen here."

"Are you fucking *kidding* me?" He was incredulous. "You're abandoning your child? Again?"

"I'm not abandoning her!" I was defensive. "I just want to be settled before I come get her."

"You're leaving your bastard daughter with *me*? At a *brothel*?"

"I figure she's safe here with you . . . unless you decide to pimp her."

"I hadn't thought about it, but now that you mention it, men would pay big time for those young little luscious lips."

My stomach turned. "You're positively vile."

"And you're no better than a common whore, using me for money," he snapped back. "Speaking of which, you have *none*."

"Unless you intend to steal from me, I came here with about eight hundred dollars."

"Oh, that'll get you far. Then again, I suppose your food bill won't be too high since your fucking jaw is *wired*."

I didn't answer him. What was the point?

"You want money?" When I remained silent, he said, "You want fucking money, Terry?" He grabbed my left arm.

"Let go of me!"

"You want *money*?"

He yanked me out of the room, and holding my left arm in a viselike grip, he opened his vault with a passcode and pupil recognition sensor.

"You're hurting me!"

"I'll give you money!"

Still gripping my arm, he shoved me inside and I hit a wall comprising a steel bank of drawers. He closed the door. We both knew I could die here and no one would know. All he'd have to do is say I left once again, and no one would doubt it.

He was breathing fire. "Open it." When I didn't answer, he yelled, "*Open the drawer!*"

I rubbed my arm and pulled out a drawer. It was filled with bank teller packets fronted with hundred-dollar bills. Neatly stacked—five wide and two across. I couldn't tell how thick the packets were or how deep they were, but it was safe to say there was a lot of money.

"Open another one!"

"Chris—"

"*Open it.*" He jerked a drawer open. "You want money?" He threw a packet at me. "Here! Take my money, bitch. Here." Another missile flew at me. "Here." Another. "*Here.*"

The last one hit my face like a bullet. Pain exploded in my head as I grabbed my cheek. My vision went blurry, I dropped to my knees, and I covered my face.

"Shit!" He was panting. "Damn it!" A pause. "Are you okay?"

"I'm fine." I uncovered my face, tried to steady my breathing. An attempt to stand, but again, I buckled.

"C'mon." He walked over and took my good arm.

"*Get away from me!*" I screamed as I yanked my arm back.

"*Jesus!*" A pause. "I'm just trying to help you up."

"I don't need your help!" I shot back. "I don't need your help, I don't need your money, and I don't need you. You *raped* me—"

"Terry—"

"You raped me, Christopher, and it wasn't the first time. Or the second or the third or the fourth, and so on and so on. But I never said a thing. I always made excuses for you in my head: *He's tired, he's stressed, he's worried, he's drunk, he's stoned, he isn't thinking clearly.* And you know what? I wouldn't have said anything this time, either, except *look at me!*" I was trying to stanch tears. "I've got two black eyes, a purple face, a wired jaw, three broken ribs, a broken arm, and I'm still pissing blood. But none of my injuries— none of them—compare to the pain and heartache I feel over *losing* my little boy. I don't know where he is. I assume he's with Devek, but I don't know. I don't even know if he's safe!" My voice stuck in my throat. "He's only five, and God only knows what he's thinking. He must be so scared!"

Tears streamed down my red cheeks.

"I know you're furious at me, Chris. And some part of me realizes it's justified. But *for God's sake*! I'm forty-two years old, destitute, and ravaged. I had nothing left except a shred of dignity that you ripped away from me. I mean, what kind of monster *does* that?!"

I was gasping for air. I tried to stand, but my head went light and I fell back down. Without asking, he scooped me off the floor, opened the vault door, and took me back into the bedroom, laying me on the bed. It was at that time that we both noticed a big red stain at the back of my dress.

"Shit!" he said. "I'll call the doctor—"

"I don't need a doctor!"

"You're pissing blood—"

"It's my period—"

"Just let me call to make sure—"

"Chris, I know the difference between my urethra and my vagina. I don't *need* a doctor!" I was so completely spent I could barely breathe. I was struggling to get my dress off. My whole body was shaking. My teeth would have been chattering, but my jaw was wired. "Can you help me, please?"

He pulled the dress over my head. I balled it up and threw it across the room. Same with my dirty panties. "You wouldn't have anything for this, would you?"

"What do you mean? Like an aspirin?"

"No, like a Kotex." I wiped tears from my eyes. "Never mind. Could you get me a wad of toilet paper?"

He got up from my bedside and came back with a bright white washcloth.

"I can't use that!" I barked. "I'll stain it."

"I don't care—"

"You won't be able to wash it out."

"Terry, I don't fucking *care*. Just take it, okay?"

I took the cloth and stuffed it between my legs. I generally had light periods. Maybe it would work until he could get me something better. I reached over the bed and pulled the valise he had given me to my side. I retrieved a dress. I undid my bra from the front, threw that across the room. "Help me put this on." Once he did, I lay down and threw the bedcovers over my face.

He pulled the sheet off and held my chin, regarding my face. He said, "You've got a nice-size welt where I beaned you."

"I'll survive." I pushed his hand away and pulled the bedcovers up to my chin and turned away from him. I was trembling under the sheets. "I've survived a lot worse." I was gulping for air. "I can't seem to catch my breath."

"You're having an anxiety attack."

"And which medical school did you go to, Dr. Pimp?"

Chris exhaled. "I have some pills—"

"I don't want any pills!" I was shivering. I softened my voice. I was tired of being angry. I just wanted him to leave. "They're probably contraindicated with kidney problems. Give me one of my sleeping pills. I'll be okay."

He exhaled forcibly. "Can you look at me?"

"I can hear you. What?"

Another exhale. "Teresa, this isn't a prison and I'm no warden. You can leave whenever you want. Just please wait until you're well enough to go and to take your daughter with you. I'll even set you up. I have plenty of money—"

"I've come to realize that."

He took a deep breath and let it out slowly. "I'll do whatever you want me to do to ensure that you'll be comfortable . . . that you won't struggle financially. It's not like when you were twenty and I had you under my thumb. You're a doctor. You can support yourself. You can support your daughter—"

"Juleen."

"I know her name."

"You never call her by her name. It's always *your daughter.* Stop depersonalizing her."

"Teresa, quit *pushing* my buttons!" He bit his lip. "Please."

I didn't answer him.

He said, "I will help you in whatever way you want my help. You're my son's mother. And . . . and I still love you very much. But if you leave me . . . again . . . that door is shut forever. I can't take the emotional upheaval. I don't care if you're on fire and I've got a hose, I'm not coming to your rescue anymore. We are through."

"Mighty fine with me," I told him.

"Peachy!" He stood up. "Nice to know that for once we're on the same fucking page!"

HE WALKED PAST Talia, trying to keep his face as unreadable as it usually was. "I'm on a call for the next forty-five minutes. No interruptions until I say it's over."

She sorted through her ledger. "I must have missed that appointment," she said. "I don't have any calls scheduled for you, Chris."

"It just came up. I'm clear, right?"

"Yes."

"Perfect. Just make sure I get privacy."

"Of course."

He went inside his office and shut the door. He plopped into his chair and threw his head back. He was breathing rapidly, his hands were shaking, and sweat had started forming over his brow and lip. He wiped his face.

He blew out a gust of air.

He took out a key ring and unlocked and opened the bottom drawer of his desk. He retrieved his kit.

Seven years of sobriety down the toilet.

Opening the zipper, he took out a packet, a spoon, a small burner, and a set of matches. Placing the powder in the spoon, he turned on the burner and heated the substance until it was a liquid. Out came the yellow elastic band that he used as a tourniquet, wrapping it around his arm above his elbow. When the vein was thick and pulsing, he sucked up the liquid in a hypodermic.

Steadying his shaking hands.

His phone buzzed.

Out of habit, he glanced at the number.

Blocked.

Well, fuck a duck!

He put down the needle and picked up the phone. "What?"

"Two hundred and fifty thousand and we'll produce the goods. Then we go from there."

"One hundred. No effort on your part. It's pure profit."

"Can't do it for less than two-fifty."

Donatti hung up. He picked up the needle and looked at his arm, judging what he was about to do. His heart was still pounding, and every time he thought about her, the tempo went up a notch.

Steadying his nerves.

His phone buzzed again.

Devek this time.

"What?" Donatti said.

"Did they make contact with you?"

Donatti said, "Yes."

"And?"

"And it's none of your fucking business." Donatti took in a breath and let it out. "When I have something to tell you, I'll call you. But I'll tell you this much. Nothing will happen, Devek, until your lawyer calls my lawyer—who is Terry's lawyer—about the divorce."

"I'm working on it—"

"Well, work fucking faster!" He hung up and took a deep breath. Once again, he aimed the hypodermic at his vein.

His phone buzzed again. This time, it was the blocked number.

Oh, fuck *it!*

He put the hypodermic down and peeled off the elastic tourniquet. By now his fingers were numb. He wiggled them for a second, then slid the icon to the other side. "What?"

"Two hundred."

"One-fifty. Text your bank wiring information to this number. It's after hours where I am, so it won't go out until tomorrow. It'll probably post the next day. When it's in the account, you call me back and show me the goods and we'll go from there."

Again, he hung up. While he waited for their text, he squirted the heroin back into a plastic baggie. The water would eventually evaporate, and he'd save most of the powder. Then he capped the hypodermic and returned that and everything else to the black bag. Stowed it away. Locked it away.

The urge had passed.

Funny.

Five minutes later, his phone dinged.

All the instructions were there, spelled out in front of him.

If only life came with a fucking user's manual.

WHEN I WOKE up, it was dark outside. The nightstand clock told me it was 12:03. My head hurt and I was parched. I was also probably hungry, but since I was on a liquid diet, hunger pangs didn't register. I waited for my eyes to adjust, and when they did, mercifully, I saw the door was closed. I wasn't sure if he was out there, but I was glad for the privacy. I turned on the lamp.

My dresses were back hanging in the closet; my foldable clothes were gone, probably back in the drawers. His leather valise was also gone, as were the dress and underwear that I had thrown across the room. A box of sanitary napkins was waiting on my nightstand along with a bottle of water.

The clean-up gremlins had come and gone and I hadn't heard a thing. I made my way to the bathroom with my napkins with wings and a fresh pair of panties. I had stopped bleeding but was still crampy. I hunted around the medicine cabinet and came out with a bottle of Advil and gulped down two tablets. Then I drained the water.

I could hide for only so long. And he had a point. He had called me numerous times during my absence. He had also written me emails and texts.

Just talk to me.

I had put up a wall of silence, ghosting, as they call it today. I was scared, to be sure, and was sitting on years of anger, but I also was ashamed. Acting the bad boy was his domain. I was the good girl. I was very uncomfortable in the role reversal. He was a brutal, cruel man. But he'd been the only one who bothered to help me when I really, really needed help. It was time to put on big-girl pants. I had a daughter to think about, and she needed to be protected.

Opening the door as quietly as I could, I took a step out into the abyss and just observed. He was wearing a long-sleeved black T-shirt and black sweats, sitting in his captain's chair, wearing headphones that pushed back his blond-and-white shoulder-length hair. He stared at his multitude of screens. While he checked out the images, he picked up a dumbbell and curled what seemed to be an enormous amount of weight—first in the left hand, then in the right—eyes always focused on the monitors. Every so often, he spoke into a mike attached to his shirt. I watched him for some time, until he got up to stretch and finally noticed me.

"Hey," I said.

"Hey." He took off his headphones. "How do you feel?"

"Better, thanks."

"Good to hear." Silence. "Do you need anything?"

"No . . . no, thanks. I was just getting some water from the fridge."

"I'll get it for you."

"No, I'll get it. It's good for me to walk."

"Suit yourself." He put the headphones back on, then took them off. "If you need anything, let me know."

On went the headphones, and he went back to work. I walked to the fridge, took two bottles of water and one bottle of strawberry protein shake. I was so sick of drinking the thick, sickly sweet stuff, but what could I do? I was always weight appropriate, but these past weeks, I had lost enough pounds to be considered thin. But I didn't look healthy. It was a scrawny thin in the wrong places.

I walked back into the bedroom, leaving the door open, and finished off another bottle of water along with the strawberry shake. Fortified, I went to do what I should have done when he first took me here, into his domain, into his bed. I came to him, and he took off his headphones. The monitors showed multiple rooms with multiple people engaged in multiple acts. He saw me looking, pushed a button, and the screens suddenly went black. His deep blues stared into my eyes—not hostile, but they were flat. He was literally looking down at me.

"What do you need?"

"Nothing." I cleared my throat. "I just want to sincerely thank you for rescuing me, Chris. I probably would have died if it hadn't been for you. Lord only knows what would have happened to Juleen. I am extremely grateful to have this place to recover and rest and to have you looking after us." My eyes welled up. "Thank you so much."

He nodded. "You're very welcome."

"Also . . ." Another pause. "I also want to apologize to you for the affair . . . for ducking out on you. I was scared, but . . ." I felt my eyes fill up. "It was a terrible thing to do . . . to leave you hanging." Wet rills on my cheeks. "I'm really sorry—"

"Stop apologizing, baby," he told me. "I was a shitty boyfriend and an equally shitty husband." He patted his legs. "C'mere."

He gently lifted me onto his lap. He wrapped his arms around my back. I laid my head on his chest and just let the tears fall. He kissed the top of my head. "I'm okay if you're okay. Are you okay?"

"Yeah, I'm okay." I picked my head up and smiled. "I'm fine." I wiped tears away and just let him hold me.

He said, "God put me here on earth to take care of you." He laced his fingers through my hair. "I talk a good case, but it's all bravado. No matter what you do, no matter how many times you leave me, I'll always be here for you. I'll always take you back. Twenty-four seven." He ran his fingers down my back. "Your own personal convenience store. I'm always open. Take anything you want."

"Thank you, Christopher. I appreciate you saying that."

"It's the truth." He stroked my back. "You have no idea how intense my feelings are for you." He shifted positions. "No idea."

I had a vague idea. He was hard underneath me. "Chris, I—"

"It's fine." He smiled. "Even a monster can occasionally control himself."

"I'm sorry I called you a monster."

"I am a monster," he said. "Just not all the time."

He continued to walk his fingers up and down my back. His breathing became labored. I looked up at his face, and beads of sweats had formed across his forehead and above his lips. He squirmed underneath my body.

"Are you okay?" I asked him.

"Fine." He pulled up the hem of his shirt and wiped his face. "It's a little hot in here."

No, it wasn't. It was freezing. Sweat continued to drip from his face. He moved underneath me. He couldn't seem to get comfortable. I tried to get off his lap, but he clutched my back. His body started to shake.

And then, idiot that I was, I figured it out. As if as an ER doc, I hadn't seen it before in hundreds of addicts. Being with me had sparked the pleasure centers in his brain. Until he had his fix, they'd keep firing until his circuits exploded. He was hooked, and sex had always been his drug of choice.

"It's okay, Chris," I said. "Go ahead."

He looked at me. "You sure?"

But he was already hiking up my dress. "Yes, I'm sure. Go ahead."

He pushed himself inside, moving slow and rhythmic. It took a couple of minutes. Afterward, he was still sweating, holding me tightly. He smelled somewhere between a musk ox and a gym locker. He wiped his face again with his shirt. He was still breathing hard. He stood up, still holding me, and I wrapped my legs around his waist.

He took me to the bedroom, laid me on his bed, and lowered his head between my legs.

"Chris, no—"

"Please—"

"I'm so tired—"

"Please—"

"I can't."

"Let me try."

"You'll just get frustrated."

"No, I won't." He probably wouldn't. It was the one thing we did where he always exhibited an unusual amount of patience. "Please. I've missed you so much. I'm begging you. Please."

I hated when he begged me. And I hated the fact that I'd left him. He had leverage now that he could use against me.

"C'mon, baby. It's been so long. Please."

I sighed. I didn't say anything, and he took it as a yes.

Leverage.

It was a weird feeling, not wanting sex but responding to it anyway. It had been such a long time, but that wasn't the reason. Well, maybe part of the reason. But in the main, Chris just knew how to play the instrument. I touched his head with my fingertips and he looked up. "Tell me when."

I fell back on the pillow and just waited for the outcome. When it happened, I pulled him toward me to let him finish us both. He said, "Tell me when you're done."

"Keep going."

About a minute passed. "Soon?"

"Keep going."

"I don't think I can."

"Go ahead then."

He climaxed with three quick shoves. When he was done, he rolled off my body. "God . . . I forgot how long your orgasms are."

"I need to sleep," I told him. "Come to bed."

He checked his watch. "I've got to get back to work."

"Whatever." I turned over and pulled the covers over my head.

The next time I was awakened, he was crawling into bed. He crept up behind me and pulled my back into his chest. We had always slept like this, him cradling me. It was so weird. I hadn't been with him in over a decade. The truth was I hadn't been with a man in over two years. He reeked of masculinity, and despite myself, I felt sparks shoot through my body.

"What time is it?" I asked.

"Four-fifteen."

"I can't move. I'm depleted."

"So am I." He was still holding me. "Go back to sleep."

I closed my eyes. I was in that fuzzy stage between awake and asleep, when he rolled me on my back. "I'm sorry, babe, but I really need you."

Code words for sex. He didn't wait for consent, but I didn't stop him because it felt comforting. It didn't take more than a few minutes. When he had finished, I was a bit nauseated but awake. I said, "I need to shower. Help me."

"Of course."

I looked at him in the light of the moon outside the picture window. His lids were droopy and his face looked worn. The stubble across his cheeks gave his complexion a tinge of swarthiness. He helped me up, and with the handheld showerhead, I washed off a day's worth of sweat and sex. Water was truly miraculous. We went back to bed, resuming the same sleeping position, except instead of being merely awake, I was now wide-awake.

I said, "You liked it, didn't you?"

He hugged me tighter. "What do you think?"

"No, not this time," I told him. "Before . . . when you hurt me. You liked it."

A beat. "No, I didn't *like* it. I felt terrible."

"Then why didn't you stop?"

"Why didn't I stop . . ." He exhaled. "Honestly, I was so in my own head, your voice barely registered."

I didn't say anything.

"Okay." He sighed. "Let me see if I can explain this to you." When I didn't respond, he said, "Are you there?"

"I'm listening."

"I could have held out for much longer," he said. "Like in high school . . . I didn't touch you until you came to me."

"That's irrelevant. Why didn't you *stop*?"

He exhaled. "Addicts have on-off switches. Once we *started*, the switch turned on." A pause. "I got really aroused. Then I got mad at myself for being so aroused, that you had that kind of power over me still, because I was furious at you. I've been nursing this anger for a very long time. You understand that, right?"

"I know who you are."

"Right. The madder I got, the more aroused I got, because, in a lot of male brains, arousal and anger feed on each other." He kissed my neck. "Like sexual psychopaths . . . which I am not."

I was silent.

"I do have control. Even at my angriest this morning, I didn't do what I really wanted. Because if I did, I knew it would be the point of no return."

I sat up. "What do you mean?"

"What do you think I mean?"

My heart was pounding. "I don't know."

"Take a guess."

"That you wanted to kill me."

"I just got you back." He laughed. "I love you. Why would I want to kill you?"

The relief was overwhelming, but I was still confused. "Well, then what do you mean?"

"If you can't figure it out, I'm not going to tell you."

"I don't know what you're talking about."

He laughed again. "Forget it. Let's go to bed."

I lay down on the pillow and closed my eyes. Then they sprang open. I sat up. "No!"

He started kissing my neck again. "No, not tonight, or no, not ever?"

"Just no."

He ran his hands across my breasts. "I should have done it when you were sixteen and madly in love with me. You would have done anything I asked back then."

It was true. I said nothing.

"Then I should have done it when you came back to me. What were you? Twenty-one?"

"Twenty."

"You were so desperate that again you would have done anything I asked."

Also true. "Then why didn't you?"

"Because I was a moron. Back then I thought there were things that you didn't do to your wife. Now you're not madly in love with me and you're not desperate. Once you heal up, you're an independent woman—much to my irritation. I know you can't stay here. You can't raise your kids in a brothel."

"As of right now, it's just a kid—as in a single child, you mean." I screwed up my courage and took a deep breath. "Chris, can you just find out if he's safe?" No answer. "Would you do that for me?"

Again, he didn't respond. I felt tears coming on. Why would he help me with my kids? They were nothing to him other than a sore reminder.

Finally, he spoke. "I will help you, but under one condition."

"Anything." My heart started racing. "Anything at all."

He laughed. "That's a good response, because I can think of lots of things."

"Please, Christopher," I pleaded. "I just want to make sure he's okay."

He said, "I will help you, Teresa, but you cannot ask me about this again. If I find out something, I'll tell you. Otherwise no questions. I won't answer them, and they'll annoy the hell out of me."

I was trying to calm myself. "Do you know something that you don't want me to know?"

"That's a question."

"Chris—"

"I don't know anything, okay?"

"But you will—"

"Stop!"

"Okay." His mood had changed. I could only push him so far. I said, "Thank you so much—"

"Don't thank me yet. I haven't done anything."

I said, "I'm sorry if I've upset you."

"Nothing you said." He hugged me and kissed the top of my head. "I know you can't live here." His hands roved across my chest. "But it'll kill me when you go."

"No, I can't live here," I whispered. "But that doesn't mean—"

"No, Terry, we *can't* be friends."

"I was going to say we can still have some kind of a relationship."

"*Sexual* relationship."

I was quiet. Then I turned over to face him and said, "If we're going to continue down this path, I need some things from you."

"Hit me."

"First and foremost, I need to see Juleen."

"I figured. You know I never touched her." When I didn't answer, he said, "Ask her."

"Oh, I will."

He said, "I'm not her father, I don't get near her. Even when I talk to her, I stand on the other side of the room. When I get mad at you, I say stupid things."

"Really stupid things. What's her schedule?"

"She has tutors until four."

"What about her meals?"

"She takes care of her own breakfast. I bring her lunch and dinner. After four, I help her with homework or with her practicing."

"How's she doing?"

"She's a smart girl. No mystery there. I imagine her father is a bright guy."

"He's a brilliant cardiac surgeon."

"That didn't stop him from fucking up his life."

"Didn't stop me either. How's her playing progressing?"

"Okay."

"She's no Gabe."

"No, she is not Gabe, but she has grit, and sometimes that gets you further than talent."

"I'll see her at four, then. I'll stay with her until she goes to sleep."

"That's around ten. She'll exhaust you, Terry. She's a chatterbox."

I was taken aback. "Juleen?"

"Yeah, Juleen. The kid you had with Devek while you were married to me."

I turned over so my back was to him. "She's normally so reserved with strangers."

"I've always had a way with girls." He pulled me to his chest. "What else do you need?"

"We need phones. I have to be able to talk to her whenever I want. I need to contact you if I need something. I'm stuck here."

"I'll get you set up in the system so you can come and go from here after you heal up. But I don't want you or her having a phone. I don't want you contacting Devek, and I don't want her contacting her father. With you, it's not a problem. But Devek is her father. It's not that I'm trying to keep her away from him, but until I know what's going on, that can't happen."

"Get a restrictive phone that doesn't allow foreign calls. I need to be able to talk to her."

"I can do that. What else?"

"If you could contact the dentist and find out when I can get my jaw unwired, I'd appreciate it. Nothing's broken. I'll be careful about chewing. I'd just like to talk better. And eat something other than protein shakes."

"I'll call the dentist. Anything else?"

"Some makeup and a blow dryer of my own would be great."

"Done."

"Shouldn't you be writing this down?"

"No need. What else?"

"That's it."

"Money?"

"Not now. What for?"

He held me tight. "Anything else I can do for you? Like right now?" He nibbled my neck. "Like turning a no into a maybe?"

"Chris, I'll do anything you want. But I am dog-tired."

I felt him pull away. "We'll wait until we're both more awake."

"I think that's a good idea, although you're very sexy."

He gave a small laugh. "But I'm also a pest."

"It's the novelty effect. You'll calm down."

"Probably not. With you, I never got enough."

"And that's why you cheated on me all the time?"

"Yeah, when I was away from home, I fucked my whores. It was part of my business."

"Right."

"When I was home with you, angel, I never cheated."

"Chris, it's past history. It doesn't matter. No sense lying."

"I'm not lying. When I was home, I didn't fuck anyone but you. Not because I'm moral—I don't know the meaning of the word—but because I didn't *want* to do anything that would drain me. I probably would have been nicer to you if I had gotten it from other women—or from other men for that matter. I'll take it from anyone. Instead, since I was depending on you for it, I became a very frustrated guy."

"We had sex all the time!"

"I'm sure it felt that way to you."

"It was that way!"

"Not to me, baby doll. You know, there were times when I was up late at night—I was always a night owl—when I was done with my work, and I just kept staring at the clock, waiting for a sufficient amount of time to pass so I could wake you up and fuck you again. Back then, I was not only younger but insatiable. I've slowed a little, but I've still got that in me with you around here. I could do it again. Right now. I've been waiting for you for a *very* long time, little girl. I haven't touched another woman since I picked you up in Los Angeles."

That would explain a lot. Still, I was stunned. "Really?"

"Yeah, really! Think I'm always this way? It's years of fucking pent-up *frustration*." He wrapped his arms around me. "But . . . I know you're tired. I can wait until the sun comes up."

I saw light shining through the top of the bedroom window. "The sun is up," I noted. "Please, let's sleep. I'm so tired. You must be exhausted as well."

"I'll cop to that." He hugged me tightly. "This is nice." He nuzzled me again and I pulled away. His beard, the few times he had one, had always been soft. But his stubble against my cheek was like sandpaper. He said, "I'll shave before I come to you. Been a long time since I've had to think about that."

A few moments later, I felt him relax. I said, "Chris?"

"No, I don't know anything about your boy, and no, I really didn't cheat on you when I was home, and no, I haven't fucked anyone since you got here. God's honest truth."

"How'd you know what I was going to ask?"

"Because I know you as well as you know me. Now go to sleep."

I closed my eyes.

For some absurd reason, his admissions made me feel better.

I had always been easily pleased.

CHAPTER 7

OUT IN THE blazing sun at eight in the morning, with temperatures already in the high seventies, Decker was kneeling in the dirt, helping his mother tend the garden. Ida Decker claimed she was only ninety-four, but certain things—like her birth certificate—didn't quite match her avowed age. He didn't dare challenge her. However old she was, she had the strength and the vitality of a woman years younger.

The patch wasn't just a few beds with a couple of plants; it was rows of peppers, squash, melons, eggplants, potatoes, and tomatoes, the veggies in every shape and variety. His mom could have opened up her own farmers' market. Decker was dressed in shorts and a T-shirt, with a hat on his head for sun protection, but he was still sweating bullets. Rina was in the kitchen making preparations for tonight's dinner. Randy and his fourth wife were coming over, and since Decker and Rina were kosher, whenever they visited, she did the cooking. Mom had accommodated them by not only supplying kosher meat but also keeping kosher pots and pans and dishes whenever they visited. Still, Rina wanted to clean the stove and oven before she cooked.

A religious Baptist, Mom had been furious when Decker had converted to Judaism. His father, Lyle, had been more accepting, but that was his style. He had been quiet and stoic, and Decker missed him terribly. He had always been closer to his father than his mother. But he gave her credit. Over time, Mom had adapted. The truth was she liked Rina way more than him. They had similar interests as well: cooking, gardening, religion—although the Gods were different—and just plain good common sense.

He stopped, picked up the garden hose, and filled a plastic cup with water. He drank with gusto. "You want some water, Mom?"

Ida looked up. "I'm fine."

"You need to drink."

"I've looked after myself for a long time, Peter. I think I can manage without your advice." A slight smile. "I appreciate the caring."

"Are we picking any of this for dinner?"

"Rina's making ratatouille with the zucchini, eggplant, tomatoes, and onions."

"Should be good. What time are Randy and Blossom coming over?"

"Around seven."

"Nice of them to come. It's a long drive."

"It is," Ida said. "He always comes over when you're here. Just about the only time."

"Mom, you know that's not true. He comes at least once a month."

"Better than you, I suppose," she grunted.

"At least you kept one son local."

"I blame the defection on that wife of yours."

"Since I met Rina in Los Angeles, you must mean Jan."

"Who else?"

"She's a nice person, Mom. We just didn't work out. Anyway, she gave you a wonderful granddaughter."

"Yeah, I suppose she was worth it for Cindy."

Mom adored Cindy. It was that old joke. Why do grandmothers and granddaughters have such a special relationship? Common enemy.

Decker's phone buzzed. He looked at the number, stood up, stretched, and took the call. "Hey, Tyler. What's happening?"

"We haven't been able to locate airline tickets for Elsie Schulung, Bertram Lanz, or Kathrine Taylor," McAdams said, "but they could be using assumed names. We're now just looking at manifests around the dates they disappeared and trying to match the names to actual people. It's going to take forever. But I'll keep at it."

"Thanks, Tyler, for picking up my slack," Decker said. "Where's Pauline's body?"

"Still in the morgue."

"What about next of kin? Didn't you tell me that Pauline had a sister?"

"I did."

"I want to call her. Get me her name and number."

"She lives on the West Coast. It's still a little early to be making calls. And I can call her, boss. You're on vacation."

Decker glanced at his mother. "That is debatable. Where is she on the West Coast?"

"In Ventura. Do you know where that is?"

"Yes. It's where my ex-partner lives. And since Pauline's body is in our jurisdiction, I think I can justify a visit to ask the next of kin some questions. Hold on . . . let me check flights from Orlando."

"Then you're planning on leaving from Florida instead of coming back to Greenbury?"

"Yes. There are lots of nonstops. Cheap too."

"Then let's meet at LAX. And we can drive up to Ventura together. Unless you want to go with Rina."

"She's staying in Florida. She's going to visit her mom. You know, you don't have to come, Tyler. I've got Margie over there." Silence.

Decker could picture the young kid sulking. Probably wasn't the most sensitive thing to say. "On the other hand, this is your case as well as mine. I think we both should be there."

"Then I'll come. Call me when you get a flight and I'll try to match the time."

"I will do that. I've got to go. Mom is giving me dirty looks."

"Tell Mom to give you one for me."

"Tyler, Marge is a very nice person and was a great partner. But now you're my partner. No need for the snide comments."

"*Moi?* Snide?" The kid hung up.

Decker smiled. He had two biological children, two stepchildren, and a foster child. Between his mother and Tyler, his "kid" count went up to seven. Rina was independent, but he still felt it was his duty to protect her. That was just the way it was with husbands. All the people in his life depending on him. But it wasn't a burden. Always better to be the hammer rather than the nail.

I WOKE UP at around nine, having had over sixteen hours of sleep between bouts of war and sex. I slowly wiggled out of Chris's grip. He was dead to the world. I went toward the bathroom on my tiptoes, and after washing up, I wrapped myself in one of his black jacquard silk robes and left the room, closing the door behind me. I made myself coffee and then settled on his black leather couch to read, trying to keep my mind off Sanjay. If I thought about what happened, I'd sink into deep, muddy waters. I still had a daughter, and I just needed to stay afloat emotionally.

My spot faced the window, and I enjoyed the light and the view. Usually when I got up, Chris was already gone, but I guess the fatigue caught up with him. An hour later, I made a fresh pot of coffee, poured myself a new cup, then padded back into the bedroom. He hadn't moved, in the same position as when I left, on his stomach, shirtless, but with sweatpants. His white hair was splayed over a black pillowcase like a cloud in a storm.

On the nightstand was his gun. It was a 9 mm, probably a Glock. He liked Glocks. He had taught me how to shoot years ago, but I hadn't fired a gun in a very long time. I transferred my coffee cup to my left hand and picked up the gun. It weighed about a pound and had good balance. I checked and saw that there was a magazine in the chamber. I held the stock in my hand and put my finger on the trigger. Firearms gave me an enormous sense of power.

"Tempted?" The voice was low and almost playful. I looked away from the gun and at his body. He still hadn't moved. He said, "Bad idea. How would you get out of here?"

I said, "There's coffee."

Finally, he turned around, sat up, and held out his hand. I offered him the gun, but instead, he took my mug. "Coffee first. What time is it?"

"A little after ten."

"Shit!" He swung his legs over the side of the bed and sipped coffee. He took down one of his many black suits and a black tee and started to dress. "I've got some business that can't wait. Good coffee, baby doll. Better than mine, that's for sure."

"I wait until the entire pot is brewed."

"Yes, I am impatient." He dressed quickly, strapping a gun holster across his chest. I gave him the 9 mm still in my hand and he jammed it into the holder. He put on red lizard-skin boots and went into the bathroom, and when he returned, he had given his hair a quick brush. He took a briefcase from the closet and left the bedroom. I heard him unlock the vault. When he returned, he said, "I've got several back-to-back appointments. Then I've got to check in with my workers. They get pouty when it's been a while, and it's been a long while. Plus, I've got your to-do list. It's going to take time. I'll shoot for two or three to be back."

"Don't rush. You have a business to run."

"You have enough food?"

"Your fridge is filled with shakes. I'm fine."

He kissed my forehead. "Don't go anywhere."

"As if."

"If it were up to me, I'd keep you locked up forever." He stared at me, then checked his watch—a gold Rolex. "Damn. I really got to go."

"And you'll take me to see—"

"The dentist. Yeah, yeah."

"I meant Juleen."

"That too. See you later."

He was off.

Chris had always been a whirlwind. He didn't require a lot of sleep, which meant he was always on. He exhausted me. It was calming to have the room to myself, but I felt more than a little frightened. I couldn't shake the images in my brain—the men bursting in, me grabbing Sanjay only to lose him. It made my heart fly from my chest to think about it. But the good news was that both Juleen and I were safe and secure for the time being. I always was pragmatic, not one to belabor what was out of reach. Instead, I always looked for whatever I could get.

"I'M LEAVING TOMORROW at around eleven, which will put me into LAX around two in the afternoon," Decker told McAdams. "We should start heading north as soon as we can, because traffic will start to get really bad on the freeway."

"What flight are you on?" McAdams asked. After getting the numbers and time, he said, "I'll leave tonight for Manhattan. I can stay over at my grandmother's and catch a ten o'clock out of JFK. That'll get me in around one. I'll rent a car."

"That'll save time," Decker said. "Are we getting compensated?"

"Five hundred apiece to pay for everything. My flight alone will cost me six times that."

"You're going first class?"

"Unfortunately, it's a business/first instead of a true first class. It was the best I could do on such short notice."

"I'm shedding a tear."

"You'll be shedding several once you're crammed into steerage."

"Rub it in, why don't you?"

McAdams said, "Console yourself in knowing that the rich inbreed. While the plebs with their genetic diversity foster creativity and divergent thinking, the wealthy end up producing drug-addicted spoiled brats and odd ducks who wear funny hats."

"Which category are you in, Tyler?"

"Life is not either-or."

Decker laughed. "I'll see you tomorrow."

"See you then," McAdams said. "I'll be the one having a tantrum while wearing my best beret."

"GET DRESSED," CHRIS told me. "I've got a surprise for you."

It was a quarter to three in the afternoon. "Juleen?"

"Uh, that's going to have to wait, because I got you a dental appointment."

"Thank you." I was trying to hide my disappointment.

"You'll see her later, Terry, but the doc cleared his last appointments for you. Get dressed so we can go."

"I am dressed."

"Do you have anything else?"

I looked at my dress, a maxi in a nice floral print. "What's wrong with this?"

"It's a little . . . Manson girl."

I let out a small laugh. "*Manson* girl?"

"Yeah, you know. Those clips of Leslie Van What's-Her-Face

singing as she was being led off to prison." When I smiled, he said, "I'm taking my bike. I want your legs covered."

I opened a dresser drawer and took out a pair of jeans. They were now a couple of sizes too big. Chris appraised me. "They'll fit you once you start eating again. Just put a belt on."

"I don't have a belt. I didn't have a lot of time to pack."

"It's fine. Just put on a shirt and let's go."

I hadn't been out of his bedroom suite since he brought me there nearly a week ago. As soon as I stepped outside, I felt like I could breathe again. It was warm. The air was perfumed with summer, and the sky engulfed me in a glorious blue wrap. A guard was keeping watch over his motorcycle. He handed Chris two helmets. Mine was too big, so Chris adjusted the strap and helped me onto the seat.

"Ducati?" I asked.

"Yep."

"You always favored Italian bikes. Cars too. I bet you own a Ferrari."

"I bet you're right."

"I used to ride a scooter in Mumbai. It's the easiest way to maneuver the streets."

"Same principle, just a bigger engine. Hold on." When I wrapped my arms around his waist, he said, "If you put your hands a little lower, I wouldn't object."

"Do you ever stop?"

"Never." He revved the engine with his hands and then he peeled off.

We went down a dirt path until we hit asphalt. The place was located in a strip mall next to a sandwich shop and a hardware store—a small-town atmosphere. Within minutes, I was seated in a dental chair. Chris asked him how long, and the dentist—a nice-looking dark-haired guy around my age—told him over an hour, maybe even two. His name was Dr. Kenneth Woodruff.

"I've got things to do," Chris said. "Unless you want me to stay with you."

"No, no," I told him. "I'll be fine."

He left, and about two hours later, the dentist took the bib off me. My bottom molars were wired to each other, but my jaw was free, although it was sore when I tried to open my mouth. But I could lick my lips for the first time in weeks. He had scraped and polished my teeth, and I felt normal if I didn't look at my face or at my arm in the cast. Chris was in the waiting room, clicking away at his phone. Next to him were two big bags. I was holding a pile of discharge instructions.

"Done?" he asked. He stowed the mobile in his pocket.

"I am."

"How do you feel?"

"More human than not."

"Take it easy for the next month," Woodruff said. "Your back teeth are still wobbly. Soups, soft vegetables, fish. No steak, okay?"

"Got it," I told him.

Chris looked at the dentist. "Thanks for making time, Doc."

"No problem, Mr. Donatti."

Chris put his arm around me. "Ready?"

"I am." I looked at the clock. It was around five when we left. As we were walking to his bike, I said, "Are you taking me to see Juleen?"

"In an hour."

"Why an hour?"

He looked at me with intense eyes. I said nothing. Another hour wouldn't make a difference. I felt better and I wouldn't even mind the contact with him. But I felt he was stalling. He said, "I've been dreaming of kissing you."

"You're not a big kisser. You mean other things."

"Maybe." He gave me the helmet. "You used to like blow jobs."

I did like them. It had been one of the few times during sex that he ceded control. He asked, "Do you still like them?"

"I suppose. It's been a while."

"How long?"

"Are you asking Devek's size, or how much time has passed?"

He broke out in laughter. "Maybe both."

"To both those questions, I say none of your beeswax."

"Seriously, how long has it been since you fucked him?"

"A long time." I paused. "He has a girlfriend."

"Did he take up with her before or after you stopped having sex with him?"

"Why are you torturing me?" He waited. "After."

"Can't blame him if he's not getting it at home."

"So now you're Devek's advocate? You love giving me a hard time, don't you?"

He ran his finger down my crooked nose. His smile turned to a grin. "Sorry."

I looked around. "God, it's wonderful to be outside. I feel like an uncaged bird." I turned to him. "Thanks for everything you've done for me, Donatti. I am very aware of the dire situation I was in."

He didn't answer. He loaded the bags on the back of the bike and then looked at me. "You really want to thank me?"

I sighed. "I already said I'll do whatever you want if you find . . ." I let the words hang. He didn't need to be reminded about Sanjay. It would only piss him off.

"I don't mean sex for once," he said. I waited. "I have an engagement tonight with a couple of clients and the women I set them up with. Drinks in the lounge at around eleven."

"What lounge?"

"I have one on the premises. It's like an old-fashioned club. Lots of the men go there to talk or read or smoke and brag—show off the women they're with. But a surprising number of business deals are done there. I'd like you to come with me." He paused. "That's what these bags are for. They're dresses for you."

I guess I couldn't go as his whore in a Manson dress. Why not? "Okay."

"Thank you."

We rode home and walked up to his bedroom in silence. After a half hour of playtime, it was about five-thirty. I got dressed, rubbed my sore jaw, and said, "Can I see my daughter now?"

"In a few minutes. Let me show you the dresses first."

Stalling. "Sure."

He straightened the bedsheets and laid them out. Three cocktail dresses—all black and all short. There were also three shoeboxes. I looked at the clothing. "Which one do you like?"

He gave the question some thought. "This one."

It had a tight, short skirt and a sleeveless, drapey bodice with a plunge in the front and a plunge in the back. "Fine."

"Try it on for me." Still stalling. He saw me look at the clock on the nightstand. "I promise I'll take you to see Juleen. I just want to see how you look, okay?"

"These clients must be important."

"They're venture capitalists. They specialize in funding vices— lots of online gambling as well as some physical casinos. This would be their first foray into brothels. I'd like to get some money out of them."

"You're expanding?"

"Depends on how much money they're willing to invest."

I nodded and took off my oversize jeans and baggy T-shirt. I slipped on the dress. Once it would have been too tight. Now it was big. I was sure that would change once I started eating. The front had two straps across the plunge so it didn't open up. He zipped up the skirt for me.

"Okay?" I asked.

"Take off your bra with it. A little side boob is sexy."

Not that there was much of that. When I lost weight, I lost it all over, unfortunately. "I'll take it off tonight." I looked in the shoeboxes—the same black backless heels in three sizes: a 6, 6$\frac{1}{2}$, and 7.

"I don't remember your exact size," he told me.

"It's six and a half." I tried them on and waited for a comment. He spun his index finger and I turned around for him. "Okay?"

"You look lovely."

He reached in his pocket and pulled out a small jewelry box sized for a ring or earrings. "Try these on."

These. That meant earrings. I opened the box. Diamond studs. My eyes got big. "These are *gorgeous*!" I grinned. "God, there's enough bling here for a sports team!" I looked at him. "Thank you so much."

"You're welcome. Try them on."

"God, I've never seen anything so sparkly." I hadn't worn earrings in a very long time. The holes were still open, but it took a little maneuvering to thread the studs in back through my earlobes. When I was done, I pushed my hair back and looked in the bathroom mirror. "These are outrageous!" I told him. "You could see me coming a mile away."

He was suddenly behind me, hands on my shoulders. "I'm glad you like them."

I turned around and kissed his lips. "Thank you."

He was staring at me. "I never got you an engagement ring, did I?"

"These more than make up for it." I walked back into the bedroom and tried to unzip my skirt. "Chris, I really do want to see Juleen."

"I know." He unzipped my skirt and undid the straps in front. The dress fell from my shoulders and to the floor. He put his arms around my waist and kissed my neck. "What about Devek? I'm sure he bought you an engagement ring."

"He did," I said. "It was beautiful—an emerald surrounded by diamonds. He sold it, along with the other pieces he gave me as well as anything else we had of value, to help pay off his debts. We were almost out of the woods, until he went back to the tables one last time, which became two and three and four, and he got us deeper into debt than the first time." I broke away and retrieved my Manson dress from the floor. I stepped into it. "Gambling never appealed to you?"

"Not a whit. I like money too much."

"Good for you." I took off my shoes and put on my slippers. "I'm ready."

He looked at me intensely. "Thank you for doing this for me."

"I'm happy to be your whore."

"You're not my whore."

"Arm candy. Whatever. I'm happy to help. For tonight, can you get me a little makeup?"

"I'll do your face. I'll also do your hair."

"Thank you." I kissed his nose. "Can we go?"

He stood rooted. "Teresa, I don't want you there as a whore. I don't want you there as arm candy. I want you there as my *wife*." I didn't say anything. "I know that's an issue right now, but it's an issue that can be fixed." He reached in his pocket and threw three rings on the bed. "Take your pick."

I regarded his eyes, then walked over to examine the jewelry. One was a solitary round diamond, one was a cushion-cut diamond surrounded by little diamonds, and the last one was two round diamonds—one with an arc of tiny pavé diamonds above it and the other with an arc of pavé diamonds below. I said, "Is this making up for past neglect, or is this moving forward?"

"What do you think?" When I didn't answer, he said, "I don't know your taste in jewelry since I never bought you gifts."

"That's not totally true."

"I'm not counting the earrings I bought you when you were sixteen."

"I still have them."

"I saw when I unpacked your stuff." He paused. "Why'd you keep them?"

I shrugged. "I guess I'm a sentimentalist. That and your mother's cross were the only things I had left from you . . . other than Gabe."

"I saw the necklace as well." His eyes grew far away. "It took me back some."

"I'm sure." I nodded. "I was going to give it to Gabe—like an heirloom—but then he converted to Judaism. My other two children are Hindu. You want it back?"

"No, no. You keep it." Chris was quiet. "My sum total of presents: a cheap pair of pearl earrings and my mother's silver cross. And a wedding band, which I didn't see anywhere."

I was quiet.

He said, "I could have done better."

"You took me out of penury. Gabe and I couldn't have made it without your support."

"You don't get a medal for supporting your family." His eyes returned to the rings on the bed. "Which one do you like?" A pause. "You can have all three if you want."

I had to make a move. There would be plenty of time to throw it back in his face in the future. To hesitate now would be bad strategy, since he was the only one helping me with Sanjay. I was willing to do anything to get my boy back. I didn't know if Chris would come through, but I did know that it was always better to have Chris on your side. I picked up the ring with the double diamonds. "This one."

His smile was a thousand watts. "My favorite too." He slipped it on my finger. "Got the size right." He pocketed the other rings and then retrieved a plain, worn white-gold band and showed it to me. "I still have mine, even though yours is probably at the bottom of the Atlantic Ocean."

He put the band on the ring finger of his left hand. "We'll work out the details later."

"Chris, I can't see Juleen with this on my finger. I'm divorcing her father. I need to explain things to her, okay?" I took the ring off. "Keep it for me. I'll put it on when we see your clients."

"Fair enough." He pocketed the ring and raised his thick blond-white eyebrows. "I know it won't be conventional. Nothing with me is ever conventional. But I do want to reach an understanding that works for both of us." He exhaled. "I *want* this to work, Terry. I *need* this to work. I can't take you leaving again. I won't survive." A long pause. "Then I have your commitment?"

"Yes, you have my commitment." I answered without pause. Dr. Pragmatic. I'd sort things out later.

He nodded. "Then take as much time as you need to break it to your daughter."

"Thank you. Can we . . ." I stopped myself.

"Yes, we can go now. You're still wearing the earrings, by the way."

"I know. I am *never* taking these off."

He laughed. "I never figured you as a bling girl."

"All women are bling girls. You just never offered me any. But don't worry." I kissed his mouth with my newly liberated tongue. "You have plenty of time to make up for it."

THERE WAS ROASTED chicken with gravy, rice pilaf, ratatouille, a leafy green salad, and fresh-baked bread. The food as well as the dinner plates and utensils sat at the end of a wooden trestle table that accommodated twelve chairs—the dining set a relic from long ago when family and friends came for Sunday dinner. After everyone helped themselves, they returned to the front of the table and waited for the matriarch to pick up a fork and start eating. Ida Decker took her sweet time. No one was going to rush her. Finally, she attacked a piece of white meat chicken.

Randy Decker had put on a few pounds since Rina had known

him. He was dark complexioned and about four inches shorter than Peter. They looked nothing alike. Why would they? Both Randy and Peter were adopted. Blossom—Randy's fourth wife—was blond and buxom with a fully painted face. She had on leopard-print leggings, a gold lamé sweater, and gold sandals. She said, "It looks delicious, Ida."

"I didn't cook anything," Ida answered. "When Rina's here, she won't let me near the kitchen. Like I have cooties or something."

Rina got up and kissed Ida on the cheek, noticing that it was all the old lady could do to not wipe it off. "You don't have cooties, and even if you did, I'm sure they'd be wonderful cooties. You should also inform Blossom that you baked all the pies, including chocolate pecan, which you told me was Blossom's favorite."

"Aw, that's so sweet." Blossom gave a heave of her chest. "Thank you, Ida."

"You're welcome."

Blossom was the favored daughter-in-law. She was the only one in the family who went to church with Ida. Her status didn't amount to much, though, because Ida was still as tough on her as the rest of them. To Rina, she said, "Did you have a nice trip?"

"It was lovely, thank you."

Blossom said, "I've always wanted to visit the Holy Land."

"Since when?" Ida piped up.

"Well, Rina makes it sound so erotic."

"Exotic," Ida corrected her.

"Yes, of course." She pinkened. "Oops."

Rina smiled. "It's a great place. When Peter finishes with our place, we'd love to host you."

"That would be lovely."

Rina looked at Peter, and Blossom looked at Randy. The brothers were eating heartily but had yet to speak. Rina kicked Peter under the table. He said, "Sure, be great to have you there."

"I'm too old," Ida said.

"Is it of interest to you?" Rina asked her. "To visit Jerusalem."

"Probably not the spots that you'd want to see—"

"Mom, that's not nice," Randy said.

"It's okay," Rina told her brother-in-law. "Ida, I've been to Bethlehem and Nazareth several times. I've also walked the Via Dolorosa and been to the Church of the Holy Sepulchre. I'd love to take you there."

Ida was quiet. "I'm in one of my testy moods."

"Who can tell the difference?" Randy said. Blossom kicked him under the table. He said, "It's true."

"Maybe I wouldn't be so testy if someone would visit me more."

Randy said, "And I've said to you many times that I would visit you more if you lived closer."

"I'm not selling my house and living with a bunch of old people."

"We could find you a lovely condo," Blossom said.

"I like my house."

"Then don't complain that we don't visit you," Randy said.

"Can we all just enjoy a lovely dinner?" Peter said.

"Said the man who comes once a year," Ida snapped.

Peter was about to respond, but Rina put her hand on his leg. "Ida, sweetheart, are you okay?"

"Yes, I'm fine." Her lower lip trembled. "Just a little testy."

Rina said, "What is it?" No answer. "How's your health, Ida?"

She bit her lip and nodded. "Fine."

Everyone started to talk, but Rina held up her hand. "Please, honey. What's going on?"

Ida said, "I don't want to talk about it."

Rina said, "That's okay. Maybe later, huh?"

Five minutes of shoveling food in silence. Finally, Decker said, "Mom, if something's wrong, you have to talk to us. We love you. What's going on?"

A pause. "The doctor found a lump."

"On your mammogram?" When Ida nodded, Rina said, "Did they do a biopsy?"

"I've got an appointment on Friday."

"Okay, so it could be nothing," Peter said.

"Or it could be something," Ida countered.

Rina said, "Whatever it will be, it's scary now. I'll come with you to the appointment."

"Me too," Blossom said.

"I don't need either of you hovering."

"I've been through this, Ida. I know the right questions to ask. My mother had breast cancer and she's still around ten years later. You'll get through this, but let the people who love you help you," Rina said. No one spoke. "How's the chicken, Ida? Not too dry."

"It's good," Ida said. "Thanks for doing all this. It would have been nice to have daughters."

Randy said, "It was your choice, Ma. I'm sure there were baby girls at the agency."

"You'd be surprised." But Ida smiled. "Anyway, I like my sons."

"I do believe that was a compliment," Peter said.

"Praise the Lord," Randy said.

Blossom said, "Can you drive me back to Miami after the appointment, Rina? Randy has to leave tomorrow."

"Of course he has to leave," Ida said.

"So does Peter," Rina said.

"Ditto," Ida remarked.

"Peter's working on an important case," Rina told her.

"He always has an important case."

Randy said, "What's going on, bro? Does it have to do with that missing nurse and the mentally challenged man you were looking for?"

"It does. We found a body. The nurse's girlfriend."

"This is not table talk," Ida said.

"I'll fill you in later." Decker turned to Rina: "Nice that both you lovely ladies are offering to come with Mom to the doctor. I'm sure she appreciates it."

Ida said, "I don't need hovering. And driving Blossom back—Miami's way out of your way, Rina."

"My mother lives in Miami," Rina said. "I'm going to visit her, so it isn't out of my way. I'll be happy to drive Blossom back."

"That's right," Ida said. "She can come here, you know. Your mom."

"She's a little frail," Rina said.

"How old is she now? Like, ninety?"

"She's ninety-seven."

"Is she all there?" Ida asked.

"Mom, that's not appropriate," Decker said.

Rina said, "She had a stroke. She has trouble talking. But she's all there."

"I'm sorry to hear about her stroke," Ida said.

"We still have fun. We watch a lot of movies together. The old ones. Maybe you'd like to visit her with me after your tests. You're a lot stronger than she is. I think you could make the car trip to Miami."

Decker looked at her. *"At meshuga?"*

Are you crazy?

They had bought a place in Israel and already he was speaking Hebrew. Rina ignored him. "Come with us, Ida. We'll do a girls' road trip."

"How will I get back?" Ida said.

"I can take you back, Ida," Blossom said. "I have a car. It's just Randy and I came in one car. And you can stay with us in Miami."

Randy started coughing.

"Nonsense," Rina said. "My mom's condo has three bedrooms. We'll be perfectly comfortable together."

Randy mouthed a silent thank-you.

"Come with us, Ida," Blossom said. "It'll be fun."

Ida puffed up her chest. "Maybe I'll do that." She stood up. "Dessert, anyone?"

"I think we're all up for your pies," Rina said.

"If I don't eat all the chocolate pecan by myself," Blossom said.

Rina said, "Why don't you two detectives talk shop while we clear the table, and we'll call you when we're set up for dessert and coffee."

"Great idea." Blossom stood up and started clearing the dirty dishes. "I'll make the coffee. I brought a special blend. It's caffeinated, though."

"Who needs sleep?" Rina stood and began taking in the platters of food. "This was fun."

"It sure was." Blossom turned to Ida. "Fun, right?"

The old woman stifled a smile. Then she mumbled, "Shoulda held out for girls."

CHAPTER 8

"MOMMY!" JULEEN RAN into my arms, and I bent down to give her the biggest hug I could muster with my arm in a cast. "Are you okay, Mommy? How do you feel?"

I was trying to keep my eyes dry. "I'm doing much better."

"You can talk!"

"Yes, I can." I let her go from my embrace and stood up, keeping her hands in mine. My son's suite was done in brown leather and suede. Red silk pillows on the sofa, and a yellow plaid blanket was draped over a modern but oversize cushy-looking chair. At least it had some warmth in it. The biggest tell that it was Gabe's was the concert grand Steinway in the middle of the room. It was also where Chris kept his cello. It was out of the case, on its side next to a music stand. Juleen's violin case and chair sat opposite, about four feet away. "Pretty nice setup."

She hugged my waist. "I'm so glad you're here!"

"Me too, *priya*, me too."

Chris was standing over a small table, looking through papers. "Is this your homework for today?"

"Yes."

"Why didn't you do it?"

"I was waiting for you to come. You're two hours later than usual."

"Well, I'm here now. That should have given you plenty of time to finish part of it."

"Can I eat dinner first? I'm hungry." Juleen looked around. "Where is dinner?"

"I'll get it for you in a minute. Start your homework."

I said, "God forbid that I interfere with her studies, but can this wait?"

Chris gave me a sour look. "Don't coddle her. I'll be back in a half hour." He started to leave, then turned around. "You can eat soft food now, Terry. What do you want?"

"I'd love some oatmeal."

"No problem." He pointed to Juleen. "Start your homework."

After he left, Juleen said, "Was he strict like that with Gabe?"

"Honestly, he didn't pay much attention to Gabe."

"Probably because he was so perfect."

"Gabe was perfect and so are you." I sat down on the brown suede sofa and patted the empty cushion next to mine. She sat and hugged a pillow.

"How are you?"

My eyes started to water. "All right."

"You look sooooo much better."

"Do I?"

"Believe me, you do." She slid over until she was under the crook of my arm. "Your eyes are still black and blue, but your face is back to normal."

"I did look pretty scary."

"Mommy, I don't care what you look like, just that you're here."

"Me too, *priya*." I paused. "Do you miss home?"

A big smile. "Not so much now that you're here."

"I missed you, too, *priya*. I need to catch up with you. What are you studying?"

"Algebra, English, no science. But four languages. It's hard. I get everything confused."

"What languages?"

"Spanish and French. But also Russian and Chinese. Why am I learning Russian and Chinese?"

My immediate thought was that he was grooming her for his foreign clientele. But maybe that was harsh. I always thought the worst of him. "I have no idea."

"Oh, and Chris has a violin teacher for me. Did you know he also plays violin?"

"I did know."

"He's so good at it. Way better than me."

"He's very talented." I took a deep breath. "Is he nice to you?"

"No, he's mean. He's very strict. And he glares a lot."

Those were all good signs. "Yeah, Chris does glare. It's just the way he is." I was silent for a beat. "He . . . he doesn't touch you, does he?"

"Touch me?" She looked confused, then made a face. "Ew, no! He stands on the other side of the room when he talks to me. Even when he's correcting my violin playing, he never touches my hands like my old teacher. He just picks up the violin and shows me."

"Okay."

"Why do you ask? Is he a pervert?"

Too many ways to answer that question. "No, but I'm a mother. He's not related to you, and you've been alone with him a lot. I just want to make sure."

"Related to me doesn't have anything to do with creepy."

"What do you mean?"

A quick backtrack. "Nothing."

"Juleen, what do you mean? Tell me!"

She sighed. "He's not like Uncle Pramod."

My heart started racing. "Why? What did Uncle Pramod do?"

"Nothing, Mommy. But he is creepy."

"How?" I persisted.

She began to imitate him. "*You look beautiful, Juleen. You look just like your mother, Juleen. If I were younger, Juleen—*"

"Oh, dear God—"

"He's a dirty old man."

"I'll kill him," I said. *Or better yet, I'll ask Chris to do it.* "Did he touch you?"

"No. Never."

"Why didn't you tell me?"

"And what could you have done? He's the head of the family. Father would never listen to me over him." She frowned. "Why doesn't Uncle Pramod like Father?"

"He does like Father, Juleen."

"Then why doesn't he give him money?"

"Because your father promised him that he wouldn't gamble. And then he did."

"He's punishing him?"

"I think so, yes." *For a variety of reasons, one that has nothing to do with gambling.*

"Why doesn't Daada help?"

"Daada is old now. He does whatever Pramod tells him to do."

"But Father is Daada's son too."

"Yes, but he's the younger son."

"Well, I think it's stupid."

"I do too."

She looked at me with her big dark eyes. "You're divorcing Father, aren't you?"

"Yes, I am." I took her hand and kissed it. "I'm so sorry."

She shrugged. "Is it because of Chris?"

"No, not at all. I contacted a lawyer before any of this happened."

"Is it because of Father's gambling?" she asked.

"Yes, and other things."

"What other things?"

"Too many questions, Juleen."

"Do you like Chris?" Before I could think of an answer, she said, "He likes you."

"Why? What did he tell you?"

"Nothing specific. I can just tell." She laid her little head on my shoulder. "I missed you so much, Mommy."

The tears came. "I missed you, too, my little *kharagosh*. I can come every day now after your studies and stay with you until you go to bed."

"Why can't you stay with me all the time?"

I sighed. "It will interfere with your studies."

"It's Chris, right? He wants you to stay with him." She looked down. "I told you he likes you."

"There are physical things I still can't do, *priya*. He takes care of me. And I think Chris is right about one thing. You should do your homework."

"Will you help me with my homework instead of Chris?"

"I can help you with math and English and French and Spanish. I cannot help you with Russian and Chinese." I walked over to the table and picked up her math sheet. "You don't need me for this. It's easy."

"I know." Juleen sat down and picked up a pencil. "Can you sit with me?"

"I can and I will." I sat down, picked up her small hand, and kissed it. "I love you so much, *priya*. I'm so sorry for everything!"

She squeezed my hand. "I'm happy now that you're here."

"I'm happy too." A pause. "So happy." I looked around. "Do you ever get out of this room?"

"I still can't walk that well."

"Ah, yes. How is your ankle?"

"Much better." She looked at me. "When it's healed, can we go for walks?"

"I would love that, Juleen."

She looked down. "Have you spoken to Father?"

"No, *priya*."

"What about Sanjay?"

"Not him either. I think he's with Father." I paused. "Would you like to go back home to Father when it's safe?"

"No!" Adamant. "I love Father, but he doesn't understand me."

"It's hard for fathers to understand daughters."

"He's very old-fashioned."

"That is true. It has good points and bad points."

"I want to stay with you."

"And I want to stay with you too."

"Have you spoken to Sanjay?"

Second time she asked that. "No, I haven't. Maybe when I'm better, I can call Father." I pointed to the math sheet. "Let's pay attention to what we can control, okay?"

She squeezed my hand again. "I love you, Mommy."

"I love you, too."

By the time Chris came back with the food, she had finished all her lessons except her Chinese and Russian homework. I couldn't even read it, let alone help her. He set the take-out boxes on the table. Curry for Juleen and oatmeal for me.

I said, "Smells good."

"You want some of mine, Mommy?" Juleen offered. "It's pretty soft."

"Maybe in a few days. Right now, I'm very happy with my oatmeal." Chris picked up her completed papers. I said, "Why is she learning Chinese and Russian?"

"She knows Hindi and English. With Chinese and Russian, she can communicate anywhere in the world."

"Do you know Chinese and Russian?"

"Enough to get by." He looked at me. "Did you help her with the French?"

"No. It's been years since I've taken French."

"You used to tutor me."

"Also years ago."

"I speak it pretty well. By the way, I've got your phones. I'll charge them up and give them to you tomorrow."

"Thank you so much, Chris," I told him. "Thank you for everything."

To Juleen, Chris said, "You don't need help for this."

"I don't know all the words in the lesson."

"That's why I bought you big dictionaries. Don't be lazy."

"I'm not lazy," Juleen protested. "Sometimes it's hard to find the words."

"I can help you, *priya*," I said. "I don't know the language, but I can use a dictionary."

"You're spoiling her." When I stared at him, he said, "I can see how this is going down." He exhaled and shook his head. "I'll pick you up at around nine."

"So short!" Juleen protested. "Why can't she stay longer?"

"Juleen, I told you she'd come and here she is. Quit complaining. And finish your homework because I'm going to check it when I come back." He turned to me. "I'm tough because she can take it. Remember that." He left.

"He's so mean!" Juleen was angry. "He isn't even my father!"

"No, he isn't. But he did get us phones."

A big smile. "Finally!"

"You won't be able to call Father on yours, *priya*."

"But we can play games together."

"Of course. Tomorrow. But now you do need to finish your homework."

"Why does he care what I do?" Juleen asked.

I wanted to say, *Because you're a source of pain to him. And he's dealing with it by appropriating you. When he bosses you around, it's not that he cares what you're doing. He's exhibiting dominance. You are no longer the other man's child; you are now part of his property.*

Instead, I said, "Chris was there for us when no one else came. Sometimes you have to take the bad with the good."

BY NINE IN the evening, the last thing I wanted to do was drink with sleazy men and their rented women. But Chris didn't ask for me to be dropped in his life, and I owed him more than a few favors. I was determined to be a good sport. After he helped me shower, I sat in a chair facing a blank wall while he combed out my wet hair. On top of his dresser drawers was a slew of makeup and hair supplies.

"Where'd you get all this?" I asked.

"I have a makeup and hair room. The women have open access to beauty products. And don't worry, everything here has never been used."

"I didn't say anything."

"But you were thinking." I didn't answer. He said, "Your hair is really long. I'd like to take it up about twelve, fourteen inches."

"You mean cut it?"

"Yes, cut it. It's very long . . . bordering on witch's length."

"It goes with my Manson girl dress."

He ignored me. "How about a foot above your waist?"

"Fine," I sulked.

He picked up a pair of scissors and began snipping.

I said, "Where did you learn all of this?"

"When I was first pimping girls and photographing them for my fledgling skin mag, I couldn't afford a professional. I did hair and makeup on all my girls. It not only made sense economically, but it was a good way to create intimacy. Make a girl beautiful, she's yours for life."

"When was this? Before we were married?"

"Before we were living together . . ." He put down the scissors. "You were still in Chicago with Gabe, and I was in New York." He started cutting again. "It was right after the trial. I wanted out. Joey eventually let me go but didn't give me squat. Which was fine. He didn't owe me anything. I was spending everything I had on you and Gabe. Money was going fast."

"I didn't know that."

"Course you didn't. I never told you. I was just about to crawl on my hands and knees and beg him to take me back when the son of a bitch died and left me money."

"Very convenient," I said.

"I didn't kill him. No one was as surprised as I was when I found out. I thought he'd written me off. And FYI, he died of a heart attack. He had a terrible diet, smoked like a coal factory, weighed about two-eighty on a five-ten frame." He stopped cutting and examined his work. "Perfect." He put some gel into my hair and started blow-drying it.

Warm air coursed through my tresses. My head felt like it had lost ten pounds.

"Of course, all of it was drug money and had to be laundered. I dumped about a third into my porno mag. Then the internet came along and that went bust. An epic failure. Luckily, I had bought some property near Columbia. Sold that for a profit. Plus, I had some illegal brothels upstate that were bringing in cash. Made enough off those to finally get something here and do it legally. That's when things started taking off. But I couldn't have done it without Joey's money. I am grateful to the old motherfucker." He took a section of hair with a round brush and began to straighten it out. "I know you think I'm hard on Juleen, but it's a hard world out there."

"She's eleven."

"And I was an orphan at thirteen." I didn't say anything. "She's under my roof. It's my rules. You don't like it, you know where the door is."

"Am I arguing?"

He took another section of hair. "What do you need to make this work—you and me?"

"A nicer attitude would be a good start."

"Sorry, I'm tense. What do you need? Besides getting Sanjay. I know that's the only reason you've agreed to marry me. And I'm okay with that. Our relationship has always been contractual. Tell me, what do you need to make *this* contract work?"

"What do you need?" I asked him.

"If it were up to me, I'd send Juleen back to Mumbai to live with her father and it would just be the two of us. But I know that's not realistic."

"Correct. I'm not sending my daughter away."

"And I know that she can't stay here."

"Also correct. She cannot live in a brothel."

He turned off the blow dryer although my hair was still damp. "This is what I need, okay?"

"I'm listening."

"You can live anywhere you want with your children as long as it's in the state of Nevada."

I smiled. "Tax benefits?"

"Tax benefits, business benefits. If I start putting stuff in your name, which is very convenient from my perspective, I want you to reside in the state where your business is. Nevada is a big state. You've got lots of choice."

"I'm sure I'll find something that's agreeable to both of us."

"Good. I know good schools and good hospitals are in the bigger cities. Las Vegas is fine, but I'd prefer if you stayed closer. Reno is a two- to three-hour drive from me. There are some nice neighborhoods and private schools there that I think would work."

"How big is the city? Population, I mean."

"Reno? About a quarter million people. Vegas is twice that. We can check out both cities. I'll go along with whatever you want."

"Okay," I told him. "What else do you want?"

He picked up the blow dryer and turned it back on. "Terry, I will support you. Anything you need to take care of your family. And I have no problem with you working, even if last time it led to your affair. I get why you had an affair. I was shitty to you. But even if I had been a peach, affairs are still exciting. Fucking someone new is exciting. I could probably handle another affair because I understand that. What I can't handle is you getting knocked up again." He yanked a little too hard on my hair. "It was completely humiliating."

"It won't happen again, Donatti. That much I can promise you."

"And I believe you. But for me to be sure—a hundred percent sure that won't happen—I want you to get your tubes tied."

I was silent. I was forty-two and had no intention of having more children, but I didn't want the choice ripped away from me.

Again, he yanked my hair. "Cat got your tongue?"

"Give me a minute." He didn't answer. Then I turned around to face him, my hair still tangled in the brush. "I don't want any more babies, but it doesn't mean that closing that door will be easy for me."

"Why? What's the problem?"

The problem was losing your biological purpose in life. But I wouldn't dare say that to him. Instead, I said, "I will do it, but not until after we're married. It's something a wife does for a husband, not something a fiancée does for her fiancé."

He thought about it for a moment. "I can live with that." He turned me around to face the wall. "The last issue is this. If you're living in one city and I'm living in another, there has to be some time for us without your kids."

"Kid." I bit my lip to prevent the tears from coming. I shook my head.

"Baby, I promise you I'll do whatever I can to get you your son back. Nothing is a sure thing, but I will try. Even so, it's going to take time." *And money.* "But I will try."

I wanted to ask him how . . . what he was going to do. But I knew it would make him angry. Instead, I nodded. "Thank you, Chris. I don't know what I would do without you."

"You're welcome." He paused. "I respect your need to be a good mother, angel. But if this is going to work, you have to respect my needs."

"What do you want?"

He put down the blow dryer. "Your hair came out beautiful."

"Can I see?"

"After I'm done with the makeup." He clipped the side of my hair off my face and studied me intensely. "Hmm . . ."

"I know. I'm a disaster."

"No, you just look like a gorgeous woman with two black eyes." He touched the bloody bags underneath my lower lids. "Let me try something to tighten this first." He rubbed some cream on me. "We'll just let that set for a minute." He checked his watch.

"What time is it?"

"Not even ten. We're fine."

We didn't talk for a moment. Then I said, "What about your needs?"

"Ah, my needs." He paused. "My hope is that you could come here every weekend. I'd fly you over or, if you're in Reno, I'd send the car for you. But I realize that you probably don't want to be away from your kids every weekend." A pause. "I'm willing to do every other week. You come in Friday night and you can leave Sunday night. That's six days a month. Surely that's not too much to ask."

"Who will take care of the kids when I'm gone?"

"Obviously you'll need a nanny. You choose, I'll pay." When I didn't say anything, his expression changed. "*What?*"

"Can you give me a minute to think about what you're asking?"

"What's to think about? You should say yes and then we're done."

"Yes, it's reasonable. Give me a sec." I paused. "I imagine that Friday and Saturday are busy nights for the business."

"Actually, it's Thursday and Friday. By Saturday morning, everyone's packing to leave for wifey and home."

"Okay, then let me come Saturday night through Monday night. Same amount of time, but that way I can be home most weekends. And I can be with you when you're not so busy."

"That actually works better. I just thought you'd want to be with your kids Monday morning to send them off to school."

"I can work around two days a month."

His smile was pure white as he took the cream off my face. "That was easy, right? We can communicate, right?" His smile had turned hungry. "I'll be *very* excited to see you whenever you do get here. We're gonna have lots of fun." He started applying foundation to my face.

"Who are we meeting tonight?"

"Yeah, I guess we should go over that. Mike Badger and George Denofrio. Mike is loud and obnoxious, but he has the money. George is the exact opposite. Quiet, but his mind is always moving. They're both married, but this isn't George's thing. He's here for Mike. George is the financial adviser, tells Mike how to spend the money. They both have been coming here for maybe six, seven years."

"And who are the women they are with?"

"Good question." He put down the makeup and picked up his phone. Made a call and got the answer. "Brie Tenerac and Kirstin Ellison."

"What do they look like?"

"Gorgeous, of course. That's why I get big bucks." He picked up blush and a big brush. Swiped the light pink powder and blew the excess off the bristles.

"What do they look like specifically? The women."

"Long blond hair. Big blue eyes. Great tits and firm, round asses. These guys are meat-and-potatoes men and I give them meat-and-potatoes girls. Nothing exotic. I think Brie is twenty-three. Kirstin is a little older. Maybe twenty-seven or twenty-eight."

"Fabulous." I shook my head.

"Don't move."

"You'd better introduce me as Dr. McLaughlin. I need some sort of competitive edge."

He smiled. "True, the women are young and gorgeous." He applied blush to my cheekbones. "But you'll be the one wearing the ring."

"Why go through this again, Chris?" I asked him. "We can just be together . . . like now."

"No, no, no." He took out a tube of mascara. "I want it official."

"But why?"

"Who can explain obsession?"

"You never seemed obsessed with me in high school."

"Of course I was obsessed with you." He stopped working. "Terry, I lived with Joey and Donna for four years. I spoke Italian fluently. Do you really think I needed tutoring in French?"

I had never thought about that. "What about math?"

"There I needed help. But I could have hired anyone. I was totally besotted with you from the moment I saw you. But at eighteen, you can't show your feelings. That's pussy."

"Could have fooled me."

"Lady, I went to prison for you. That's pretty obsessed."

I had no comeback.

He said, "You've always been my girl. You'll always be my girl. Look up." He applied mascara on my lower eyelashes.

"I'm not a girl anymore. I'm forty-two."

"I know your age." A pause. "See, that's the difference between women and men. You see me as a forty-four-year-old man. I still see you as a sixteen-year-old girl." A pause. "I think you're the most beautiful woman on the planet. But you know what is really hot about you?"

"Besides everything?"

He laughed. "Your voice. It's whispery and low when you talk and throaty when you laugh." He blew out air. "It is sex personified. I'd never whore you. But if I did, I wouldn't put you in the rooms. I'd put you on the phones." He put down the mascara brush. "Your eyelids are purple. I'm going to work with that, just soften them."

He mixed some eyeshadow and applied it to the lids of my eyes. Then he stepped back to admire his handiwork. "Baby, those young ones have nothing on you."

"Can I see?"

"Of course." He took out the hair clips and wrapped a couple of tresses around his fingers. Then he helped me down from the chair.

I went to the bathroom and looked in the mirror. Stared at the whole woman looking back at me. My eyes started to moisten. He spoke from behind my shoulders. "Don't do that. You'll ruin all my hard work."

"How did you *do* that?"

"I'm an artist. You're a great canvas. I'll touch it up right before we go."

I turned around and faced him. "Thank you."

He stared at me with his brilliant blue eyes. "You're welcome, baby." He smiled. "So when can I do your ass?"

I hit his shoulder and moved around him, walked into his living area.

He followed me. "I don't mean at this very moment."

I hit him again, this time with my cast.

"Ow. That's a lethal weapon." He said, "You know you're gonna do it. I can talk you into anything."

"Can we change the subject?" I was irritated. "It's always so cold in here."

"That reminds me. I bought you a pashmina for tonight. You want it now?"

"I'll just use your robe. It's warm." When I came back, he was in his captain's seat, monitoring the rooms on the screens.

He said, "Make me some coffee, babe."

Like nothing happened. "Sure. I could probably use it myself."

He didn't answer me. His eyes were glued to the screen.

Chris was all work and all play—and never a dull boy.

CHAPTER 9

THE SPACE WAS next door to the main brothel, a three-story building that resembled residential condos done in wood and glass and befitting the environment. This structure was two stories, with the patrons' area upstairs and a staff cafeteria downstairs that was dark. The lounge was dimly lit, woody and clubby, harkening back to a different era when men were kings and it was acceptable to pinch and grope and wink with untold freedom. There were lots of old bars and cocktail lounges around that still looked like this, but they were threadbare and worn. This was clearly the update that proprietors would do if they had the money.

A long mirrored backbar was fronted by two men in white suits, ready to pour on request. An array of spirits, glasses, and silver shakers sat on shelves cut into the mirror. The room was furnished with tables for two, four, and six, set apart from one another for privacy. On each table were several candles and several small vases of fresh flowers. Women waited on tables, and their attire was surprisingly modest. By that I mean form-fitting tuxedo jackets over black leggings and pumps with high heels. The jackets had a deep V in the front, but nothing was really hanging out. I'd seen more revealing clothing at any wine bar. The nicest part of the space was a wall of glass that probably showcased the mountains in daytime. Since it was dark, the panoramic view was basically a black blob with some landscape lighting below. But dark or light, a window always gave the appearance of freedom ahead.

It was a few minutes after eleven when Chris escorted me through the door and to a table for six situated in a corner next to the window. It was summer, but the mountain temperature always dropped at night, and I noticed a ceiling heat lamp. It was turned on, and the women, wearing sleeveless dresses, seemed quite comfortable. Which was good. I was always cold. When Chris and I started living together, the minute he would leave, I'd turn the AC off.

The men, and then the women, stood as we approached. When we reached the table, Chris went into charm mode. He shook the men's hands and gave each woman a kiss on the lips. Then he made introductions. The girls looked as I had expected, but the men did not. I had created a picture of Mike Badger, given what Chris had told me, as a Falstaffian man—big and sanguine with a deep voice. Instead, Badger was small and slight and spoke as if he were talking through a reed. He appeared to be in his late fifties, with graying hair and bags under his brown eyes. George Denofrio was taller in height and larger in girth, but not by any means a big man. Chris was a big man. His stature usually dominated. It would be interesting to see how he acted when someone else was holding the cards.

He said, "This is my fiancée, Terry McLaughlin." I stared at him and he grinned. "Dr. Terry McLaughlin." He pulled out my chair and helped me take off my shawl. I sat between Chris and George Denofrio.

The women squealed out a chorus of congratulations. Badger wasn't interested. Immediately he asked me if I was an MD.

"Excuse me?" I said.

"Are you a real doctor?" he said. "You could be a PhD."

I remembered Chris's words: *loud and obnoxious*. His brown eyes were focused on my face. "I'm an MD."

"Where'd you go to medical school?"

Okay. We're playing this game. "Loyola in Chicago."

"Decent school. I went to Northwestern."

Which is a higher-ranked university. I nodded. "Great place."

"Especially for medical school. What's your specialty?"

I looked at Chris, who appeared to be listening to the conversation. "I did ER/trauma. I haven't worked in a couple of years."

"Where'd you work?" he asked.

Really pushy guy. Chris was still silent. I said, "For a while I worked in Manhattan at several locations—Weill Cornell and Columbia/Presbyterian. Then I worked in Mumbai for a while."

"Mumbai?" When I nodded, he asked, "How'd you get to India?"

I looked at Chris, who gave away nothing. I said, "Many planes fly there."

An irritated smile. "Okay, I'll rephrase the question. What brought you to India?"

"Same answer."

Badger regarded Chris. "She's a funny one."

Chris raised his hands up in the air and shrugged. I didn't know if he was throwing me under the bus for bringing up India or if he was just giving me free rein. His face was totally flat.

Badger persisted. "What was it like to work in India?"

I looked at Chris and then turned back to Badger. "ER is ER."

"But there must be differences."

"Of course." I thought a moment. "In America, there were lots of gunshot wounds. In Mumbai, there are many more stabbings with knives and swords, believe it or not. So India is messier but less lethal, while America is cleaner but more lethal."

To Chris, he said, "I see you keep illustrious company."

"She's one of a kind," Chris answered. He nodded and a server appeared from the mist. "WhistlePig neat, ice on the side." To me: "What would you like?"

"Coffee, please."

"You sure?"

I lifted my right arm encased in a cast. "I'm still on medication."

"What happened?" Badger asked.

Chris smiled, but his eyes were cold. "That's what goes down when someone crosses me."

When no one spoke, I said, "He's kidding. I was in a car accident."

"Omigod," Kirstin said. "Are you okay?"

"Obviously not," Badger answered.

Kirstin turned bright red.

I said, "I'm fine. Just a little bruised."

Chris said, "What can I get everyone?"

After all the drinks were ordered, conversation resumed with Chris directing. The drinks came, and everyone toasted to a good time. Things started out light, with the men doing all the talking. While Brie and Kirstin were beautiful, they were ornaments. For some reason, I no longer felt competitive. Instead, I had morphed into a protective den mother. Physically they looked as Chris had described them, but there was something worn and haunted in their eyes. I could relate: life was not turning out as we had pictured.

Twenty minutes went by with talk of stocks and bonds and mutual funds and real estate. Badger was spouting about his latest ventures that were printing cash. Denofrio was sitting stoic, nursing a jalapeño margarita. But he did have a notepad out. Chris had barely touched his drink, meaning he intended to stay sober for the evening.

I can control myself.

Kirstin caught my eye and smiled at me. "Congratulations."

"Thank you very much."

"Beautiful ring."

Her voice was small and girlish. I looked down at my hand. "Thank you."

"Did Mr. Donatti pick it out?"

"He did."

"He has good taste."

"Excellent taste."

Brie said, "How did you two meet?" A pause. "Or is that too personal?"

I looked at Chris, who appeared to be deep in conversation. But then he said, "We went to high school together."

That was a conversation stopper.

"High school?" Badger looked at me. "How old are you?"

"Not much younger than him," I retorted.

"What are you? Like forty?"

Chris finally intervened. "It's unseemly to ask a woman her age."

"It's no secret. I'm forty-two."

"You preserve well," Badger said.

"Just like a jar of strawberry jam." I smiled. "Thank you."

"Were you high school sweethearts?" Brie asked.

"Something like that."

Chris said, "Actually, Terry is my ex-wife."

"You were married?" Denofrio said.

The man could speak.

"He was and he's masochistic enough to try it again," I told him.

Badger chimed in. "Why'd you break up in the first place?"

Chris was about to speak, but I got there first. Trying to be polite, I said, "Youth . . . inexperience. Vistas we've seemed to conquer over the years."

"No, I really want to know," Badger insisted. "What kind of woman marries a man who runs whorehouses?"

I was shocked by his rudeness. Chris said nothing. Of course, the question was directed to me. I said, "He didn't run brothels at eighteen."

"But at some point you had to know that the man you were marrying was . . ."

"Unconventional?" I filled in.

"I think the word he's looking for is *criminal*," Chris said.

Badger said, "All I'm saying is that you must have known what he was."

"Obviously. But first loves have a way of making you do impulsive things."

"That's so romantic," Brie said.

Glad you think so, I thought.

Badger steamrolled on. "Then you knew about Joseph Donatti."

I looked at Chris. He actually seemed to be enjoying this. "Eventually, yes, I did find out about his uncle."

"What do you mean 'eventually'? Donatti is not a common name."

"He was Chris Whitman in high school."

"Oh." A momentary pause. "Then how'd you find out about his past?"

"Mr. Donatti, né Whitman, told me."

"So, you knew. And you married him anyway."

"There are many compelling reasons to get married." I gave him a sweet smile. "Our son is now twenty-four. I think you can do the math."

Kirstin said, "You're Gabe's mother?"

I looked at her. "You've met him?"

"Yes. He was at last year's Labor Day party."

I turned to Chris. "Interesting." I smiled at Badger. "Surely you gentlemen have more pressing matters to talk about."

But the man wouldn't let it go. "I'm interested in your opinion of him."

"Pardon?"

"What do you think of your fiancé now? I mean he's rich and good-looking and all that. But now you know who he is. You're marrying a man who owns whorehouses."

I said, "I'm marrying an astute businessman who is very wise."

"Ah, the devoted woman." He grinned in self-satisfaction. "I love it."

I said, "Mr. Donatti has lots of devoted women."

"They're called whores."

I could see Chris's eyes darken, not for me—I could take care of myself—but for the women with them. I squeezed his leg. "You mean these two beautiful ladies?" When he didn't answer, I said, "If you don't approve of whom you're with, Mr. Badger, perhaps Mr. Donatti can help you set up a harem of your own."

"I'd love the idea." He winked at me. "But only if you came with it."

"That's *not* going to happen," I told him. Then I leaned toward him with a sly smile on my face, peering into his pugilistic eyes. "But if you behave yourself like a good boy—and I mean a really, really good boy—one day . . . I just might let you *watch*."

Chris burst out into unrestrained laughter. He licked his finger with his tongue and made an imaginary tick in the air. "Switch seats with me, Teresa."

"Of course."

The rest of the evening went by without incident, with Badger ignoring me and turning his attention to a bottle of Jack Daniel's. Seated with the ladies, I steered the conversation away from anything personal and chatted with my young friends about foundation, lipstick, nail polish (we all three liked the color Wicked), the benefits of Botox even at twenty, and whether the current bachelor was on crack cocaine when he dumped Amber for the evil Edison. At one point, the conversation switched back to Gabe. They both thought he was cute and sweet. All he talked about was his piano and his fiancée, which just about summed up my son's interests.

When it was time to go, I smiled sweetly to George, who shook my hand, and afterward, I allowed Mike Badger to kiss my hand gallantly as if nothing had happened.

He winked at me and slurred out, "The offer still stands."

"You couldn't afford her," Chris told him. "We'll talk later?"

Badger nodded and staggered off, his arm draped around Kirstin's shoulders, using her for support. Denofrio and Brie walked behind Badger and his date, tailing them like Secret Service agents. A few minutes later, I was in Chris's upstairs office at the lounge, taking off the heels and putting on flats. The man had offices in every building he owned. This one was like his main office downstairs from his suite, done in brown leather with a little color in the accessories, plus some nondescript framed pictures on the walls. There was an antique portable bar with stemware that seemed beside the point because there was a big bar downstairs. I said, "Did I ruin your deal for you?"

"Are you *kidding* me?" He grinned. "You *crushed* it, baby. The asshole was smitten."

"Did you get what you want?"

"Pretty much." He kissed my nose. "Thank you."

"I'm glad it helped." I was drained. "I'm tired."

"Do you want me to bring the bike so you don't have to walk?"

"No, I'm okay."

The walk was a silent one. When we got to his suite, I headed for the bathroom and washed off all the makeup. I was pale and thin and had two black eyes. I looked like a Keane painting from the sixties. He helped me take off my dress—my cast got in the way of everything—and I slipped on my nightgown and went under the covers. It was a little before one in the morning.

Chris hung up his clothing, took out his sweats, and then plopped down beside me. "I'm horny."

"As long as you don't get mad if I fall asleep." I waited for him to get on top.

"I'm feeling pumped. Turn around."

"Nothing funny, Chris. I don't want that."

"No ass, I promise," he said. "Turn around."

"Please don't be rough."

"Just let me know, angel," he said. "I'm listening."

He pulled back the covers and lifted up my nightgown. When he was done, he kissed my lips gently. "You do know that I love you."

I touched his face. "You're one of a kind. Thank you for everything, Donatti. I don't know how I would have survived those early years without you. Like I told Badger, I knew what I was getting into. I made a conscious decision to come back."

"You were penniless with a kid, living in a cold-water flat in Chicago. I threatened to take Gabe away from you. I forced your hand. You had no choice but to do whatever I wanted."

I touched his face and brushed his golden-white hair from his cheek. Somewhere inside, there was an eighteen-year-old boy whom once I would have died for. "You always have a choice," I told him. "And I chose Donatti." I closed my eyes. "I'm really tired."

"Go to sleep, baby. I won't bother you." He got up to go to work. When he was at the door, I said, "Chris?"

He turned around. "What, angel?"

"Why did you invite Gabe to a party here?"

"Not to corrupt him. He's incorruptible."

"I know that. Why'd you ask him to come to a party with all these yucky people?"

He came back and sat on the bed. "Lots of these men . . . they envy me. I'm rich, I'm good-looking, I can have any woman—any person—I want, I have an enviable life. But lots of them, like Mike, they may envy me, but they also look down on me. To them, I'm nothing but a procurer of whores. And I recognize that's what I am. Fine. I'll accept it. But a lot of these guys . . . they also have shitty kids—drug-addicted washouts. Probably because they're shitty fathers. I was a shitty father. But my son had a great mother."

"Do you mean Rina or me?"

"Maybe both, but it doesn't matter. Whatever the reason, Gabe is a marvel. I bring him out to those motherfuckers . . . introduce him to them—my good-looking concert pianist son who got accepted to Harvard but turned it down to go to Juilliard at sixteen. I look them straight in the eye when I brag about him. I may be just a pimp. But my kid can kick your kid's ass any day of the week."

AT TEN-FIFTEEN IN the morning, they announced boarding. Decker placed his phone on the sensor that read his e-ticket. When he finally looked at the seat assignment, he realized he was in first class. It was definitely his name on the ticket. He sat in the second row on the aisle, a grin on his face. His kids had upgraded Rina and him on their international flight to Israel, and now it looked like McAdams had upgraded him on this coast-to-coast journey.

As Decker settled in, stretching out with newfound legroom, the window seat next to him remained empty even though the plane was packed—anything to Los Angeles was always full. He called McAdams as the last few stragglers were coming into the cabin.

"Thank you, Tyler, you didn't have to do that. But the room is much appreciated."

"You're very welcome," McAdams answered.

"How's it going?"

"Pretty good." McAdams entered the cabin. "How's it going with you?"

"Great!" Decker looked up, put the phone down, and stared.

"Fancy meeting you here." McAdams tossed his leather bag onto the window seat.

"What are you doing in Orlando? I thought we were meeting up in Los Angeles."

"I've never been to Epcot," he said. "A little dated, but I suppose it was revolutionary in its time."

"Tyler, I'm serious. Why did you come out here?"

"Impulsivity, I guess. Blame it on my prefrontal cortex." He slid inside and picked up his bag. "Figured we can chat on the way to the West Coast."

Dumbfounded, Decker had nothing more to say. Tyler was approaching thirty, which gave his face a bit more gravitas. But he still had youth and good looks, with hazel eyes and dark, curly hair. He wore a black T-shirt under a lightweight denim-colored seersucker jacket and jeans.

McAdams peeked inside his bag. "I'll just take out my notes. So how was your call to Pauline's sister?" He consulted the papers. "Marion Vanderberg."

"She took it fairly well." Decker paused. "She didn't seem too shocked. She hadn't heard from Pauline in years."

"How many years is years?"

"I don't know. It could be two, it could be ten."

"You didn't ask her?"

"Since we're going out there anyway, I thought I'd ask the questions face-to-face."

"Yeah, can you remind me *why* we're going out—except for you to see your old partner?"

"Marge is picking us up at the airport, plus she knows the area very well." Decker paused. "What's bugging you, kid?"

McAdams was silent. Then he said, "If she's driving, do I have to sit in the back?"

Decker regarded the young man. "Tyler, I don't mind stretching out in the back. It's just that half the time you zone out and wind up playing with your phone instead of talking. I understand. Long car rides can be boring. But you can sit up front with Marge. I'm fine with it."

"I'm being a brat." McAdams had turned sour. "I just hate to be marginalized. My father did that to me all the time."

"I'm not your dad, I'm your partner. Your current partner. Marge is a fabulous person and a great woman to bounce ideas off of, but she's no longer my partner. It's typical of her to offer to drive us around. I don't care where I sit. Now, where are we on the autopsy?"

"Pauline had multiple stab wounds, but not one was, by itself, lethal. She probably bled out. The biggest wound was in the leg. It narrowly missed the femoral artery." McAdams thought a moment. "Odd place to stab someone. You'd have to be thrusting down or even kneeling."

"If you were aiming at the chest and your victim stepped back, you could miss the chest and get the leg," Decker said. "I probably know the answer to this, but have we gotten anything definite that puts Lanz, Schulung, and Kathrine Taylor in Germany?"

"No," McAdams stated. "We've sent out bulletins to police departments in Düsseldorf. The Lanzes live just outside the city. It's a wealthy area, lots of industrialists."

"How big is Düsseldorf?"

"It's a major city." McAdams tapped on his phone. "Over six hundred thousand. It's the state capital of the North Rhine–Westphalia area. Biggish Jewish population, by the way. Bet you could find a kosher restaurant." Still tapping. "There's a kosher market. And a Chabad."

"When people land on Mars, they'll find that Chabad had beaten them to it." Decker paused. "I'm wondering if instead of poking around Germany, we'd be better off trying to put pressure on the Taylors. They've heard from their daughter at least once. I'm betting they've heard from her again."

"They are not going to do anything to endanger their daughter's life."

Decker said, "Eventually the Taylors will want to see Kathrine. Now that we have a body, maybe they'll open up. Because they're going to worry about her. Kathrine might feel safe, but she may be slow to recognize danger. And with Bertram's history of manslaughter charges, that danger may be a real factor."

Announcements were made to turn off large electronic devices. Smaller ones may be used if in airplane mode.

McAdams said, "Then you're going to call them?"

"Once I find out all there is to know about Corbett, I can talk to them with more authority. They're a good bet to locate Bertram and friends."

"And how is visiting an estranged sister going to help us find out about Pauline Corbett?"

"I'm hoping they weren't always estranged. Pauline is our victim, and I need to know all I can about her."

"How's that going to help us find Schulung?"

"It might not. And while Elsie Schulung is at the top of our list, I can't have tunnel vision. It's possible that talking to her sister will lead us down a different avenue of inquiry."

McAdams nodded and stowed his phone. He had turned quiet.

Decker said, "What is it now?"

"I hate when I'm a petty asshole. I don't know what comes over me sometimes."

"We all have our egos."

"I just get in these moods. You can blame that on my prefrontal cortex as well."

"Or maybe you're just an asshole," Decker said.

McAdams laughed. "Watch your mouth, old man, or you'll be riding coach on the way home."

DECKER GRINNED. "THAT'S my girl!"

"Who?" McAdams asked. "The waving maniac at the end of the staircase?"

"It is she."

Trim and fit, Marge was wearing jeans, a white blouse, and beaded sandals on her feet.

Decker waved back. "She looks great!"

"Seeing as I have no basis for comparison, I'll just have to take your word for it."

"Tyler—"

"I'll be charming, don't worry." McAdams watched as Decker and she embraced in a big hug worthy of pre-COVID days.

"Look at you," Decker said. "I like your hair."

"Do you?" Marge preened.

"Yes, I do. It's very youthful."

"Will thinks it's too short, but he likes the color. I'll take one out of two." Marge faced McAdams. "You must be the kid that this guy is always raving about."

"And you must be the partner to whom I can never measure up." McAdams stuck out his hand. "Pleasure to meet you."

"Likewise." Marge hooked her arm around Decker. "You didn't tell me he was so cute."

"You think?" Decker said.

Marge hit him. She looked at her watch. It was two-thirty in the afternoon. "When are you going back?"

"Ten p.m. red-eye out of LAX," McAdams said.

"We should be up there around three-thirty, four. Maybe an hour to interview." She thought. "We can maybe squeeze in an early dinner. Do you have any luggage?"

"Just carry-on," Decker said. "And we're first class."

"Wow!" Marge whistled. "How'd you pull that one off?"

"He didn't," McAdams said. "But I did."

"Pete, you've found a worthy partner." She smiled. "Marion Vanderberg lives in Camarillo, about twenty minutes south of me. Actually, she lives close to that kosher winery. I don't know about dinner, but the wine tasting room will be open. They serve tapas if you're interested. Quite good. Will and I have gone there several times."

"Tapas sounds great," Decker said. "My treat."

"You're in my territory," Marge insisted. "It's my treat."

"Oh no, you don't," Decker said.

"I'm not arguing about this," Marge said.

McAdams tried to hide his annoyance. "Just flip a coin."

Decker said, "How about we split the bill and treat the kid?"

Marge agreed. Her car was a four-door Ford Focus, maroon red, and it had seen better days. Although the cloth interior was frayed in spots, it was clean and smelled good. She said, "I want to hear all about this case."

"Mind if the kid sits up front?" Decker said.

McAdams said, "It's fine—"

"I'd prefer it," Marge said. "Not that you're not handsome, Pete, but there's nothing like youth." A pause. "I'll just put on my glasses . . . ah, you're still good-looking."

McAdams felt his face getting hot.

Marge grinned as everyone took a seat inside the car. She patted McAdams's leg. "Now tell me all about this case."

"The boss hasn't told you?"

"Of course he's told me. But I want to hear it from you."

"Sure." McAdams took out his notes, but Marge put her hand over the pad.

"Tell me what you *know*. From memory. You'll retain the info better that way."

McAdams stowed his notes. "You're as tough as he is."

"True, but I'm a lot better to look at."

ONCE THEY WERE on their way, McAdams gave Marge a recap. Bertram Lanz had started out a Missing Persons case. After paying a visit to Bertram's residential home, Decker and he discovered that Lanz had been befriended by a nurse named Elsie Schulung. She had been fired for a few reasons, mostly because she had a tendency to go rogue. Decker had headed out to Elsie's house to talk to her, but no one was home. Since it was the summer, it wasn't odd to think that she may have gone on vacation, but after the mail continued to pile up, Decker and the local police decided on a welfare check and found blood in the house.

"It didn't look like a murder scene, but there was more blood than a spoonful," Decker said. "Then the local police took over and basically booted out Greenbury. They kept in touch but clearly wanted to handle it themselves."

"Silly people. Do they realize who they had?"

"No wonder you like her," McAdams said. "Can you boost my ego as well?"

"When you earn it, sure."

"Tough as *nails*," McAdams said.

Decker said, "In Schulung's house, there were pictures of Bertram Lanz and his girlfriend, Kathrine Taylor. She lived in another residential home where Bertram used to reside. That's how they met. Then we discovered that Kathrine was missing as well."

"What about Schulung's car?" Marge asked.

"Missing at first," McAdams said. "We eventually found it hidden by brush in the woods."

"If Elsie fled, how did she escape without her car?"

"Schulung had a girlfriend named Pauline Corbett," Decker said. "We think she used her car."

"Corbett is the body you just discovered," Marge said.

"Yes," McAdams said. "And the blood in Elsie's house matched Pauline's blood. We have a few theories; one of them is obviously that Elsie killed Pauline."

"Or someone in Elsie's house killed Pauline," Marge said.

"Exactly," McAdams said. "Since Bertram, Kathrine, and Elsie have all seemed to have disappeared around the same time, we're thinking there's a connection."

"She took them as hostages?"

"Maybe."

"And how did they get to where they were going after they ditched Elsie's car?"

McAdams said, "The short answer is we don't know. But Pauline's car is missing."

"If Elsie took Pauline's car, who drove Pauline's car to the spot where Elsie ditched her car?" Marge asked.

McAdams said, "We don't know the answer."

"Could Elsie also be dead?" Marge asked. "Buried in the woods?"

Decker said, "My guess is that she's with Bertram and Kathrine. And we know Kathrine was okay as of about three weeks ago because her parents spoke to her."

The car turned silent. Decker added, "Bertram was charged and found guilty of manslaughter in a bar fight back in Germany about ten years ago. It was one of those brawls and a lot of punches were thrown. But Bertram's fists killed a man."

"Then he's not afraid to fight," Marge said. "You're thinking that Bertram might have stabbed Pauline? Why would he do that?"

"We've kicked around several things," McAdams said. "But we really don't have a strong motive."

Marge said, "Any ideas on how Pauline's death is relevant to your Missing Person?"

"No," Decker said. "But now, at the very least, we have a body. That's why we want to talk to the sister . . . find out more about the victim."

"Basic Homicide 101." Marge smiled, then cocked her thumb toward the backseat. "Pay attention, young'un. You can learn from this guy."

THE WINDING ROADS cut through California farmland and ranch house residences. Decker had forgotten how much he loved the West Coast, with its sunny skies and varying terrain. Since it was August, it was hot and dry, but the ethers were deep blue and the air in these parts was clear and clean. Current crops were peppers, table grapes, artichokes, all sorts of melons, and lots and lots of big, beautiful strawberries. Fruit and vegetable stands dotted the streets, brimming over with all that was fresh. There were also citrus orchards—lemons, limes, and oranges— along with acres of avocado trees, some of which acted as a wind-break for the citrus. Lots of guacamole was featured in restaurants.

Marion Vanderberg lived in a wood-sided one-story house painted the color of a robin's eggshell. The front area hosted two big avocado trees sitting in dirt and crabgrass, the patch bisected by a cracked con-crete walkway to the front door. It was warm, and Decker was glad he'd opted for a polo shirt and jeans rather than his usual brown suit. He rang the bell, and the woman who answered was barefoot, wear-ing Bermuda shorts and a white T-shirt. She was around fifty and tall and rawboned—a big woman with gray-streaked, coffee-colored hair pulled back in a ponytail. Pecan-colored eyes, full lips, and a mottled complexion of different shades of bronze. After introductions were made, she told the trio to sit wherever they wanted.

The place was cozy. Tables held fresh flowers. The sectional was brown Ultrasuede and worn at spots. Wide-planked natural oak floors were covered with napped area rugs. Shelving units, bolted on the walls, held books and old stereo equipment, along with dozens of framed photographs. The TV was on a blank wall with wires trail-ing down to a cabinet unit.

Marion sat on the smaller sofa of the L-shaped sectional while the three of them sat in a row on the larger sofa. Her eyes were far away.

Decker said, "Thank you for seeing us." The sister nodded. "Nice trees in front."

"We have about thirty more in back," Marion said.

"How many acres do you have?"

"About five."

"All avocado?"

"No, we also have lemon, orange, grapefruit, apricot, peach, plum . . . several varieties of plum." Marion perked up. "There's a big open-air fruit and vegetable stand about two blocks away. It's more like a trading post for the area. We trade our stuff for tomatoes and peppers and eggplant. In the winter, we trade citrus for lettuces and onions. Works out well."

"I'm sure it does," Decker said. "I used to have a ranch in the east valley decades ago. I had some fruit trees on the property, but I bought it for the trails. I had horses back then."

"What happened?" Marion asked.

"I got married and had kids. Living in an isolated area wasn't good for them."

"Yeah, that's why I like it here. You get your privacy but there are neighbors." She sighed. "Sorry about the temperature. AC is on the fritz."

"We're fine." Decker waited in silence. Then he said, "I'm very sorry for your loss."

"Thank you." Again, the faraway look. "She was my baby sister."

Marge said, "How many siblings in the family?"

"Five," Marion said. "Three girls, two boys, plus a worn-out mother and an alcoholic father. He sold insurance up north."

"Where up north?"

"San Luis Obispo area."

Marge said, "How'd you get from there to here?"

"Marriage. Thank God it's been a good one. Joe manages several big farms in the Santa Paula area. For years, we've talked about having our own farm, but it's too much responsibility. We're happy here with our trees and our chickens and our goats. We make our own cheese."

"Sounds ideal," McAdams said.

"After coming from my family, it's as close to heaven without seeing Saint Peter himself."

"Are you close to your siblings?" McAdams asked.

"I'm close to my brother and my older sister. We all live within an hour from each other. My brother's a farmer and has about fifty acres. My sister is a lawyer and lives in Ventura."

Marge said, "I'm with Ventura PD. Great community."

"Yeah, she loves it." Marion paused. "Then you're not with them?"

"Detective Decker was once Lieutenant Decker from LAPD. I worked with him in Homicide for years."

"And you?" She was referring to McAdams.

"I work with Detective Decker in Greenbury PD on the East Coast. It's a small police department, but we're determined to find justice for Pauline."

"Thank you," Marion said. "My older sister and I were obedient children. Pauline was always a spunky kid. At loggerheads with my father. He hit her several times. Not as bad as he hit my mother, but he wasn't shy with his hands. I could never get her to understand that if she just buttoned up when he was in those moods, she wouldn't get hurt. But she was like a moth to a flame. Whenever he was mean, she'd provoke him further." A sigh. "It was no wonder she started with drugs."

"In her adolescence?" Decker asked.

"Yes, but it continued way past."

"How way past?"

"Pauline would have been . . ." She tapped her foot. "Forty-three. We didn't have much contact for the last four years. She'd text me on my birthday . . . Christmas. I'd text her back. Couple times she asked for money."

"Did you give it to her?" Marge asked.

"Sent her fifty bucks two . . . maybe three times."

"Do you have the address where you sent it?" Decker asked.

"Yeah, but it's not current. My sister moved around a lot."

McAdams said, "Pauline's current address put her in a studio apartment in Baniff, Pennsylvania. Greenbury PD along with Baniff PD went to her place to retrieve items for DNA when we found out she was missing. It's hard to believe that she ever lived there. A few clothes, an old toothbrush and hairbrush, a bed and a chair, and that's about it."

Marion said, "Did you find drugs?"

"No, and we did a thorough search. Her medicine cabinet was empty except for Advil."

"You didn't find weed?"

"No."

"Was that her drug of choice?" Decker asked.

"Among others. I know she took meth. She had meth mouth."

McAdams said, "Fractured teeth?"

"Fractured . . . missing," Marion said. "It doesn't surprise me that her place would be empty. I think she primarily lived with Elsie, who wouldn't have put up with that."

Decker said, "Then you do know about Elsie."

"Sure. I was all for it. For one thing, Elsie paid for Pauline's new teeth."

"Do you know that Elsie is currently missing?"

A long pause. "No, I didn't know." Another pause. "Do you think she murdered Pauline?"

"We don't know. What's your opinion of her?"

"I will tell you this. Before Elsie, Pauline had one bad relationship after another. She liked sparring with mean men. When Elsie came along, I was shocked. I'd never known my sister to be interested in other women. At the time I thought, well, at least she was with someone who probably won't beat her up."

"Did you ever meet Elsie?"

"No. Talked to her a couple times on the phone. I had the feeling she didn't want me in Pauline's life. She was possessive."

"We've heard that Elsie marched to her own drumbeat," McAdams said.

Marion said, "Elsie and Pauline might have had something going on, but I can tell you one thing. My sister was not gay. That girl loved men. The meaner the better."

"Then why do you think she branched out to Elsie?" Marge said.

"I could just say money, but it might have been more." Marion paused. "Whatever Elsie was, she impressed me as a healer. In one of her Christmas cards, Pauline wrote to say that Elsie got her off drugs. I don't know if that was totally true, but even if part of it was true, it was a step in the right direction."

McAdams said, "That also fits the way that other people describe Elsie. She cared about people and she really wanted to help them."

"Then it sounds like Elsie wouldn't want to hurt her," Marion said.

"We certainly hope not," Decker said. "You described some of Pauline's past relationships as abusive."

"Yes."

"How many abusive men are we talking about?" Decker asked.

"She was married three times. All of them hit her. I suspect that she also had many boyfriends that I didn't know about."

"Can you give me the names of her husbands?"

"Sure, but I honestly don't see them as coming back and killing her. Her last husband was four years ago. If I were you, I'd look at who she was currently dating."

"Do you think that she dated men while she was with Elsie?" Marge asked.

"Oh, for sure," Marion said. "My sister had been fooling around with boys since she was thirteen. By the time she was done with high school, I think she slept with every boy on the football team. My opinion? Once she was off drugs, her sexual appetite went up and not down."

"Where would she find her men?" Marge asked. "It would help us zero in on who she might have been seeing."

Marion said, "If I had to guess, I'd say probably bars."

"Online, perhaps?" Marge asked.

"Maybe." A pause. "At one time, she had a website . . . with pictures of herself. Some of them were in bathing suits. Some were topless."

"Would you know the URL?" McAdams took out his phone.

"No."

Silence ensued. Then McAdams said, "Can't find anything under Pauline Corbett. Maybe it was Facebook? Or a members-only account on Instagram?"

"No, it was her own website. But this was at least three years ago. A lot could have happened since then."

McAdams said, "Can I look at your computer?"

"Sure." Marion stood up. "It's in the back."

As soon as she left, Marge turned to Decker. "She just widened your suspect list."

"By her exes and a lot of unknown people." Decker shook his head. "Now we have to consider that Pauline and an abusive boyfriend got into a fight at Elsie's house. But then why would Elsie take off like that? Why not just report the incident to the police?"

"Maybe anonymous bad guy threatened Elsie if she told anyone about what happened," Marge said. "Elsie was frightened not only for herself but perhaps for Bertram."

"Then who buried Pauline?"

"Anonymous bad guy?"

Decker said, "Her body was buried too close to where Bertram disappeared and too close to Elsie's abandoned car to be random."

"Agreed," Marge said. "Maybe anonymous bad guy left the scene and Elsie and Bertram buried her."

"We went over Elsie's car," Decker said. "We didn't find blood evidence of a body."

Marge said, "How about this? Anonymous bad guy kills Pauline in Elsie's house. He puts Pauline in *his* car and then gets Elsie to help him bury her."

"Then why was Elsie's car found in the brush?"

"They went back together in anonymous bad guy's car." Marge made a face. "It sucks as a theory, but you have to start somewhere."

Decker smiled. "Our assumption is that Elsie took Pauline's car when she disappeared. She left her own car in the brush to throw the police off."

"Or maybe she wasn't worried about the police. Maybe she was afraid of someone else looking for her."

"We're back to anonymous bad guy," Decker said. "We know there had to be two drivers in order for Elsie to abandon her car in the woods."

"Then who's your likely candidate for driver number two?"

"Don't have one yet. I just got back from vacation."

Marion and McAdams returned. She said, "I've been a terrible hostess. Anyone want coffee?"

Decker smiled. "I'd be delighted."

Marge said, "Times two."

"Me three," McAdams said.

"I'll be right back, then."

When she left, McAdams said, "I found Pauline's site in Marion's browser history." He showed Marge and Decker a copy of the home page. "It looks like Pauline took it down about six months ago, but maybe we can apply for records from the server. Find out who contacted her."

"I don't know if we have the authority to do that," Decker said. "She's deceased, but the people she corresponded with are not."

"Our suspect list has just ballooned," McAdams said.

Decker said, "Margie and I were just talking about that. That perhaps there was an anonymous bad guy who did the killing and threatened Elsie if she told anyone."

Marge said, "We were just going over the car situation."

McAdams said, "The boss and I just assumed that Elsie drove her car and Pauline drove her car and they left together in Pauline's car. But now that Pauline is dead, it's a big unanswered question. There had to be a third driver." McAdams turned to Decker. "It could have been Bertram."

"He doesn't have a license," Decker said.

McAdams said, "But that doesn't mean he doesn't know how to drive."

CHAPTER 10

H**E HAD JUST** started his foray into outer space when his phone vibrated on the nightstand. He should have turned the damn thing off, but now that it buzzed, it was distracting. He grabbed the cell, intending to silence it, but then he saw the caller.

"Shit." He jumped off her body and clutched his sweatpants in one fluid motion. "I gotta take this."

"Why didn't you turn it off when we started?" Terry asked.

Her tone annoyed him. "Because it's twelve in the afternoon and some of us have to work for a fucking living." He put on pants and grabbed a T-shirt. "Stay here!" He slammed the door to his bedroom, harsher than he meant to. Into the cell, he said, "Donatti."

"You asked for the goods. I have them."

"I don't see anything."

"I can change that." A moment later, a frightened little boy appeared on his phone's screen. Then the screen went dark. "Satisfied?"

"No, I'm not," Donatti said. "I need to show the image to someone."

"That wasn't the deal."

"You've got a population of almost one and a half billion people with probably half of them kids." Donatti locked the door to his suite. "I have no idea who you're showing me."

"There has to be trust."

"There's trust . . ." Donatti was running up the stairs to Gabe's suite. "A hundred and fifty thousand worth of trust on my part. I haven't seen anything from you yet. Just hold for a few seconds."

He opened up the door and caught Juleen just as she was taking out her violin in anticipation of her lesson in a half hour. The little girl's eyes went as wide as pancakes. To her, he said, "I'm going to show you someone. I think it's your brother. Ask him a question that only he would know the answer to. Got it?"

The girl nodded.

Donatti said, "Okay. Show me the kid again! Go!"

His phone screen showed a little boy sitting on a big couch, clutching a pillow. As before, he looked absolutely terrified. He showed the image to Juleen. "This him?"

The boy's face lit up. "Sister!"

Juleen felt tears. "How are you, Sanjay?"

"I *miss* you."

"I *miss* you, too, *priy*. Are you all right?"

Donatti tapped her shoulder. "Ask him a question *now*."

"Sanjay, what is that video game that you always play with Gabriel?"

"You mean Firefox?"

"Yes, that's it."

The screen went dark. Donatti darkened his screen as well. "That's him?"

Through tears, she nodded. "Yes."

"Go into your bedroom and close the door!" When she didn't move, Donatti said, "*Now!*"

The sound of his voice spurred her into action.

Alone, he said, "Okay. I'm here."

"Satisfied?"

"For now, yes."

"All that stands between the boy and safety is money."

"Give me a figure."

"The man owes two and a half million. Add another one hundred thousand for interest."

"I can get it, but it'll take me time."

"How long?"

"Long. Maybe two months."

"We can't be responsible for a child for two months."

"How about this?" Donatti's brain was whirling. "I'll pay you another quarter mil now if you release him to his father. You don't want the kid's death on your conscience."

A small laugh. "If we release the kid, we have nothing."

And, of course, that was the truth. "How about if I bring his father to the boy?" Silence. "It'll calm the boy down and you'll have two hostages instead of one."

The laugh got louder. "I see you know nothing about Devek."

"He's the boy's father. He'll do it."

"Good luck with that. Send the two hundred and fifty thousand and we'll be in touch."

The bastard hung up. Donatti cut the line and exhaled. He felt a release of tension but not in a good way . . . more like the way he used to feel after he iced some stupid bastard. He called Devek, who answered after two rings. "It's Donatti. Listen, I just spoke to your son. He's okay for now."

"Thank God!" He sounded groggy. Not surprising because it was well past midnight in India. Devek said, "Are they going to release him?"

"Not until I pay them a lot of money, and I'm not going to do that just yet."

"How much did they ask for?"

"They asked for what you owe with interest. You said you could probably get a half million from your brother?"

A pause. "That will take time."

"Devek, the one thing we don't have is a lot of time. I'm paying them in installments, but it's a lot of money out and I'm not going to do that forever."

"I'll do whatever I can. I swear. Thank you so much, Chris. How is Juleen?"

"Fine."

"Can I talk to her now?"

"No," Donatti told him. "Listen, Devek, I think I got them to agree to let you come and stay with Sanjay while we're both working out the money situation. I'll let you know the details as soon as I have them."

"What do you mean let me stay with Sanjay?" Devek asked.

"Just that. They'll pick you up and at least you two can be together while the negotiations continue."

"What do you mean?"

"Are you fucking deaf?" His voice went up a notch. "What's not to understand?" A pause. "They will pick you up from some undisclosed location and take you to your son and you will stay with him until your debts are paid off. You will not only be good collateral for them, you will be a comfort for your child. Get it?"

"I can't do that!" Devek said. "They'll kill me!"

Donatti stared at his phone. "Are you fucking *kidding* me?"

"You don't understand. I mean it when I say they will kill me. I can't go!"

"They won't kill you as long as you're worth money to them!"

"You don't know that!"

"Jesus fucking Christ, Devek, this is your son. If it was my boy, I would have been there yesterday."

"So, you go."

"No, I won't go, because Sanjay isn't *my* son. Jesus, if Terry knew about this, she'd be on the first plane over to Mumbai."

"Then let Terry go. Sanjay is her son too."

"I don't believe this!" Donatti was now officially angry. "Terry isn't the one who owes money, asshole, you do. What the fuck is wrong with you, Devek? No one can be that much of a coward!"

"You don't know what these people are capable of."

"Yes, I do know. I'm one of them. I've terrorized dozens of men, so stop being a pussy and listen to me. I'll call you back when I know the next step. Until then, you work on getting the money and getting your divorce papers signed. You get me those two things and I can make this happen where everyone wins. I'll call you when I know something!"

"Donatti, you don't know what you're asking me to do. It's walking into a death sentence!"

"I realize you're scared, Devek, but right now, you've got no choice. Because if you don't do what I tell you, I'm going to come over to Goa and put a bullet in your brain like I should have done eleven years ago! Which I just may do anyway because at least it would save me money on Terry's divorce. Now stop being a fucking pussy and man up, for Christ's sake. Think about what I said, and I'll get back to you as soon as they call me."

He hung up.

"Fucking asshole."

Donatti looked up and saw Juleen staring at him, a terrified look on her face. He said, "I told you to stay in the bedroom." When she didn't answer, he said, "How much did you hear?"

She still didn't speak.

Donatti said, "You can't breathe a *word* of this to your mother. She cannot know what's going on. It'll kill her if she knows." No response. "Juleen, you need to answer me. Not a fucking *word*!"

She nodded.

"Good." He checked his watch. "Your teacher will be here soon. Go practice your pieces and I'll talk to you later."

She didn't move. Tears in her eyes.

Donatti exhaled. "I got you a phone, by the way. Limited internet, but you can call your mother, Gabe, and me. I'll bring it to you when your mom comes to see you later." He started to walk away.

Juleen whispered, "You were talking to my father, weren't you?"

He turned to face her. "I was."

"You said you'd kill him if he didn't do what you said." She swallowed hard. "Don't deny it. I heard you."

"I'm not going to kill him. Stop worrying."

"You called him a coward for not going to Sanjay."

"You shouldn't eavesdrop."

"I didn't eavesdrop. You were shouting."

He had been shouting. He exhaled and then said, "Your father's not a coward, Juleen." He walked toward her, then stopped. "He's just a man who's . . . out of his element. He's scared! And he should be. The people I'm working with are not nice."

"You would go if it was Gabe, right?"

"Yes, I would go."

"Then my father is a *coward*. He's a coward and a gambler and I hate him!"

"Don't talk shit about your dad," Donatti said.

"It isn't shit! It's the way I feel. And I can feel however I want!" She burst into tears. "I hate everything! Except Mommy."

"Mommy is worth loving."

Juleen continued to wail. Donatti shook his head. Gabe had been a pain in the ass, but never like this.

"Stop crying. You're giving me a headache and I'm already in a bad mood."

The little girl clamped her hands over her mouth to soften the sobs.

"Listen to me." Donatti rolled his eyes. "Are you listening?"

"Yes."

"Juleen, your father is a good man. He's a doctor. He heals people." Donatti paused. "I'm not a good man. I used to shoot people dead. And I've been shot before—several times. I don't want to die, but I've come close to death, so maybe it isn't as scary for me."

She didn't respond.

"Like if I was in an operating room," Donatti said, "I'd be scared. Everyone has different things that scare them, okay?"

"But you think he's a coward. You told him to man up."

"I was giving him a pep talk, that's all."

"Will Sanjay be okay?"

"I sure as hell hope so."

"The bad men want money, right?"

"Right."

"And you're paying them, right?"

"Right. But you can't tell your mother that."

"Why don't you just pay them and they'll release Sanjay?"

"That's really none of your business." When she didn't talk, Donatti said, "Juleen, people like these men . . . you just don't do what they say right away. They won't respect you. And if they don't respect you, they won't listen to you. I don't know everything, but I know how bad people think."

"And what you're doing will help Sanjay?"

"I hope so. But nothing is certain." He went over to her and knelt down. He put his hands on her small, bony shoulders. "What I need you to do is to be a very good actress. Because Mommy is going to ask you questions. You need to pretend that you don't know what she's talking about. Can you do that?"

She nodded.

"Good girl." Donatti stood up.

"You love Mommy, don't you?"

He paused. No sense lying. She was going to find out eventually. "Yes."

"Are you going to marry her?"

"She's already married to your father."

"They're divorcing."

"I know."

"Will you marry her after she and Father are divorced?"

"Yes."

"Why did you divorce Mommy?"

"None of your business."

But she persisted. "Did you divorce Mommy because of Father?"

Donatti looked at her. She was bright and she was curious. Traits both good and bad for survival. "There were lots of reasons for our divorce. Your father was just one of them."

"Was it because you beat her?"

"I was a terrible husband, Juleen," Donatti said. "I'm sure beating her sealed the deal. Now no more questions. You have your afternoon studies to think about. You need to forget about this and concentrate on your lessons."

"Can I skip my lessons today, Chris?" Her eyes watered. "I'm feeling a little sad."

"No, you may not skip your lessons, Juleen. You want to feel ordinary again, do something ordinary."

"Poor Sanjay." Tears rolled down her cheeks.

"I know you feel bad for him," Donatti said. "But you can feel bad and still be educated at the same time. Go take out your violin and run through some scales before your teacher gets here, okay?"

She nodded.

"Good." This time, Donatti made it to the door. His mind was still reeling from his conversation with Devek. Chickens were perceived as cowardly, but the males of the species were quite the opposite. Roosters were vicious. There was a reason a dick is also called a cock.

He shook his head as he climbed down the stairs. Despite his degrees, Devek was a weakling. If he wouldn't willingly go to Sanjay . . . well, then Donatti had no choice but to make him see the light.

McADAMS TOOK A sip of the bar's featured wine, a red called Variations
Five that had a good nose and was very drinkable. He, Decker, and
Marge Dunn were sitting in a spacious wine tasting room during
happy hour. The area featured high ceilings, a concrete floor, and
a U-shaped bar that enclosed the servers who poured wines available for purchase. There were also raised tables and stools spread
in the area. On the walls and in the bins were bottles of wine and
drinking paraphernalia for sale, along with some edibles. It was
becoming crowded with people piling in after work. Decker picked
up a lamb slider and bit into it. It was worth coming out just for
the kosher food.

He wiped his mouth and said, "Pauline's past makes everything
harder, but it does give us a starting point."

"The exes," Marge said.

"They are, at the very least, known quantities."

McAdams said, "I'll get contacts for them as soon as we get back."

"Good, because we'll want to eliminate them first," Decker said.
"Especially if they were violent."

"What do we do with Baniff PD?"

"I'll notify them," Decker said. "We've already canvassed Elsie
Schulung's neighbors. Did we ever talk to Pauline's neighbors?"

McAdams said, "No, just checked the apartment."

Decker said, "Which was empty."

Marge said, "At some point prior to meeting Elsie, she probably
lived there full-time. Why not go back to the neighbors? Maybe
there's a bar in the area where she hung out."

"Right," McAdams said. "We've already looked Pauline up in the
computer. No wants or warrants. No previous, either."

"Then no drug convictions."

Marge said, "Maybe she was more of a known quantity in
Baniff PD."

McAdams said, "We talked to Baniff PD about Pauline. They weren't helpful."

"Territorial," Decker said. "Elsie is their case."

Marge said, "Pauline's murder is in your jurisdiction. That should make them more amenable to sharing."

Decker said, "In a perfect world, that should happen. I'll call Baniff PD as soon as we get into Greenbury." He checked her watch. "It's almost six."

Marge said, "We've got plenty of time to make your flight."

"Yes, of course," Decker said. "I was thinking that even if I wanted to call Baniff, it would be almost nine in Pennsylvania. I'll leave it for tomorrow."

McAdams said, "Are you sure you want to drive us back, Marge? It's way out of your way. We could Uber."

"I'm staying in L.A. with a friend," Marge said. "It's Will's poker night, so everything works out perfectly." She gave each man another two-ounce pour until the bottle was empty. "You're not driving, so have fun."

McAdams said, "Just because Pauline has a past doesn't mean that Elsie and Bertram weren't involved in her murder. We found her body near where Bertram disappeared and near where Elsie left her car. That's more than just a coincidence."

"Agreed." Decker finished his wine.

Marge said, "You see the size of the tapas here? They're huge."

"Jewish tapas," Decker said. "I think I'll get an order of the fish and chips."

"Make it two," McAdams said. "I'm hungrier than I thought."

"Marge?" Decker asked.

"I think I'll try the ribs."

"That sounds good also," Decker said. "Let's get two orders of ribs too. Why choose?"

"I like your philosophy." Marge gave him a wide smile. "Just like old times, Rabbi."

"Yep." Decker finished off his slider and licked his fingers. "Only the food's a hell of a lot better."

I FELT ARMS go around my body as he pulled me to him and his breath on my neck. I had been asleep, but I was a light sleeper. I croaked out, "What time is it?"

"Four-thirty. Go back to sleep."

"I have to go to the bathroom."

"You need help?"

"No, I'm okay." After I came back, I was more awake. He put his arms back around me. I said, "Did you get your business done?"

"What?"

"Your business in the afternoon. Whatever it was, it must have been important for you to stop in the middle of sex."

"It was important. I don't want to talk about it. I'm tired. Go to sleep."

"Did it have anything to do with—"

"Stop it, Terry." His sigh was exasperated. "Let me sleep."

"He's my son, Chris. I just want to know that he's safe!"

"And when I have news, I'll let you know." He paused. "You've gotta stop, baby. All it's doing is pissing me off!"

It was counterproductive to make him angry. He was a prime manipulator, but being with him all those years, I had learned a thing or two. "Do you want to make love?" I turned over and faced him. The blinds over the window let in slits of moonlight. I could see him staring at me. "Yes or no?"

He didn't answer right away. Then he said, "I've been pestering you nonstop for over a week. Now, all of a sudden, you're horny?"

I tucked an errant hair behind his ear and stroked his cheek. "You're a very attractive man, Donatti."

He smiled. "Think so?"

"I do." I kissed his lips. "You are my silver fox."

"More like your white fox."

"Even rarer."

He kissed me with passion. "I know what you're doing and it's not going to work."

"What am I doing?"

"You are *not* going to weaken my resolve, little girl."

"Resolve about what?"

"Terry, we fuck and then we go to sleep. No talking."

"Okay." I pushed his head between my legs. I closed my eyes and let him begin to work his magic.

A moment later, he picked his head up and said, "You know, I might be more loquacious if you let me do your ass."

"No ass. And stop talking."

"Yes, ma'am."

When it was time, I pulled his chest to mine and let him finish both of us. Afterward, he scooped me in his arms, and within a minute, he was sleeping. His words played in my head.

You are not *going to weaken my resolve.*

Which meant he was doing something. And for now, that was all I cared about. I had to think that Sanjay was okay. To think anything else was way too frightening. Chris was smart. He could do this.

I turned on my other side and he pulled me deeper into his embrace, my back against his chest. His body was still lean, his arms muscular and strong. He was delicious in his toxic masculinity: tough and brutal and mean.

The men who beat me up and took away my son were also tough and brutal and mean.

Fight fire with fire.

CHAPTER 11

T HAD BEEN great to see Margie, to be taken back to an earlier time when Decker was at the top of his game. Not that Greenbury didn't have its crime, but mostly, it was a sleepy little college town. Pauline Corbett's murder was the exception. It brought out the real detective in him, injecting a bit of youth and making him more determined than ever to find out what really happened. For the last hour, Decker had been on the computer, trying to dig up a current address for Blake Baer, Pauline's second husband.

McAdams was sitting at his desk, across from Decker's. He said, "Well, we don't have to worry about Jerome Neisman."

"Who?"

"Jerome Neisman, a.k.a. Jerry," McAdams said. "Pauline's first husband. He's dead."

Decker looked up. "Scratch him off the list and go to number three."

"Cal Bruckner. They divorced four years ago."

"Why can't I find this dude?" Decker said. "I keep getting a soccer player and guys who I think are too young."

"How young is too young?"

"In their mid-thirties."

"Not really. Pauline was forty-three."

"Yeah, you're right. I'll check them out." Decker's phone rang. It was Jake Quay of Baniff PD. "Hi, thanks for calling me back."

"What's up? Did you find Elsie Schulung?"

"Not yet, but we did find her friend, Pauline Corbett. Unfortunately, she's dead."

Silence. Then Quay said, "Where'd you find her?"

"Buried close to the spot where Elsie Schulung left her car. Corbett's body is in our jurisdiction, but we know that Pauline's blood was at Elsie's house and that's your jurisdiction. We need to work together on this."

"Yeah." A pause. "Wow. When did this happen?"

"We found the body about two, maybe three weeks ago."

"And you're first calling now?"

Decker forced back irritation. He was doing the man a courtesy. He didn't need his permission to investigate his case. "I was on vacation, and it took us a while to dig her up and confirm her identity with DNA."

"Yeah. Okay. Sure." Quay paused. "What's your next step?"

Decker said, "Pauline kept a studio apartment before she moved in with Elsie Schulung."

"We checked. Nothing's there."

"I know that. But I'd like to canvass Pauline's old neighborhood now that we have a body. I'll come and bring some officers; you come and bring some officers—a joint effort."

"I have no problem with that, Pete. I never had a problem with working together. But I have to run all operations by my captain."

"By all means, Jake, follow your protocol," Decker said. "I've got a few things to wrap up here and then I'll come to Baniff. By then you should get your clearance."

After he hung up, Decker turned to Tyler. "You're coming?"

"I was planning on it." Pause. "Okay, this is interesting. I think I might have found Cal Bruckner. He's fifty-eight. He's a long-distance trucker."

"Where is home base?"

"Massachusetts." A pause. "Right over the New York line, just east of Albany."

"Give him a call."

"I've got to get his number first." McAdams typed into a backward directory. "It's a 413 area code. Probably a cell phone." He called and after two rings got voice mail. He left a message. "How many names did you pull up for husband number two?"

"I found eight Blake Baers. I think we can safely eliminate the soccer player."

"Give me the numbers and I'll start making calls. If that doesn't work, I'll start checking social media."

Decker wrote down three phone numbers with names:

Blake R. Baer
Blake T. Baer
Blake M. Baer

He slid the paper across the desk and began calling up the remaining Blake Baers.

Two didn't answer the phone. Decker left messages. The remaining two were the wrong Blake Baers. When McAdams finished, he said, "Two messages, and one was not the right person."

Decker looked at the list of names of Pauline's husbands. "I wonder if Marion Vanderberg got the name wrong."

"Why?"

"At the end of the name *Blake Baer*, there's a question mark." Decker paused. "I could check marriage licenses. They should have the proper names."

"Where did Pauline get married?"

"Good question." He checked his watch. It was a little after nine PDT. Not too early. He picked up his cell and gave Marion a call. When she answered, he said, "Mrs. Vanderberg, it's Detective Decker from Greenbury PD. How are you?"

"I'm fine, Detective. What's up?"

"We're in the process of contacting Pauline's ex-husbands. I noticed you had a question mark after Blake Baer. Any reason for that?"

"Yeah, I should have called you," Marion said. "I was blanking and I knew I got the first name wrong. It's Brook Baer. I should have remembered his name. What I do remember was that he was a real idiot."

"An idiot?"

"Yeah, and a dangerous one."

"I'm going to put you on speaker so Detective McAdams can hear you." Decker pressed the button. "Okay, Mrs. Vanderberg, we're both here."

McAdams said, "Hi, Mrs. Vanderberg."

"Hi, young man, how are you?"

"Just fine," McAdams said.

Decker said, "We can hear you perfectly. Can you tell us how Brook Baer was an idiot and a dangerous one at that?"

She said, "You know, it started coming back to me after you all left. Her history with guys. She married Jerry at around seventeen, right out of high school. He was a nice boy, but a loser. Couldn't keep a job because he was high all the time. The marriage lasted about two years. A year later, she met the supposed love of her life—Brook. I hated him from the get-go."

"Why was that?"

"Brook just had to be the star of the show. He talked too much and he laughed too loud. He flirted with anything in a skirt and he drank. Now, he was good-looking, I'll give him that. Never a shortage of female admirers. But he was mean, especially when he drank."

McAdams said, "Did he beat her?"

"Oh yes, but she only told me about the abuse around two years into their marriage."

"Then Pauline would be about twenty-two or twenty-three?"

"Something like that. She was turning into a real good-looking woman by then. Her acne cleared up and she lost a little weight. Guys were noticing, and Brook didn't like that. They got into an argument and he slapped her at first. Then it escalated. She left him when she was about twenty-five."

"Then what happened?" Decker asked.

"Brook was crazy. After she left him, he started stalking her. He called her a million times a day. He followed her home from work and followed her around on weekends. She had a couple of break-ins that we think he did. She finally did get a restraining order, but you know what that's worth."

"Not much," McAdams said. "How long did the stalking last?"

"About three years after they divorced. It would stop for a few months, then it would pick up again. Back and forth. She finally got so nervous, she moved out of state."

"Where was she living at the time of the stalking?" Decker asked.

"Denver, I believe. Anyway, she finally had enough. She picked up and left for Texas. I forget where. She moved around a lot."

"Did the stalking persist after she moved?"

"I don't know. She stopped complaining, though. A few years later, she met Cal. That marriage lasted longer than it should have."

"Meaning?"

"Same old, same old. They'd get high or drunk and start arguing. But they were married a while. She divorced him about four years ago."

"Did he stalk her?"

"Cal? Nah. He remarried as soon as the ink was dry on the divorce papers."

"And she never heard from Brook again?" Decker said.

"If she did, she didn't tell me," Marion said. "Like I said, we lost touch except for a few cursory texts." A pause. "I hope this helped."

"It does help," Decker told her. "Would you happen to know where Brook is living now?"

"Don't know and don't care."

"But she was living in Denver when she was married to him?"

"Around those parts, yes."

"Let me just repeat a few things. She was living in Denver with Brook. Then she moved to Texas with Cal."

"No, she moved to Texas first and there she met Cal. She and Cal moved a few times. They settled somewhere in the Midwest—Kansas or Iowa. Some farm place. After they divorced, she moved to Philadelphia."

"How did she meet Elsie?"

"I'm not exactly sure. Pauline worked as an aide at a nursing home. Elsie was a nurse. Maybe they met in a work situation or something."

McAdams said, "Do you know where Pauline worked?"

"Just somewhere in Philadelphia. No names come to mind."

Decker said, "We might call you again for information. Would that be okay?"

"Call as often as you'd like, Detective," Marion said. "Do you know when the body is going to be released? We'd like to bury her."

"I'll let you know when we're done. Do you have a mortuary in mind?"

"Jeez, no, I don't." A pause. "I'll call my brother and sister, and we'll call you back when we've made a decision."

"I'll wait to hear from you," Decker said.

"Keep me updated," Marion said. "She was my sister, and even though we weren't close, family is family." Her voice had turned tearful. "Call any time."

"Thank you." Decker hung up.

McAdams said, "I'm already on Brook Baer."

A moment later, the station's phone rang. It was Cal Bruckner.

"Hello, sir, thank you for calling me back."

His voice was deep. "No problem, Detective. What's going on?"

"I'm going to put you on speaker so Detective Decker, my partner, can hear the conversation." He pushed the button.

Decker said, "Hi, Mr. Bruckner, thanks for talking to us."

"No problem."

McAdams said, "We're calling about your former wife, Pauline Corbett."

"Pauline?" A sigh. "What's she done this time?"

"I'm sorry to tell you this, especially over the phone, but she is deceased."

"Deceased." A pause. "You mean dead?"

"Yes, sir. We think she died about a month ago. Murdered." Bruckner didn't speak. Decker said, "When did you last have contact with her?"

"Years ago."

"Two, three, four?"

"Last time I saw her was in court four years ago. And that was fine with me. Haven't heard from her—except maybe two years ago, it was . . . She sent me a Christmas card. I don't even know how she found my address. I can tell you one thing, though. My wife wasn't too happy that my ex was still sending me a Christmas card."

"How long have you been currently married?" McAdams asked.

"I married Rayette as soon as I divorced Pauline. It wasn't what you think. I didn't meet Rayette until after the marriage blew apart."

Decker said, "Then the last time you had contact with your ex, other than a Christmas card, was when you both were in court four years ago."

"That is the truth."

"What did she say on the Christmas card?" Decker asked.

"Is that important?"

"I don't know," Decker said. "Is it?"

"I don't know," Cal said. "I think she said that she was happy but she missed me. That's what pissed off the wife." A pause. "I have no idea how she found me. I moved to Kenenntock so my wife could be with her family. It's a small town. But that was Pauline. She was good with a computer. I'll give her that."

"How did you meet?" McAdams asked.

"Online," Bruckner said. "I'm a long-distance trucker. We used to text a lot and it helped pass the time. Eventually we met up. She was coming off a bad relationship with her crazy ex. I think she was happy to keep me at a distance for a while."

"What was she like?" Decker asked.

"Pauline?" A pause. "She was hot. But she smoked a lot of weed and was a meth head. Now, I'm not passing judgment. As a trucker, I've been known to take some pills. But her behavior went wacky. I didn't want to be married to that."

"How long were you married?"

"Seven years, although we were together longer than that. I gave it my best shot, but you can't control everything. Why are you calling me? There must have been someone more recent in her life."

"There was," Decker said. "She's missing as well."

"*She?*" Muttering over the line. "Pauline was with a woman?"

"That seems to be the case."

"Was it a friend thing or something more?"

"We don't know."

"A woman. That flips me out. Not that I care, but it's still weird, you know."

"People change," McAdams said.

"Maybe but . . . anyway . . . are we done?"

"Just to repeat," Decker said, "you haven't seen her in four years?"

"That would be the truth." A pause. "Pauline and a woman. Jeez."

"Thank you for your time, sir."

"Yeah, fine," Bruckner said. "I wish I would have known sooner. The marriage wouldn't have lasted, but I wouldn't have minded experimenting with another woman. It might have made us both a little happier."

WITH PHONE IN hand and a new Nevada area code, I dialed the New York number. It rang twice, then it connected.

"Dad?"

"No, it's Mom, actually."

"Mom!" A pause. "How *are* you?"

"Much better, thanks." My eyes felt wet. "Your father got me a new phone. Now I can bug you all the time."

"Any time. I'm so happy to hear you sounding well. How's Juleen?"

"Learning about four languages. Chris's idea, not mine."

"Yeah, it sounds like Chris. How is he treating you?"

"Very well."

A pause. "You can tell me if he isn't."

"No, he is." I bit my lip. "He's being . . . great."

"Hmm, well, I'll take your word for it. You're healing okay?"

"Yes. The dentist unwired my jaw. I've still got my back teeth wired together, but I can eat things other than shakes. How are you, honey?"

"I'm even better now that I know you're on the mend."

"I am. We're all doing—"

"Can you hold a second?" Muttering. "Sorry. I'm glad you're

fine, Mom. It's really good to hear your voice. Your number was blocked. That's why I thought it was Dad."

"I'll give it to you right now."

"Perfect. Just let me get to my contacts. Okay. I'm ready."

I gave him my new number. "Have you recorded anything new that I can listen to?"

"Yeah, I have. I'll send you my latest CD—hold on." More muttering. "I'm back."

"Honey, you sound busy."

"Um, can I call you back in about an hour?"

"Of course. Whenever it's convenient. I love you, Gabriel."

"I love you, too, Mom. I'll come see you soon. Heal up."

The line disconnected.

A good conversation for us. I felt that our relationship, though damaged by my actions, was slowly repairing. Part of it was he felt sorry for me. But I'd take whatever sympathy he was willing to give me. Charity begins at home.

It was half past nine. I'd been up for over two hours and could use a fresh cup of coffee. I made a pot, poured a mug for myself and another for Chris. I took them both into the bedroom. He was still asleep. I put his mug down on the nightstand, then I sat down next to him. The movement of the mattress woke him up. He grunted out a request for the time.

"Almost ten."

He sat up and took the mug from the nightstand. Then he looked at his phone and put it back down. "Denofrio called me yesterday. I didn't return his call on purpose. He just called me again an hour ago. That's a very good sign. Thanks again for coming with me the other night. Badger is an ass; I know it wasn't fun for you."

"It wasn't bad, actually. Nice to get out."

"Good." He took a sip of coffee. "Good stuff."

I said, "I called Gabe."

"And?"

"Nothing. It was nice hearing his voice. He sounds like you."

"He does." Chris took his Rolex and latched it onto his wrist. "Are you hungry?"

"I could eat."

"Starving?"

"Not at all."

He beckoned me forward with a crooked finger. When I slid back under the covers, he drew me into his arms. "Any requests?"

"Whatever you want, except—"

"I know, I know." He grinned. "You're my wife, baby."

"Not yet."

"Don't get technical with me, little girl. Nothing should be off-limits between us. I can only be patient for so long."

"You just don't know what it's like . . . being a woman."

"No, I don't," he said. "But I know what it's like to be sodomized. So don't play the victim card on me, little girl."

I leaned my head on his chest. "Poor Chris." I meant it.

After we finished, he said, "Give me about fifteen minutes and I'll get us some breakfast."

"Thanks." I looked at the nightstand, at his phone specifically. I couldn't help but wonder if there was news about Sanjay. He must have followed my eyes, because he took my hand. "I'll help you shower."

When we were both clean, I kept the towel wrapped around my body. I sat on the bed and said, "Chris, is there anywhere we could go out for breakfast? I'm feeling a little cooped up."

He put on his pants. "There's a coffee shop where the dentist is. It's pretty basic, but we can go there."

"Where do your clients go if they want breakfast?"

"They order up room service. The food usually comes with other services that they pay for."

"Got it." I took off the towel and slipped on one of my Manson girl dresses. I gathered my hair and pulled it back into a clip. "What about your workers?"

"I've got an employee cafeteria."

"Can we go there?" When he stared at me, I said, "Or is it verboten for the boss to eat there?"

"No, no, I go there all the time."

There was a prolonged silence. He put on a black tee and then his shoulder harness for his gun.

I said, "You don't want to be seen with me?"

"No, not at all. Everyone knows we're engaged." He tucked his Glock in his holster and put on his jacket. "When I go there, my workers expect attention."

"Understandable. Everyone wants attention from the boss."

"I do more than a pat on the back. It's a lot of flirting. It makes them feel important. They are important. Without my ladies and my gents, I don't have a business."

"And the problem is?"

"I don't want you to feel bad."

"Why should I feel bad? It's business." I slipped on my flats. "Can I get oatmeal at the cafeteria?"

"You can get anything you want."

"Let me just put on a little makeup and then we'll go."

"Okay. Remember this was your idea."

As soon as we were outside, my lungs filled with fresh, warm midmorning air. The business was unsavory, but the location couldn't have been more beautiful. The hour was redolent with summer smells and the birds were having a gabfest. It was about a fifteen-minute walk. The cafeteria was located directly under the lounge where we had been a couple of nights ago. As soon as Chris opened the door, the ambient noise of conversation died down to a hush. I looked around at the tables and chairs. Mostly women—around 80 percent—but some young-looking studmuffins as well. I didn't know if the pretty boys were for men or for women. Maybe they did double duty. It wasn't air-conditioned inside, and the women were dressed in casual clothing: shorts, T-shirts, sandals. Nothing glamorous. I fit right in. He escorted me to a back table where he could see everything, and before my backside hit the seat, a server was there. She was wearing an apron around her waist, but it wasn't a sexy French maid costume. She wore a long-sleeved black shirt and black pants. She looked to be around my age and, like me, had her long hair tied back. She held a coffeepot and two cups. After pouring, she said, "Good morning, Mr. Donatti. How can I help you?"

"I like your new hair color, Karena."

"It's not too dark?"

"It makes your eyes stand out." He turned to me. "This is my fiancée, Dr. Teresa McLaughlin. You take good care of her, okay?"

"Of course. Congratulations, sir. To you too, ma'am."

"Thank you," Chris said. "She wants oatmeal. Get her fresh, not from the buffet. I'll take my usual."

"Scrambled eggs whites and turkey bacon—six slices crisp."

"Perfect."

Karena smiled—an A student.

I said, "Scrambled eggs sound good . . . not egg whites. The real thing."

"You want eggs instead of oatmeal?" Chris asked me.

"Can I have both?"

"WTF, Terry." Chris laughed. "You can have whatever you want."

"I'll have both, then. And orange juice."

He laughed again. "Get her anything she wants. I'll be back." He turned to a bodyguard. "You watch her like a hawk."

"Yes, sir."

I hadn't even noticed another body until Chris had spoken to him.

A moment later, he was working the room. The transformation was eerie. He had become the popular boy I had known in high school—the guy with male friends who had emulated and admired him, the guy that girls had been in love with. I hadn't been an exception, sitting on the sidelines, watching Chris and his posse hold center stage, his girlfriend on his lap, stroking his face and probably stroking other things that I couldn't see. Back then, he had kept me his secret. We never mixed in public. He didn't even acknowledge me with more than a nod. We weren't sleeping together yet, but he was drawing me in the nude and, at sixteen, that constituted an intimate relationship to me.

Then his high school girlfriend wound up dead. Chris was arrested and sent to prison for the crime until Detective Decker proved otherwise and got him out of jail. But by then I had discovered things about him, and I broke off our relationship, until a child and poverty had me crawling back.

"More coffee, ma'am?"

I looked up. "Yes, I'd love some, thank you."

She poured me another hot cup. "Beautiful ring."

"Thank you." I looked at her face. She was smiling, but she seemed sad. All the women here had that same reaction to me. A distant melancholy that I seemed to bring out. An awkward silence. I said, "Do you have half-and-half instead of milk?"

"Of course. I'm so sorry."

"No, it's fine. I just like half-and-ha—"

She had left in a flash. I was alone. I smiled at the bodyguard and then realized I probably shouldn't be smiling at random men. She was back with my half-and-half and my oatmeal with all the trimmings. I thanked her again. I said, "How long have you worked here?"

"About five years."

"Long time."

"Mr. Donatti is a great boss. I heard you were high school sweethearts." She turned red. "Or is that too personal?"

"We've known each other since high school."

"Wow. You don't look old enough." A pause. "I mean your age. I should stop talking."

"It's a compliment. Thank you."

"More coffee?"

"I'm fine for right now, thank you."

"I'll let you eat in peace. I'll bring the eggs when Mr. Donatti sits back down. I want them to be fresh."

"Good idea." I poured half-and-half in my coffee, took a spoonful of my oatmeal, and watched Chris. What struck me in specific was how happy he looked, going from table to table, listening as his employees talked to him, nodding, smiling, engaged. He was never that way with me. Sexual? Yes. Funny? The boy had a great sense of humor. Excitable? Duh. Honest to the point of brutal? Check. Angry? All the time. Did he love me? He said he did, but sometimes I wondered. He never looked happy when we were together. Looking at him with others, he was airborne. With me, he seemed earthbound.

About twenty minutes later, he sat back down. His breakfast appeared moments later. He looked up and said, "Where are her eggs?"

Karena's face darkened. "I'm so sorry. I'll get them right now." She was off.

I said, "Don't yell at her."

"You're too nice. She messed up."

"Don't yell at her. Promise."

"My promises aren't worth anything. But I won't yell. How's your oatmeal?"

"Perfect."

She was back a minute later with food and coffee. "I'm so sorry—"

I put my hand atop hers. "It's okay. Thank you." I suddenly felt very blue. I'm sure Chris was a very good boss, but he was still exploiting people. They were commodities. Witnessing the depersonalization hit me hard. I pushed my eggs away.

He noticed. "Not hungry?"

"Oatmeal is filling," I told him. "How often do you come here?"

"Two, three times a week."

"The employees seem to like the attention."

Chris looked at me, recognizing something in my voice that was less than admiration. "I realize that this is a lot for you to absorb. That's why I always kept business and personal separate." When I nodded, he shrugged. "You didn't get what you expected in me. Whatever I could have been, you got in our son."

I put down my spoon and hid my face behind a coffee cup, looking at my first love across the table. Chris was a survivor, having grown up abused sexually and physically by a violent father, only to be adopted and abused sexually and physically as an adolescent by an equally violent stepfather. I didn't really know what it was like, but I had a hint. My father was a drunk. He had problems holding down jobs, and it was my stepmother who brought in the cash. When I turned fifteen, Dad often made nocturnal forays down the hallway to my room, trying to force the lock as I shivered under my covers, terrified and helpless. My stepmother eventually caught him twisting the doorknob in the wee hours of the morning. I heard her shocked and angry voice. I was petrified that she'd turn her rage on me. Jean was a taskmaster—I cooked, I cleaned, and I babysat my younger sister while she worked. But I was so grateful to her when she told me the next morning in a calm voice that I shouldn't worry. The nighttime visits were over.

I felt my eyes go moist. I laid my hand on Chris's arm. "I think you've done an amazing job with your life, Donatti."

He regarded my face. He ran an index finger under my eyes and wiped away my tears. He tickled my nose, then he smiled. "Right back at you, Doc."

CHAPTER 12

THERE WERE SEVERAL Brooke Baers—all of them female. No Brook Baer, which didn't mean he didn't exist, only that he wasn't a fan of social media. McAdams said, "Does Brook Baer pop up in any of your databases?"

"No, but ours are limited." Decker checked his notes. "Okay, Marion said that Pauline was living with Baer in Denver somewhere."

"Didn't she say near Denver, not in Denver?"

"Gotta start somewhere. I'll put in a call to them."

He checked his watch. It was two p.m. their time. At twelve in the afternoon mountain time, most of the detectives were probably out in the field. Those left behind were probably on lunch breaks. He looked up Denver PD. It was divided into six districts. He started with District 1, and after a few transfers, he was disconnected.

Maybe he'd have better luck with District 2. After being transferred several times, Decker was relieved to hear a voice on the end of the line.

"Detectives. This is Barron."

"Hi, this is Detective Peter Decker of Greenbury PD in Upstate New York. I'm working on a homicide, and it was my understanding that our victim had lived in or around Denver maybe fifteen years ago. I'm actually trying to track down her ex-husband so I can eliminate him from my investigation. You have a much bigger database than I do and maybe he's in your files. His name is Brook Baer—"

"Could you mean Brock Baer?"

Decker paused. "Possibly." A groan on the other end of the line. "You know him?"

"Unfortunately, yes, I do know Brock."

Decker said, "I'm putting you on speaker, Detective, so my partner can hear the conversation." He pressed a button. "Can you still hear me?"

"Loud and clear."

"Tell me about *Brock* Baer," Decker said.

"Scumbag," she said. "I arrested him several times for domestic violence. Couple times it was pushing and shoving with both parties involved. About six years ago, he was slapping around his girlfriend and fired a shot at her head." She laughed. "Detective Decker, did you just randomly call up this district or . . ."

"I started with District 1 and got disconnected. So I went on to your district. How's that for luck?"

"Sometimes the stars align."

"They do indeed, and call me Peter," Decker said. "Did Baer serve time?"

"Four years, but out in twenty-eight months for good behavior," she told him.

"How long ago was this?"

"Sentencing was four years ago. Means he's been out for a year and a half."

"Kept his nose clean?"

"He hasn't come to my attention," Barron said. "I can check our files and see if he's reared his ugly head elsewhere in the area."

"Thank you, that would be great."

"Who's your vic?"

"Pauline Corbett."

There was a pause. "The name is familiar."

"She and Baer divorced about eighteen years ago, then she left the area."

"I was in uniform back then. Not in this district, though."

"Corbett's sister told us that Baer beat her up a few times. She also told me that Baer stalked her for some time afterward. Do you have a Threat Management Unit—something that deals with stalking and harassment?"

"We do now. I have to check if we had a dedicated unit eighteen years ago. What happened with the stalking?"

"Pauline moved to Texas, and I think it finally stopped. But I'm not really sure of anything. I'm just starting the investigation."

"Then her homicide was recent?"

"Do you have a moment, Detective Barron?"

"It's Olivia, and yes, fill me in."

Decker started from the beginning, with the disappearances of Bertram Lanz and Elsie Schulung. The search eventually led him, along with the local police, to do a welfare check at Elsie's house, where they found blood. The DNA of the blood matched Elsie's partner's DNA.

"Her partner being Pauline Corbett," Olivia said.

"Yep," Decker said. "Then several weeks ago, we found Pauline's body, buried near where Bertram Lanz was last seen. Now it could be that Baer had nothing to do with Pauline's murder. Elsie Schulung has done a runner and that makes her look guilty."

"Or scared," Barron said. "Or even dead."

"Exactly. I need to start finding people and eliminating them as suspects. Since Pauline had a series of rocky relationships, I need to investigate those contacts before I start elsewhere."

"I'll check our databases . . . see if our boy has been up to mischief lately."

"Do you know Baer's parole officer?"

"Not offhand, but I can find that out. Give me your number."

Decker gave her three phone numbers. "The first set of digits are mine, the second belong to my partner, Detective Tyler McAdams, the third is the main line for Greenbury PD. We're a small department. Your message will get to us. Thank you so much, Detective Barron."

"Olivia," she said. "I'll get back to you as soon as I have some information."

"Appreciate the help. Stay safe out there."

"Yeah, right." She laughed. "Remember when we were the only ones saying that to our officers in the field?"

"It was not so long ago, Olivia," Decker answered. "Since COVID crept into the universe, it seems that the entire world has co-opted our first amendment."

McADAMS HUNG UP after talking to Marion Vanderberg. "Yes, it was Brock, not Brook. She's very sorry for the mix-up."

Decker was looking at the computer. "Brock has a lengthy record."

"For?"

"The usual: mostly domestic violence, but also assault, armed robbery, illegal possession of a firearm. Like Olivia said, he was released on parole a year and a half ago. His last known address was in Philadelphia. And we have a name and number for a parole officer." Decker picked up the phone. "Let's see if our boy has been following the rules."

"Who are you calling?"

"Baer's parole officer."

"Is there a phone number or an address in the rap sheet?"

"Yeah." Decker read the digits out loud. "It's probably not current, but try it out anyway." The line kicked in, a woman on the other end. He said, "Yes, this is Detective Peter Decker with the

Greenbury Police Department in New York. I'm looking for Ivan Dublitz." A pause. "He's retired. Okay . . . do you know who has his case files?" Another beat. "Yes, I'll hold. Thank you."

McAdams said, "The phone number you gave me is disconnected."

"What about social media?" Decker asked.

"My next step . . ."

A moment later, the woman returned to the line. "The case files were given out to three different people. Who are you looking for?"

"Brock Baer. He was released from prison about a year and a half ago."

"Let me look up the name in the computer . . . We have more than one list . . . What?"

"Excuse me?" Decker said.

"No, I wasn't talking to you. Sorry. We're jammed right now. Why don't I call you back?"

"Sure." He gave her three phone numbers. "And who am I talking to?"

"Oh, sorry. Vicki Laslow. I'll call you back in about twenty minutes."

"Thank you." He hung up. To McAdams, he said, "She's calling me back. What's going on with social media?"

"He has a Facebook account, but his last post was four years ago." A sigh. "Nothing since he's gotten out of prison."

"He didn't shut it down."

"No. And Facebook never shuts down old accounts because a lot of subscribers look good for ad accounts." As McAdams read, his face darkened. "Man, he's an angry man. Come take a look."

Decker read the posts on the Facebook page, starting with the most recent one.

U WONT get away with this, TANYA. UR a HORE and you know what happens to HORES!

TANYA, you lying, slut BITCH, drunk-assed HORE. UR fucking toast!

TANYA, UR a BITCH and WHORE. I DIDNT fucking lay a finger on you. LYING BITCH.

McAdams said, "At least the last time, he spelled *whore* correctly."

"Scroll down," Decker said. "See if you can get a last name for Tanya."

"Got it . . . okay, here we go. Tanya Robertson."

"Does she have social media?"

"I'm sure she does . . . here we go." McAdams turned the computer to face Decker. "And hers is recent. Looks like she's done some hard living."

Decker regarded the pictures. She was wrinkled and very, very thin. Her hair was tied in a topknot and she was wearing a sleeveless shirt that showed emaciated tattooed arms. "Can you tell where she's posting from?"

"You mean what city?"

"Yes."

"No, but let me see if she says something about where she's living in her posts." McAdams scrolled down her posts with Decker looking over his shoulder. "She has several pictures of the same group of women."

"Any captions that say names?"

"Let me scroll. Okay, here we go: Sam, Karina, Boz, and Kelsey. They're all wearing summer clothing."

"Yes, they are."

"I can look up all these addresses of people posting to her. We can see who matches whom."

Decker was still staring at the picture. "The landscaping looks like a desert climate. Look at this photo, at the house that the women are standing in front of." He stood up. "That's adobe."

"There are probably zillions of adobe houses in the country."

"Mostly in southern Arizona and New Mexico. Try New Mexico. Albuquerque, specifically. It seems to be a place where people run to when they want to hide."

"Did not know that. If Tanya is hiding, her posts don't reflect it."

"Maybe she was hiding, but now she feels safe."

"Brock is out of prison. Why would she feel safe?"

Decker shrugged. "Maybe Brock isn't after her anymore. Maybe Brock was out to settle an older score."

McAdams looked skeptical. "Tanya seemed to be the one who put him in prison."

"That is true," Decker said. "But look at the dates of all these posts. They're recent. If she was nervous that he was coming after her, do you think she'd be putting her life online?"

"Probably not. I'll see if I can find a number for her or any of her friends."

"Great." Decker's phone rang. It was Vicki Laslow. "Thanks for calling back."

"No problem," Vicki said. "His current parole officer is Melody Simpson. If you have a pencil, I'll give you her number. She's not in right now, otherwise I'd transfer you."

"I'm ready when you are." He wrote down the numbers as she recited them. "Thank you. This helps."

"No problem." She hung up.

McAdams said, "Why are you always right?"

"You found a listing for her in Albuquerque?"

McAdams shook his head. "I yield to your superiority, oh wise man."

Decker said, "Call her up."

"Yes, sir!" McAdams was connected to her answering machine. He left a message and hung up. "What now?"

"Now we wait."

McAdams checked his watch. "Getting near lunch. Hungry?"

"Why not?" Decker put down his pencil. "When all else fails, there's always coffee."

I HAD BEEN seeing Juleen on a regular basis, the highlight of my day because I loved her and it made us feel close and closer to what was once normal. We could almost pretend that everything was okay. I FaceTimed her in the morning, and after her studies, we spent the evening together, including dinner. We rarely brought up what had happened. Instead, we'd watch a movie or play a game or talk about her future in America, specifically in Nevada, where she could live a freer life. She always had something to chat about, much more loquacious than she had been at home with family and friends. She seemed to be thriving in a barren climate. I suppose in almost every ecosystem, there was always something beautiful that could pop up even under the harshest of conditions.

What was a bit concerning to me was her relationship with Chris. She seemed to hunger for his approval, which he doled out in small dollops. I hoped that this wasn't a snapshot of her life to come, seeking attention from men by being obedient. I knew the trajectory of that road. I longed for the day when we lived alone in our own house and I could convince her of the power of self-reliance. I dreamed about a future with her and Sanjay. When my mind drifted to my little boy, I turned it in another direction. It was just too painful.

Today was an abbreviated lunch with my little girl. Chris had stuffed her itinerary with extra lessons twice a week. Did I approve? Yes and no. He was running the show, but she seemed to be okay with it. There was no need to step in unless there was a problem. He walked me back to his hermetic space so Juleen could continue uninterrupted with her education.

It had been nice getting out in the morning even for oatmeal. After he closed the door and turned the locks, I said, "When are you going to put me in your high-tech system so I can get out and visit Juleen without your help?" When he didn't answer, I said, "At the very least, I'd like to take a walk. It gets claustrophobic after a while. You told me you'd do it as soon as I got a little better."

"I'm responsible for your safety, Teresa."

"No one is going to break in here. You've got a guy on me and guards everywhere."

He looked at me, blue eyes focused on my face. "You're already in the system. I just have to set you up with fingerprint and pupil recognition."

I was quiet. Then I said, "When did you do that?"

"Right after you asked me to do it."

"Why didn't you *tell* me?"

"You didn't ask about it so I didn't say anything." When I stared at him, he said, "The truth is I prefer to keep you locked up. It's safer."

"You can't keep me locked up forever."

"Actually, I could. Who'd stop me?"

And what could I say to that? He waited for an answer. I finally said, "No one, I suppose."

"Think about that." He glanced at his watch. "I've got to go back to my office. I'll set you up with the system tomorrow morning."

"Why can't you do it now?"

"Because it'll take time and I have a lot of business to take care of."

"Then you'll do it tomorrow?"

"Yep."

"Promise?"

He smiled at me. "What are my promises worth?"

"Zero."

"More like fifty-fifty." He laughed. "Tomorrow I'll show you how to get your freedom." He bit his bottom lip. "I'm not sure how much I'm liking that idea."

"What freedom, Chris? I can't go anywhere. I'm completely without resources. What are you worried about?"

He raised an eyebrow. "So, if you had resources, you'd leave?"

"That's not what I meant." I walked up to him and stroked his cheek. "Look, I know you don't trust me—"

"I don't trust you at all."

"Well, I don't trust you either." A pause. "What a relationship, based on mutual distrust." He didn't answer. I said, "I won't leave you, okay?"

"Well, that's not true," he said. "As soon as you get your kids, you'll move away."

"And when will that be?" I asked.

His face turned unreadable. If he had something, he wasn't going to tell me. There was no sense nagging him.

I said, "I'll be here every other weekend. I promised you and I do keep my promises."

"Mostly."

"I will marry you, Donatti. I will get my tubes tied, and I will come to this place just like we talked about. And when you see that I'm fully committed to you, you'll probably dump me because I won't be challenging anymore. I know men. You're only in it for the hunt. Besides, you can't keep up this sexual pace. You'll die. I'll die."

He raised his eyebrows. "It's called a little blue pill."

I wagged my finger. "You shouldn't take that unless you need it. And obviously you don't need it."

He grew serious. "I'll never tire of you. Never! I've always loved you, Terry. But now, with you here with me, I've fallen back *in love* with you. Those intense feelings that I had when we first got together. Only better, because you're the only person in this world that I trust."

"You just said that you didn't trust me."

"I don't trust your commitment to me, but I do trust you with my life. And by that I mean that every night when I go to sleep, I leave my gun on my nightstand. In the beginning, every time you moved, I woke up. Now . . . I wake up and you've been up for hours. Don't hear you get up, don't hear a thing. And I'm naked in the wind. You could take me out and I wouldn't even know what was coming."

"No, I'm not going to shoot you," I said. "That's a pretty low bar for trust, Donatti."

"You'd be surprised. You get pretty mad at me."

"Stop it."

"Also," he continued, "and this is truly, truly remarkable . . . you've never asked me for money."

"You always gave me money."

"You never asked for anything more than I gave you." He shook his head. "Your woman gene must be defective."

"Stop it."

"Even when we divorced, my lawyer had to beg you to retain a lawyer so we could get the process going. You know, at that time, you owned my entire ass. It took a while to transfer it to Gabe. Everything I had was in your name. You never skimmed *a penny* from me."

"I know."

"Did Devek know what was going on?"

"He knew you had money. He even told me that if we didn't marry, I could get alimony. I told him where to go with that idea."

"Not a bad idea."

"It was a terrible idea," I said. "I wanted Juleen to have married parents. And the last thing I needed was to antagonize you. I was *scared* of you, Chris. I knew what you were capable of doing. I told him that my divorce was my business. That I'd handle it. And I did."

"Not to your benefit. Even when I finally offered you a settlement, about a tenth of what you should have gotten, you gave it all away to Gabe."

"It was your money. I figured that's what you would want."

"Terry, I was already supporting him. We were *married*. You were *entitled* to something." He shook his head. "I used to think, *God, this woman must really hate my guts if she won't even take my money.*"

"I didn't hate you. I just thought it was best to cut ties."

"You certainly did do that."

I didn't say anything.

He looked at me for what felt like the longest time. "Probably a good thing. If you would have taken the money, Devek would have just gambled it away."

"That is true." I paused. "Christopher, I promise I won't ghost you again. I swear I'm committed."

He ran his tongue in his cheek. "I can't stand to lose control. I especially can't stand to lose control of you. And when you're here with me, I'm always in control of everything."

"Nobody is in control one hundred percent of the time."

"I'll take ninety-nine-point-nine, then." Another glance at his watch. "One thing I learned about myself while you were gone is how truly warped I've become. I can't live in the real world, Teresa. Things that annoy normal people make me homicidal. Which was why I shot heroin. It numbed me enough so I didn't go around murdering people, which I wanted to do all the time. When I built this place—this physical construct where I am king—I didn't need drugs anymore. I rarely, *rarely*, hear the word *no*. You leaving me for the purpose of properly raising your children—even under my terms—is a big, fat *NO* to my face. And I don't like it."

His eyes studied my face. It was an expression I had seen long ago, right before he was about to tie me up to sketch me in the nude. Oh, those carefree teenage years.

"But I do deeply love you and I want you to be happy," he said. "So . . . I'll take a big breath and let you leave when the time comes. And now I really do have to go attend to my affairs." He walked over to me and kissed me gently. "I know this has been hell for you, but it's been great for me. Just like in high school. I was walking around in a fog until I met you. Now, like back then, the fog has been lifted and I can see again." He slowly backed away and then turned and closed the door behind him, locking me in my tomb.

It was hermetic. Sometimes I didn't mind. After all the noise in my life, the quiet was pleasant, even peaceful. I'd work out on his weight and exercise machines; I'd listen to music. I'd read; I'd take a nap. I was still very tired and sleep was a welcome refuge.

But sometimes the quiet left me alone with my thoughts, which immediately went back to that dark day. And that was never a good thing.

CHAPTER 13

AT TEN THE next morning, Decker glanced at the station house message machine. A plain red light indicated no one had called. McAdams was already at his desk. "You're here early."

"No, you're later than usual."

"I am," Decker admitted. "Without Rina's coffee, I decided that nothing was worth getting up for."

"You can make your own coffee, you know."

"I can, but my coffee doesn't turn out like her coffee."

McAdams smiled. The station house's line rang and he picked it up. "McAdams."

"This is Tanya Robertson. I believe you left a message for me."

"I did. Thank you for calling back, Ms. Robertson. I'm putting you on speaker so my partner, Detective Decker, can hear." He pressed the button.

"Hi, Ms. Robertson," Decker said. "We're looking for information on your former boyfriend, Brock Baer—"

A big groan. "That son of a bitch. What did he do now?"

"Uh, we're not sure he did anything," he said. "We're trying to locate him—"

"Don't ask me. I don't know where that mofo is."

"You know, he's out on parole."

"Yeah, I know. He came over to my house, when he was first sprung, asking for help. Can you imagine the nerve?"

"When was this?" Decker asked.

"When he was first released. About a year and some change ago. Asking *me* for help!"

"I take it you said no," McAdams said.

"I said if he didn't get his ass off my property, I'd call the police. Then he got loud—screaming and yelling and calling me names—as usual. I got out Sassy Sally and fired it in the air. I told him the next round of buckshot was calling his ass. He left."

"And?"

"And that was it."

"He didn't return?"

"If he had returned, he'd be in a pine box."

"Got it," Decker said. "He posted some pretty awful things about you. Can I ask what that was all about?"

"What can I say? He'd get drunk and we got into it. Nothing new there. He slapped me around. Not new either. But then he fired a gun in my wall to show me he was serious. That was new. I talked him down. Finally, he left the apartment. I called the police, and when they took the bullet from the wall, they had a case to arrest the asshole. I think he got four years."

"And he came to your house about a year ago?" McAdams asked.

"Yeah, that sounds about right."

Decker said, "And you have no idea where he might have gone?"

"Don't know and don't care."

"Did he ever talk to you about his ex-wife?"

"He had more than one."

"Pauline Corbett."

"Ye-ah, he talked about her all the time. Mostly in the negative. Whenever we'd fight, it was always, 'You're just like Pauline. I'm gonna get that bitch.' Yadda, yadda, yadda. He hated her. But that didn't stop him from yakking on and on about her. He was obsessed with her. Is she okay?"

Decker said, "No, ma'am, I'm sorry to tell you that she's dead—murdered."

A long pause over the line. "The bastard finally did it."

"You think that Brock murdered Pauline."

"He talked about it all the time. Until he pointed the gun at me, I thought it was hot air. How'd she die?"

"Stabbed to death."

"Not shot?"

"No."

"Up close and personal," Tanya said. "Poor woman."

McAdams said, "Did you ever meet Pauline?"

"Not in person, no. But I could tell you what she looked like. He had several shoeboxes of photographs of her. Some were old, like from when they were married. Others were more recent. By recent I mean before he went to prison. But you could tell they were on the sly. Brock was stalking her, taking pictures without her knowing."

"Yikes," McAdams said.

"That's Brock. Has to have something or someone to bitch about. When I found the shoeboxes underneath the bed, I asked him about all the pictures of Pauline. He told me that it was none of my damn business and hid the boxes somewhere else."

Decker said, "You wouldn't by any chance still have those photographs?"

"I do have them. I found them when I moved. They were hidden on a closet shelf. I threw away almost everything that belonged to him, but I kept the photos. Then when he showed up, I was gonna give them back to him. I was about to say something, but then he started getting loud. WTF. Why should I do that bastard any favors?"

"But you didn't throw them out."

"No, I still have them somewhere. I have to look."

"Could you do that?" Decker asked. "And if possible, could you mail them to me?"

"Sure."

"That would be great," Decker said. "How about if I give you a FedEx or UPS number?"

"Sounds good."

Decker gave her the digits. "When you have a tracking number, if you could email it to me, I'd be much obliged. I don't want anything lost."

"No problem," Tanya said. "God, that asshole actually murdered someone?"

"We don't know," Decker said. "We've just started looking into Pauline's death. Baer may be totally innocent."

"The words *Baer* and *innocent* don't go together," she said. "If there's trouble, Brock is involved."

Decker said, "We'll be in touch. And, Tanya, keep an eye out."

"'Preciate the concern, but I got Sassy Sally," Tanya said. "I'm ready for anything."

SITTING AT HIS desk inside his suite, eyes on his computer, Chris called out to me, "You've got to look at the screen next to the code box."

I was outside trying to sync my retinal scan with the machine. "I *am* looking at the screen."

"It's not registering." He regarded my craning neck and smiled. "You're way too short." He got up and rolled his desk chair out the door. "Can you balance on this without falling on your ass?"

"Remains to be seen."

"I'll get you something to stand on later, but try this in the meantime."

"You don't have a stepladder?"

"Why the hell would I need a stepladder?" He helped me onto the seat. "Just kneel. You should be eye to eye with the screen."

When he took his hand away from mine, I wobbled.

"Okay?" he asked.

"Fine."

"Just stare into the screen and don't move until I tell you to."

He went back to his computer and I did as he instructed, always a good student. It took a minute.

He said, "Great. Now put your right thumb on the screen."

I complied.

When he was done, he helped me off the chair and we went back inside the room. He pulled out three keys. "The pupil and thumb recognition will allow you to unlock the door once it gives you the green light. These are your copies. I know they work because I've tried them out. First, let's see if you can go outside by yourself. Then we'll see if you can get inside."

Everything worked. But it was a strain. The door was enormously heavy to open and close. But I managed to do it and lock up without the alarm going off. After it was over, he handed me the keys. "Your partial freedom."

"Partial?"

"We'll have to program the entrance and downstairs elevator to get you up here. And then we'll have to program you into the system if you want to get in and out of Gabe's room to see your daughter."

"That would be great. When can we do that?"

"Some other time. But I'll do it. I promise."

"Thank you."

"No problem." A pause. "Terry, I have beeps on my computer that trigger when someone is going in and out of the doors upstairs and using my private elevator. I also have cameras all over the place. But my eyes and ears can't be everywhere at the same time."

"I'll let you know what I'm doing beforehand."

"Please. I'm responsible for your safety. And Juleen's safety. I have enough going on without having to chase you down."

"I understand." I gave his face a hard stare. "Who did this to me, Chris? Who hurt me and took my baby? Was it Devek?"

"I told you: no questions."

"I have a right to know."

"And you will know when the time's right."

"Is my son safe?" When he didn't answer, I choked up. I said, "Is he even alive—"

"He's alive." When I started to say something, he put a finger to my lips. Tears were running down my face. He wiped them with his thumb and said, "I'm doing the best I can. But there are no guarantees. That's all I can say right now. No more questions, okay?"

I nodded. "I think I need a change of scenery."

"Probably. Let's go out for dinner. Wait . . . I can't tonight. Tomorrow?"

"Sure." My second outing in less than a week. I was a veritable party girl. I wiped my tears with my dress. "Where?"

"I own a small Italian restaurant in the same strip mall as the dentist. It's casual and it's certainly not gourmet, but it's passable. The locals seem to like it. So do my workers. I know you still can't eat perfectly, but the minestrone is good and it's vegetarian. Sound good?"

"Great." Again, I dried my eyes.

He took me in his arms. "I'm sorry you have to go through this, baby doll. I truly am. I hate to see you suffering. And I know you're suffering."

The tears came back. "Thank you."

He held me for a few moments in silence. "Terry, I need a favor from you."

"Can it wait a few hours? I could use a little break."

"It's not sexual."

"Okay. What do you need?"

"Every year around Labor Day, I throw a big bash for everyone who has been here in the past year: my guests, my clients, my workers, my employees . . . It's usually around a hundred to a hundred-fifty people. I have a band and food and an open bar—we do it in the lounge, where I took you to meet Mike Badger. He comes every year, by the way."

"Do you want me to help plan something?"

"No, Talia will take care of everything. She does it every year. She has it down to a science." A pause. "I would like you to come to the party, okay?"

"If you want me there, of course I'll come."

"I do want you there. You're my fiancée. You're going to be my wife. It would reflect badly on me if you weren't there."

I paused and broke away from him. "What are you trying to tell me, Chris?"

"The way these things work, I have to be available to anyone who wants to talk or dance with me, including my workers. My parties are their time—when they can let their hair down with the boss. So, while I want you there—I need you to be there—I'll also need my space."

I took a few moments to answer. "Like the scene in the cafeteria?"

"Times a hundred."

"So, what do I do? Sit in a corner by myself and smile?"

"More or less."

I threw my arms out. "It's fine, Chris. Do what you need to do. I'm the interloper here."

"You're not an interloper—"

"Your whore, then."

"You are not my whore." His expression darkened. "You trade places with any of my workers for one day, and you'll find out exactly what it really means to be a whore. Any one of them would jump at the opportunity to be in your shoes. You were my wife, you will be my wife again, and, in my mind, you have always been my wife, regardless of who you've been with. You're just doing what wives have done for their husbands over the centuries. So stop saying you're my whore. It's ridiculous."

"Yeah, yeah."

"And stop shining me on!"

"Don't you *dare* get mad at me." I tried to control my anger. "You have a business to run. I won't get in your way. Besides, I'm used to standing on the sidelines while you party."

He walked over to me and picked up my chin. "Terry, this is not high school—"

"It is, actually." I freed my face from his hand. "Except we're all adults now and I know what to expect from you, which is a lot of sitting in the corner by myself."

"That isn't fair."

"No?" I walked away and began to pace. "God, even in high school, I had a boyfriend, who, by the way, adored me. Maybe I should do that now, Chris. Get my own boyfriend. Maybe Mike Badger. He sure seemed to like me. And since you're borrowing money from him, I betcha he's doing fine in the bucks department."

His voice got low and menacing. "Stop it."

"Yeah, he is pretty ugly. I could do better—"

"Did you ever screw him?"

Confused, I turned to face him. "Are you kidding me?"

"Not Mike," he said. "Daniel Reiss. Did you fuck him?"

He was still on my high school boyfriend. "How could you ask that?" I snapped. "You know I was a virgin when I came to you."

"It could have been your period."

"It could have been, but it wasn't. Although maybe it would have been better if I had done it with Daniel. It certainly would have been better circumstances."

"Cut it out, Terry."

"This isn't about me or anything I've done, Donatti, so stop deflecting the conversation to make you look like the victim, okay?"

"Then stop pushing my buttons and talking about other guys. You know how jealous I get." He bit his lip. "Look, are you going to come? Yes or no?"

"Do I have a choice?"

"Of course you have a choice. I can make excuses. The workers would probably feel freer if you weren't there. But it's not what *I* want."

It was times like this that I remembered precisely why I had an affair. Something to call my own. The pregnancy, however, had been unplanned—the one of two consequences from my second disastrous marriage that turned out well. With Devek, my anger had always been a continuous simmer. With Chris, it was and had always been a hot blue flame. "Don't worry. I'll be there and I'll be all smiles."

"You're pissed."

You better believe it, I thought. I held up the keys. "At least I have my partial freedom." When he didn't react, I shrugged. "Go have your fun, Chris."

"It's not fun, Terry, it's work."

That made me even madder. "Okay, then go have your fun work. Go screw whoever you want. I don't give a damn what you do."

"And you never did," he told me. "That was part of the problem."

"That's utter horseshit! Stop feeling sorry for yourself because I bested you *one* time in the screwing department."

He turned red in the face. "Okay. You got your revenge. You totally humiliated me. You totally trashed me. Good for you. I'm sure I deserved it. I certainly suffered because of it."

"You don't have a lock on suffering, you know."

"You're right. So maybe it's time for both of us to move on."

"I *can't* move on with my child missing, Christopher! Get my son and then I'll be *happy* to move on."

He suddenly looked weary. His voice turned soft. "It's going to take a while longer, baby doll. And like I said, there are no guarantees. I assure you I'm doing whatever I can."

Suddenly a stupid party seemed trivial. Tears sprang up from nowhere. "Is he suffering?"

"No, he's not suffering. He's probably scared, but he's okay." He flipped his hair out of his eyes. "I'm sorry, but this isn't an easy fix. Just be patient and trust me, okay?"

I wiped my eyes, wondering who had my son. And if Sanjay had been taken by horrible men because of Devek's debts, why was he still alive? And then it dawned on me, idiot that I was. "You're paying off Devek's debts, aren't you?" I waited for an answer. All I got was silence. "How much is it costing you?"

"None of your business."

"I'll pay you back, Christopher. I'll pay you every penny no matter how long it takes."

An eye roll was his response. He said, "I don't want to talk about this anymore. Don't bring it up. For both our sakes, okay?"

"Okay." My eyes were still wet. "Thank you for all your help. I'll come to your party and I'll be a good sport. I promise."

"Thank you." He blew out air. "I'll be back in a little bit."

"Where are you going?"

"To see my staff. The more contact I have with my employees, the harder they work. And while I'm in the cafeteria, I'll put in the lunch order for your daughter. Do you want anything?"

"No, but I'll come with you," I said. "Practice being a good little wife—"

"Teresa, my love, I've run out of juice for this conversation." He headed for the door. "I'll see you later."

"Chris, I need to get *out* of here." He stopped walking and turned to me. I said, "And I wouldn't mind a fresh cup of coffee."

"Okay." His eyes softened. A big intake of air and then he exhaled. "Baby doll, I want you at this party because your presence is my Valium. Even in high school, after you pulled away from me and I pretended to ignore you, even if you weren't with me, I always knew where you were."

"You stalked me?"

"Always."

"What about when I was in Mumbai?"

"I kept tabs on you. Not me personally, but I hired people over there who were watching for me. That's how I found out that Devek owed money." He paused, then he said, "Are we still on for dinner?"

"Of course." A weak smile. "And I still want that cup of coffee."

"Then let's go."

As I walked to the door, he took my arm and held me back. I looked up and smiled again, but his face was unreadable.

He said, "I'm a hard case. Impenetrable. And I'm never going to change because I don't want to change. I like my psychopathy. But it's not easy for you. Thank you for putting up with me. Don't think I don't notice."

"Just get me . . ." I stopped talking.

He dropped my arm. His voice was even. "I know, baby, but no more. Please?"

"I'm sorry." My voice cracked, but I held back tears. "Thank you. Let me practice opening the front door."

"Go for it."

I knelt on his office chair and found my balance. "Could you please get me a stepladder, Chris? You might not need it, but I do, and as of right now, there are two of us here."

"I'll get you a stepladder."

"And while you're at it, would you mind getting some colorful throw pillows and blankets? And something nice on the walls. I know you like to keep things simple, but I find looking at black and white day after day a bit depressing."

"Go online, pick out whatever you want, and send it to Talia," he told me. "You can decorate any way you'd like."

"Also, if it's not a problem, it would be nice to have another elliptical for me. I'm tired of adjusting your machine and then readjusting it when I'm done. You have the space."

"Consider it done."

"And one last thing," I said. "I want to make sure that I get the cast off my arm before your party. It will have been over six weeks by Labor Day, so that shouldn't be a problem."

"I'll make an appointment." He gently stroked my cheek. "Is there something more I can do for my beautiful and brilliant wife?"

Like a lot of sociopaths, he was not lacking in the charm department. I'd seen it too many times to be fooled, but even when I knew what was coming, he could still get to me, such was his skill. I sighed, then I stared into the high-tech screen on the wall for pupil recognition. After that was accepted, I placed my thumb over the screen. I heard the clicks. I got down from the desk chair and used my three keys to undo three bolts. Then I struggled to crank open the metal-clad door.

He had the good sense not to offer help.

"No." I kept my voice even. "Beautiful and brilliant wife says there's nothing more."

CHAPTER 14

DECKER AND McADAMS scoured the computer data. They made numerous phone calls. They looked on various social media sites. It was an exercise in frustration. No one seemed to know where Brock Baer was holed up . . . or even if he was still alive.

McAdams said, "I should try the obits." Silence. "Hey. Earth to boss."

"I'm here, I'm here," Decker said. "Obits are a good idea, although each county keeps their own death records."

"I'll try the more populated counties in Pennsylvania first—that's where he was living when he got out—and if that doesn't work, I'll give New Mexico a whirl since he followed Tanya to Albuquerque." No response. McAdams said, "What's on your mind, Deck? Wanna clue me in?"

"I don't know if it's age or vacation or jet lag or hunger, but I just thought of something that should have been obvious days ago."

"What's that?"

Decker said, "Pauline sustained multiple stab wounds."

"Exactly what we thought the cause of death would be."

"Except that there are way too many stab wounds for the amount of blood we found at Elsie Schulung's house. And when we checked Elsie's car, we didn't find any blood there."

McAdams said, "She was stabbed and did most of the bleeding somewhere else. Then she somehow made it home." He paused, then said, "We're missing a crime scene."

"Exactly." It was almost seven and Decker was cranky. He'd been on airplanes for the last two and a half weeks. Combined with long hours of desk work, his stiff back had been on strike, shooting little sparks of pain. He got up, and it took him a few seconds to stretch to his normal height. "I need some sustenance. Are you interested in dinner?"

"Theoretically yes." McAdams returned his eyes to his computer. "What do you have in mind since Rina isn't here to feed us?"

"Our choices are limited to takeout," Decker answered. "Vegetarian or the kosher deli."

"Vegetarian. Tell me what you want and I'll place the order online."

"I usually get the Asian stir-fry with noodles and a side of tofu chicken wings."

"That sounds good, actually." McAdams looked at the computer screen. "There's nothing about Brock Baer's demise in Philadelphia."

"That would be too easy. I'm betting that he's still alive." Decker placed his hand on the small of his back and arched his spine.

"You okay, boss?"

"Just sore."

"Deck, how are you going to do backbreaking work like remodeling an apartment, and in a foreign country to boot? Do you even speak Hebrew?"

"Not really, no." He blew out air. "Hasn't anyone ever told you that you don't hit a man when he's down?"

"Sorry. I'll place the order now. When do you want it delivered?"

"I'll pick it up. I need to walk."

"Whatever you want." McAdams placed the order. "Okay, it's done. Ready?"

"Yep."

The two men walked in silence. It was still light outside, but the summer heat and humidity had dropped a notch. The shops were closed, but the restaurants and bars were bristling with business even though things were usually quieter in the summer. There were some classes being held, but the student population was about a quarter of what it was during the school year. In several weeks, the kids would start streaming in with their parents. Another semester, another year, and time ticked on and on and on.

McAdams said, "I was thinking, Deck. We're not making any headway locating Brock Baer. Even if we find him, he may have nothing to do with Pauline's murder."

"Of course."

"And if we're looking for another crime scene, it *has* to be close to Elsie Schulung's house. Otherwise, how did Pauline manage to get there, still alive, with mortal stab wounds?"

"You're right."

"But . . . if Elsie didn't stab Pauline, why didn't she just immediately call an ambulance for her when she saw her poor condition? Why didn't she call the police? And who buried Pauline?"

"What are you saying?"

"I think that Elsie probably had something to do with it. But there was also someone else involved. Either Elsie felt the need to protect the second party or she was scared of him."

"Who's the second party?"

"Bertram Lanz is certainly up there. But given the brutal nature of the crime, we need to consider Brock Baer."

"Which is exactly what we're doing," Decker said. "What we need is a recent link between Baer and Corbett. I know that Jake Quay showed Pauline Corbett's picture around. But now, Corbett's death is our case. When we go to Baniff, we need to show Corbett's picture *and* Brock Baer's picture around the town and see if anyone remembers them hanging together."

"That's actually a good idea. How much cooperation are we getting from Quay, do you think?"

"He sounded eager. Hopefully, he'll get clearance from his captain. Guess we'll find out tomorrow."

They were in front of the restaurant. McAdams checked his watch. "Food is probably not ready yet. I'll go in and wait."

"Let's walk some more, Harvard. The exercise feels good." With that, they continued to stroll around the area.

McAdams picked up the conversation. "In my mind, Elsie Schulung's still in the hot seat. Why has she disappeared?"

"Maybe she disappeared because she's dead."

"Why do you think that?"

"Because Pauline's dead." Decker shrugged. "Maybe someone killed both of them. And since Bertram disappeared, he's also in the hot seat."

"Do you think he's capable of burying two bodies?"

"Don't know, Tyler, but from his police record in Germany, we know that he isn't afraid to use his fists."

"Why would he kill Elsie?" McAdams said. "Everyone said they were friends."

Decker threw up his arms. "Maybe Pauline's death has nothing to do with Elsie's disappearance."

"Except that Elsie's car was found near Pauline's body."

"Too close to be a coincidence," Decker said. "If Elsie is dead, where is her crime scene? It certainly wasn't at her house. Forensics went over it thoroughly."

McAdams said, "And if Baer is responsible for Pauline's death and Elsie's disappearance, how does Bertram Lanz fit in? He disappeared very close to where we found Elsie's car. That's too much of a coincidence as well."

"Yes, it is."

"Deck, as of about a month ago, Kathrine Taylor's parents told you that Bertram and Kathrine were in Germany. You've always said to me that you believe that Elsie was with them. Why would you suddenly think Elsie was dead?"

"I don't know." Decker exhaled. "All I am saying is the blood at Schulung's house is *not* the total picture with regards to Pauline. We'll find out more when we go to Baniff."

"Let's buy some deli sandwiches for the ride tomorrow while we're waiting for our dinner," McAdams suggested.

Decker let out a small laugh. "We're ingesting nothing but salt and fat. My wife is going to chastise me when she gets home."

"It serves her right for going on vacation while we're in the middle of a case."

"It's not exactly a vacation. She's visiting her mother."

"A woman who has lived most of her life, I might add." He pointed a finger at his chest. "What about the future generation?"

Decker said, "Just wait until you're that age, Mr. Millennial."

"Okay, boomer," McAdams said. "And, FYI, I probably won't even get to *that* age."

"That's downright morbid." Decker was concerned. "Why in the world would you say that?"

"Because I'm part of the worst status category: unmarried male."

"That can be rectified, McAdams."

"Find me a woman."

Decker put his arm around the kid. "Son, some things you just have to do for yourself."

THEY LEFT AT eight the next morning. With light traffic, the drive was a little over three hours. They reached the outskirts of Baniff around eleven-thirty with a full sun in the sky. The air was warm and pleasant. Soon, the area would ease into autumn with cooler temperatures and the promise of brilliant colors. The trees would be glorious. Hopefully, he'd be done with the case soon and he could do his leaf watching closer to home.

It had been a couple of months since Decker and the local law had done a welfare check on Elsie Schulung. Inside the house, they had found a pool of blood after they moved the refrigerator. Then Pauline's missing case file had become a homicide. The same players—Elsie Schulung and Bertram Lanz—were still considered suspects, but a good investigation meant other avenues had to be considered. Decker wanted a thorough probe of Pauline Corbett's life.

Baniff was a small town built around a central square park. The wide lawn had lost some of its emerald-green hue, but the area had many oak trees that provided ample shade. There was a large water fountain in the middle of the area with metal benches parked around the perimeter, perfect for sitting, relaxing, and passing the time. Municipal buildings, commercial stores, restaurants and bars, and other businesses sat closest to the greenery and then disappeared after several blocks in any direction. Beyond them were the residential areas: mostly small, one-story brick bungalow homes, but some apartment complexes as well.

Corbett's former residence was four stories, fronted by a yellowing grass strip planted with small maple trees. Access to the individual units was by way of outdoor staircases. The apartments had balconies. Some were outdoor spaces filled with furniture and potted plants. Others were junk heaps. Pauline had lived on the second floor. Her balcony was empty, and when they had last checked, her apartment was bare-bones. No surprise, since she had moved in with Elsie about six months prior to her death. As Decker pulled the car into one of the visitors' spots, he spied Jake Quay standing in a sliver of shade. He wasn't a really big man, but wearing his uniform tans along with a big hat and an overloaded duty belt, he looked like authority. Decker rolled down the window and gave Quay a wave. The gesture was answered with a nod from Quay. They convened on the sidewalk.

Decker said, "Everything square with your captain?"

"Yep. We all want to get to the bottom of this, pronto." Quay pulled something from his pocket. "Here is a map of the area—all the stores and restaurants."

"Thank you."

"How do you want to divide it up?"

"You take half, McAdams and I will take the other half." Decker showed Quay a photograph of Brock Baer. "This man is Pauline's second husband. He's a bad apple, and we can't seem to find him. You can keep this picture. We have others. Show it around, and maybe we can establish a connection between Pauline and him."

"Are you looking at him as her murderer?"

"I'm open-minded," Decker said. "Elsie Schulung is missing, so she's still on the list, because of Pauline's blood in her apartment. But there wasn't much of it, and I believe that Pauline was attacked elsewhere."

"Not in her old apartment," Quay said. "Forensics didn't find anything."

"No, she wasn't murdered in her apartment. I'd bet that she was murdered closer to Elsie's house. How far is the center of town from her house?"

"Hmm . . . Elsie's a little farther out. About a half mile to the north."

"Which is here on the map you gave me?" Decker pointed to a spot.

"Yes."

"Then McAdams and I will start there. It would be helpful if you started where Pauline had lived . . . see if someone remembers her with Brock Baer."

"That's fine." Quay hit the picture with his fingertips. "He looks like a bad apple."

"That's good," Decker said. "Bad apples are memorable. It's the good-looking apples that are the most dangerous. If you don't believe me, just ask Snow White."

CHAPTER 15

CLOSING THE DOOR to his downstairs office and tapping his phone, Donatti said, "Yes?"

"We got him." It was the same voice he had been talking with for the past weeks. They were becoming fast friends.

Donatti smiled. Devek wasn't much of a team player. He'd been dragging his heels with the divorce papers. He was reluctant to go to Sanjay. He needed a push, something to put fire under his ass. Which was exactly what Donatti gave him. "Thank you."

"No need to thank me. Just pay up the extra cash you promised me to do the deed."

"I will when I'm positive it's him. I'll need multiple images. And two newspapers. The *Times of India* in English and *Dainik Bhaskar*. And I want at least six pictures of him with the kid and with the newspaper. Send them in five minutes."

"Donatti, it's him."

"Seeing is believing, and since I'm writing the checks, I want something more than your word."

He hung up and grabbed two sheets of paper. He was already out the door to Gabe's room. He waved to the guard on duty outside the girl's door.

"How's it going, Jeff?"

"Fine, Mr. Donatti. Is everything okay?"

"Perfect." He went through his usual rigamarole to get into his son's private space: pupil recognition and then the code. He opened the door, interrupting Juleen's Spanish lesson. Her teacher was one of his workers. The woman was brunette and buxom and every bit the image of the Latina bombshell that men fantasized about. She was trained as an educator in her native Venezuela, but since money and food were scarce and she spoke English, she was elected by her family to go to America and send back U.S. dollars. There were more respectable ways to put bread on the table, but none was as fast as sex work.

"Session's over," Donatti announced. "Thank you, Daniela. Juleen will see you tomorrow."

Confusion registered on her face. Still, Daniela gathered up her materials. She was used to taking orders without questions. After she left and the door was closed, Donatti's phone rang.

The voice said, "I'm sending them over now on WhatsApp. They'll disintegrate in thirty seconds."

"I'll need more time. Two minutes at least."

The line disconnected. Donatti beckoned Juleen forward with a finger. The girl was wearing a sleeveless yellow top and white shorts. The bandage had recently come off her twisted ankle, allowing her to wear flip-flops. These were pink with red hearts. When she was close to him, he pulled her closer and showed her the screen of his phone. "I'm going to show you some images. If you recognize the face, I want you to tell me who it is, okay?"

She nodded, looking as serious as ever. Donatti heard the ding and pulled up the images. He turned to her. "Who is that?"

Juleen's eyes moistened. "That's my father."

"Scroll through all of them."

She swiped the phone. There were six images. "It's my father."

"You're a hundred percent sure?"

"Yes."

"Because if you're not sure, tell me right now. It's costing me money."

"It's him. He has that little mole on the side of his face." The tears were falling down her smooth brown cheeks. "I'm sure."

Donatti took the phone away and looked at the newspapers, then looked at the printed copies he was holding in his hand. The copy of the *Times of India* matched the newspaper that Devek was holding, headline for headline. He showed Juleen the copy he'd made of the front page of *Dainik Bhaskar*, a widely circulated Indian newspaper written in Hindi. Then he showed her the newspaper that Devek was holding.

"Do these two papers match?"

She wiped her eyes and looked them over. "The headlines match."

"Read the lead article. Tell me if it's a word-for-word match."

Juleen read for around thirty seconds, her eyes dancing between the two copies. Then she looked up. "The image is pixelating . . . dispersing."

"Did they match?"

"From what I saw, yes."

"Okay." He waited a few minutes, tapping his toe. The girl sat quietly, fresh tears down her cheeks. Donatti's phone dinged. New images popped up. He showed them to the girl. "Who's this?"

Her lower lip trembled as she scrolled through the images. "It's my father and my brother."

"You're sure?"

"Positive." She let out a small sob. "He looks happy. Sanjay. He's smiling."

"I'm sure he's very happy to see your dad. I'm sure it's a relief.

Now go to your room, and don't come out until I tell you. Not like last time. No eavesdropping on my conversation."

Her head drooped. "Yes, sir."

Donatti caught her arm. "Juleen, it'll be okay."

She bit her lip and nodded. He let her go.

A moment later, his phone rang. The voice on the line said, "Satisfied?"

"I need a video of the two of them from you. I need to hear their voices."

"That wasn't part of the agreement."

"Well, now it is. You change conditions all the time and so do I. This is what I want on the video. I want the two of them to be comfortable. I want them to be smiling. I want the boy to say, *I'll see you soon, Mommy.* I want the man to say, *Thank you, Chris, for all your help.* Then afterward, I want you to take the man and put the fear of God in him and get him to sign the papers he needs to sign. I'll send you one hundred now and four hundred when I get the video."

Donatti hung up and was about to knock on Juleen's door when his phone rang. The voice said, "Four hundred now and one hundred after I send you a video. It will take time. I have to make it first. I need to charge you extra for it."

"This is what I'm willing to do: two-fifty now and two-fifty after I get the video."

There was a pause. "We'll talk in twenty-four hours."

"Fine with me, but you're not getting a penny more than two-fifty until I see the video."

"I'll need more from you now that we have the man. The boy takes directions. The man is a liability."

"The man is a coward and he's scared shitless. I'm sure he'll be no problem."

"He can be stubborn."

"I'm sure you're used to dealing with stubborn people."

"What we do with stubborn people is arrange a permanent solution. Of course, that will cost you more."

"Right now, I'm not interested in a permanent solution."

"Every day he's alive is a liability. If you neutralized him now, there is no need for him to sign papers. But as I said, that will cost you more. Neutralizing has to be planned carefully."

"Keep him healthy," Donatti said. "I'll send you the two-fifty and the second installment after you send me the video. And it needs to be exactly like I said. I'm showing it to her, and if I don't have a smiling kid, it's useless to me."

He hung up.

His heartbeat had slowed during the conversation. His breaths were even and deep. Not even a scintilla of anxiety. If it weren't costing him so much money, he'd be enjoying the process. He went over and gave a hard knock on Juleen's door. "You can come out now."

She opened the door. Her eyes were red.

"Were you eavesdropping?"

"I didn't hear a thing. I lay down on my bed and put a pillow over my face."

"That's a little extreme."

"I didn't want you yelling at me."

"Don't take my yelling personally." Donatti checked his watch. "Your next tutor will be here in forty-five minutes. You can take a break until then." Her eyes focused on the floor. "Not a word to your mother."

"I know." She looked up at him with Terry's face but her own dark eyes. "My father went to be with Sanjay?"

Once they put a gun to the back of his head. Donatti said, "Yes, he did."

"So, he's not a coward."

"Nope. He's a brave man and a good father."

She nodded, tears bursting from her eyes. "Will they be okay?"

"I hope so, Juleen. It's costing me a lot of money for them to be okay. Does your mother ever talk to you about it—about what happened to Sanjay?"

"No." Juleen shook her head. "We don't talk about that day."

"She doesn't ask you questions about Sanjay? What I might be doing?"

"No. I don't think she wants me to think about it."

"That's good." Donatti paused. "What do you want for dinner?"

"I'm not hungry."

"Rule number one: Take care of yourself. I repeat, what do you want for dinner?"

"I'm glad my father is with Sanjay. It won't be as scary for my brother."

Donatti looked at her downtrodden face. "I know you miss them both. I'm really hoping we can get everything settled. Then you can see them again."

"You'd allow me to see my father?"

"Of course, once everything is over. You won't live with him, of course. You and Sanjay will live here with your mother. But you can visit him in Mumbai . . . or Goa. I think he's living in Goa now. And he can visit you. Your father is your father, and he will always be your father."

"Then we are going to live here?"

"Not here with me, but you'll live in Nevada with Mommy."

"Nevada?" She looked puzzled. "Is that a city or a state?"

"It's a state."

"Does it have an ocean?"

"No, it's inland. But it does have mountains and a desert and a big, natural lake called Lake Tahoe where a lot of movie stars have homes. One side of the shore is Nevada and the other side is California. You and Sanjay and Mommy could live there. Or you three might like a bigger city called Reno or maybe a bigger city called Las Vegas. No matter what Mommy chooses, the place will seem tiny compared with Indian cities."

"I've heard of Las Vegas," she told him. "My father talked about taking a holiday there."

I bet he did. Donatti said, "Mommy will visit me some weekends, but most of the time it'll be the three of you. Do you want spaghetti for dinner?"

She nodded. "Spaghetti is fine. Mommy likes spaghetti. Can she even eat spaghetti yet?"

"I don't know, but Mommy's having dinner with me tonight. But we'll make it around eight, eight-thirty, so she can spend time with you."

"Thank you, Chris." More tears.

Donatti stared at the girl. "You need to be happy, Juleen. If you're sad, then Mommy gets sad. And I like a happy Mommy instead of a sad Mommy. A sad Mommy is a pain in the ass."

She blurted out, "Do you hate me?"

He regarded her face: so earnest it was comical. "No, I don't hate you. Why would I hate you?"

"I'm not your child." She looked down. "I feel like a burden."

"You're not a burden," Donatti said. "But the reality is I don't have much use for you. You take Mommy away from me and you don't make me money, so from my standpoint you don't do me much good. But I don't hate you."

"But you like Sanjay?"

"I don't even know Sanjay enough to like or dislike him."

"But you're paying money for him."

"That's for Mommy. I want her to be happy."

"Would you pay money for me?"

"Of course I'd pay money for you. Mommy loves you. She'd *really* be unhappy without you. My goal in life is to keep Mommy happy."

"Do you love Gabe?"

"Lots of questions, Juleen."

"Do you? Love Gabe?"

He rolled his eyes. "Gabe is my son. I'd do anything for him. If that's love, then I guess I love him."

"Why is Gabe's last name Whitman and your last name is Donatti?"

"I was born Christopher Whitman. When I met your mother, I was Christopher Whitman. When I started working for my uncle, Joseph Donatti, he asked me to change my name to his."

"So why didn't Gabe change his name?"

"I didn't put the name on your brother's birth certificate, Mommy did. Now no more questions."

"Mommy loves me, you know, even if you have no use for me."

"I do know that."

Her chin jutted outward with defiance as she spoke. "She loves *me* more than she loves *you*."

"That is for damn sure. For the last time, what do you want for dinner?"

"I thought we agreed on spaghetti."

"Yes, we did. My bad." He started to walk away. This time she caught his arm. "What?"

"Thank you for helping Mommy. And thank you for helping me, especially since you don't have any use for me. And no, I'm not being sarcastic."

He took his arm back and studied her. "You're a pretty girl, Juleen. One day you'll be a beautiful woman. My sole advice to you is to keep your legs together. You don't want to end up like your mother with a dog like me. You can do better."

"I don't like boys."

"Yeah, you already told me that. One day you'll change your mind."

"No, I won't!"

Donatti thought a moment. "Do you like girls?"

"No. Gross! I mean I love Mommy, but she doesn't count." She sighed. "I'm sorry if I was rude to you, Chris." Tears in her eyes. "I'm . . . I'll do better. I'm sorry."

He knelt down, put his hands on her shoulders, and stared into her eyes. "It's hard to live in chaos. You're holding up well."

"Thank you."

"But you've got to remember that I'm the boss here. You don't mouth off to the boss. It's not good to be mouthy, period. It pisses people off."

"I'm sorry."

"I'm not chastising you, Juleen. I'm just telling you that it's a poor strategy to disrespect anyone. It's a really poor strategy to disrespect me."

"I know."

"On the other hand, it's not good to be a dishrag, either, especially because you're a girl. Guys are going to try to push you around and talk you into things. Don't get sucked into their bullshit. Choose what's important to you and go for it. If anyone gives you a hard time, you tell *me*. I'm not your father. I will never be your father. Furthermore, I don't want to be your father. But you are Mommy's daughter, and because of that, I will take care of you forever."

"Thank you." Juleen dried her eyes on her yellow top. "And you'll take care of Sanjay?"

"Once he's here, of course I will."

"And Mommy too."

"Especially Mommy."

Tears overflowed from her eyes. "She needs protection."

"Yes, she does." Donatti nodded. "I've got it covered."

CHAPTER 16

McADAMS TRIED THE doorknob of Micky Anderson's Bar and Grill. Discovering it locked, he knocked on the door. When there was no response, he peeked through the window. All seemed quiet, chairs upside down on tabletops and the ceiling lights off. He called Decker. "I'm not having any luck. Anything nice is closed until four in the afternoon. I've gone into two coffee places, both of them to-go. One of the baristas recognized Pauline, but he didn't know Brock Baer. The other was blank on both."

"The one you got a hit on . . . What did he say?"

"He said that Pauline would come in and buy a cup of coffee—a mochaccino, I think. Pauline was friendly, but it was like a thirty-second interaction. Did you get anything?"

"Like you said, the nicer places aren't open. I went to a bakery/coffeehouse. No one remembered Pauline. Then I went to a sandwich shop in the supermarket. The person behind the counter remembered Pauline's face, but that was about it. There was a seventeen-year-old stock boy in the market who definitely remembered her. He said she was flirtatious."

"Wow. She's picking them a little young."

"He didn't mind," Decker said. "But then he told me that she stopped showing up, which was consistent with the checkout cashiers that I talked to. A few remembered her, but they hadn't seen her for a while—months more than weeks. And that would jibe with her moving in with Elsie Schulung."

"Is there a grocery store that's closer to Elsie's house?"

"Don't know for sure, but I seem to remember an independent grocery store about five minutes away. I never bothered talking to anyone because it wasn't our case and Quay made it clear that we should stay away."

McAdams said, "How far is Elsie's house from town?"

Decker said, "Walkable. Fifteen to twenty minutes, I'd say."

"Are there restaurants near there?"

"Not that I remember. I think there's a convenience store at a gas station where you can buy coffee and a doughnut, but nothing sit-down."

"Then if you wanted a legitimate restaurant, you'd have to go into town," McAdams said.

"Looks that way," Decker said.

"Well, nothing is open now. Where do people eat lunch?"

"At home. Lots of the lunch trade was wiped out by COVID."

McAdams said, "I'm looking at my map and there's a place called Burgers and Dogs about two blocks away. I don't know if it's a counter takeout or an eat-in, but I'm going to try that next."

"Burgers and Dogs," Decker echoed. "It's five blocks away from me. Wait for me."

"I'm kinda hungry. You want a burg— Wait, what am I saying? I don't suppose they have vegetarian options."

"It's fine. But I could use something to drink. It's hot out here."

"It is," McAdams said. "Let's go in and bother the locals."

A few minutes later they were standing in front of a diner. The interior smelled like fried meat, bacon, and melted cheese. The floor space held about a dozen tables with linoleum tops that held settings for two to four people. The seating was mismatched: a combination of metal, wood, or cane-backed chairs. The counter was generous and doing a brisk business. They found an open table, and a server came by with menus. She was in her twenties with a long blond ponytail, a round face, a prominent forehead, and wide-set blue eyes. She wore a long denim dress over a long-sleeved black T-shirt. Her name tag said MARY.

She said, "Our soup is navy bean, and our pie is strawberry."

"Thank you." After she left, Decker looked at McAdams. "Remember Eli Wolf?"

"She's Mennonite?" McAdams said. "Could be. The dress and the look. We're in the right geographical location. I mean not Baniff specifically, but we're not that far away from Lancaster." A pause. "You ever speak to them? The Wolfs?"

"No." Decker shook his head. "If I thought about all the suffering people that I've met . . ." A sigh. "It's really hard, but you just have to close the case in your head and go on to the next." He looked at the menu. "I'll stick with coffee. I wonder if they have iced coffee."

"There's a veggie burger."

"Fried on the same grill as the burgers. But get what you want, Tyler."

"I'll take the veggie burger."

"You can have the real thing."

"Trying to watch my intake of red meat." McAdams put the menu down, and Mary hopped up and came to the table.

"What can I get you, folks?"

Decker said, "Do you have iced coffee?"

"We sure do."

"Thank you."

"That's it?"

"That's it."

"How about a scoop of ice cream with it?"

"Actually, that sounds pretty good."

"Whipped cream?"

"Sure."

She turned to McAdams.

"A veggie burger, no fries."

"You want to sub a side salad?"

"Sure."

Decker said, "How long have you been working here, Mary?"

The server looked momentarily stunned. "Me?" Decker nodded. She said, "Five years."

"Long time."

"Yes. I'm very grateful to have this job."

"I bet." Decker pulled out a picture. "Have you ever seen this woman before?"

"That's Pauline. She used to come here two, three times a week."

"Used to come here?"

"I haven't seen her for a while. Why are you asking?" When Decker pulled out his badge, she said, "You're the police?"

"Detectives," McAdams said.

"What happened to Pauline? If you're here, it must be bad."

"It is. She's unfortunately deceased."

Mary looked at the pad in her hand. "I gotta put these orders in."

Decker said, "If you have a moment . . ."

"I hardly knew her."

"Anything you can tell us." Decker looked around. "Obviously not now. It's busy. But maybe in an hour or so?"

Mary nodded and was off. When she brought over the food and drinks, Decker sensed a cooler attitude.

So did McAdams. He picked up his veggie burger and said, "We'd better leave a nice tip."

Decker sipped his ice cream and coffee. "This is really good."

"Tasty," McAdams said after taking a bite. "Want to split this?"

"No, I'm fine. I suppose we should let Quay know what we're doing."

McAdams said, "I think she'll talk more freely if the local law isn't here."

"That's a good point. I'll text him and tell him we're eating lunch in our car. That way, he won't want to join us." Decker's fingers tapped across his phone. A moment later, he heard a ding. He read the text and responded. "Quay's going back to the station. I told him we'll phone him in an hour and compare notes."

"Did he find anything?"

"No idea." Decker polished off his iced coffee. "I could use some water."

"So could I." McAdams managed to get Mary's attention. He mouthed, "Two waters." Within a minute, the glasses were on the table. Her disposition hadn't turned any friendlier.

When they paid the bill with a credit card, they left an enormous cash tip. Mary noticed. Right after she squared the tab and handed them back the plastic, she sat down at their table. "I can give you five minutes. But honestly, you won't even need that. Like I said, I didn't really know her."

"Ever see her with this guy?" Decker took out the snapshot of Brock Baer and placed it on the tabletop.

She stared at it. "Not with Pauline. She was alone when she came in here. After she moved away, she came in a couple of times with Elsie."

"So you knew Elsie?"

"I didn't *know* her. Pauline introduced her to me." Mary bit her lip. "They were living together. I sensed that they were more than just friends." She shrugged. "Modern world."

"Indeed." Decker tapped the picture. "Then you don't recognize this guy?"

"I never said that. He was in here once. I remember because I waited on him."

"Really!" Decker felt a flash of excitement. "Did he talk to you about Pauline?"

"He mentioned her. This was maybe four months ago." She was still staring at the photograph. "He looks mean in the picture. In person, he's got a nice smile. He's kinda cute."

"And he talked to you about Pauline?" McAdams said.

"It wasn't like . . . 'Do you know Pauline and where can I find her?' "

"Okay," Decker said. "What was it like?"

"I think he mentioned he was a friend of hers from way back. I told him I haven't seen her around lately." She took in a deep breath and let it out. "That was really about it."

"Perfect," Decker said. "And you think this might have been like four months ago?"

"Three or four, yeah," Mary said. "After Pauline moved in with Elsie."

"What was Pauline like?" Decker asked.

"She was friendly—you know, talking to other tables across the room. She came in for lunch." A pause. "I don't think she had a job."

McAdams said, "Why?"

"I don't know," Mary said. "You just get a feel for people. She never seemed in a hurry. And she left the same tip no matter what she had. Three dollars and fifty cents. Not the most generous if she's having a full meal, but she left it even if she stopped in for a Coke. It all evened out." Mary stood up. "I have to get back to work."

"Thank you for your time," Decker said.

"Thank you for your tip," she replied. "I suppose it was for the service *and* the information. Although it wasn't much information."

"It was great information." Decker paused. "Out of curiosity, what's your last name, Mary?"

"Yost. Why?"

"Just curious."

"If you say so." Mary walked away.

After she left, McAdams said, "For a Mennonite, I was thinking Yoder, but Yost is about the same thing. Anyway, we now know that Baer was here."

"It establishes a recent link, especially since he mentioned Pauline to Mary," Decker said. "At least it doesn't feel like a waste of time."

"What do you think he wanted from her? To rekindle an old relationship? Retaliation? Just passing through and thought he'd say hello?"

"Doubt it was the last one. Let's see if we can find out." Decker checked his watch. "It's a little past three. What time do you think the bars open?"

"Happy hour usually starts at four."

"We can keep canvassing. Or we can call Quay now and find out if he has anything."

"Let's keep canvassing," McAdams said. "My motto is the fewer people to muck things up, the better."

Decker said, "What do you think about an overnight stay here?"

"How long do you think our business here will take?"

"I don't know. But I want to investigate this area thoroughly, which means I want to talk to all the restaurant and bar people. Plus, I want to go back to Elsie's house and canvass there. Why rush it if Rina's not home anyway?"

"For one thing, I didn't pack anything."

"I know you're used to the good life, but you can survive without a change of clothes." Decker looked at his phone for inns. "Sorry, Harvard, I don't see a Ritz nearby."

"Anything Relais & Châteaux will do, old man." McAdams smiled. "Would it be too much to ask for something clean?"

Decker looked at his map. "There's a MotoInn about a half mile away. There's also what looks like a boutique hotel called the Lancaster's Red Rose that's a few blocks away. Should we check it out?"

"What's least likely to give me bedbugs?"

"Don't know, but the local place is way more likely to give us information."

McAdams sighed. "Then the Lancaster's Red Rose it is."

AT THREE-FORTY-FIVE, THEY checked in to their respective rooms. Decker's was small and furnished with Victorian repros. There was a worn dresser with a ceramic washbasin sitting on top of it—unnecessary because the place did boast indoor plumbing. The bed was small but sufficient for one person. The mattress was lumpy and the coils squeaked. The nightstand held fresh flowers in a small vase. The bathroom had shampoo, soap, and plenty of hot water as amenities. Decker showered, re-dressed, and met McAdams in the lobby a half hour later. They called Jake Quay, who said he'd meet them at the hotel at five. In the meantime, they found a drugstore, where they bought toothbrushes, toothpaste, a bag of disposable razors, and two combs.

They went back to the hotel, and Decker left the bag with the front desk. The woman in charge had short lemon-colored hair, a pale face, and brown eyes. She looked to be in her fifties. Her name tag announced her as Beth. She said, "Would you like me to put these up in your rooms?"

"We'll get them on our way back." Decker looked to his right. The hotel had a small bar and cocktail lounge. He took out a picture of Pauline Corbett. "Do you know this woman?"

"That's Pauline," Beth said immediately. Her eyes narrowed. "Why?"

Decker took out his badge. "We're looking for information about her."

"Why? What did she do?"

"Ongoing investigation."

Beth regarded the billfold and said, "The badges look real enough. But so did the other guy's badge."

Decker and McAdams exchanged looks. Decker took out a picture of Brock Baer. "Was the other guy this man?"

Beth's eyes went to the photograph. "Will you excuse me for a
moment?"

"If you're thinking about calling someone local, try Sergeant
Quay," Decker said. "He'll vouch for us. As a matter of fact, he
should be here in about five minutes." He tapped the snapshot with
a finger. "What did this guy want?"

"He asked if I knew Pauline Corbett. I told him I knew her.
When he asked where she lived, I became suspicious. I told him I
didn't know, even though I did. I know she's missing . . . Pauline is."

"Unfortunately, she is deceased, and she died in my jurisdiction."

The woman appeared stunned. At that moment, Jake Quay
walked inside. He was wearing civvies—a black polo shirt and jeans
and high-tops. He came to the front desk and noticed the look on
Beth's face. He said, "I guess they told you what's going on."

"It's true, then? Is Pauline dead?" When Quay nodded, Beth
said, "Like, was she killed or . . ."

Decker said, "It's a homicide."

Beth gasped. "What about Elsie? Has she been found?"

"Not yet." Quay noticed the picture of Brock Baer. He picked it
up and showed it to her again. "You've seen him before, Beth?"

"He was asking about her . . . Pauline."

"When was this?"

"A while back. Maybe three months ago. Before Elsie disappeared."

"And?"

"I didn't think much about it, because the next day she met him
for drinks in the bar. They looked like friends."

"Then they weren't fighting or anything?"

"Not to my eye, no."

"Did he stay here?" Decker asked.

A pause. "I know *I* didn't check him in. But Eddie could have been on shift. Want me to check the register?"

"Please," Quay said.

"It might take me a little time. I don't remember the exact date."

"We can wait."

Decker said, "You said they had drinks together in the lounge?"

"I remember they walked into the lounge. I'm assuming they had drinks."

"Do you remember who was behind the bar?"

"No, I don't remember that. Sorry."

"And that was the last time you saw him?" Decker asked.

"Yes." Beth started going through the register books.

Decker said, "While she's checking the records, let's see if the bartender has anything to add." Quay nodded, and the three of them walked into the lounge.

The carpet was a deep floral maroon and smelled musty. The furniture was old but polished; same with the bar top. At this hour, the place had few customers. The man behind the bar was bald with a young face. His shirtsleeves were rolled to the elbows, exposing colorful tats. CHET was on his name tag.

Quay showed him the picture of Baer. "He was in about three months ago, Chet."

"Vaguely familiar." A shrug.

Quay said, "He was with Pauline Corbett."

A spark. "Ah. That's right. What about him?"

"You tell me," Decker said.

Chet shrugged. "They met up around eight."

"Did they come in together?"

"I've got to think." A long pause. "I believe he came in first. Then she came in and sat down next to him." He pointed to the end of the bar on the right side. "There." A pause. "My opinion? They seemed to be warming up."

"Meaning?" Decker asked.

Chet said, "After a while on this job, you can kind of tell if people are in for a friendly how-do or if they're gearing up for a night of getting hammered."

Quay said, "So they were in it for the long haul?"

"Seemed that way to me, Jake, but I don't know. Check with the Mule or with Tobacco's Road."

Jake nodded. "Will do."

"How long were they here?" Decker asked.

"About an hour."

McAdams asked, "Did they seem friendly with each other?"

Chet said, "Don't remember them fighting." A pause. "Don't remember her hanging on him or whatnot. They had a few beers, got up, paid the bill, and left."

"How many each?"

"Two, three bottles. They seemed to be walking okay when they left. What's this about?"

Decker said, "The man that Pauline was with is a person of interest in a homicide."

"I know that Pauline and Elsie Schulung are missing." He looked at Quay. "We talked about this a few months ago, right?"

Quay said, "Yes, we did."

"Are they dead?"

Decker said, "Pauline is deceased."

"Wow." Chet looked upset. "And Elsie?"

"Still missing."

"What happened to Pauline?"

"Ongoing investigation," Decker said. "Pauline was found in my jurisdiction in Greenbury. That's why I'm here with Sergeant Quay."

"Where is Greenbury?"

"About three hours from here."

"What was Pauline doing there?"

"I'm trying to figure that out," Decker said. "How many times did you see Pauline with this guy?"

"Just the once . . . about three months ago." Chet looked at Quay. "Right before Pauline and Elsie went missing, obviously. Do you think he had something to do with it?"

"We are checking everything," Quay said. "Thanks, Chet, you've been helpful."

"No worries."

They went back to Beth at the front desk. She looked at Quay and said, "I don't think he stayed here, Sergeant. Probably this place was too rich for his blood. He was more like a sleeping-in-his-car kinda man."

"Did he look shabby when you spoke with him?" Decker asked.

"I don't remember. Sorry."

"Thanks anyway, Beth." Quay turned to Decker. "Both of the places that Chet mentioned should be open by now. The Mule is closer. Let's try that first."

CHAPTER 17

RED LETTERS SPELLED out THE MULE with a blue-lit logo of the pack animal trudging under the weight of side bags. Quay said, "You know, I did interview people here when Elsie went missing. We're a small town, but I take my responsibility seriously."

"I know, Jake. I'm only here because new things turned up in my area. And I haven't interviewed anyone with regards to Pauline. And that means that McAdams and I have to go back to the beginning."

"I just want you to know that I haven't been sitting on my ass."

Decker placed a hand on the man's shoulder. "McAdams and I work in a small town. We know how dedicated we are. I'm sure you're the same way. Let's get this done together."

"Yeah, well . . ." Quay opened the door. "Thanks."

Inside was dark as befit a bar. The floor space held a pool table, currently unoccupied, with about ten small tables around the perimeter. The bar was U-shaped, and the stools looked recently upholstered. Three men and two women took up space, munching on bowls of mini pretzels that sat on the countertop. A white-aproned bartender stood in front of shelves holding a wide selection of libations. There was also a chalkboard featuring a sizable menu from the kitchen.

The bartender was rotund and red-faced—maybe mid-fifties. He looked at Quay and nodded. "What's up, Sarge?"

"The usual, Jim. Trying to nail bad guys." Quay made introductions.

Upon hearing the detectives' names, Jim said, "Then this is business?"

"Yep, but it's hot outside. I'll take a beer." Quay looked at Decker and McAdams, both shaking their heads no. "You don't mind?"

Decker said, "Not at all." He pulled out a picture and laid it on the bar top. He spoke to Jim. "Have you ever seen this man?"

Jim gave it a quick glance as he pulled the beer tap. "Looks familiar. Who is he?"

"Maybe you've seen him with this woman?" Out came the picture of Corbett.

"That's Pauline." He let the suds run over the rim of the glass, then gave it to Quay.

"Ever see them together?" Decker asked.

"Maybe like a while back . . . like three months ago."

"That would be about right," Decker said. "What can you tell me about them?"

"I gotta remember first." He wiped his hands on his apron and appeared to be thinking. "They sat at the bar. They were here for maybe an hour. They were making the rounds."

"Meaning?" McAdams asked.

"They'd been drinking before they came in. I could smell it."

Quay sipped his beer. "Behaving badly?"

"Nothing out of the ordinary. Pauline's a friendly gal. She'd talk to anyone." His eyes were far away, bringing up a memory that was still etched in his mind. "He was quieter, but not by much. I know that Pauline's missing. The sergeant and I had a conversation about it, right?"

"We did," Quay said. "You said that Elsie and Pauline would come here."

Jim said, "Pauline used to be a regular, but after she hooked up with Elsie, the visits weren't so often. They'd pop in . . . play pool for about an hour. They ordered sodas and bar food. I think Elsie was trying to keep Pauline sober."

"Pauline could throw them down?" McAdams asked.

"She could hold her own."

Decker tapped the photo. "What did Pauline drink when she was with this man?"

"What did she drink?" A pause. "Not soda, that's for sure." Another pause. "Don't hold me to it, but I seem to recall both of them putting back shots with a beer chaser."

"How many shots?"

"Maybe three or four over an hour. Nothing crazy."

A patron yelled, "Hey, Jim, can I get a refill?"

"Sorry, Barry. Coming up." He looked at the trio. "Excuse me."

They waited until he was done serving. Quay drank his beer, then took a handful of pretzels. "Not much lunch today."

Jim came back over. "Refill, Sarge?"

"Nah, this is fine."

"Okay." A pause. "Is Pauline dead?"

"She is deceased, unfortunately," Decker said.

"And you think this guy in the picture did it?"

"He's a person of interest. Elsie Schulung is still missing, so she is also a person of interest."

"I can't see Elsie harming Pauline. They were . . . you know."

"Involved," McAdams said.

"Ye-ah. A surprise to me. Pauline liked men. But I guess she was a switch hitter. Who is this guy, by the way?"

"His name is Brock Baer," Decker said. "How many times did you see him with Pauline?"

"Just the one time, as far as I can recall."

Quay said, "If you happen to see him again, let me know."

"No prob," Jim said.

Decker said, "And you say they stayed here for around an hour?"

"About."

"Do you remember when they left? The time?"

Jim thought a moment. "After ten probably. The place was still crowded."

"Did you sense any tension between them when they left?"

"I don't remember," Jim told him. "I was busy. They weren't yelling and screaming at each other, if that's what you're asking." Another shout, calling for the bartender. People were coming in. "I've got to run."

"Thanks so much. Just one more question," Decker said. "Any idea where they'd go after they left the Mule?"

"Probably another bar," Jim said. "They didn't look like they were done for the night. You know, when people drink, it doesn't take much to go from a good time to one too many."

"Did they appear to have had one too many?" McAdams asked.

"I don't remember perfectly, but I'd say they were on the edge," Jim said. "Whatever happened doesn't surprise me. Nothing surprises me anymore. I'm just glad that when trouble came, it wasn't here."

FIFTEEN MINUTES LATER, Decker, McAdams, and Quay stood in front of a brick building with a wooden sign, the name TOBACCO'S ROAD burned black into the planks.

Quay said, "The place is bigger than the Mule. At this hour, things start to get busy. Don't know how much we'll get out of the bartender."

A glance at his watch. It was half past six. Decker said, "Let's go."

As Quay predicted, there was a lively crowd. The atmosphere inside was dim and smoky. The bar was packed with patrons sitting elbow to elbow, drinking and eating and laughing. A big-screen TV was mounted on the wall with multiple images of baseball games. Scattered tables and chairs were positioned around three pool tables, all of them occupied.

They threaded their way up to the bartender. She had short blue hair to match her blue eyes and a body inked with tats. Gauges sat in her ears and a ring in her nose. She noticed Quay first. "Hey, Sarge. What can I get you?"

"Beer is fine." He looked up at the chalkboard. "And an order of baby backs."

"Got it." She turned her eyes to Decker and McAdams, who said, "Baby backs sound good for me."

"They go fast. And to drink?"

"Give him a beer also," Decker said. "I'll take a Diet Coke."

"Been there." Meaning she thought he was an ex-alcoholic. "Anything to eat?"

"I'll take a giant pretzel."

"Hot mustard?"

"Live dangerously," he said.

She smiled as she poured two beers from the tap. Then she handed Decker his Diet Coke, picked up two empty beer glasses from prior patrons, and wiped the counter. "I'll put this in to the kitchen."

"Hey, Maddy," someone shouted.

"Be right with you." She put in the order and was off serving others. Five minutes later, she handed them their food. "Refills?"

Decker nodded. "Thanks."

She looked at Quay, who nodded, and at McAdams, who said he was still nursing the first.

Quay picked up a rib. "Maddy, these two are detectives. When you get a moment, they'd like to ask you a couple of questions."

Maddy took away his dirty glass and gave him a fresh mug. "About what?"

Out came the picture of Brock Baer. Decker said, "Ever see this man before?"

She turned the snapshot so she could see it better. "Looks familiar. What did he do?"

"We're not sure," Decker said. "How about this woman?"

"That's Pauline." Maddy paused. "Oh yeah. Now I remember." Her eyes rolled. "They were here together." Another eye roll.

Quay looked perplexed. "Did you tell me this before?"

"Nope. But right after these two idiots went at it, I went on a monthlong trip to Thailand. You probably talked to Aaron."

"That's right," Quay said.

"What do you mean 'went at it'?" Decker asked.

"It was on the late side when they came in. Around eleven, but that's not crazy. We're open until twelve on weekdays, two on weekends." A pause. "It must have been a weekday. Thursday, I think, because I left on Saturday. They started off okay—a little loud, but par for the course. About fifteen minutes before closing, I made a last call. Five minutes before I locked the door, the guy wanted another. I told him no. He started getting belligerent with me. She started yelling at him not to yell at me. Then he started yelling back at her. There was some name-calling. Luckily, there were several customers still here, including Big Eric. Helped me escort them outside. They were both skunk drunk."

"Eric is a big guy." Quay took a bite of his ribs. "Good stuff."

"We try."

Decker said, "Do you know what happened to them after they left?"

"No, I do not," Maddy said. "But I didn't hear yelling anymore. I cleaned up, left about an hour later. No one was in the parking lot. I went home. The guy was a psycho."

"Why do you say that?" McAdams asked.

"The eyes ... flat, dead, just empty. Then again, it could be he was drunk. No one looks sweet when they're shit-faced." Maddy heard her name. "That's all I remember. I've got to get back to work."

"Did you ever see these two together after that one time?"

"Nope," Maddy said. "But like I told you, I was gone for a month on vacation. Wish I was back there now."

"I'm sure." Quay wiped his face. "Thanks for your help, Maddy."

"No worries." Maddy licked her lips. "You know about Occam's razor?"

"We do," McAdams said. "Simplest is best."

Maddy said, "If you guys think that he did something to Pauline, then he probably did."

AFTER RIBS AND libations, they left the bar. Quay said, "I think we're pretty much done for the night. No other places are as big as the two bars we just went to. And it sounds like they ended their evening here."

"I think you're right," Decker said.

"Looks like they took the fight over to Elsie's," Quay said. "We'll put out a BOLO on Baer's car tomorrow morning, see if we can find the son of a bitch."

"Does Baer have a car?"

"No idea, but if he does, I'll find it," Quay said. "You two hitting the road tomorrow?"

Decker said, "Unless something happens, we will be going back home."

"What could happen?"

"Earthquake, fire, flood, pandemic," Decker said. "Who the hell knows?"

Quay smiled. "In the meantime, have a good night."

"You do the same." Decker turned around to go back to the hotel and McAdams followed. When they were a block away, and Quay was clearly out of hearing range, Decker stopped walking. "Let's go back to the bar."

"Because . . ." McAdams said.

Decker said, "Like I said, we're missing a crime scene."

"You think he did something to her inside the bar?"

"No, not the bar. But maybe the parking lot."

McAdams looked around. It was almost eight in the evening, but there was still lingering daylight. "Sure."

They reversed directions and went back to Tobacco's Road. Standing in the parking lot, they were a good fifty feet from the entrance.

Decker said, "Okay, they came out of there." He pointed to the door. "Maddy said she didn't hear anything like screaming outside once they left, but maybe it happened too far away for her to hear. Let's look around."

"Fine."

"Careful, Tyler, cars are coming in and out."

"Okay, Dad." After a half hour of scouring the pavement for . . . something . . . McAdams said, "I don't see anything nefarious."

"Agreed." Decker turned and looked at the road. Across the street were small one-story businesses. No CC cameras in view. To his immediate right and left, there were stores as well.

McAdams said, "No good place to do the deed. Everything's in the open. What if Baer had a car? Could have done it there."

"Certainly possible." Decker organized his thoughts. "They left the bar, skunk drunk, continued the fight in the car, and then he stabbed her there, making the car the crime scene."

"How do you stab someone when you're driving?" McAdams said. "At some point, you have to pull over."

"Maybe he stabbed her when the car was parked." A pause. "Or maybe it happened in Pauline's car. She was driving and he reached over and stabbed her."

"Then she would have lost control of the car," McAdams said. "There would have been an accident, don't you think?"

"Okay . . ." Decker said. "Let's say there was an accident. Some-one lost control of the wheel. That means there should be swerving tire tracks somewhere."

"It happened a long time ago, boss. Even if there had been tracks, with all the summer rain, they were probably erased."

"Maybe not." Decker thought and shrugged.

McAdams said, "If it happened in Pauline's car, then that's our crime scene. We have no idea where her vehicle is. If it happened in Brock Baer's car, then the crime scene is there. We don't know if he owned a car or if he rented one. Whatever the case, sticking around here won't tell us anything."

"I'd still like to come back in the morning and take a look." Decker's eyes scanned the area. "Which direction is Elsie's place?"

"Let me get the map." McAdams sighed. "Northeast, which is . . ." He took out his phone and opened a compass app. "That way."

"Okay. Now which direction is Pauline's old place?"

"Hold on . . ." Another look at the paper map. "Southeast, which is that way. Why are we interested in Pauline's place when the blood was found at Elsie's place?"

"Elsie's was within walking distance. What if they were on foot and it happened while they were on their way home?" When Mc-Adams sighed again, Decker said, "Yes, I realize it's a long shot, but we're here anyway. Let's just check it out, okay?"

"When?" McAdams said. "Now?"

"No, it'll keep until the morning,"

"Good idea. I'm tired and hungry, and it's almost dark."

Decker said, "Let's find you some food."

"What about yourself? At least I ate a couple of ribs."

"I'm all right."

McAdams said, "You can't think clearly on a pretzel with mus-tard as your dinner. Let's find a convenience store. We can pick up cereal and milk." Out came the map. "There's a gas station about three blocks from the hotel."

"Sounds good, Harvard." Decker smiled. "Thanks."

"Rina's not here." McAdams shook his head. "Someone has to feed you."

"Aw, you care."

"Yeah, I care." A pause. "I'm also a little afraid of your wife."

"Buddy, that makes two of us."

CHAPTER 18

I HAD TWENTY-FOUR HOURS to think about Donatti's party and my new role as his fiancée. Chris was good at protecting things; Juleen and I needed protection. Even more important, he was paying an enormous ransom for *my* son. Whatever he wanted was my new motto, and tonight, he wanted dinner at a strip mall. I would have preferred to be alone and read, take myself to an alternative universe. What I did was slap some makeup on my face and fix my hair. I was all smiles when we went out the door. It put him in a good mood.

The sun sat low over the undulating crests. It was colder than I thought it would be. That was how it was in the mountains. Out here, as soon as daylight faded, the temperature dropped. As Chris brought out the Ducati from the garage, I rubbed my arms. He noticed. "You didn't bring a jacket?"

"I forgot. I'm okay."

He took off his leather bomber jacket. "I'm fine. It's a five-minute ride." He gave me a helmet. "I got you a smaller one. It might still be too big. Try it out and we'll see if it works."

I put on the jacket. It almost went down to my knees. The helmet was just a little too big. He tightened the straps. "Let's roll. Are you hungry? I'm starved."

"I could eat."

I got on the back and wrapped my arms around him, hoping that the cast wasn't too uncomfortable. He took off and I was transported back to the first time I had ever ridden on a motorcycle. I was sixteen. We had finished his tutoring session and he invited me out for a hamburger, assuring me it wasn't a date. We picked up dinner at a fast-food place and started out in miserable traffic. As soon as he hit the freeway, he merged to the left and we flew. I was petrified, but it was a sense of freedom I had never felt before. He took me into the mountains near where we lived, and we ate, staring at the horizon until the sun vanished and it was dark. We didn't talk much. We sat close, but he didn't do anything physical to me. I knew he hated to be touched, but even so I believed back then that he just wasn't attracted to me.

Night was falling now, but lights emerged a few minutes after we left. The place was located in a block of small shops. He pulled the bike around to the back entrance, killed the motor, and we both hopped off. Hanging the helmets on the handlebars, he walked the bike through a rear door. A bodyguard was there to meet him.

To me, he said, "I'll take the jacket."

"Of course." I gave it to him.

We went through the kitchen and came out into the restaurant. It was a typical kind of Italian restaurant—no Chianti bottles hanging from the ceiling, but checkered tablecloths and posters of Italy. It was busy with townsfolk in casual clothing: T-shirts, jeans or khakis, and flip-flops or sandals. There were several tables of knockout women. Chris nodded to them and they nodded back. He chose a table near the kitchen with visibility to the front door. He pulled a chair out for me, then he sat down. A moment later, there were two glasses of red wine, two glasses of water, a basket of bread and butter, a salad for him, and a bowl of soup for myself.

He said, "I don't know if you're still on medication. Are you drinking wine?"

"I can have a glass."

"You want white instead of red?"

"No, red is fine, thank you." He offered me some bread and I took a slice. "Thank you."

"Soup okay? I thought it might be easier than salad."

"It's great, Chris, thank you."

"Third time you've thanked me."

"I was taught well."

We ate in silence for a few moments. Then he said, "You look a little stunned."

"I haven't been out very much." Silence. "It's disorienting."

"I'm sure it is." More silence. He said, "Can I help?"

"No, I'll be fine." I put down my soup spoon. "Just a lot has happened."

His eyes focused on my face. He did that when he was in listening mode. It was part of why I had liked him. When I talked, I had his full attention.

"It's like . . . I went to bed. Had this . . . eleven-year dream that turned into a nightmare. And I woke up and I'm right back where I started . . . except I'm older and I'm still missing a son. Like some kind of Einsteinian time warp."

He picked up his wine and sipped. "Not easy."

"Not easy at all."

"Did you like India?"

The question threw me. "Yes. Especially at first. I'd never traveled anywhere, and Mumbai is a very exotic place. After a while, I found it exhausting. You couldn't turn a corner without running into people. Mostly men. I mean, there were women on the streets, but it's a little creepy being out there by yourself. I was a real alien, constantly looking over my shoulder." He nodded. I sipped some wine and said, "Maybe I was looking for you."

He smiled but said nothing. His eyes were constantly jumping between me and the door. Since I had been away for eleven years, I'd forgotten what it was like to sit with him in a public space. His vigilance: it bordered on paranoia, especially when he drank.

I filled in the silence. "Have you ever been there?"

"To Mumbai? Yes, I have."

I was surprised, but kept it to myself. "What did you think of it?"

"Sensory overload."

"Yeah, really. All the people, all the colors, the traffic, the noise, the smells . . . lots of smells. The good ones are the street food. The bad ones . . . well, no need to talk about them." He smiled again. Enigmatic. I said, "When were you there?"

"Around five months after you left me."

I grew quiet. Luckily some white-aproned server came to the table to hide my embarrassment. He was young—really young. Gabe's age. He looked at my finger and said, "I hear congratulations are in order."

Chris smiled, but it lacked warmth. "This is my fiancée, Dr. Terry McLaughlin."

He looked at me and said, "Pleased to meet you, Doctor. I'm Scott. What can I get you?"

I didn't have a menu. "Uh, what do you have?" I asked.

"Scott can get you anything you want," Chris told me.

"I'm sorry," I said. "My mind's a blank."

"How about ravioli?" Chris said. "It's probably soft enough for you to eat."

"Perfect."

"Bring her some ravioli. Make sure it's vegetarian. I'll have my usual boring dinner. Refill on the wine."

"Certainly, Mr. Donatti." He scooted away.

I remained quiet. Then I said, "What brought you to Mumbai?"

"You. I knew you were there. I went to hunt you down."

Weird choice of words. But maybe it was exactly what he was thinking. I said, "Did you find me?"

"Of course." A long pause. "Took me a while because I was given a different name."

"What name?" I asked.

"It was a while ago. Singh Rajut?"

"Peresh Singh Rajut?"

"Yeah, I think that's it."

"That's Devek's nephew, although they're almost the same age. They were in New York at the same time."

"Yes, I know that now. But for a while, I was confused. Didn't matter. I found you." A smile. "Nice house you lived in. How big was it?"

"Big . . . around five thousand square feet. We sold it."

"How much did it sell for?"

"Thirty-six crores . . . about five million dollars. But Devek didn't own it. His father did."

"Ah."

"It went to pay off his first set of debts. Afterward, we didn't have any savings. I know he had to ask his father—well, actually it was his older brother—for spending money. He swore he'd never gamble again."

"Never trust a dog. I should know."

"Right you are."

"Where'd you move to afterward?"

"A very nice apartment . . . which we didn't own. It was his brother's. I don't know if we paid rent or not. Devek handled the money. A big mistake."

"Devek has a money problem. He can't seem to hold on to it."

"I realize that now." I paused. "So . . . you were at our house . . . our first house?"

"I was."

"The inside?"

"No, just the back. The gardens were lovely. Lots of green and lots of places to hide." I didn't answer. He said, "First time I saw you, you were with Devek . . . strolling with him, hand in hand, in the garden. You looked happy. You were heavily pregnant."

"I'm sure I looked like a cow."

His voice dropped in volume. "You looked absolutely stunning. You've got to remember that I never saw you pregnant with Gabe. I found out after the fact."

"I was wrong. I should have told you."

"I was married. I had another life. It was a violent life, and I'm sure I scared the shit out of you. I don't blame you for staying away. But at that moment, I realized what I had lost."

My eyes moistened. "Sorry."

He said, "You must have loved the garden. You sure went out there a lot."

I stared at him. "How long were you there?"

"Long enough. You used to cry a lot."

I felt tears coming. "I missed Gabe. Believe it or not, Chris, I also missed you. I was out of my element. The garden was the one place where I could be alone with my emotions. I was stoic when I was with Devek. He didn't want to hear about my past. He'd tune out when I talked about Gabe. He expected me to forget my own son."

"Understandable."

"Maybe from his point of view. From my point of view, it was spiteful and idiotic."

Chris thought a moment. "If I would have showed up at your door, would you have come back with me?"

"I honestly don't know." I sighed. "I was scared. It wasn't your baby, and I knew you were beyond furious. I know you tried to contact me, but I couldn't get myself to answer you. I didn't think you'd ever forgive me."

"Back then, I probably wouldn't have," Chris said. "Obviously not the case now."

"You've truly forgiven me?"

"Totally." He sat back in his chair. "I was horrible to you." He paused. "I won't say I'm a different man. I'm still a nasty son of a bitch, but as God is my witness, I will never, ever beat you again. I am truly sorry about that. I crossed the line—even for me."

I didn't respond.

"Do you believe me?" he asked.

"I do, although . . ." I stopped talking.

"You're thinking about sex," he said. "That's not the same thing as beating you. You're my wife. Sex is part of the contract. I get in moods. Go along with it and we'll both be fine."

I didn't answer him. There was no point in starting an argument. I said, "So what happened with India? Did you just decide to leave?"

He looked me in the eye. "I came there with a purpose, Terry." A long pause. "Obviously, I wasn't after you, because I had plenty of opportunity."

I felt my heart racing and looked down.

"I kept waiting for him to come out alone. Several times, you two came out together. I didn't want you there when it happened."

When he stopped talking, I said, "So far as I know, Devek is still around." I licked my lips. "You decided not to or . . ."

"Not exactly." He drank water. "I finally did get my chance. Devek was in the garden . . . alone. He was in my sight. A super-clean shot. Easy-peasy, as my ladies say. What I *should* tell you is I had a sudden change of heart. That I had some kind of moral awakening."

I waited.

He shrugged. "I missed."

I was stunned into silence.

"I was aiming right here." He pointed at the back of his head. "I should have gone for the chest . . . bigger target. But I wanted to take him out in one shot, and I suppose I was a little cocky. As soon as I squeezed the trigger, I felt the gun kick to the left. That rifle was my workhorse. It was a custom job. And at that moment, it decided to go gnarly. The bullet flew right by him. He felt the wind, must have heard it as well. Picked his head up and looked around like a prairie dog."

The lightbulb went on.

"What?" he asked.

"I remember now. He ran into the house and told me he'd been shot at. He told me it was you. Well, what he said was: 'That fucking maniac husband of yours just tried to kill me.' I told him he had to be imagining things, that if you wanted him dead, he'd be dead."

"You'd think after all my experience that would have been the case." Two more glasses of wine were placed on the table. He raised his to his lips. "He definitely wasn't imagining anything. I took the miss as a sign. I left."

My heart was thumping. "After he came and told me what happened, I went outside to look. I didn't see or hear anything. Not a rustle, not any kind of movement."

"I'm a pro, honey, although at the time I sure didn't feel like one. I was so pissed that when I got back, I dismantled the gun and furnaced the parts." A pause. "The end of an era." He finished the wine, then pushed it away. "Don't let me have any more."

A moment later, our dinner had arrived. On his plate were four chicken breasts and steamed broccoli. He said, "Dig in."

My dish was something cheesy and saucy. The smell made me sick to my stomach. Chris was unperturbed. He sliced a grilled chicken breast into neat little rows, speared the meat, and placed it into his mouth. He had never been much of a foodie. His meals consisted of hamburger, chicken, steak, French fries, pasta, the occasional salad, and green beans. The broccoli on his plate was a first in my memory. I picked up my water glass and sipped.

"Want any of this?" he asked, pointing to his plate.

"I'm fine. You want any of mine?"

"Nah, it looks a little . . . white."

"It does." I played with the strings of mozzarella.

"Not hungry?"

"I'm fine." I ate a bit just to prove it to him. "Good."

"There's no punishment if you don't clean your plate." He regarded my face. I'm sure I looked as shaken as I felt. "Stop fretting. There won't be a repeat. You don't have to worry."

I put down my fork. "Whatever Devek is, he's the father of my children."

"I know that too well." He pushed my wineglass toward me. "You're pale. Have a sip."

I did as he ordered and watched him eat. Finally, I said, "You never came back to India?"

"Nope. I hired people to look after you, to make sure you were okay. But that place is nothing but bad memories."

"I agree with you there." I paused. "I'm sure that's cold comfort."

He polished off a chicken breast and put down his utensils. "When I came back home, I was still furious at you. And I was humiliated . . . that I couldn't even do the one thing that I was always good at. But more than anything, I was really depressed. I could have tried again. I knew I would have gotten it right the second time. But I also knew that it wasn't a smart move. I had all this emotion and no way to let it out. So I acted the way most angry, humiliated, and depressed men do. I went for chemical relief. I was already drinking a lot. It numbed me a little, but it wasn't enough." A shrug. "Heroin is a great drug. I went from not being able to get out of bed in the morning to 'Life ain't so bad, I can handle this.'"

I drained my wineglass.

He said, "This country is never going to solve the opiate crisis. I had a lot going for me and I succumbed. Poor people with shit lives . . . why shouldn't they escape?" He gave me some of his broccoli. "You like veggies. Eat something, angel."

I picked up a floret and nibbled at the buds. He picked up his flatware and ate another breast, followed it up with forkfuls of broccoli.

He said, "It wasn't my first rodeo with the hard stuff. I had experimented in high school with all sorts of shit. Then, after you left me the first time, I went full force. I was upset about being dumped, but it wasn't just you. It was also being under Joey's thumb. It was being married to Maria. It was shooting people. I just couldn't cope."

"I'm sorry."

"It's in the past," he told me. "I don't think about it much. All I'm saying is the shit helped me get over the hump twice. Second time I used it, after you left me, I was developing this place and the drug gave me peace of mind to work. Not optimally, but I could concentrate enough to get my enterprise off the ground. Talia was helping with the details. She kept me on track. And she was also convenient."

I didn't say anything.

He said, "She wasn't the only one, Terry. Not by a long shot. I was thirty-four. I was in good shape physically . . . Well, maybe my liver wasn't so hot. But I had anger to dispel and I had *energy*. I was fucking everything in sight. Two, three, four times a day, weekends even more. Threesomes, foursomes, orgies, every kind of fantasy I could create. Girls and guys, I didn't care." He looked at me. "I love women, but sometimes a great blow job from a cute guy is just primo. Men know what feels good."

I stared at him. "Did you always feel that way? About men?"

He shrugged. "Does it bother you?"

"I dunno." I picked up my fork and put it down. "I just never . . . realized."

"My first experiences were with men."

I nodded.

He said, "Terry, my love, I'm not homosexual, I'm not heterosexual, I'm not bisexual. I'm just sexual. I'll screw anything. And back then, I certainly did. That much fucking . . ." He took a bite of his chicken. "Even at thirty-four . . . you need help. I was taking a lot of little blue pills along with shooting up. Then, one day, I woke up horny and realized I couldn't get a hard-on." He finished a third chicken breast, then pushed his plate away. "This was about four, maybe five years ago. I'd say approaching forty was my midlife crisis, but my life has always been one crisis after another. Whatever it was, I knew I had to change. All that debauchery took its toll. I was an addict, an alcoholic, and a fat-ass to boot. I was around fifty pounds overweight. It took about six months, but I finally got off the shit. I stopped smoking; I cut down on my drinking. I told Talia it was over personally and started exclusively paying for it, which slowed me down sexually. I began to eat right and exercise something other than my dick, and the weight came off. That's when I started concentrating on work. I turned it around."

I managed a smile. "Good for you."

"I wasn't happy exactly . . . more like calm." Quoting me. Then he grinned. "And God rewarded me by fucking up your life."

That was the Chris Donatti I knew. "My life certainly did get fucked up."

"Hey." He picked up my chin and stared until my eyes met his. "I dropped everything and came to you when Gabe called."

"Yes, you did." I leaned over the table and tucked white hair behind his ear. "Thank you for saving my life. And thank you for saving Juleen's life. I'm sure she's a sore spot for you."

"I don't hold it against her. Plus, it helps that she looks like you." He paused. "I will do everything I can to get your son back." He took my left hand, played with my engagement ring, and then he kissed it. "You want dessert?"

"I'm okay."

"Do you want to go back?"

"Please."

He peered at me with his intense blue eyes. "You okay?"

"I'm fine." I gave him a weak smile. "Thank you very much for dinner."

"You're welcome. Can I see you again sometime?" I tried another smile. He shook his head, stood up, and tousled my hair. "Terry, my love, don't look so scared. It was over a decade ago. I'm assuming that Devek is still alive." He pulled out my chair and helped me up. "And if the man's heart is no longer beating, I had nothing to do with it."

CHAPTER 19

DECKER WOKE UP with the sun, mainly because the curtains in his room were threadbare. He showered, he shaved, then he went down to the lounge for a cup of coffee. McAdams was already there, his breakfast consisting of toast, juice, and a mug of java. He was reading the *Wall Street Journal.* When he didn't look up, Decker said, "Good morning."

He put down the paper. "You have a very light step."

"Years of sneaking up on criminals." Decker sat down. "You're up early."

"The window faces east and the place doesn't provide you with eye masks."

"Yeah, I could have used one of those this morning," Decker said. "I'm hungry."

"They don't have much of a kitchen, but they do have bagels."

The server came up, a woman in her sixties with a gray pageboy framing her face. "Good morning. I'm Sandra. Coffee and OJ?"

"That would be great," Decker said.

"And we have toast, muffins, croissants, and bagels."

"Bagel, please."

"Plain, onion, or cinnamon raisin?"

"Cinnamon raisin."

"Toasted?"

"Sure."

"Butter or cream cheese or both?"

"Cream cheese."

When she left, Decker said, "Too many choices this early."

McAdams smiled. "What's the plan, boss?"

"I want to go back to the bar now that it's daylight and poke around the area."

"Businesses that are open during the day aren't usually open at night. I'm sure no one saw or heard anything. And if they did, how well are they going to remember something from three months ago?"

"We can check for CCTV. Also, let's retrace several routes from the bar to Elsie's place to see if we can find anything."

McAdams was perplexed. "You mean like a crime scene?"

"That would be the best-case scenario. Worst-case scenario would be spending hours looking and finding nothing."

The server was back with food and drink. She filled up the coffee cups and put the pot on the table. "I'll just leave this here."

"Thank you." Decker took a sip of coffee. Next, he slathered cream cheese on his bagel and took a bite. "This is my thinking. Baer wouldn't have done anything to Pauline in the commercial area. Too many people around. Plus, the town's sidewalks are very well lit and there's CCTV. But if they were walking back to Elsie's, they might have been using residential streets. Baer would have had the cover of darkness."

"Neighbors can hear or see things. And there's CCTV in residential areas too."

"So maybe they cut across a park or empty field somewhere. Plus, the neighborhood backs up to forest."

"If Baer killed Pauline on the way to Elsie's house, why is there so much blood there?"

"I'm thinking just the opposite. If Baer stabbed her at Elsie's, why isn't there more blood?" Decker said. "Maybe he stabbed her on the way back. Somehow she made it to Elsie's and she bled out."

"Or maybe they took the argument back to Elsie's house and that's where he did it. Or maybe he had nothing to do with it."

"You're absolutely right." Decker finished his bagel in five bites. "Any of those things might have happened. But we've established a link between Pauline and Baer. Let's just hunt around a little more."

Sandra was back. "Another bagel?"

"Yeah, actually, that would be great."

"And you, sir?" Looking at McAdams.

"I'm fine, thanks."

She left, and Decker said, "Never made sense to me, that whatever happened in Elsie's house was an accident. There was no attempt to take Pauline to a hospital."

McAdams said, "If we're thinking about Brock Baer as the bad guy, then why would we think Bertram was involved at all?"

Decker said, "Maybe he wasn't involved in the murder. But maybe after Pauline was killed, Elsie panicked and enlisted Bertram's help to escape to Germany."

"If Baer killed Pauline," McAdams said, "why didn't he kill Elsie also?"

"Maybe she got away before he could do it. She fled, and when she thought she was safe, she called Bertram and asked him for help."

"How would this go down?" McAdams asked. "Baer comes to Elsie's house with Pauline, whom he just stabbed. Elsie panics and jumps in her car and flees? And he doesn't go after her?"

"Maybe Baer didn't have a car."

McAdams said, "Why would Baer go back to Elsie's house with Pauline if he had just stabbed her?"

Decker thought a moment. "Maybe he dumped her outside, and Elsie found her and took her into the house. What if Pauline died a few minutes later, and Elsie panicked and fled?"

"Instead of calling 911?" McAdams made a face. "The only reason Elsie wouldn't call 911 was if she was involved."

"Or if Baer scared her," Decker said. "Maybe he kidnapped her and forced her to help him bury her."

"If Baer forced Elsie to help him bury Pauline, they'd need a car. Elsie's car has been gone over forensically. No blood was found."

"Then we're back to Pauline's car," Decker said. "We know from witnesses that they were arguing in the bars. What if they continued the argument while they were driving back to Elsie's house?"

"Who was driving?"

"If we're assuming that they had Pauline's car, let's say she was driving. The argument gets heated. She pulls over—maybe she tries to kick him out, maybe she leaves the car in a huff, maybe she even leaves out of fear. He follows her, stabs her, and puts her back in the car. Then he takes her to Elsie's."

"Why?" McAdams said. "Why not leave her there to die? And why choose to bury Pauline three hours away?"

"Somebody doesn't want the body anywhere near Baniff."

"Then what?" McAdams asked. "Pauline dies and Baer convinces Elsie to help him bury her three hours away? I think if I were Baer, I would have just killed Elsie too."

Decker said, "What if eventually Baer did kill Elsie?"

"Then why was Elsie's car found near Pauline's grave site?" McAdams said. "And what does that have to do with Bertram Lanz?"

"We obviously don't have all the pieces yet," Decker said.

"I don't think we have enough of the puzzle to know that there are pieces missing."

Decker said, "We do know that after Pauline was murdered, Elsie picked up Kathrine Taylor in her car. Why would Elsie do that unless Bertram was involved?"

"Okay, let's run with that," McAdams said. "Baer brings Pauline to Elsie's house. Elsie panics and escapes. She comes back a few days later, gets her car, and then she calls Bertram and asks for help. They decide to meet up at the diner. And as a reward for helping her escape, Elsie picks up Kathrine Taylor for him and they all three take off for Germany."

"It would explain why Elsie waited a few days to retrieve Bertram from the diner."

"But, Deck, why would Elsie ditch her car in the woods? And how would she get from the diner to wherever she was going? She'd need another vehicle, since Bertram didn't drive. And why is Pauline's body buried in Greenbury if she was murdered in Baniff? And if it was Baer who murdered Pauline, why wouldn't Elsie just call 911 . . . tell the police what happened?"

"Very good questions, Harvard. I have no answers. Let's just hang around. I'm sure it will amount to nothing, but we're here, so why not." Decker wrapped the second bagel in a paper napkin. "I'll save this for later. Sooner we get to it, the sooner we can leave. Ready?"

"Sure." McAdams left a twenty on the table as a tip, and the two of them took off.

THE FIRST THING they looked for were closed-circuit cameras. There were two of them at the Mule: front and back entrances. The rear door's CCTV was broken. The front camera was operable and did record, but the disc had been erased a month ago. Washout there.

Not a lot of cameras in the immediate area. Those that existed yielded nothing. It was the same refrain: either the equipment was broken or malfunctioning, or the tapes or CD had been erased or changed out.

If you would have come sooner . . .

"What now?" McAdams asked.

Decker was clearly running out of options. "I want to check the main road between Tobacco's Road and Elsie's place and see if we can find evidence of a struggle."

"A struggle that's months old."

"I'm sure we won't find anything, Tyler. It's a long shot. But let's try."

They went back to the last place where Pauline and Baer had been seen together. There, they consulted the map and began on foot along the two-lane motorway that was the most direct route from the bar to Elsie Schulung's house. No sidewalks, with greenery on either side of the asphalt trail. The planting was thick with shrubbery and trees, providing a barrier for the residential areas behind the road. The street wasn't that busy, but it wasn't devoid of cars either.

McAdams tripped on a tree root but caught his balance. He was constantly looking down because the ground's detritus—leaves, rocks, and dirt—hid lots of things. "If a bear shits in the woods, odds are I'll step on it." A pause. "What are we looking for?"

"Can't tell you, but if I see it, I'll know it."

"That makes one of us. It's getting hot."

"You'll survive," Decker said.

"Someone's grumpy."

"Someone is constantly complaining about an hour round-trip walk," Decker said. "Count it as your daily exercise." His eyes were constantly scanning the area as well as sweeping over the ground. He took out his phone.

McAdams asked, "Who are you calling?"

"Quay." The line connected and the sergeant answered on the third ring. Decker put the phone on speaker so McAdams could hear. "Hey, it's Pete Decker here."

"Hey, Pete. What's up?"

"We're leaving soon."

"Find anything?"

"Nah, not really," Decker said. "Did the BOLO go out this morning for Brock Baer?"

"Put it in as soon as I got here."

"Great," Decker said. "From my records and research, it doesn't appear that Baer owns a car. Can you double-check for me?"

"Checked this morning. He has a driver's license with an old address in the Philadelphia area. I couldn't find any registered vehicle assigned to him. But he could be living anywhere and could be driving anything."

"One of Baer's former girlfriends lives in Albuquerque. Maybe we should call the local police and see if his name sounds familiar to them."

"Sure, you can do that," Quay said. "Let me know if you come up with anything."

Passing the buck to him. Or maybe not. Pauline's body was in his jurisdiction. Decker said, "Will do." He hung up, and then he stopped walking. "Regarding Pauline Corbett's car . . . any news on that?"

"If there was recent news, you'd know about it," McAdams said. "A BOLO went out for Corbett's vehicle when Elsie went missing. If Brock Baer is using the car, there haven't been any sightings of the vehicle."

"Do we know that for sure?"

"No official has called us."

"We're a small town," Decker said. "We don't have access to current databases that the big cities have."

"What are you talking about?" McAdams asked. "You don't think the BOLO went out nationwide?"

"No, I'm sure it did, but there are better ways to capture the license plate info," Decker said. "Most major cities have automated license plate readers on the back of their patrol cars. It's a camera, like a tollbooth camera or a red-light camera, that uploads thousands of license plates that pass in front of the lens. When police see a vehicle that they think is suspect, if they are equipped with ALPRs, the suspected plate number can be uploaded and run through the database, which will spit back info about the car in seconds. Furthermore, if they are hooked up to the system and the patrol car cameras happen to scan a vehicle in the database, the system will alert the officers. Then they can act on the information."

McAdams regarded Decker. "You're just telling me about this *now*?"

"First of all, it's a newer technology, ten to fifteen years old. Secondly, the database isn't a governmental system like CODIS or AFIS. Big-city departments usually contract out to private companies who can accommodate that much information. We're talking thousands of cars in a day. Certainly, our little department is too small to pay for something like that, mainly because we're low crime and we don't need that much information. I suspect it's the same with Baniff. But Philadelphia is a big city. Let me call Cindy and see if the city has ALPRs on their patrol cars. Maybe I can have her enter Pauline's plates in the system."

"That would be helpful." McAdams paused midstride. Then he said, "Don't you think that Baer, if he was using Pauline's car, would change the plates?"

"Maybe. But guys like him are usually lazy. Let's at least get the plates into the system. The companies that own the databases also store info about tollbooth cameras, and there are a lot of tollbooths in this area. Maybe Baer went through a tollbooth in Pauline's car before he changed plates."

McAdams said, "It's a good idea."

"Thank you." Decker took a deep breath and let it out. "I'll call Cindy when I get back. Also, you call Kev. Ask him to start contacting tollbooths from Baniff to Greenbury and see if we can take a peek at their cameras. Elsie Schulung lived here; she'd know how to avoid the cameras. But Baer is not from this area and just might not be so clever."

"Okay." McAdams sighed.

"I know," Decker said. "It's hot and we're not finding anything. We're almost at Elsie's place. Let's just finish up there."

"Sure," McAdams said.

When they arrived at Elsie's, Decker said, "Thanks for putting up with my crazy ideas."

"No stone unturned," McAdams said. "Want to cross over and look at the other side of the road?"

"No, I want to retrace our steps on the same side and look again. If they pulled over it would be on the right side going to Elsie's house. Keep your eyes on the ground, Tyler. Your eyesight is better than mine."

McAdams paused. "What am I looking for exactly?"

Decker said, "Old dried blood that hopefully hasn't been washed away."

"Or a knife?"

"That would be too lucky."

McAdams said, "Got my eyes glued to my feet."

They walked for ten minutes in silence, looking up and down and sideways. The earth did not give up her secrets happily. As they were nearing the finish line, under the protective canopy of a big oak, McAdams felt something wet and squishy underfoot, something that caused his heel to slide forward. "Damn it. I think I stepped in shit!" He stopped and looked at the underside of his right shoe, the sole covered in brown. "Damn!"

Decker was about twenty paces ahead. "Just wipe it off on the ground."

It smelled, but not the smell he expected. More like metallic. McAdams took off his sunglasses. The color was more reddish brown than turd brown. "Peter?"

Decker stopped and pivoted around. McAdams rarely called him by his first name. "What is it? What'd you find?"

McAdams said, "Not sure, but I may have just stepped in your evidence."

WITHIN AN HOUR, the spot was crawling with officials from Baniff. Already found, before any cars pulled up, was some rust-stained clothing that leaked liquid of the same color. The discarded apparel appeared to be a shirt. Hard to tell whether it belonged to a man or a woman. A few yards away was a hunting knife, the blade discolored with spots and blotches. Lady Luck had kissed the ground. No bodies found, but the area was still being searched.

To McAdams, Quay said, "I thought you were leaving."

"When the boss gets an idea into his head, there's no stopping him." McAdams looked at Decker, who was ten yards away, meticulously searching the ground. "Turns out we found something. Not sure what, but it is something."

Quay squinted into the sunlight. "Could be irrelevant to your case."

"True, but how much crime do you get here?" McAdams was annoyed. "We were searching here because Decker figured that Baer and Pauline might have been walking back to Elsie's house. They'd been arguing before; maybe they were still arguing. Maybe it got heated. Maybe he stabbed her and then dumped the knife."

"He takes off her clothes here but buries the body three hours away?"

"Don't have an answer for that," McAdams said. "We've got a shirt, Sergeant. It could be his shirt. It could be anyone's shirt. We'll just have to wait for the forensics on what we found."

Quay said, "That's going to take a while. We don't have a lab here." A pause. "Do you have a lab?"

"Not in-house. We send the information out to the next town over. It's a referral center for all the smaller towns around it. And yes, it takes a while for us too."

Decker came back. "We need more evidence bags. We found a ton of stuff: cigarette butts, soda cans, beer cans, food wrappers, water bottles—"

"You're not going to turn all that in for processing," Quay said.

Decker stared at him. "There is a potential crime scene. Everything needs to be collected." He looked around. The sun was rising to its full height and the temperature was climbing to triple digits. "The first thing we'll do is process the knife and shirt for DNA."

"Whose DNA?" Quay asked. "Pauline, Elsie, or Baer?"

"We have a profile on all three of them. Well, I don't have Baer's profile, but he's a felon, so he's bound to be in CODIS. All we need is a match."

McAdams said, "The sergeant was just saying that the labs he uses don't process any faster than the labs we use."

"Then we'll wait," Decker said. "In the meantime, there are other things I can do."

"You know, if this is Pauline's blood . . ." Quay shuffled his feet. "Then the murder happened in our jurisdiction."

Decker stared at him. "Jake, you're not going to get all territorial on me."

"It's not me, it's my captain, Decker. I know him. He hates anyone coming into his city and telling him what to do."

Decker cursed internally. "Is he coming out here . . . to look at the evidence? I'd like to meet him. Maybe explain my situation."

"He's on vacation for the next two weeks, but I'll have to let him know what's going on."

"Look, Jake, until we know that this is Pauline's blood, her death is in our jurisdiction. Her murder is our case. And even if it turns out to be Pauline's blood on the knife, no one knows exactly where and when she died. It behooves us to have cooperation between the teams. If your captain is that protective, can you do me a favor and hold off on notifying him?"

Quay shuffled his feet again. "How long?"

"A week?"

"If he finds out I went a week without telling him about this, he'll have a shit fit."

"How long can you give me?"

"What day of the week is it? Wednesday?"

"Yeah."

"How about if I tell him next Monday morning? That's almost a week, but it's over the weekend."

"That's fine," Decker said. "I appreciate it."

"Yeah, sure . . ." Quay's phone buzzed. "Excuse me." He walked off.

McAdams said, "I don't know about that guy. If it's Pauline's blood on the knife, we may be booted."

"But the thing is, Harvard, we have the body."

McAdams gave him a double thumbs-up.

"Damn right," Decker said. "This time, I'm not going down without a fight. To these silly turf wars, I say may the best man win."

CHAPTER 20

NO MATTER WHAT he did or where he went, Chris always wore his wedding ring. Even now, though we weren't married yet, it was a constant companion. He used to play with it all the time, twirl it around his finger, so much so that I once asked him if it was too tight. He said no, he just liked to touch it. It tethered him. Otherwise he felt he'd drift away. I thought it was his way of telling me how much he needed me. He had needed me, but not in a healthy way. I had always been his emotional rainy-day account, something to dip into when things went haywire. It was a tiring, thankless role. And it took me a while to learn that things were never going to change.

Unless you've been there, it's very hard to imagine what it's like to live with an abusive partner. All the things that people tell you to do, all the things you tell yourself to do. Just put your foot down. Just leave him. Just divorce him. Just shoot the bastard. It was a little more complicated than that, especially because Chris's controlling behavior wasn't typical. He didn't check my phone or constantly ask where I was going or who I'd been with. He gave me *just* enough freedom for me to think I'd be okay. Until I wasn't.

The first time I left Chris, I was seventeen and pregnant. After my father and stepmother kicked me out of the house, I knew I was headed for destitution until my late mother's parents—my grandparents—offered to take me in. I don't know what I would have done without them, although I would soon find out. For eighteen months, I was riding high. I had free babysitting while I was in school, I had food and shelter, I had warmth in the winter. When they decided to move to Florida to a retirement home, I didn't dare stand in their way. They were older, and dealing with me and an infant had been difficult for them. Still, they asked me all the time if I'd be okay. I said I'd be fine.

I wasn't fine. I tried to stay in college, but eventually I had to drop out and work to support my son and myself. I wasn't qualified to do much at twenty, and getting a babysitter for Gabe was not financially feasible. I finally found a job at a twenty-four-hour diner with a very kind boss who allowed me to waitress at night and bring Gabriel with me. There was a crib next to the dishwasher, and I think the constant swishing acted as white noise. Thank God he was a good sleeper. Most of the customers were decent, some were scuzzy, and a few were downright creepy. The work was grueling, and the hours were long. I spent a lot of time there. I made friends with other waitresses, some who let me know that there were less arduous ways to get quick cash.

Especially with a face like yours.

I was never tempted.

When Chris found me, Gabe and I were living in a cold-water studio in the middle of winter in Chicago. He took us to a hotel and up to his suite. He fed us dinner. Then he had rough sex with me in the bedroom while Gabe watched cartoons in the living room. I figured he got his revenge and that was that. No one was as surprised as I was when he showed up the next day and told me to pack my bags.

He moved us into a two-bedroom apartment. It had heat. It had actual hot water. It had a shower that worked. The refrigerator was big enough to actually hold food. There was real furniture. It even had a piano for our son. He gave me money for food and proper clothing. He paid for my college tuition. He paid for a babysitter. In exchange, all I had to do was give him sex on demand. He was separated from his wife at the time. A few months later, his marriage had been officially annulled because his wife couldn't bear children. Later, when she remarried, she had four kids. But at the time it was Chris with the child, so it couldn't have possibly been his fault that a baby had never been conceived.

After college and medical school, he said he wanted to get married. I told him it wasn't necessary, but he insisted. He wanted to make it official. He said it tethered him. We were married in a church, and I moved to New York to be with him. It was our first time living together, and that was when the trouble started.

Being with a controlling man . . . you get so used to it that it seems normal. And you do a lot of rationalization, which is a fancy word for lying to yourself. *Yes, he's having sex with other women—and men, as it turns out—but he doesn't really care about those people. Yes, he's cruel and heartless, but only when he's drunk or stoned or angry or frustrated or jealous . . . or maybe it's because the sun is in the wrong astrological sign. Look at all the good stuff he does. He supports you, he gives you money, he pays for your schooling.* And, stupid person that you are, you convince yourself that it's okay.

At least, he doesn't beat me up.

Until he did.

The kicker was that when I started the dalliance with Devek, I wasn't in a bad place. Chris was gone a lot, working on a grandiose plan to develop a super-brothel in Nevada, which I thought was a very stupid idea. Shows you what I knew. But I never voiced any opinions on his plans, and he never asked me what I thought. It was his life and his money, and at least he wasn't killing people. Plus, it had the added benefit of keeping him away from me and Gabe for stretches at a time. When he came home, he'd still want lots of sex, but that was okay with me. He was really good in bed and anxious to please when he was sober.

Then Devek came along. Devek was attentive. Devek was sweet. Devek was smart. Devek was funny. Devek was a doctor. I said to myself, *I deserve a man like this.* Okay, he wasn't great in bed. Okay, he wasn't very exciting. Okay, he wasn't good-looking. But look what great in bed, exciting, and good-looking got me.

Then I found out I was pregnant. Luckily Chris mistook my half sister's abortion papers—an abortion that I had paid for—as my abortion papers. He thought I had gotten rid of *his* baby. I had no idea what he would have done had he known the truth. He beat me up because he thought I didn't want his child. Backhanded me hard across the face, two or three times. Not nearly as bad as what I had just gone through, but I had black eyes, cuts on my cheeks from his ring, and a bruised face. He might have done more, but then Gabe came in. That stopped Chris in his tracks. He stormed out. Later, he was dog-faced apologetic. He swore he'd never do it again. He begged me to come back to him.

I told him I'd think about it. Then I fled.

Luckily, he didn't discover the truth until after I had escaped with Devek to India. We got divorced and I got remarried. I had left Gabe, who was almost fourteen, with the Deckers, figuring after a year or two, I could bring him back to live with me. A couple of problems with that: Devek didn't want him, and Chris wouldn't have ever let him go. So I abandoned my son, something for which I had yet to forgive myself. I never forgave Devek for being so cold to Gabe the few times he came to visit me. It made it much easier to leave him and come back to the States.

Once I decided to leave Devek, things didn't go as planned. They never do. I expected a bad custody battle, but I never expected to wind up in a hospital with broken bones and with Chris not only nursing me back to health, but protecting Juleen. Eleven years later, I was back where I started. Recovering from a brutal walloping and without a son. But at least I had a place for my daughter and me . . . time to think. As long as I acceded to Chris's wishes, I'd be okay. In a couple of months, I'd be in my own house with my kids, divorced from Devek, and away from Chris for the most part. I'd be working as a doctor. I'd be living a quiet and normal life.

Ergo, if he wanted me to go to his stupid party and be his pretty, devoted prop while he cavorted with his staff, I'd do it with a smile. Chris was the key to retrieving my son. There was a better future in the distance.

If I could just hang on a little longer.

If . . .

AT SIX IN the morning, Decker smelled the coffee. He reached over to Rina's side of the bed and it was still warm, her smell filling the bedroom with all that was good. He showered, shaved, dressed, and walked into the kitchen just as the toast popped out.

"God, it's great to have you home," he told her.

"It's really good to be home." She gave him a smack on the lips. "Sit down. Coffee's ready."

"How about if you sit down, and I'll serve you?"

"Even better." Rina sat. She had her hair pulled back into a pony-tail. This morning, she wore a lightweight ecru linen blouse and denim skirt. Comfortable clothes. It was hot outside. Slippers were still on her feet. "I missed you."

"I guarantee it was not as much as I missed you." He poured her coffee and buttered the toast. "My outlook is definitely rosier now that you're back." He took the food and drink to the table and sat opposite her. "But I'm glad you saw your mom. I'm sure it made her very happy."

"It did. Her caretakers are very nice but very gabby."

"Did they get on your nerves?"

"You know . . . they take such good care of her, I don't mind. And she seems to like them. I can't believe your mom is so independent."

"Too stubborn to need help. Except when she does." Decker sipped his coffee. "Thanks so much for going to her medical appointments. I hope it wasn't too much trouble."

"Once she got the news that everything was benign, she was a different person."

"I'm sure."

Rina was smiling. "You should have seen the four of us—Blossom, my mom, your mom, and me—going to the market. Oh my God. The mothers stopping in front of every single item on the shelves, discussing its merits and detriments. It took us over an hour for a routine trip, and that's not counting loading and unloading time. And I don't mean groceries. I mean them."

"You are a patient person."

"Actually, Blossom and I work well together." She dumped cream in her coffee. "I know they're old and that can be challenging sometimes. But really, it's a privilege still having them around."

"I'm sure they loved your company." Decker took a bite of toast. "Personally, I'm thrilled that you're back. And Tyler is as well. He missed your dinners. He missed your sandwiches for the road."

"Nice to be appreciated." Rina got up, washed her hands, and said the ritual blessing over the bread. Then she took a bite and sat back down. "So, tell me about Brock Baer."

"Nothing's changed since the car ride home last night. He's a strong person of interest, but that doesn't mean that Elsie Schulung has been taken off our list of suspects. I need to talk to her. But first I have to find her . . . if she's still alive."

"Are you still searching for a body?"

"I don't have any reason to allocate people for that yet. Maybe when DNA results come back from the knife and shirt, we'll have more to work with. We're hoping to get them by next week, but I suspect it might take longer. We're testing for Pauline's blood, for Elsie's blood, and also for Baer's blood. If he stabbed the women, maybe the knife slipped in his hand and he cut himself."

"Did you find any mixed blood at Elsie's house?"

"I don't know. Baniff did all the testing. From what I've been told, it was Pauline's blood only."

"Any theories?" Rina asked.

Decker shrugged. "Baer stabbed her and he took her to Elsie's house. She died there and then Baer forced Elsie to help bury her. But that doesn't make a lot of sense because Pauline was buried three hours from Elsie's house."

"Near the diner."

"Yes. I'm just trying to figure out why Elsie or Baer would bury her so far away."

"They didn't want her body associated with Baniff."

"Still, you take a chance . . . carrying a corpse so far away."

"I agree. But I don't think it's a coincidence that Bertram went missing so close to the burial spot."

"Absolutely." Decker refilled Rina's mug with coffee. "The investigation is kind of on hold until we get the DNA back."

"But you're actively looking for Baer."

"Yes. He and Pauline got into a massive fight right around the time that Elsie and Pauline went missing. If there's Baer's DNA in the blood we found, then we have a compelling case against him."

"And you think that Elsie's dead?"

"Maybe."

"I thought you figured that Elsie was in Germany with Bertram and Kathrine."

"That's also possible. I've called Bertram's parents' secretary no fewer than five times. I've called their local police two or three times. It would certainly be helpful to know if Elsie was or still is there. Then I don't have to search for another body."

"It's odd that no one is calling you back, especially the local police."

Decker shrugged. "I'll keep trying."

"How does Bertram Lanz fit in?"

"Maybe Elsie called him to help her escape. Or maybe he was a witness to the murder." Decker took another sip of coffee. "In the meantime, McAdams and I will be back to righting tipped mailboxes and recovering lost pets."

"Bringing a dog or cat back to its family can be very meaningful."

"You're not kidding." He smiled. "Animal owners can be the most grateful people on earth. They love their pets." He squeezed her hand. "Good to have you home."

She said, "Barbecue tonight?"

"I'd love it. So would Tyler. Unless you'd rather be alone."

"No, Tyler can come. He's like a fixture here at dinner." She gave him a smile across the table. "You know, we're alone now."

Decker smiled back. "Yes, we are indeed." He stood up and wiped his mouth. "I guess that stranded cat is gonna have to wait."

CHAPTER 21

A WEEK BEFORE THE party, I got my cast off. It had been six weeks and my fracture had healed and I felt liberated, as if the beating were a distant memory and times ahead were bound to be better. Hope is like that. No matter how bad things get, it's always tucked away in a back pocket.

The night of the bash, I noticed that the dresses that Chris had bought me were tighter. I had put on weight, but I had also gotten some of my curves back and that wasn't a bad thing at all. The black number I decided to wear was all silk and sequins with a boatneck front, a plunging back, and a very short skirt. I shimmied when I walked and reflected any illumination that came my way. Chris was too busy to do my hair and makeup, so I did both myself. I looked older—crow's feet and smile lines were visible—but I was less painted. More like myself and less like one of his girls. Chris was also too busy to walk me over to the lounge. That job was entrusted to one of his bodyguards, Jorge, who was medium-size but packed guns both muscle-wise and weapon-wise.

When he pulled the lounge door open, the space looked like an updated high school prom. Lights and streamers all over the place, a full band playing loud music, several bars, lots of conversation and laughter, servers passing out copious amounts of drinks and food. Chris had told me to come at around eleven, but by that time, it appeared that the party had been in full swing for hours.

My heart started racing.

It wasn't that I was shy. I could make conversation with people. I did it all the time as an ER doctor. People came in with unknown disorders, and you had to know how to draw out information. But this was different. I was on my own, but I couldn't be myself. I had a role to play, but I wasn't sure what it was.

Chris was on the dance floor with women around him, gyrating and junking with multiple partners to the beat of something thumping and bass-heavy. It was a big mass of bodies, flesh against flesh in a free-for-all freak boogie. I'm sure Chris noticed me when I came in—his eyes were never far away from the entrance of any building—but he made no attempt to welcome me. That was expected. That he'd leave me to flounder took me by surprise. He knew I had no idea where to go or what to do. I suspected he was relishing my discomfort. I knew that although he had forgiven me, there was still lots of stray anger.

Okay, I said to myself. *You have all your bones intact and your face doesn't look like grape jelly. Keep your eye on the prize.* With my head and body erect, I scanned the room for somewhere to sit. Suddenly an arm hooked around mine. It was Brie. She was clearly tipsy, but she was also a familiar face and that grounded me. She had squeezed her formidable body into a gold sheath minidress. She bumped her hip with mine.

"Wanna dance?"

"Maybe a little later." I looked around. "Where are you sitting?"

"Wherever I can find a *lap*." She broke into giggles.

"Uh, that wouldn't work for me."

She giggled again. "Why not? The boss is having fun. So should you."

"I like your reasoning, but maybe I should sit first and find out what the boss wants."

"Good thinking. Men get so weird sometimes."

"Honey, that is the truth."

A server came up with a tray of champagne. Brie took two flutes and gave me one. "C'mon. What's a party without the bubbly?"

"Thanks." I took a sip. "I love your 'fit."

"You think?"

"Yeah. Your body looks killer in it."

"Aw, too kind, too kind." She squeezed my arm tighter. "I like you. You're not stuck-up like that other cunt."

"Which other cunt are we talking about?"

"Her!" She cocked her head in Chris's direction. He was freaking with Talia.

I said, "She was a cunt?"

"God, she was the worst! Everyone was happy when he dumped her sorry ass." She turned and smiled at me. "And now you got the ring, so hahaha."

I smiled. "Thank you."

"Sure you don't want to dance?"

"No thanks." I smiled again.

Just then a panicked Jorge took my elbow. "Sorry, Doctor. This way."

I held up my glass to Brie. She did the same. We did an air toast. Jorge and I wended through the throng until he deposited me at a table. He said, "I'll be right behind you if you need anything, Doctor."

"I'm fine." Jorge was pale. I said, "Are you all right?"

"I just thought I lost you. The boss would kill me."

"I would never let that happen," I told him.

Jorge smiled at me. First time ever. I sat with my bubbly and watched Chris do his thing, reliving high school all over again.

When I first broke up with him, before the first time I *really* broke up with him . . . I was still a teenager in love with him, and every time I tried to approach him to make amends for our rift, he used the opportunity to make out with his girlfriend.

Just to spite me.

Which in retrospect was weird, because Chris wasn't into kissing. As we went further in our relationship, I came to realize that whenever he kissed me repeatedly, whenever he was romantic, he was feeling insecure.

I felt a presence, looked up, and saw Mike Badger standing in front of my table. I said, "Have a seat."

He sat. "You're not joining the festivities?" A smirk. "Or is he calling the shots?"

I turned my head and looked into his eyes. "Are you going for round two, Badger, or are you going to be nice to me?"

He looked down. "Yeah, I'm kind of an asswipe."

I smiled.

"But I can get away with it because I'm so good-looking and I have such a sparkling personality."

I laughed. "I'm curious, Mike. Why'd you give up medicine?"

"Way more money in real estate." A pause. "And women like money."

"Do you miss it? I mean, all that talent and training. I'm sure it was hard to make the change."

"It was. Sometimes I do miss it."

"Nice to do something for humanity, huh?"

He stared at me. "You are very easy to talk to."

"Thank you." I looked at Jorge. "Could you get Mr. Badger a glass of champagne?"

"I'm not supposed to leave you, Doctor."

Badger stood. "I'll get it. Would you like anything . . . what should I call you?"

"Terry is fine, and I wouldn't mind a club soda."

"Sure."

I turned back to Jorge. I had to shout to be heard. "Would you like something to drink?"

"I'm fine, ma'am."

Badger regarded my face. "You're a beautiful woman. Not being flirtatious. Just a statement of fact."

"Thank you." My eyes returned to the dance floor. Suddenly Chris's eyes were steely. They shot me a glance. I looked away and thought, *Really? Mike Badger? Seriously?*

Badger said, "I'll be right back."

"Take your time," I told him. "I'm not going anywhere."

After he left, I watched my fiancé. He was dancing with two girls and a guy, his long limbs moving gracefully. His face was flushed and his eyes were bright. He was enjoying himself.

Another presence at my table. The man was maybe ten years older than me. Slim build. Dark hair speckled with gray. Brown eyes. Maybe six feet. He was wearing good-quality clothes. And he was nice-looking. He said, "Mind if I sit?"

I should have told him no. I heard myself say, "Not at all."

"I don't think I've ever seen you before."

I held out a hand. "Terry McLaughlin. I'm Mr. Donatti's fiancée."

"Bard Fenton." He shook my hand with a quick eye on my ring finger. "Mr. Donatti has good taste."

"The ring is a good one."

"I wasn't talking about the jewelry."

I smiled. "Thank you, Bard." I was shouting above the noise. "Can I call you Bard?"

"You can call me anything you want," he shouted back. "How'd you meet Chris?"

"We went to high school together."

"Really? High school sweethearts?"

"Something like that."

"That's enigmatic."

"Sometimes less is more." God, the din was loud.

Badger was back. He set down my club soda and took the seat next to me. He looked at Bard. "How's it going?"

"It's going." Fenton looked back at me, then at Mike. "Ms. . . . What's the last name again?"

"McLaughlin," I told him.

"Ms. McLaughlin is being very enigmatic."

Badger said, "Actually it's Dr. McLaughlin."

"I stand corrected," Fenton said. "That's impressive."

"ER doctor," Badger said.

"You two have met before?"

Badger said, "Yeah, we had drinks together . . . with Donatti, of course."

Fenton said, "She was just about to tell me how she met the illustrious Mr. Donatti."

"In high school," Mike said. "They were married before . . . to each other."

"How'd you know that?"

"She told me."

Fenton looked at me. "What happened the first time around?"

I looked at Mike. "You want to answer for me?"

Badger smiled. It softened his face. "Sorry."

"No, it's very nice not having to explain myself." I looked at Fenton. "Chris and I were together for a long time. We had a baby, we got married, we got divorced, and then we got back together. The order is correct."

"What happened to the baby?" Fenton suddenly held up his hand. "Sorry. None of my business."

"The baby is now a twenty-four-year-old concert pianist."

"You mean Gabriel?" he said. "You're Gabriel's mother?"

"Yes, I am."

"You don't look old enough."

I smiled widely. "Thank you." My head was beginning to split apart.

"It's the truth."

As if on cue, the music stopped, and the singer announced that the band was taking a little break. The music turned from live to recorded—a slow song. Bard stood and held out his hand. "May I?"

"I don't think the boss would like it," I told him.

"The boss likes regular clients who keep coming back and paying him money."

"That is true, but I'm going to pass."

"Aw, c'mon," he told me. "You don't want me to make a scene, do you, Terry?"

I wagged a finger at him as I got up. He put his hand on the small of my back to lead me to the dance floor. I hadn't taken more than a few steps before Chris was there.

He said, "Thank you for bringing her to me, Bard. I can take it from here." He took my elbow and led me onto the floor. He took my right hand in his left and put his other arm around my back.

A Hollies song, more of my father's generation than mine. The first note—distorted and sustained—then breaking into a woozy, boozy, bluesy electronic melody. I knew the song well. I used to play it over and over when I was sixteen, thinking of Chris every time I heard it. Someone so besotted with love for another that all he needed for his existence was air. It was how I felt about Chris back then. I would have drunk poison for him.

I regarded him now. His eyes were flat, but his mouth was smiling. His voice was very soft and low. "Are you trying to make me look bad?"

"What are you *talking* about?"

"Keep your voice down." I didn't answer him. He said, "You're my woman. You don't dance with other men."

"He *insisted*," I whispered. "I didn't want him to make a scene. I didn't want to embarrass you."

"Well, you just fucking did."

I had had it. "Are you effing *kidding* me? This is what you're saying to me after you've been basically . . . screwing your girls with your clothes on?"

"Smile." I forced out a smile. His voice was a growl. "Smile like you mean it. This is *my* party."

I consciously relaxed my face and gave him a soft smile, trying to follow his dance steps. He was a good dancer. He was good at everything.

I hated him.

The voices in four-part harmony—like angels coming from the sky—singing how she was his sustenance, his sole reason to live.

Chris took my hand and laced his fingers with mine. "Jealous?"

"No, I'm not jealous." I remembered to smile. "I don't care who you screw."

He said, "Your anger is a strange reaction for someone who doesn't care."

My teeth were gritted. "I'm not jealous, Chris, I'm sad. I feel like I'm in high school. Mr. Popular with *everyone* around him and I'm on the sidelines. It gets old." Listening to the lyrics and the electric twang of the guitar made me even sadder. "What's really galling is you look like you're actually having *fun*. You never have fun with me."

"We have fun."

"No, we have sex," I said. "I don't even know why I'm here. It would be better if I went back."

A few moments of silence. He said, "I want you here."

A big exhale. "I'm sorry if I embarrassed you. I won't talk to anyone. I'll sit in my corner until you give me permission to go back to your space."

More silence.

He drew me closer. I felt his body relax even though I was as tense as tetanus. His eyes softened as he widened his baby blues and attempted to get my attention, but I wouldn't look at him. He let go of my hand and picked up my chin and tried again. I sighed again. I leaned my head on his chest and he kissed the top of my head. He pulled me closer. Despite myself, in his arms, I felt my body slowly release its stress.

"You know how jealous I get," he told me. "You're my fiancée."

"And you're my fiancé," I said. "How do you think I feel?"

"Am I dancing with anyone else?"

"Do what you want," I told him. "Like you said, it's your party."

He peered into my eyes. "You are positively . . . the most beautiful woman . . . in the world."

"You're an idiot!"

"No, I'm not an idiot. I'm a prick." Boozy guitar riff. "C'mon. You know how I feel about you. You're absolutely, and without a doubt, the only woman I've ever loved."

He was about to kiss me, but then the band came back, the recorded music disappeared, and the combo broke into "You Wreck Me."

Chris took my hand. "Come here, gorgeous. Let's dance."

"I don't feel like it."

"C'mon. You like Tom Petty."

"I don't want to."

"You say you want fun, have some fun." He yanked my arm. "Come *on*."

He took me into the center of the floor, and immediately, he was surrounded by his ladies wanting to cut in, but this time he shook them off. His hand around my waist, he led me around with moves I had forgotten, but obviously he had not. Light on his feet, he guided me through a series of routines that I hadn't done in years.

I was floating—as light as dust. This time when I smiled, I meant it. I was enjoying myself. When the band hit the guitar solo, I broke free of his grip and danced on my own, twirling with my hair spinning around my body like blades of a fan. Moving my hips to the beat, my arms high about my head, I rocked to my internal rhythm until I was across the room from him.

He pointed to his eyes, then to me, silently saying, *I'm watching you.* He slowly approached me in step to the music.

I turned to him, crossed my hands across my chest, and tapped my foot.

He caught back up with me and we had the dance area to ourselves, a circle of people around us clapping to the music and watching us heat up the floor. In the end, he dipped me and kissed me on the lips.

Final applause. I curtsied as he bowed.

King and queen of the prom.

My smile was genuine.

He, on the other hand, had a strange look on his face. He took my hand. "C'mon."

"Where are we going?"

"You'll see."

"What?"

"You'll see."

He led me out of the lounge and through a corridor, opening a series of locked doors with keys from a ring he pulled out of his suit pocket. It was dim and I had no idea where we were. He settled upon a final door and opened it. We stepped into a room, and he switched on the lights. There was a bed, an open closet with robes, an adjoining bathroom, and a patio with a Jacuzzi. A hotel room but not exactly.

I was in one of his brothel rooms.

He reached up to a corner where I saw a camera. "Don't worry, I'm turning it off." He pointed to the bed. "Get up."

"Chris, I don't want to."

He didn't answer me. He pulled out a condom and some lube from the cabinet. "Get up."

"Please don't do this to me."

He picked me up and plopped me on the bed. Turned me around until his groin was at my ass. Then he hiked up my dress. I felt the tears come. "Why are you doing this to me?"

He didn't answer. Instead, he started to ease his way into my anus.

I yelled, "You're hurting me!"

"Because you're fighting me." Another shove. "Just relax." He hit my butt cheek. "Relax, relax."

I started to cry. "It hurts!"

"It usually does the first time. You'll get over it."

"Why are you *doing* this?"

"Because you're *mine*!" Another thrust. "You shake your booty for other men, you can shake it for me!" A third push.

"Chris, please—"

"Just count sheep. It'll be over soon."

"*Please!*"

"Terry, stop talking and let me finish!"

I closed my eyes and tried to go into a different space. That was what I always did whenever he raped me. The pain was sharp and throbbing at the same time. It seemed like forever as I nearly bit through my lip trying to deal with the violation. He moved deep within my body faster and faster until he climaxed. It took him about five minutes—a very, very long five minutes. Not the longest five minutes of my life. That five minutes belonged to when I had lost Sanjay. But it was close. He pulled out, threw away the condom, and zipped up his pants as I collapsed on the bed, trying to stanch my tears.

He offered me several wipes. "Here."

I took them but I didn't move.

"C'mon." He waited a moment. "Terry, I gotta get back."

"Go," I whispered.

"I can't leave you here. It's a locked corridor."

"Pick me up in the morning," I told him. "I want to sleep."

"You can't sleep here." When I didn't answer, he took the wet towels and wiped my butt. "You're bleeding a little. It'll stop."

I didn't answer him.

He pulled up my panties and pulled down my dress. Then he picked me up. "C'mon."

"I don't want to go back," I told him. "I want to go to bed."

"You can't. Buck up. You'll be fine." He looked at my face. "Your makeup is smeared." He went to the bathroom. He brought back an array of products and laid them down on the bed. He checked his watch and sat me on the bed. Then he picked up a wipe and took off my makeup. "Hold still so I can do this quickly."

Tears ran down my cheeks.

"Terry, I can't do this if you're crying." His voice was matter-of-fact. He blotted my tears and went to work. Silently . . . quickly. Then he stood up, turned the camera back on, and took my hand. "Let's go."

It was hard to walk, but I followed him back like a zombie. When we got to the lounge, I pulled my hand away. I said, "If you want me smiling, give me a few minutes."

He looked at me, turned, and went back inside.

I leaned against the wall, trying to calm down. I just couldn't face the crowd. I felt something wet coming out from my insides. The ladies' room was right down the hall. I walked inside—there was a full crowd—and I quickly locked myself in a stall, wiping my bloody backside. I was sore, but it was the psychological indignity that hurt the most. I stuffed some toilet paper into my panties to sop up whatever else would come out.

I flushed the toilet and put on my brave face. Brie was there. So were Kirstin and several other women I hadn't met. They were all young. They were all lovely. I washed my hands. I said, "I think I like the action in here better than out there."

"For sure," Kirstin said. She was wearing a red strapless tube dress. "This is Bethany, Amanda, and Jess."

Bethany was blond, Jess was brunette, and Amanda was a redhead. Chris's angels.

"Terry." I shook their hands after I dried mine.

Jess had agate-colored eyes. "We all know who you are. Congratulations."

I looked at my ring. I should have flushed that down the toilet. "Thank you."

"Pretty good dancing," Amanda said.

"We took lessons a long time ago," I said. "The boss has probably kept up with it more than I have."

"You looked like a pro," Brie said. She held up an uncorked bottle of champagne. Then she released paper mouthwash cups from a dispenser. "Anyone?"

"Sign me up," I said. As soon as I downed the first cup, I asked for another.

Bethany said, "How long have you known the boss?"

Was *way too long* the right answer? "We met in high school." From head to toe, I was in pain. "Anyone have an Advil?"

Amanda produced a bottle. "Help yourself."

"Thanks." I washed down two tablets with champagne.

"We were just talking about the cunt," Brie said.

Kirstin said, "Brie—"

"Oh, she knows how I feel," Brie said.

I gave her a genuine smile. "I do."

"Is she that way with you?" Amanda asked.

"She's been okay," I said. "I've hardly had anything to do with her."

"Aren't you the lucky one," Bethany said.

"Are you living here with the boss?" Amanda asked.

"Temporarily, yes," I said. "I have my daughter with me, so I'll probably opt for suburbia once we get things figured out."

"How old's your daughter?" Amanda asked.

"Eleven." I pulled out my phone and showed them pictures of Juleen that I had recently taken. Lots of oohs and aahs.

"Any pictures of Gabe?" Kirstin asked.

"Not on this phone except . . ." I reached into the back of my phone case and pulled out a well-worn photograph. "The boss took this. Gabe was five. Look how blond he was."

"Is that you?" Brie said.

"Yep." I stowed it back. "I was so young. It's depressing."

"You really haven't changed at all."

"Can I take you home with me?" I asked her. "Do you have kids?"

"Not yet," Brie said. "I have a boyfriend, but I'd like to stop doing this before I have kids."

"Yeah, wouldn't we all," Kirstin said. "I have a little boy."

"Can I see?" I asked. The next five minutes were spent in exchanging phone pictures of boyfriends and children. After showing me her freckle-faced son, Kirstin placed her phone back in her purse. She said, "I bet the boss will buy you a big house. He's crazy about you."

How about if you skip the last two words? I thought. I said, "We're working it all out."

"Where does he keep you?" Bethany asked.

"Keep me?"

"You don't live in the dorm," Jess said.

"Oh, right. I'm staying in his suite." I laughed. "Might be more fun in the dorm."

The girls laughed with me. Kirstin said, "Yeah, the boss can be pretty intense."

I smiled, not wanting to say too much. I'm sure he had the place bugged.

Jess looked in the mirror. "I really don't like this lipstick. It's too pink."

"That's because you're a true autumn," Amanda said. "You need like purple or burgundy."

"I have like a dark red," Brie said. "I'm a summer. Dark reds look good on summers and autumns."

"Can I try it?"

"Yeah, sure."

Jess took the lipstick. "Thanks."

Just then someone knocked and the door swung open.

"There you are." Chris's demeanor was calm, but his eyes were dead fish. He grabbed my wrist. "If you'll excuse us." He yanked me out of the bathroom and not so gently leaned me against the wall, boxing me in with his arms. He whispered, "You said a few minutes! What the fuck are you trying to pull?"

I shook out my wrist. "I had to wipe my ass because it was bleeding." I spoke in a low, calm voice. "Then I got to talking to your ladies."

He took in a deep breath and let it out. A wave of alcohol washed over my nose. He said, "I'm responsible for your safety, Teresa. Jorge couldn't find you. I couldn't find you. In case you don't remember, your son was—" He stopped himself.

"What?" My heart started pounding. I was in full-blown panic mode. "Has something happened—"

"No, no, no. As far as I know Sanjay is fine. But he was taken from you. I don't know who's out there. I thought the worst."

My hands were still shaking. "Are you lying to me about Sanjay?"

"No, Terry, I'm not. I swear."

I was trying to stave off a panic attack. I said, "You go back inside and tell Jorge I'm here. I need to calm down."

"Not this time. Calm down at your table."

He took my arm, but I shook off his hand. "Please do not touch me."

He held up his hands. He opened the door for me and accompanied me back to my table.

If there had been a lull in the party during my absence, I didn't detect it. Within a few minutes, Badger was back at my table. So was Fenton. He brought a buddy named Oliver Keaton. They talked among themselves, they talked to me, each one trying to out-flirt the other. They tried to ply me with drink; I demurred and drank club soda. Another man pulled up a chair—white hair and probably in his seventies. He was well preserved. He owned property. He regaled me with stories about how wealthy he was. They all conspired with me to get the coveted reaction.

Steely eyes constantly swept my way.

I should have acted aloof, yea even frosty. Instead I met him stare for stare and flirted back with my table companions. Sweet smiles, throaty laughter, and a touch here and there. The more relaxed I became, the tenser he got. The drinks in his hand began to come in rapid succession. Three, four, five, six, and then I stopped counting. He said he had cut down on alcohol consumption, but tonight was an exception. Alcohol made him act looser. He laughed more often, he talked a little louder, and his motions became exaggerated. His complexion had blossomed pink. With every glance he gave me, his eyes became angrier and angrier, but for the crowd he held it together. All people saw was a man having a good old time.

About two in the morning, the crowds started to thin, lasting another hour until the lounge was emptied. We walked back to his place in silence. I was wrecked from exhaustion and pain. He was staggering a bit, reeking of booze and hyped up on anger. As soon as we got into the room, I whirled on him and said, "If you lay a single fingertip on me, Sanjay or no Sanjay, I am leaving you forever. And if you think I'm bluffing, you'll have to use a gun to stop me."

"Don't fucking worry," he spat back. "I don't want you and neither does anyone else."

"Well, we both know that's not exactly true."

His eyes turned dead. "Fuck off, bitch."

I should have answered him back with anger and called him names in kind. Anger didn't make him angry. He understood anger. Instead, I laughed. Not a big laugh. One of those little derisive laughs that said, *You're ridiculous.*

Although his gun was still holstered, his left hand was on the butt. He whispered, "Get the fuck out of here!" I was debating just where to go when he yelled, *"Get! Out!"*

I ran into the bedroom and closed the door. Which did no good whatsoever because there wasn't a lock in the jamb. He came in a moment later. He was already starting to shake, sweating out the poison. He reached up into one of the higher cabinets and pulled down a comforter. He grabbed pillows and he left.

I let out a sigh of relief. I changed out of my tight dress, put on a loose dress, and fell into an exhausted sleep.

I woke up about two hours later, around the time that Chris usually came to bed. I was parched and drained the water bottle I kept on the nightstand. I turned on the night-light and went to the bathroom to get more Advil. After I downed the tablets, I was about to return to bed. Then I sighed. I slowly opened the door. The window shade was still up and there was moonlight streaming in through the glass. He lay curled up, his face buried in a pillow, his contracted body pushed against the back of the couch. He was in full-blown shakes. The place smelled like a cross between a gym and a distillery.

I said, "C'mon, Chris. Come to bed." When he didn't answer, I walked over and placed a hand on his trembling shoulder. "C'mon—"

"Go away." His voice was muffled behind the pillow.

"Chris—"

"Go away!" He yanked his shoulder from under my touch. He turned over, his face awash in sweat. "I reek like garbage."

"We've been through this before," I said. "I'll run you a shower."

He turned back over and put a pillow over his head. In a muffled voice, he said, "Just get out of here."

I went into the bathroom and turned on the water. When it was ready, I walked back with a face towel and wastebasket. I said, "C'mon."

"I can't move."

"I'll help you up." I began to pull on his arm, and he slowly got to his feet. He started to reel and sat back down. "I'm gonna be sick."

I handed him the wastebasket and held his hair as he puked. Afterward, I gave him the towel. He wiped his face. His complexion was chalk. "I am utterly putrid."

"You'll feel better after you've showered. Give me the basket. I'll clean it out in the other bathroom."

"You don't have to clean up my vomit."

I took the basket from him and placed it on the floor. "C'mon." I took his arm. "Let's get you cleaned up. Can you walk?"

"Yeah, yeah . . ." He made it to the bathroom before he began to rock on his feet. He knelt down at the toilet and threw up for a second time. When he was done, he went into the shower, hunched over like an old man. I retrieved the waste can, dumped the vomit in the toilet bowl, and flushed everything down. I rinsed the basket in the sink. When it was clean, I went back to the couch and picked up his comforter and the pillows. I started to strip them but decided that everything needed to be dry-cleaned. I opened the door and took the linens to the laundry chute outside. Jorge said, "Everything okay, Doc?"

"Just doing some housekeeping."

"Evan is coming on in about twenty minutes."

"That's fine. Have a good one, Jorge."

"Thank you, ma'am."

The water was still running when I came back. I retrieved two water bottles and a bottle of Advil. Five minutes later, Chris staggered out and I handed him an extra-large bath towel.

He dried off his body and put on a fresh pair of sweats. "Go to sleep. I'm okay now."

I gave him the water bottles and the medicine. "I threw your bedding in the chute. It all needs to be cleaned."

He opened both water bottles and gulped them down. Then he popped four tablets into his mouth. "Thank you." He looked at me. "Can I sleep in the bed?"

"It's your place. You can sleep anywhere you want."

"You know what I mean."

I shrugged. "The bed is big enough to accommodate both of us."

I slithered under the covers. Usually when he came in, I moved over from the edge, because we spooned as we slept, until I wriggled from his grip so we could both have a little room. Tonight, I remained stock-still, not giving up an inch. He got the message. The man was anything but dumb.

He went to the other side, got under the sheets, and curled up. He started trembling, shaking the bed in intervals. I felt as if I were lying next to a drunken passenger on an overnight flight with inter-mittent turbulence. I didn't know if he could talk, but mercifully, he chose not to.

Eventually, the motion of his DTs rocked me to sleep.

CHAPTER 22

I WAS UP BY ten, feeling wasted and hungover. Chris was sprawled out on the bed, snoring but no longer shaking. The room smelled rank, and all the noises from last night were still ringing between my ears, enough to give me a massive headache. I took a quick shower and grabbed the bottle of Advil. Once out of the bedroom, I gulped water, then I started the coffeemaker and went to the half bath in Chris's office area. My ass was still sore but no longer leaking blood.

There were lots of strong women out there: true leaders. I was not one of them. I am and always was a subordinate. First to my stepmother, and then of course to Chris, who is an apex predator. But even with Devek, who was weak, I'd let him call the shots. It didn't bother me. I was always an obedient student and excellent at taking orders. God made me that way, and I've come to grips with who I am. But there were times with *both* men where they knew they had gone too far. When my hatred was so apparent, they both buckled.

Two cups of coffee later, and after the pain medication kicked in, I called Juleen.

"When are you coming?"

"As soon as he gets up. He's still asleep."

"When will that be?"

"Don't know, *priya*. We got to bed very late."

"Did you have fun?"

"Yes," I lied.

"So like when, Mommy? An hour? Two hours?"

"I don't know, Juleen. I'll come as soon as I can."

"Okay." Her voice brightened. "Can I send you some pictures of the shoes I want?"

"Of course. We can look online together."

"I'll send you the website."

An hour later, I heard the shower running. I called Juleen and said, "Chris is up. Let me take care of him and then I'll see you."

"So, about the shoes. You're sure I can get three pairs?"

"Yes. Get the three pairs. But no more."

"Thank you so much."

"You're welcome. I've got to go. See you soon."

After we hung up, I started the coffeemaker a second time after putting in freshly ground beans. When he came out, I handed him a mug of coffee and four tablets of Advil.

"Thank you," he muttered. I was silent as he drank. He said, "You're not having any?"

"I had my coffee earlier. I'd like to see Juleen now."

He said, "She's busy with her studies."

"It's Saturday, Chris."

"Right." He took another sip. "I thought we could spend some time together."

"No," I said. "I told her I'd come as soon as you could take me. She knows you're up. She's expecting me."

"Can I finish my coffee?"

"Of course."

He sipped again. "Terry, why don't you grab a cup of coffee and let's talk for a couple of minutes."

"I don't want to talk, and I don't want any more caffeine. I want to see my daughter."

"Fine." He put his mug down with a thud. "Let's go."

"I wouldn't have to bother you if you'd enter me into the system."

"Not now."

"When?"

"I don't know, Terry, just not now." A pause. "I feel like shit." I didn't respond. His voice dropped in volume. "Did I make an ass out of myself?"

"Not at all." I opened the door to his suite. Evan was there. I smiled at him and looked back at Chris. "I'm ready."

Wordlessly, we walked upstairs to my daughter's room—Gabe's room—and he opened the door. Juleen's smile was wide. She looked so happy and innocent that I felt my eyes getting teary. Her face fell. "What's wrong?"

"Nothing, *kharagosh*." I hugged and kissed her. Held her in my arms with an unusual ferocity. "Nothing at all."

Chris cleared his throat. We both looked at him. "What do you two lovely ladies want for lunch?"

"Curry and rice," Juleen said.

"You should vary your diet," Chris preached.

"What's wrong with curry and rice?" I said.

"She has it every day."

"You eat the same thing every day. Bring her what she wants."

He exhaled. "Okay. What do you want?"

"Nothing."

"Some rice maybe?"

"I'm not hungry now."

"You should eat."

"And I will when I'm hungry."

Chris bit his bottom lip but said nothing. He was turning to leave when Juleen called out to him. He turned around and she said, "I've been practicing the Halvorsen piece a lot. I mean, just the first couple of variations. Wanna hear?"

Hungering for his approval.

Chris looked at his watch and then he looked at me. I said, "Are you busy?"

"No, I'm fine." He sat down on the piano bench. To Juleen he said, "Go ahead."

She took out her violin and he played a middle A from the piano to tune her instrument. He gave her a thumbs-up or thumbs-down on each string, depending on whether the note was sharp or flat. Gabe had inherited his perfect pitch. When she was all tuned up, she raised the instrument to her chin, then brought it back down. "I'm a little nervous."

"Want to know a secret?" Chris said. "Your brother gets nervous every time he gives a concert. He paces in his dressing room. But once he's onstage, he's fine. Just go for it."

She took a deep breath, let it out, and played. It didn't sound like a piece for beginning students. There were lots of double stops and some rapid passages, but she seemed up for the challenge. When she stopped, Chris nodded. "Pretty good."

Her smile was radiant. "Really?"

"Still some room for improvement, but I can tell you've been practicing. If you keep it up, we can play the duet next week for those variations."

"You'll *play* with me?"

"Unless you know another cellist around here." He stood up and checked his watch again. "I'll have Evan drop off your lunch."

He left and she was still smiling. "It did sound okay, right?"

"It sounded beautiful."

"I don't know if I'd go *that* far."

"Chris is a tough critic. That he's willing to play with you is high praise." I smiled at her. "Let's look at the dresses you picked out. You can't have all six."

Juleen put her violin back in the case. "Are you okay?"

"Of course." Kids pick up on everything. "Why do you ask?"

"I don't know. You seem . . ." She shrugged.

"At loose ends?" She nodded. I told her, "I'm pretty much healed up. I'd like to get out of here and start our life."

"Chris doesn't want me here, right?"

"Juleen, *I* don't want you here. We need a normal house in a normal city with a normal backyard. You need school. You need friends."

"What about Sanjay?"

"I will never stop looking for him, *priya*, and I have hope that Chris will find him and bring him back to us. But whatever happens, you need to move forward with your life. And I will do everything I can to make that happen."

"Where will we live?"

"Somewhere in Nevada. Maybe Reno. Maybe Lake Tahoe."

"Chris mentioned Las Vegas."

I looked at her. "You've talked to Chris about this?"

"Just that he told me that we can't stay here."

"He's right about that."

"He doesn't want me around, you know. He told me he doesn't have any use for me."

I sighed. "He's a certified idiot."

"At least he doesn't treat me like a baby."

"That is true," I said. "He used to say terrible things to Gabe too. Don't pay attention to him."

"I don't care. He's not my father." She thought a moment. "Not that Father is much better."

"Don't be disrespectful."

"He gambled away all our money."

"I know. But he loves you and you still can't be disrespectful." I tried out a weak smile. "What else do you and Chris talk about?"

"Mostly my studies. He's not here so much now that I have you." She snuggled close to me. "Sometimes I ask him questions. He answers me honestly, but sometimes his answers are very mean. Sometimes he can be quite comforting. And I remember what you said. You take the good with the bad."

I kissed her forehead. "As long as he isn't creepy. You would tell me if he—"

"He's not creepy, Mommy. Gabe and I talk a lot. He gives me pointers on how to handle him. It's helpful."

"Gabe would know." A pause. "Hey, I've got an idea. Do you want to look at houses online together?"

She brightened. "Yes. Let's do that."

We spent a long time on real estate, looking at everything from houseboats on lakes to tacky mansions in Vegas. Then we ate. We topped the evening off by watching three movies. It was after ten when we turned off the TV. I couldn't put it off any longer. I called Chris and asked him to take me back. When we got to his suite, I headed straight for the bathroom and turned on the shower. I got out, a towel wrapped around my body, and found him waiting for me—fully clothed—on the bed. The room had been cleaned. It smelled like bleach and air freshener.

"Can we talk?" he asked.

"No. I'm too tired."

"It won't take long." He raised his eyebrows. "I loathe to ask, but I need a favor from you."

"Let me get dressed first." When he didn't move, I said, "I'd like some privacy."

He got up and left. I put on my Manson girl dress and drew back my hair in a ponytail. I came out and he was already at work. "Hey," I said loudly.

He took off his earphones and got off his captain's chair. He pointed to the couch. "Have a seat."

"I'd rather stand. What do you need?"

"I'm having a get-together—"

"No."

"Can you hear me out?"

"The answer will still be no."

"Okay. Your answer is no. Just hear me out."

I crossed my arms and waited.

"Some of my best clients are here the entire weekend. Rich clients. Some were at your table last night. I usually give them a send-off. Since it's Labor Day weekend, it'll be Monday night. Maybe forty, maybe fifty people in my office downstairs. All you have to do is make an appearance and then you can go back upstairs. That's it. Okay?"

"What is the purpose of my coming down and then going back up?"

He washed his face with dry hands. "My girls like you. The ones that were in the bathroom." He looked at the ceiling. "I may not have made a total jackass of myself, but I fucked up." I waited. "I grabbed you yesterday, yanked you out of the bathroom."

"Yes, you did."

"Even in my haze, I knew I did the wrong thing. I could see it on their faces. Suddenly I wasn't the nice, sensitive, understanding boss anymore. At that moment, I was every asshole man they had ever met."

You are an asshole. I said, "I'm sure it's no big deal."

"It is a big deal, Terry. I could tell this afternoon when I was in the cafeteria. They were respectful, but I could sense it. I figure if you come to the party and they see you acting nice to me . . . and I'm acting solicitous to you . . . they'll figure all is forgiven."

I was quiet.

"Terry, this is my *business*. My livelihood. My employees work hard. They do it for the money, of course, but they also work hard because they like me. It's the difference between doing okay and doing well. Kirstin, Amanda, and Jess have been with me for a while. They teach the newbies what to do. I've got lots of new girls coming in when you leave, and I need the older ones to show them the ropes. They've bonded with you."

"Oh *please*!"

"I know they like you because I see how they are with you and how they were with Talia. They didn't like her." When I chuckled, he said, "Why? What did they say?"

"Not important."

"She was kind of a diva." Chris looked at me. "Is she okay with you? Talia?"

"I don't have much face-to-face with her. Whenever I email her or text her for something, it comes pronto."

"Okay. Let me know if she gives you attitude. I'll fire her on the spot."

"She's fine. Are you done?"

"Will you come? To the party?"

I closed my eyes and then opened them. He was my key to San-jay. What could I do? "What are the rules?"

"No rules," he said. "Talk to whoever you want, flirt with who-ever you want, be your charming, sweet self. Just be . . . warm to me . . . like you actually like me. Can you manage that?"

"I'll come."

"Thank you."

"I'm tired. I'm going to bed. You want me to sleep on the couch?"

"You can't sleep on the couch. I'm working tonight." He regarded my face. "Why can't we both sleep in the bed . . . like last night?"

"As long as you stay on your side, that's fine."

He gave me a plaintive expression. "Teresa, you know how much I love—"

"I don't want to hear it." I put my hands over my ears.

I went silent and so did he. Then he said, "I'll get you a new dress for Monday night."

"I still have a black dress I haven't worn."

"I'd like to see you in red."

"Whatever you want."

"You can pick out some new shoes."

"I have heels. If you don't like them, pick out something else. I don't care."

"You want an evening bag?"

"What on earth for? I'm not carrying anything except a phone."

"You might want something to hold that's pretty or exotic. I can probably get something from Vegas by tomorrow. Ferragamo or Prada or Gucci, maybe."

The silence was stony.

"Can't buy you off with a bag, huh?" When I didn't answer, he said, "Any way I can speed up a détente?" I still didn't respond. He said, "You left your engagement ring on your nightstand."

"I don't wear it when I visit Juleen."

"She knows we're getting married."

"I'm still divorcing her father. I don't have to throw it in her face."

I could see frustration in his expression. He said, "I *expect* you to wear it Monday night."

He was trying to control the situation and I wasn't letting him. Probably a mistake, but I was too angry. "I'm about"—I showed him a millimeter of space between my thumb and forefinger—"about this close . . . to walking out that door and never coming back. Don't you dare threaten me!"

He glared at me, eyes flat and cold. "You do realize that if you leave me, I stop making payments. And whatever happens after that is on you, babe."

I stared back, blinked hard and fast. His cruelty was beyond belief, but he was right. I was totally dependent on his largesse.

We were both silent for about a minute, maybe even longer. Then he backed down, exhaled and closed his eyes. "Sorry." He walked over to me and put his big hand on my shoulder. "Sorry." I shook him off and remained silent.

He said, "Tell you what, Terry. Next week, I'll open up a joint account for you and me and put enough money in there . . . so if something happens to me, you'll have sufficient funds to pay off these bastards. But, for now, let me handle it, okay? I promise that no matter *what* happens between us, I'll handle your son's situation to the best of my ability." He exhaled again. "After this is all over, you can keep the money in the account. All yours."

I looked down and noticed tears dripping from my eyes, falling onto the floor. "Don't bother. Either you'll continue to help me or you won't. I'm not about to profit from my son's ransom." I looked up. "Go back to work. I'm going to bed."

"You want me to sleep on the couch?"

"Please."

IN LOS ANGELES, crime took advantage of holidays. People got together, people drank, people got into trouble. In a small town like Greenbury, holidays were filled with lazy mornings, pancake brunches, a parade in the afternoon, and barbecues for dinner. Labor Day was the official good-bye to summer. The town emptied of part-timers, but quickly swelled with the population of college kids. Parents moved in their progeny, some with trepidation, some with relief. Disoriented kids would be oriented a few days later to begin their first taste of advanced education and living without Mom and Dad.

Sunday morning, Decker had actually slept in for the first time in years, rising at ten in the morning, well beyond his usual time. Rina was up. He could hear her puttering around, then he could hear the sliding doors to the outside patio open and close. He brushed his teeth, combed his hair, and put on a bathrobe. He trudged out to the yard.

"Hey there."

She was at the barbecue. "Good morning."

"More like afternoon."

"No, it's still considered morning, although not by much."

He noticed all the outside tables had been set up. "What's going on?"

"Well . . ." She smiled. "It started out with just Jake and Ilana driving up. I told you they were coming."

"I'm sure you did."

"You don't remember. Anyway, they're spending the night."

"Lovely." A pause. "By all the tables, it looks like we're expecting more than two people."

"Well . . . then Sammy decided it would be really fun to rent a big RV and take the kids up here and do an overnight campout in the RV. I think he and Rachel did that once during COVID and decided it was a lot of fun."

"Then they won't be staying in the house."

"No. But . . . when Hannah got wind of it, she asked if there was room for her family. So Sammy rented an even bigger RV, and Hannah and her crew are hitching a ride. They *will* be staying in the house."

"We have two guest bedrooms. Where are they going to set up with the baby?"

"Probably in the office."

"Sounds like a plan."

"We're not done yet," Rina said. "I got a text from Cindy this morning at around seven. She and Koby are both off and asked if it was okay if they came up. Which was just politeness because any of them are welcome any time."

"You're sure about that?"

Rina smiled. "We've got the whole gang except for Gabe and Yasmine, who are in Los Angeles, visiting her parents for the holiday." Rina looked at her husband. "You look stunned."

"Maybe a little. Where are the Kutiels staying?"

"They're going to leave this evening after the barbecue. They have to work tomorrow. They left earlier than the others and should be arriving momentarily. The rest will be here around the time of the parade. So . . ." Rina wiped her hands on her apron. "You can either go with them to the festivities or stay here and help me prepare."

"Is that a serious question? You or a gang of noisy interlopers?"

"They're your children and grandchildren."

"That doesn't make them any less noisy." He walked over and snaked his arms around her waist. She was grilling vegetables: asparagus, onions, mushrooms, squash, and tomatoes. He said, "I'm a whiz with tongs."

"Wanna take over?"

"Can I shower first?" He looked at his backyard. "Next time wait for me to bring out the tables and chairs."

"I think that's a good idea," Rina said. "My strength maybe isn't what it used to be."

"Neither is mine." He turned her around and gave her a smack on the lips. "We'll grow feeble together." She hit him gently. Then he said, "Do we have enough food?"

"What a question. We're having hamburgers and hot dogs. You can take them out of the deep freeze at around three."

"Should we invite you know who?"

"Already done. He's making blondies and brownies. Maybe a chocolate babka. He's baking everything here because I have all the pareve ingredients. He should be here in an hour."

"Then I should hustle. Never greet anyone in a bathrobe."

"Not a good idea at all." She kissed his cheek. "Go get ready. There's coffee in the kitchen, by the way. But it's from like seven in the morning."

"I'll make a fresh pot when I come out."

He'd just finished dressing when he heard a knock on the door. As soon as he opened it, the whirlwind started. His grandsons had reached double digits in age and their heights were off the charts, not surprising since Mom and Dad were tall. They had mocha-colored skin—a cross between Cindy's pale and Koby's black complexions. They were named after their grandfathers, Akiva for Decker and

Aaron for Koby's father. Though identical twins, Akiva was slightly taller than Aaron, and was the easier going of the two. Aaron was intensity squared. The boys had auburn curls and large, dark eyes with long lashes. They wore T-shirts, shorts, and sneakers. Each one was dribbling his own basketball; Decker had put up a hoop on the garage several years ago. They often talked at the same time, asking in unison if Grandpa wanted to play.

Decker said, "You guys start without me. I promise I'll be with you in a bit."

Cindy was holding several bags. He kissed his daughter and took the bags.

"Come into the kitchen. I was just about to make coffee. How are you guys? It's been a while."

"Too busy for our own good." Koby was carrying an ice chest. He placed it on the kitchen counter and began to pour the excess water from homemade ice packs into the sink. "Can I refreeze these bags for the way home?"

"Of course."

Koby put the chest on the floor. "I should keep an eye on the boys."

Decker said, "They're fine . . . unless you want to shoot some hoops."

"I'd like to move a little. It was a long ride."

"Have fun. I'll be out soon."

Cindy was unpacking the bags. Decker regarded his daughter. She was on the dark side of forty. Just where did the time go? She looked muscular and fit. Her hair, by and large, was still flaming red, although a few strands of errant gray had snuck in. She wore jeans and an Eagles T-shirt. "We brought a few kosher items that Rina likes." She looked around. "Where is Rina?"

"Outside grilling."

"I'll say hello in a minute," she said. "By the way, did you find that guy you were looking for? Brock Baer?"

"Good memory. Not yet."

"I remember his name because I entered it in our database. As far as I know, he's not in Philadelphia," Cindy said. "But I have a call in to the data center that scans the automated license plate readers. I'll let you know if his number was spotted anywhere."

"Thank you, honey. It would be really helpful if you got a hit. Because right now, we're sort of floundering."

"Did the DNA come back?"

"I thought it would come on Friday, but I think the holiday weekend is pushing everything back a couple of days." Decker started making fresh coffee. "I'm not even sure we're pointed in the right direction."

Cindy turned to her father. "Daddy, if you think it's related to your case, it's related."

"Love your confidence." He kissed his daughter's cheek. "It's great to see you, princess."

"I know . . . Gotta treasure each moment, right?"

Decker said, "Indeed we do. Are you okay?"

"I'm fine." But her expression was off. "How's Grandma?"

"She's okay now, but she had quite a nasty scare."

"I know. I talked to her. When I did, she sounded stoic as ever. I'm thinking that we might go visit her next time we both get off. Take the kids to all the amusement parks. Then I think maybe I should speed it up. No one lasts forever. Not even Grandma."

"She's pretty close to immortal."

"I always tell Koby when the world comes to an end, the only survivors will be cockroaches and Grandma." Cindy's eyes watered. "It's good to see you."

Decker hugged her. "What's wrong, Cindy?"

"It's all good, Daddy, honest." She exhaled. "I don't know why I'm so emotional."

Decker said, "Just get it out. You'll feel better."

"Okay." She smiled. "I've transferred to Homicide. Starting right after the holidays."

Decker was taken aback. "Really?"

"Yeah, you think you're the only one who can call himself elite?"

"Congratulations." He laughed. "I thought you were happy in CAPS. You've certainly been there long enough. Shows you what I know."

"I was very happy in CAPS. Moving wasn't my idea."

"So, what happened?"

"I have a friend in Homicide. She kept bugging me."

"Brought you to the dark side, huh?"

Cindy smiled. "I had CAPS down pat. I think I'm a little nervous about Homicide. I'm a little on the old side to be a newbie. Are you going to buck me up?"

"You don't need it, Cyn. You'll be a fantastic homicide detective."

"Except I'm used to living victims."

"There are many, many living victims in Homicide. The main one just happens to be dead." He hugged her tightly. "You'll do great."

"Thanks. Any words of advice?"

"Well . . ." Decker considered her question. "It's long hours, honey. And it's grueling work. Because our victim is deceased and can't speak, we feel compelled to do it for them. It's an obsessive business." He paused for several seconds. "The one thing I will say is remember that you have a life away from work. You've got a husband and children and friends. Getting your mind *off* the case is as crucial as thinking about it."

"I wouldn't have done it, but Koby said I'd be sorry if I didn't grab the opportunity."

"I agree. The department is lucky to have someone as gifted as you are." He smiled at her. "Do you know any of your colleagues beside your friend?"

"I know a few. Naomi Ristra is the one that recommended me. She's a detective sergeant. I'll be working under her."

"It's imperative to have a good mentor."

"I've already had the best mentor ever." She hugged her father. "Wish me luck?"

"No need, Cyn. You are a natural." He held her as if she were a teen going to college for the first time. "I love you, pumpkin. Whatever you need, I'm always just a phone call away."

Cindy hugged back, then broke away. "Thank you, Daddy. I'm sure you'll be sorry for that offer." A smile. "I should say hello to Rina."

"Go on. I'm going to watch the boys play basketball."

"You should play with them. With Koby, it'll be two-on-two."

"I have many virtues, Cindy, but speed isn't one of them. Although I am still taller than the boys. I suppose I could just stand under the basket and shoot."

"That's called a lane violation, Daddy." She laughed. "I'll be helping Rina. Let me know if you need anything."

"Other than CPR?"

"No worries," Cindy said. "My doctor husband has got you covered."

CHAPTER 23

WE WERE BOTH neat people and we were both sticklers for being on time. It was unusual for me to dawdle, but I did.

Chris opened the bathroom door. "Teresa, I need to get down there. How long?"

I turned off the water and took a towel from the rim of the shower door. I wrapped it around my body and stepped out. "So go." I turbaned my wet hair with another towel. "I'll have Jorge take me down."

"It's Ben."

"Jorge, Ben, Evan . . . whoever."

"Why did you wash your hair?"

"Because I'm a clean woman?"

He pulled out a blow dryer. "C'mon. I'll do it. I'll do your makeup too."

"Chris, just go down and I'll be there in about a half hour."

"I want to see how you look in the dress."

I gave out an exasperated sigh and took the dress from the bed. I said, "Can you wait in the other room?"

"Why?"

"Because I want privacy . . . Go."

He left me in the bedroom, and I closed the door. I took the dress out of the plastic. It was a bright red bandage minidress. After I put it on, I looked in the mirror. Going a size up felt better. It was tight, but I could breathe. I put on my ring, my earrings, and clipped up my wet hair. I opened the door and said, "I'm confused about this neckline. Is it off the shoulder or like a cold shoulder?"

Chris came in. "You can wear it both ways." He pulled the straps down. "I like it off the shoulders."

"Fine." I spread out my arms. "Approved?"

His eyes went up and down my body. "You look lovely."

"Go down and I'll be there in a bit."

From inside one of the dresser drawers, he brought out a flat velvet box. "Just to gild the lily . . ." He opened it. Inside was a diamond necklace—a rivière, to be exact—starting with small round diamonds in the back and culminating in a sizable central diamond in front. It sparkled like fireworks. He took it out of the box. "May I?"

I shook my head. "Thank you, but no."

His face fell. "C'mon. Please?"

"I don't want the necklace."

His eyes went flat. "Terry, it'll make me look good, okay?"

"Yeah, but it'll make me look bad . . . like you're placating me with jewelry."

"Just do me a favor and wear the damn thing."

"No, Chris. I'm already doing you a favor, remember?" He didn't answer. I said, "It's too much bling with the earrings and the ring. I know how women think. They'll think I'm overdoing it or lording it over them. I'll wear your mother's cross. It means more to me than that. I don't want it. Take it back. It's getting late. Go."

He threw the necklace on the bed and left.

As promised, I came down a half hour later, resplendent in his mother's silver cross. The chain was long, so I had knotted it up so it would fit my neckline. There were around forty people—about thirty men and ten women. He had two bars going as well as passed trays of hors d'oeuvres and free-flowing champagne. Talia was flitting around the room, flirting with the men, but mainly making sure that everything ran like clockwork.

I saw Badger and Fenton and gave them each a peck on the cheek as they went to join the men in manly conversation. I headed toward the women. Kirstin was with Amanda, Jess, and someone I didn't know, standing off to the side of the bar, drinking—what else?—champagne. I walked over to them. "Hiya."

Kirstin said, "You look nice."

"Right back at you." I turned to the one I hadn't met—dark brown complexion with a head of tight black curls. She had emerald-green eyes and the requisite big bust. Exotic and beautiful. "Terry McLaughlin."

"I know who you are. Everyone does."

"Never felt so popular in my life."

The woman smiled. "Elodie Anderson. I love your ring."

"Thank you."

"I like your necklace," Jess said. "It offsets all the sparkle."

I smiled as I regarded Chris. He had a drink in his hand. "The boss gave it to me when I was sixteen. It belonged to his late mother."

A chorus of *awws*.

"That's so sweet!" Jess said.

"Yeah, you can imagine how I felt," I said. "This big, gorgeous guy giving me something so personal. I was kinda geeky back then."

"I'm sure you were anything but geeky," Amanda said.

"No, I was." My eyes on Chris. He exchanged an empty glass of booze for a full one. I said, "I wasn't his girlfriend in high school. I was his tutor. He had another girlfriend who he was . . . you know. Anyway, it was actually a good thing. We became friends before it happened."

"That's really romantic," Elodie said.

"It was, actually," I said. "I was smitten."

"Who wouldn't be?" Amanda said. "My high school boyfriend was a jerk. All he wanted was sex."

"That's all men," I said.

"Yeah, at least you got a cross out of the relationship. All I got was an abortion and a bouquet of wilted daisies."

Kirstin said, "She got more than a cross. The boss is nuts about her."

Try just nuts, I thought.

Amanda asked, "Was the boss a good student?"

"Not bad." A paused. "He paid me a lot." Chris had polished off the second drink and was asking for a third. "Nothing has changed in that regard." I winked and they laughed. I said, "Will you excuse me for a moment?"

I walked over to Chris and intercepted the drink just as he was about to put it to his lips. "Thanks so much!" I took a sip. "Wow, strong. But good stuff." I turned to the three men to whom he was talking. "Mr. Donatti only believes in good stuff." I took the empty glasses that the men were holding. "Who'd like a refresher?"

Nods all around. Chris introduced me, and I said to him, "You want another one since I stole your Scotch? Maybe a soda chaser?"

"Sounds good," he said.

I smiled demurely. "I'll be right back, gentlemen."

I dumped the glasses, including his Scotch, and waited at the bar for the new orders. There were four glasses to carry back, and I asked the bartender for a tray. Talia came up to me. "Need help?"

"Yeah, I do actually, thanks."

"No problem," she said. "Beautiful ring. I helped him pick it out . . . all three of them, I mean."

"You've got great taste. All three were lovely." I picked up two whiskeys. I said, "The club soda goes to Chris."

"Got it."

We went back to the circle of guys. I looped my arm around Chris's and chatted for around ten minutes, until my head started to

pound. I stood on my tiptoes and whispered in his ear that I wanted
to go back. He nodded and excused himself. "I'll take you back."

"You don't have to leave your party. Ben can do it."

"I want to walk you up."

As soon as we got into his suite, he pressed me against the wall,
holding my hands in his. Looking at my face with longing in his eyes,
he went in for a kiss.

Insecure little man.

I turned my head to the side.

He pulled back but kept my hands in his. "How long are you
going to keep punishing me?"

"I dunno," I told him. "How long are you going to keep raping me?"

He exhaled. "You know I get in moods. If you'd just go along
with it—"

"I should go along with you raping me?"

"If you went along with it, it wouldn't be rape, would it?" He
dropped my hands and checked his watch. "I've got to get back." He
regarded my face. "Thank you for coming tonight. And thank you
for stopping me from overdoing it." He motioned a glass going to
his lips.

"No problem," I said. "I'll be asleep when you come up." A forced
smile. "Have a good night."

I HEARD HIM come into the bedroom at around four-thirty. Instead
of going to his side, he slapped my ass. "Move over." When I remained motionless, he said, "I'm not going to do anything. Just
move over. I'm tired of this war of attrition, okay?"

Reluctantly, I scooted to the middle. He went under the sheets
and scooped me into his arms. He had his groin against my ass.
He was hard. I said, "Don't even think about it."

"I miss you, baby."

"No sex."

"Do you miss me?"

"No, I don't actually. And the last thing I want from you is *sex*."

He pulled away from me and sat up. He sighed. "You just don't get it."

"Get what?"

"Men."

"I get men," I told him. "I get that they like sex. But the vast majority out there don't rape."

"That's just it," he said. "Out there, they don't rape. Out there, I don't rape. But we're not out there. We're in here. And in here, I do what I want." A pause. "I'm not *normal*, okay?"

"Obviously." I turned over and pulled the cover over my head. "What's the use? You'll never stop."

"You're right about that," he said. "I'm a violent man, and I come from a long string of violent men. My father beat me and sodomized me whenever he drank, and he drank all the time. My uncle also beat me and sexually assaulted me. Worse than that, he turned me into a killing machine. I *finally* got out from under him and switched to illegal brothels, pimping underaged girls. When I got enough money from that, I clawed my way up to this setup. Now I run a legitimate business. I'm a regular tax-paying citizen. This may not be your idea of a respectable profession, but from where I started, it's pretty high on the food chain."

"And the point is . . . ?"

"The point is I'm still a product of my upbringing, and when I get these unstoppable urges, if you'd just wait it out, give me my five to ten minutes of whatever I want, afterward I'm mush. I'll do anything you want. I don't understand why that's so difficult."

"How did you feel when your father raped you? Did you give him his five minutes?"

He turned me around so we were face-to-face. "I was eight when it started, and he wasn't mush afterward. There was a reason I tried to off myself as a kid—twice." He was quiet. Then he exhaled. "What can I do to make it right?"

"Stop raping me." Silence. "That's never going to happen."

He said, "I rescued you, I nursed you back to health, I provide you and Juleen with shelter. I'm educating your daughter. I swore to you that I will do everything possible to get your son back, and you know it's costing me. I'm also paying for your divorce. I'll buy you a house, I'll buy you a car, I'll pay for your kids' education, I'll give you money for expenses and frivolities and for whatever you want . . . Just what am I getting out of this deal?"

I didn't answer him.

"I am doing everything in my earthly power to make you happy, Teresa. All I'm asking for is a little understanding when I get in these moods. Don't take it personal."

"How should I take it, Donatti? Like one of your sex workers? It's just sex, and I'm getting paid so shut up?"

"Stop it, Teresa. You are not one of my sex workers, you are my queen. I'm still the king—whatever the king says is still law—but trust me, no one likes it when the queen is unhappy, least of all the king.

"You see, when the king is unhappy, you give him a leg of mutton. If that doesn't do it, you give him a couple of wenches. If he's still pissed, you give him a couple of enemies to torture on the rack or in the iron maiden or with the emasculator—"

"The emasculator?"

"Yeah, the emasculator. Vets use it on large animals. Cuts the tendons on one side and clamps off the vessels on the other side. Gets the job done with very little bleeding."

"That is *disgusting*!"

"Don't look at me. I didn't invent it. It is a nifty product, however."

I put my palms over my ears. "I don't want to hear, okay?"

He took my hands from my head and said, "What I'm trying to say is it doesn't take much to make the king happy. The queen is a different story. The king's ministers come to the king. They say, 'The queen is unhappy.'

"'Okay,' the king says, 'bring in the royal florist.'

"The ministers say, 'We tried that. It didn't work.'

"'Okay,' the king says. 'Try the royal jewelers.'

"'Already went that route,' the ministers say. 'She doesn't want a new tiara. She wants to talk.'

"'No problem,' says the king. 'Bring in the royal companion.'

"'That's a no-go,' say the ministers. 'She doesn't want to talk to the royal companion, she wants to talk to *you*.' So . . ."

He exhaled.

"So . . . the king girds his loins, preparing himself for the onslaught, and goes to his queen." A beat. "And then . . . after hearing a nonstop litany of complaints, a blow by blow of everything the king has done wrong since Jesus first walked the earth, replete with times and dates—on end and without pause—because woe be he who tries to defend himself only to be accused of interrupting her, talking over her, and bullying her. After he hears everything—a complete syllabus of Bad Husband 101—then maybe, just *maybe*, she'll forgive him." A pause. "And then she'll accept the royal florist and the royal jewelers—"

"That is *not* fair."

"It doesn't sound a *little* familiar?"

"Yeah, the part about interrupting and talking over and bullying."

He sat back and looked at the ceiling. "I'm sorry I hurt you, okay?"

"But you're not sorry, because you'll do it again whenever you're in a *mood*."

"That still doesn't mean I'm not sorry." He made a face. "Terry, what do you want from me? Not in a cosmic sense, I mean right now. And don't tell me nothing. Help me out here."

"You rape me. Then when I don't immediately capitulate to your whims, you threaten to abandon my son to a pack of hyenas—"

"I said I was sorry."

"Chris, I'm not in a forgiving mood, okay?"

"Will you forgive me after I go to India and bring back Sanjay?"

Hearing my little boy's name put a lump in my throat. It was a low blow—certainly not the first time he'd used my son as collateral, probably not the last, but . . . We both knew that he was the *only* one helping me. If I wanted Sanjay back, I needed him on my side. I emitted a sound, something between a sigh and a stifled sob. Finally, I said, "It would be nice if, once in a blue moon, you'd let me lead."

"Lead?" A pause. "You mean like in sex?"

"Yes, sex. It would be nice for me to feel empowered."

He picked me up and put me on his lap. We sat face-to-face. "Baby, if you want to throw a dog chain around my neck, force me on all fours, and stomp on my back with spiked heels from thigh-high, lace-up black leather boots, I am all in."

Despite myself, I smiled. "I never figured you for a submissive."

"I'm not. But for you, I'd do anything." He picked up my hand and kissed it. "Yes, I was awful. I'm a jealous guy and I hate when men stare at you because I know what they're thinking . . . what they're doing in their heads."

"I'm not *doing* anything."

"You did eleven years ago."

"And most of that was your fault," I snapped back. "I wouldn't have cheated if you hadn't been such a . . ."

"An asshole?"

"Yeah, that too. I was thinking a horrible husband."

"I was a horrible husband. But I do love you." He kissed me hard. "Can we officially call a truce? I can tolerate your anger, but I hate it when you're so cold to me. It makes me feel worthless."

"You deserve it."

"I'm sure that's true. I'm a rotten person. But forgive me anyway." He felt my breasts over my dress. "Whoa! I just got to second base. Can I slide into home?" I pushed his hands away and he sighed. "Okay. I get it. Let's go to sleep."

I was still on his lap. I thought long and hard. Then I said, "Do you keep condoms here?"

"Not here. For what purpose?" A pause. "Why do you ask?"

"Can you get them?"

"I have them in my office downstairs. Why?"

"Stop asking questions. You'll like it. Go get condoms and some lube, okay?"

He jumped out of bed, knocking me off his lap. "I'll be right back."

"I bet you will." I got up and went to the bathroom and brushed my teeth. I put on makeup and perfume. He hadn't bought me any sexy lingerie, but I did find a white tank undershirt in his drawer and put it on. I combed out my hair and waited.

He was back in a flash, trying to contain a grin. He stared at me. "God, don't you look heaven-sent." He started to take his pants off, but I stopped him.

"Not yet. Come here." He jumped into bed, and I pushed his head between my legs.

He complied without hesitation. When I was sufficiently aroused, but not yet there, I pushed him off. I said, "Now you can take off your pants and put the rubber on."

"Okay." It took him five seconds. "Now what?"

I presented my backside. "Slowly, Christopher. And use a lot of lube."

"Baby, you don't—"

"I'm in charge, remember?" He didn't answer. I repeated, "Slowly."

I felt him ease his way in. The pain was immediate.

"You're tense," he said. "It's hurting you."

Duh. "Just keep going." I felt him push deeper and I winced. "Tell me when you're all the way, okay?"

"Yeah." His voice was soft. A final shove. "Okay. I'm in."

"Don't move," I told him.

"Don't move?"

"Don't move!" I was deep breathing, adjusting to having something where it shouldn't be. I looked up at him and took his left hand. I licked his fingers and placed them between my legs. "Softly."

I could hear him breathing hard. He said, "Like this?"

"A little higher . . . softer . . ."

"Good?" he asked.

"Yeah." I moved his hand again. "Here."

"Just let me know, angel."

"You're moving your body. Don't move."

"Sorry. It's a reflex." After a minute, he said, "Can I put my other hand in your pussy?"

"As long as you don't poke me."

He licked his fingers and slid them inside of me. "I just want to massage you where I can feel my dick. It feels really good for me." When I didn't answer him, he said, "Is it okay?"

"Yes, yes . . . don't talk."

He was silent. He had graceful fingers and a wonderful touch. After a few minutes, I felt the buildup. A few minutes more and I felt the release, closing my eyes and aware of my body responding to him. He felt it, too, grabbing my hips and giving a couple of hard shoves. It hurt as a cramp, but not as raw pain because I was still coming. After a minute, he stopped, and I disconnected from his body. He was still on his knees, his breathing labored, his sweat copious. And he was still hard. I slapped his ass and said, "That's how you do it to someone you love."

"You're right," he said breathlessly. He took off the condom. "You're right, you're right, you're right."

I was about to get up, but he pulled me back down and got on top of me. He started kissing me, again and again, his sweat dripping onto my chest. "You are poison." Another kiss. "Just pure poison."

His mouth smashed against mine. His kisses were fire. He kicked my legs apart with his knees. "Unadulterated shit. Worse than shit. I can resist smack. I can't resist you." He jammed himself inside of me.

He climaxed quickly. "Ah, Jesus!" He was panting. "Let me die now."

I pushed him off my body, but his arm shot out and held mine. Slowly, he put my hand on his solid erection. "Please?"

"I'm sore."

"Suck me."

I paused. "Did you take something?"

"I'm almost forty-five. What do you think?"

"Chris!"

"You can't offer a starving man a buffet and expect him not to gorge." I pulled my hand away from his grip and was about to go down on him, but he stood up. "C'mere."

"What?"

"Just come here." I complied. He placed me, back against the wall, and pushed me down on my knees. "Please?"

"Get me a pillow."

He turned around and got me one. I put it under my knees. He caged me with his body, then he put his hand around my neck and brought my mouth forward.

I said, "Don't you dare shove it down my throat." Of course, that was exactly what he did. I gagged and then slapped him hard. I pulled away. "The next time, I bite."

He smiled. The second time, he was a *bit* gentler. He said, "Can I come in your mouth?"

I nodded yes.

"Can I come on your face?"

I nodded again.

"Can I come on your tits?"

A third nod.

"Can you be my sex slave for the rest of my life?"

I shook my head no.

"Damn!" He climaxed in my mouth.

This time when I pushed him off, he didn't hold me back. I made a beeline straight to the shower. When I came out, I immediately put on my nightdress and pulled back my hair. He was sitting up in bed, pillows behind his back, stretched out and bare-chested with his sweatpants on. He was looking at his phone, his face covered by his blond-white hair. Fit and buff, he was a gorgeous guy. I understood why I fell for him at sixteen. But now, I should know better. Sunlight was streaming underneath the shade covering the window. It was probably close to seven in the morning.

He looked up and said, "C'mere."

"I'm not interested," I told him.

"I've got my pants on. Although they could be off in a second if you wanted."

"I don't want."

"C'mere!" A pause. "I want to show you something."

I went over to the bed. He patted the mattress next to his body. I slid over and lay stretched out next to him. He was fiddling with his phone. I said, "I'm here."

"Hold on." He showed me his phone and pressed the play arrow on a video.

I gasped and brought my hand to my mouth. Bit my lip as I watched.

My little Sanjay was sitting next to Devek, clutching his arm. He had a wide smile on his face. He said, "Hi, Mommy. I'm happy now. Father is with me. And he's happy too. So, we're both happy. We're playing video games and reading books . . ." He smiled at Devek and Devek smiled back at him. "I miss you, Mommy. Say hi to Juleen. I miss her too. But I have Father."

The camera switched to Devek. He looked anything but happy. Tension was etched deeply in his face. He said, "We're okay, Terry. Please thank Chris and tell him we hope everything will be coming soon and this will be over—"

The screen went blank.

Tears were running down my cheeks. I whispered, "When did you get this?"

"A couple of days ago."

"And you're just showing it to me *now*?"

Chris said, "You weren't speaking to me a couple of days ago."

I looked up at him. I could barely find my voice. "Are they really okay?"

"As far as I know, yes."

"Can you tell me what's going on?"

"You know what's going on. They took your son because Devek owes money."

"They kidnapped Devek as well?"

"Something like that." Chris put his phone down on the nightstand.

"When will it be over?" I asked.

"I don't know. They're waiting on more money from me. I'm waiting on a few things."

"What things?"

"Things that take time. I told you in the beginning that this wasn't an instant fix. So far, so good. I'm doing my best, but no promises."

"Do you know where they are?"

"Other than India, no."

"Could you find out?"

"I could, but then what?" He put his arm around my shoulders and drew me closer. "Your little boy is under constant guard. I can tell you that much. Baby, he can't outrun a bullet."

I nodded, trying desperately to hold back tears. "He looks happy."

"He does."

"Can you send it to me? The video?"

"No," Chris told me. "It'll make you too emotional. It's not good for you, it's not good for Juleen, and, frankly, it's not good for me."

"Can I see it again?"

He gave me a look but retrieved his phone and the video. He pressed the play arrow.

And then the tears came in buckets. For my little boy who was snatched from me, for my big boy whom I had abandoned when he still needed me, for my sweet girl confined to a room in a brothel, for my life that could have been a lot better. But it also could have been worse. Whatever it could have been, it was mine and it was useless to live in regrets. I gave him back the phone and snuggled closer to him. "Thank you, my love. Thank you, thank you, thank you."

"You're very welcome." He put his phone down and wiped my tears with his thumbs. "I know I do horrible things. I say horrible things. But I do adore you. And I want to make you happy." A beat. "Should we get some sleep, baby doll?"

It was a little after seven. "I'm too wired. You sleep."

"I have a business meeting at eleven," he said. "I've set the alarm for ten-thirty." He stroked my arm. "Stay with me until then, angel."

How could I possibly refuse him? We went under the sheets, and he brought me close to his body. His hands were around my waist and he was nuzzling my neck. I was exhausted but awake, trying to hold back the nausea you feel when you've had inadequate rest. I felt his breathing slow. I said, "Thank you again."

"My pleasure." His voice was sleepy.

My eyes were still wide open. "You know what would cheer me up?"

He looped his leg around mine and pulled me closer. "What?"

"A big bouquet of flowers."

A pause. "Roses?"

"Yes, please, but also lilies and peonies and orchids. Just a huge bouquet that I could put on the dresser. Something beautiful and colorful that would brighten up the room."

"No problem." He kissed the back of my neck, then didn't talk. I thought he had fallen asleep. But then he said, "Do you want the necklace also?"

"Thank you, Your Majesty, that would be divine."

CHAPTER 24

I DIDN'T HEAR ANYTHING until the alarm went off at three-thirty in the afternoon, my reminder that it was time to visit Juleen. But I knew I'd been having bad dreams because my heart was racing and I was in a cold sweat. I was disoriented, panicked that I was not with my children in my Los Angeles apartment, until slowly, slowly things came into view. The bedroom was empty, the curtain was still drawn, and after last night, I felt exhausted, mentally and physically. I dragged my body out of bed and put on one of my loose Manson girl dresses. When I walked into the living area of the suite, Chris was sitting on the couch, typing on a laptop. He took off his glasses, glanced at his Rolex, and looked at me. He said, "You've been sleeping for a while."

"I don't feel well." I gave myself a mental shake. "I'll be okay. Can you take me to see Juleen?"

"Maybe you should cancel?"

"No, no. I'm just a bit logy. Let's go."

He gave me a look and took me to see my daughter.

I lasted until nine. I called him to take me back. I headed straight for the bedroom.

He said, "You didn't eat anything."

"I'm not hungry." I pulled the bedsheets over my head. The next time I woke up, he was coming in from working. I muttered out for the time.

"Three-fifteen. How are you feeling?"

"Okay." I sprayed minty droplets down my throat and rolled onto my back.

"You're sure about this?" he said.

"I'm fine." He was quick, and I was grateful. Afterward, as I was lying in his arms, he said, "Anything I can do for *you*, baby?"

I didn't mind having sex with him. That was the deal we struck when I came back to him three years after high school—sex for support. I could close my eyes and be far, far away. But at the moment, his lugubrious voice made me cringe. "I'm okay, but thanks."

I got up to wash off. When I came back, I went to the other side of the bed and buried myself in the covers.

He finally spoke. "You're still pissed at me."

And of course I was. When I was married to him, I was so used to being sexually mistreated, it felt almost normal. But after eleven years with Devek, eleven years of a reprieve, I realized just how utterly abusive he had been. I was seething inside. *But*, if I wanted to see my son again, I had no choice but to swallow the indignity. Seeing Sanjay in that video gave me infinite heartache, but it also gave me hope. I said, "I'm fine, Chris. I'm just tired."

"And that's why you're on the other side of the canyon?"

"I'm not myself," I said. "I need space."

He was quiet. Then he said, "Do you also need all the bedcovers?"

I picked my head up. The duvet was falling off my side of the bed. "Oh, sorry . . ." I yanked the heavy bedcovers off the floor and gave him his fair share. "Sorry."

"S'right. Just want to know the rules." I didn't answer. A moment later, he said, "You want to talk about it?"

"There's nothing to talk about. I'm not mad. Let's just go to sleep."

A sigh. "Okay . . . I'll take you at your word."

The next thing I remember was someone shaking me. My heart was beating out of my chest. Chris's voice. ". . . having a bad dream."

I slowly roused. "A nightmare." My eyes were wet. I was panting. "Did I wake you up?"

"Your arms were flailing. You bonked me in the face."

"I'm sorry."

"No prob. Are you all right?"

"Yeah . . ." I rubbed my eyes. Tears streamed down my cheeks. "Sorry."

"Stop apologizing. Do you remember what you were dreaming?"

"I was . . . being beaten. I was defending myself. Probably why I was moving my arms." He was silent. I said, "Sorry."

"Forget it!" A pause. "Was it me?"

I thought, then shook my head, then grasped that he probably couldn't see me. "No." I wiped my eyes. "It was someone Indian. Not Devek . . . but someone."

He said, "I realize I'm not your favorite person right now, but if you want a little physical comfort, I'm here."

I didn't answer him.

He added, "I don't mean sex, Terry. Just . . . comfort."

I bit my lip and scrunched my eyes to stop crying. I didn't move. I couldn't move.

He hesitated, then he came to me, until my back was tucked against his chest. He wrapped me with his limbs. He had shaven. He smelled good. He kissed the back of my neck. It was like stepping into a warm bath. "You're safe, angel. No one's going to hurt you. Not as long as I'm around. I will protect you with everything in my power, including my life."

"Thank you." I wiped my cheeks. Despite my antipathy toward him, the solace was reassuring. "Juleen too?"

"Of course Juleen too."

I didn't talk for a moment. Then I said, "Do you like her?"

"What?"

"Juleen . . . Do you like her?"

He paused, then said, "I think she's a good kid."

"Thank you." But he hadn't answered the question. "Do you like her?"

He exhaled. "What I feel is irrelevant, baby doll. She's important to you so she's important to me."

"So, you don't like her?"

"Teresa, I don't like anyone. On the other hand, I don't dislike anyone. To me, people are just . . . tools. They help me get what I want, and if they don't help me, they're useless and I throw them away in my mental trash can. Like Mike Badger. I know he's an asshole, but he has things that I want, so I'm nice to him. He thinks we're friends." A derisive chuckle. "When I get what I want out of him, he's history. Same with my employees. They are constantly telling me their problems. I listen like any good therapist, because it makes them feel better, and when they feel better, they work better. I don't give a shit if their mothers are dying of cancer or their kids are sick. While they're talking to me, I nod sympathetically. But in my head, my brain's going: 'What's this gonna cost me?'"

I didn't say anything. Then I said, "What about the Deckers? Are they just tools?"

"Of course. We owe them because of Gabe . . . like a debt. When Decker calls, asks for help, I try to accommodate him. Once I feel I've paid him off, it's over."

"Oh, sure," I said. "And that's why you took a bullet for Rina?"

He was silent. Then he said, "Rina's spooky. She can read minds. Like she has this direct pipeline upstairs. I want to keep on her good side. When it's all over, we'll be going to different places. But maybe she can put in a good word for me."

I smiled, but he couldn't see it. Which was probably good. He sounded serious. I said, "What about Gabe?"

"Gabe is my son. I would die for him." A pause. "I admire Gabe. He's had some tough times, but he's done well and he's his own man. But if I never saw him again, I wouldn't miss him much."

Then I said, "What about me?"

"Yeah, you." He was quiet. "Do you remember our conversation when you dumped me?"

"I asked you for the drawings, and you wouldn't give them to me."

"No, the second time. Right after we graduated high school."

"You mean the time you tried to kill me?"

"I didn't try to *kill* you."

"You *shot* at me."

"Exactly. I shot *at* you. *At* is the operative word. If I had wanted to kill you, you would have been dead."

"You could have missed."

"Not at that range . . . We're getting far afield. Do you remember our *conversation*?"

I sighed. "We talked about the gigs—"

"After that."

I thought a moment. "You said that if I talk about the gigs to anyone, you'd kill me—"

"Before that."

"You have a very specific time frame in mind." I thought a moment. "You said something about a pit bull . . . that if the pit bull was trained to kill, was it the dog's fault if he did what he was trained to do."

"Right on the cheddar."

I waited.

"Only I'm not a pit bull, I'm a Neapolitan Mastiff. You know what that is?"

"I know what a mastiff is."

"Not an English Mastiff. A Mastino is different. It's a big mother-fucking dog with an enormous head and a massive body. Mine was around a hundred and seventy pounds of pure bone and muscle—and drool." He chuckled. "Duke died about six months ago. I was thinking about getting another one, but then you came along and I figured it wasn't the right time."

"You named your dog Duke?"

"Ducati Italiano. Duke for short."

"Oh." I shrugged. "I like dogs. Don't let me stop you."

"Mastinos are not regular dogs, Terry. Not only are Mastinos very wary of strangers, a lot of them attach to just *one* person. For Duke that one person was me. He was better than my gun because he re-acted quicker and on instinct. He was fiercely protective and would have died for me, but he treated everyone else like a potential dinner." A pause. "I am your Mastino. I will protect you to my death because I am attached to you. But only you. It's always been only you. For better or worse."

"But for me, you'll protect Juleen, right?"

"Absolutely."

"And Sanjay too?"

"And Sanjay too. I will do everything in my power to get your son and protect your kids because I love you utterly and completely. I may have something missing upstairs, but there aren't many guys who would shell out millions of hard-earned dollars on other men's children just to make their women happy—especially since the kids are from the man who stole my wife."

That was the truth. Whatever he was, he rescued me. "Thank you, Chris. I mean it."

"No thanks necessary, baby. Just please stop being *pissed* at me. It's not my fault, Terry. I'm a dog—an unneutered male. My mind is basically occupied with three things: feeding, fighting, and fucking. Sometimes finances. Beyond that, I don't give a shit about anything.

So, pet me and give me treats and I'll be your loyal companion for life." He exhaled and hugged me. "Can we *please* have makeup sex?"

"No."

"Can we do something sexual?"

"No."

"Can you watch me while I do it to myself?"

"Eww. Gross. No!"

"Can I watch you while you do it to yourself?"

"No."

"Can I pay you?"

"You mean like one of your sex workers?"

"I only give them their cut and tips. I'll pay you the entire amount."

"No."

"Can I buy you something to persuade you? Like a diamond ring?" I held up my left hand.

"Can I buy you a house?"

"You're going to do that anyway."

"Can I beg like a pathetic dog?"

"No."

"Can I lick the dirt off your feet while you tell me everything I've done wrong in my life?"

"No. It would take too long."

"You win." He sighed. "I'm a broken man."

"Go to sleep."

Ten minutes passed and my brain was still whirling. One thought leaping to another. A minute later, I asked, "How many women did you sleep with while I was mad at you?"

"Ah, so *that's* what—"

"I have multiple reasons to be angry with you, Donatti. Just answer the question."

"Jealous?"

I turned over to face him. "*Answer* the question."

"Zee-ro." Silence. "I've haven't touched anyone since you got here. And I won't touch anyone until you leave. I told you that."

"Your word isn't worth anything."

"Terry, if I fooled around while you were still here, the girls would have told you."

"Yeah, right! Narc on the boss."

He paused. "You know, if I had hooked up with anyone else, my ladies would have torn her to shreds. But they know you're different. You're older—"

"Thanks a lot."

"To me you're the most beautiful woman in the world, but your age is a fact."

"Keep digging that grave."

He ignored me. "You're older, you're a doctor, you were my wife, we have a son and over twenty-five years of history together. They know they can't compete against that. So they've taken you as one of their own. They look after each other, Terry. That means they look after you. In their eyes, it would have been disrespectful. They would have been mad at me. You would have been mad at me. I'm an amoral guy, but sometimes things, even sex, aren't worth the hassle."

WEDNESDAY MORNING, DECKER showered, shaved, and dressed. He was ready to greet the day and walked into the kitchen just as the coffee machine beeped. As thank-you gifts for their hospitality, the kids had picked up a variety of fresh jams from a farmers' market on the way to the house. Decker opened one of the jars and slathered rich marmalade onto his toast. Rina was on the phone with a real estate broker from New York, trying to negotiate a rock-bottom price for a bigger apartment for Hannah and Rafi. She was determined to get a good deal for the kids.

When she hung up, Decker said, "How's it going?"

"It's a buyer's market in New York." She poured herself a mug of java. "I've just got to convince the sellers of the situation."

"Some people are very stubborn."

"Indeed." For her jam choice, Rina decided on raspberry. After saying the ritual blessing, she took a bite of toast and sat down. "Last weekend was nice."

"It was fun seeing all the grandchildren." Decker exhaled. "I can't believe how big the twins got."

"Length, yes; girth, they've got a way to go."

"Yeah, they are skinny," Decker said. "Aaron wants to weight lift."

"He's a little young."

"He is. But he's very intense."

"He is," Rina said. "I know that he's seriously looking at college ball."

"Yeah, Cindy mentioned that. Akiva is equally bright, but way more mellow. But their differences make it fun." Decker paused. "Why do they talk at the same time?"

"No idea." Rina smiled. "It was a loud weekend. Lily has quite a set of lungs on her." Decker laughed and Rina laughed with him. She said, "What's on your schedule today? More cats in jeopardy?"

"Depends on whether or not we've got DNA results from the clothing we found. It's taking a while. I think they've cut down on their staff."

"Like everyone else." Rina took a good, hard look at her husband. He seemed far away. "What's on your mind?"

Decker sat back in his chair. "I'm so proud of Cindy. I'm just so happy for her."

"She's been a detective for a very long time, Peter," Rina said. "It's just a different unit. She'll do fine. Stop worrying about it."

"I'm not worried at all." Decker sipped his coffee. "But with her joining Homicide . . . it really does seem like I'm passing the mantle."

"Feeling usurped?"

"More like coming to grips with the future."

Rina nodded. "Second thoughts about Israel?"

"Not at all."

"The place has gone up since we bought it. We could sell for a profit. Are you sure?"

"Positive. This is a new adventure and I love adventure. I'm looking forward to it."

"I'm glad." Rina smiled. "You know you're only taking a leave of absence. You're not resigning. You can always go back."

"But in reality, I probably won't go back."

"If you don't go back, I'm sure you'll chart a very interesting future. As a matter of fact, you already have. Israel was your idea."

"Are you okay with it? I kind of feel like I've dragged you along with my vision."

"I'm great with it." Rina took a final bite of toast and wiped her mouth. "The only problem is this current case. You're not going to leave for sabbatical until you get it solved."

Decker thought. "I've got time before we leave."

"And if a new case comes up?"

"I'm not going to take it."

"Yeah, we'll see about that." Rina patted his hand. "What about Tyler?"

"The kid has many options. He can stay in law enforcement either as a cop or in the district attorney's office."

"Or public defender's office."

"Bite your tongue."

"Everyone's entitled to representation."

"It's the American way," Decker said. "Tyler will figure it out. He'll be fine."

Rina regarded her husband. "You do seem melancholy, darling. It's okay to mourn something that has been a part of you for so long."

"Too busy to mourn. I'm focused on solving this case. I want to go out a winner."

"You've always been a winner in my book."

Decker smiled. "Thank you for the wonderful life you have given me."

"You're welcome. Luckily, it isn't over yet."

"Right." He stood. "I'll see you tonight. What are we doing for dinner?"

"No idea," Rina answered. "But whatever we decide, Tyler can join us."

McADAMS HUNG UP the phone as soon as Decker walked into the detectives' room. He said, "There's a mixture of blood on the clothing. Most of it belongs to Pauline, and they're working on separating Pauline's blood from the second sample to do a DNA typing."

"How long will that take?"

"They're hoping this afternoon or tomorrow. Baer is in CODIS, so it'll be either a yes or a no. I am really impressed that you insisted we look for something on the roadway. Like how did you know?"

"Been doing this for a long time. Detectives do a lot of legwork and a lot of it is monotonous . . . not to mention dirty."

"I know. I've been through enough trash cans in my days here, old man." McAdams smiled. "Hey, I'm going to get some coffee from across the street. Want anything?"

"No, I'm fine. By the way, you're invited for dinner."

"Great." McAdams picked up his wallet. "Even if the second blood type belongs to Brock Baer, is that enough to convict him of anything other than being with Pauline when she was injured?"

"I don't know," Decker said. "But you have to ask who else if not Baer."

"All Baer would have to say is that they were both hurt by an anonymous third person. And the blood in Elsie's house got there because Baer brought her over while she was bleeding."

"Already thinking like a lawyer," Decker said. "Okay. Then why would someone bury her? Why not just call the police?"

"Baer had a record. He didn't trust the police."

"Why bury her so far away?" Decker asked.

"He had been jailed for domestic violence. He didn't want the finger pointed at him. Or . . ." McAdams paused. "Baer could say that he stabbed her, realized what he'd done, and was hoping Elsie could save her. That would knock down the first-degree murder charge. If I were him, I'd go with the anonymous person, although juries don't like things like that."

"You've found your calling in law." Decker smiled. "Too bad it's for the other side."

"I'm not pleading his case, boss, I'm just saying if I were to plead his case . . ."

Decker thought a moment. "If Baer brought Pauline back to Elsie's house, and she was already dead, that would explain why there was no spatter in the kitchen."

"But it wouldn't explain why Baer would bring the body to Elsie's house and then bury her far away. Why not just leave her where he killed her?"

Decker's brain was filled with jumbled ideas. "What if Baer forced Elsie to help him bury the body? I'm beginning to think that Elsie was complicit in some kind of way. It would explain why she didn't go to the police."

McAdams said, "If Elsie was complicit, why would she choose a spot so close to the diner to leave her car and bury Pauline? She had to know that once Bertram was reported missing, we'd be looking there."

"Burying the body near the diner had to be done on purpose," Decker said. "Meaning Elsie had to know about the field trip. What if Bertram was there when Baer brought Pauline into Elsie's house?"

McAdams said, "If you were Elsie and you saw Baer was at the door with a body, and you knew that Bertram was in the house, what would you do?"

"Tell him to hide."

"Exactly."

"But suppose he sees what's going on and he hears everything. How do you think that would affect him?"

"He'd be totally traumatized," McAdams said. "Anyone would."

"So how about this?" Decker said. "Elsie helps Baer bury Pauline near the diner knowing that Bertram has a field trip there. Once she gets back to her house, she tells Bertram to go back to Loving Care and stay quiet about what happened. She tells Bertram that she'll meet him at the diner and they'll escape together with Kathrine if he doesn't tell *anyone* what happened. He agrees. In the meantime, she plans everything. It takes time to get tickets and passports and all the stuff you need to go abroad."

"It still doesn't explain why she'd leave her car there, pointing the finger at her."

Decker formulated his thoughts. "If Bertram disappears from the diner, Elsie *knows* we're going to scour the area looking for him."

McAdams said, "She wanted Pauline's body to be found?"

"It would certainly ensure an investigation into Pauline's death."

McAdams said, "Elsie convinces Baer to bury the body far away—in Greenbury—knowing that she's going to meet Bertram at the diner and take him back to Germany because he was traumatized by what he saw and wanted to go back home."

Decker nodded. "Trouble is, Harvard, no one we spoke to at the facility said anything about Bertram being traumatized."

"And if he was traumatized, you'd think he'd talk to someone at Loving Care about it."

"Let's rewind the discussion." Decker paused. "Weren't you going to get coffee?"

"Yeah, it can wait. Unless you want some."

"I'm fine for now, but you go get coffee. Let me think about this for a moment, okay?"

"Be back in ten," McAdams said. When he returned, he said, "Got you a coffee anyway."

"If you buy it, I will drink it. Thanks." He took a sip. "Wow, way better than the station's swill." Another sip. "I was thinking about what we were saying, Tyler. If Bertram witnessed such an event, he would be traumatized. And the people we talked to said he clearly wasn't traumatized. He was excited. What if Bertram had nothing whatsoever to do with Pauline and Brock Baer? What if he wasn't at the house at all? What if Elsie's plan to kidnap Bertram and Kathrine predated Pauline's death?"

McAdams said, "The parents never called the police with a ransom demand."

"Maybe *kidnap* isn't the right word. Maybe the right word is *rescue*. I keep going back to the pictures of them that Elsie had on her bookshelf. Maybe she just thought that Bertram and Kathrine should be together and she was going to make it happen."

"Friar Lawrence to Romeo and Juliet." McAdams shrugged. "Could be."

"Let's say Elsie had all her ducks in a row—the passports, the tickets, the money—she had all this planned before the mess with Pauline. Then Baer shows up, forces Elsie to help bury Pauline . . . Elsie knows she's about to escape. She's in the process of taking Kathrine, which could be construed as kidnapping even if Kathrine was willing to go with her. Elsie's not about to go to the police. But she does want Pauline's body to be found. If the DNA is his, I think that we've got enough circumstantial evidence to arrest him." Decker waited a beat. "Maybe not to convict him, but we can possibly hold him long enough to convince Elsie to come back to the States and make a statement."

"Why would she do that?"

"We can strike a deal with her . . . tell her we're not prosecuting her for kidnapping Kathrine or for helping Baer or anything else like that if she'll tell us what happened to Pauline. Maybe then she'll want to come in and do the right thing."

"You have a lot of faith in humanity," McAdams said.

"I hedge my bets," Decker said. "I expect the worst and hope for the best."

WHEN THE BLOOD mixture came back containing Brock Baer's DNA, the case was catapulted into action. The first step was to find the man—a lot more difficult than sending out a BOLO and waiting for the information to come rolling in. Ten days of fruitless searching: sending out countless emails and checking out wire services and making numerous calls to numerous agencies. The man was a ghost. Decker tried to remain positive, but the frustration was mounting and the clock was ticking. Six months until retirement sounded like a lot of time, but cold cases are often measured in years, not days.

McAdams hung up the phone. It was eleven in the morning. "Well, that was a bust. The perp was named Brad Bayer."

Decker push the end button on his cell phone. "Sorry, I didn't hear you."

"Not important. Just venting. What's up with you?"

Decker said, "Guess who I just got off the phone with?"

"Santa Claus?"

"Almost as good. Mila and Kurt Lanz's private secretary. His name is Joseph Jager and he speaks English very well. We actually could communicate."

"That's always helpful. So where are the Lanzes this time? Nepal? Djibouti? Kathmandu?"

"Still currently unavailable, *but* Jager did say that Bertram Lanz is with his parents and we can stop looking for him. I told him before I can call this a closed case, I'd like to speak to Bertram."

"And?"

"He said he'd try to arrange something. I also told him that I'd like to speak to Kathrine Taylor as well."

"He confirmed that Kathrine's there?"

"He didn't say yes or no. All he told me was that he'd try to arrange what I asked for. Once I talk to Bertram and Kathrine myself—make sure they're okay—I can close that case. Inroads, Harvard, inroads."

"Why do you think he's suddenly cooperative?"

"Maybe it was all the calls that we made to the local police. Maybe it's been long enough for Bertram's parents to feel comfortable about taking Kathrine. Who knows?"

"Are you going to call Kathrine's parents?"

"I will once I've spoken to her. I'll also call Lionel Lewis and Renee Forrester. I'm sure they'd want to know that Bertram and Kathrine are okay."

McAdams said, "And Elsie Schulung?"

"She's the question mark," Decker admitted. "When I asked about her, Jager told me that she came to Germany with Bertram and Kathrine, but she took off and he doesn't know where she went."

McAdams said, "Do you think he's telling the truth?"

"Don't know," Decker said. "I did tell him that if Elsie contacts them, it's imperative that she call us back. She's needed in a murder investigation."

"As a witness."

"As a witness, as a perpetrator, as a coconspirator. I don't know yet because all the evidence isn't in. Not knowing the details, I could sure use Elsie's help."

"And what are the odds that Elsie will call back?"

"Don't know," Decker said. "If she's frightened of Baer and if we find him and put him behind bars, she might be more inclined to help. First we have to find her." He shook his head. "We haven't been able to find a local felon. How are we going to find someone in a foreign country?"

McAdams paused. "If Bertram is at home in Germany, maybe we could go and talk to him there. Maybe he can shed some light on this mess. He certainly cost us enough money and manpower. A couple of tickets to Europe would be a drop in the bucket."

"True. Want me to get the coffee this time?" Decker asked.

"We should get a pod machine."

"We should," Decker said. "Since you bought the last pod machine, how about if I buy a new one?"

"Buy a better one than I did," McAdams said. "That lasted all of six months. Why are you buying anything when you're leaving soon?"

"My parting gift to Greenbury."

"Won't be the same without you," McAdams said. "Do something especially obnoxious so I won't miss you so much."

"I'll miss you, too, Harvard. Believe it or not, I probably learned as much from you as you did from me."

Decker's cell rang and the screen showed Cindy's name. She had started Homicide last week and he hadn't heard a peep from her. No news is usually good news, but with children there was always this low level of anxiety that the other shoe was about to drop. Or maybe it was his own anxiety about moving away.

He swiped the icon. "Hi there, stranger. How are you?"

"Doing okay. And you?"

"Can't complain, can't complain." A pause. "How's Homicide treating you?"

"Well, a certain homicide detective is getting a sore backside from getting kicked in the butt."

"Nature of the beast," Decker said. "It's either an easy solve or leads that go nowhere."

"That's what they tell me. Right now, I'm doing a lot of computer work for ongoing cases when the detectives are out in the field."

"Computer work is part of the training."

"It is and I'm comfortable in front of a screen. My compulsive nature is an asset here. Any detail I do point out at a crime scene is truly appreciated."

"Fabulous."

She sighed. "I've been on two death notifications. Does it ever get easier?"

"No."

"I was afraid you'd say that," she said. "I suppose that's what motivates us more than anything. Trying to get some answers for the families."

"Truth, justice, and the American way," Decker said. "Are you integrating okay?"

"Very well, actually. My colleagues seem happy with my can-do attitude, even if I border on hyperbolic. I smile through my frustration and no one is the wiser."

"Good for you."

"Thank you." A pause. "I'm not actually calling about me. Remember you asked me to check on Brock Baer with the ALPR data center? I got a hit. I think your guy has been arrested in Kelbo, Missouri."

"Really?" Decker brought up Google on his computer screen and typed in Kelbo, Missouri. "What charge was he brought in on?"

"Burglary."

"Where the heck is Kelbo, Missouri?"

"It's in the Ozarks."

"Okay, here it is." Decker enlarged the map. "Where's the next largest city?"

"It's about twenty minutes from Springfield, Missouri, which, in turn, is about forty-five minutes away from Branson, Missouri—the country music city."

Decker paused. "Don't tell me our guy is in a band?"

"He might be, but he's more likely to steal a guitar than to play it. I believe that your guy was moving back and forth between all three places. When he was arrested in Kelbo, they searched his motel room and found stolen property linked to cases in Branson and in Springfield. Kelbo PD is a small operation. They have about twenty uniforms and ten detectives in a Criminal Investigative Division."

"I'll give them a call. Thanks, princess. You don't know how much this helps."

"Least I could do after torturing you and Mom as a teenager. I've got a name and number. Do you have a pen?"

"I do."

"Contact Sergeant Loretta Stoltz." She spelled it, then she gave Decker the phone number. "Stoltz heads Burglary, which is not only the biggest department in the detectives squad but also the most active department. I looked up their stats. Not an exceptional amount of violent crimes, but a lot of property crimes."

"And where is Brock Baer at the moment?"

"I think he's behind bars, but I'm not positive where he is. I'm sure Stoltz knows."

"I'll call her as soon as I hang up with you," Decker said. "Sergeant Kutiel, if you ever want a position in Greenbury, I'd be happy to give you a letter of recommendation."

"No, thanks," Cindy said. "I've been ordered by my sons that if we ever make a move, it must be to a city that has all three major league sports teams. We not only have the Eagles, the Phillies, and the Seventy-Sixers, but as icing on the cake, we also have the Flyers. Sorry, Charlie. Greenbury just cannot compete."

CHAPTER 25

TWO WEEKS AFTER the Labor Day debacle, I was reading my divorce papers, sitting in Chris's desk chair in his downstairs office—the space where he often held his intimate parties. There was a lot of legalese in the contract, things that had to do with Devek's taking full responsibility of the debt incurred during our marriage. Since I wasn't asking for any financial remuneration—there was nothing to be had—I was asking for full custody of both children. The office door was closed and I had privacy. But Chris kept on coming in and out, searching for papers he needed, or looking up something on his computer, or just asking me if I had questions.

I had a lot of questions. The next time he came in, I said, "Am I reading this correctly or does it say that Devek gets Sanjay over the summers?"

"That is correct," he said.

"That is unacceptable."

He sat on top of his desk. "Baby, it was his set-in-stone demand from his lawyers. I have to speed the process along. The longer Devek and Sanjay are under threat, the more that threat becomes a reality."

I became weepy. "Once Devek has Sanjay, I'll never see my son again."

"Terry, he's signed the papers, and by law, if he reneges, he'll get jail time."

"They'll never prosecute him. He'll just run away with him."

"No, he won't."

"How do you know?" My voice had risen a couple of notches. "I'm a little emotional right now."

"I know." Chris was preternaturally calm. "Teresa, listen to me. I know there are some divorced men who are good fathers. But judging from *my* experience with divorced men—which, granted, is biased—what I see is that once men start new families, they discard the children from their exes. Men are attached to their kids because they are attached to their wives. Once they're done with their wives, they lose interest in the kids."

"You never lost interest in Gabe," I countered.

"Because I never lost interest in you," Chris said. "This may sound harsh, but I'm pretty sure that Devek will remarry. And once that happens, you and your kids will be relegated to souvenirs."

"What do you know of him?" I said. "You've never met him."

"I've talked to him."

"You *have*? *When*?"

"Mostly, I talked through lawyers, but there were times I had to talk to Devek directly. Specifically, when it came to Sanjay. And our conversation has been mostly civil."

"Mostly?"

"He's a frustrating guy." Chris laughed. "Devek is a little . . ."

"Weak?"

"I was going to say wimpy, which is surprising because most doctors think they're a step away from God. He's probably weak because he's always been under the thumb of his older brother"—he looked at me—"who seems to have a thing for you."

I felt myself turning red. I looked down.

"Good for you for saying no," Chris said.

Tears spilled down my cheeks. I whispered, "Devek told you what he did?"

"I dragged it out of him. In all my experiences, I don't recall knowing another man who tried to pimp his wife to his brother. What's his name? Pramod?"

I said, "Then you're aware of Devek's character. He's not going to let Sanjay go. If for no reason other than spite."

"Nah, that won't happen." He looked at me. "Listen to me, Terry. Devek is a respected doctor who comes from a rich and prominent family. He's an idiot, but on paper, he's a pretty good catch. I guarantee you that once he gets a new wife—and a much younger wife—she won't want anything to do with Sanjay. Eventually Devek will stop asking for visits. He will, in fact, ask you to keep Sanjay for the summer because he'll have other plans with his new family. You'll get him back. In the meantime, this concession got him to sign the papers."

I wiped my eyes. "What if he doesn't give him back . . . I mean now?"

"Baby, I'm going to India and picking Sanjay up personally. If Devek wants to remain alive, he won't fuck with me. This time, I promise you I won't miss."

"Are you really going?"

"I promised Sanjay's . . . guardians . . . a big final payout. Until I get the boy in my hands, they won't get it."

"Thank you for everything, Christopher. I can't tell you how much . . ." I smiled through tears. "Can I come with you?"

"Absolutely not!" Chris snapped back. "I've got contacts there, but I'm still a stranger in a foreign country. If those guys get their hands on you, they'll bleed me dry." He got up. "The lawyers are going to be here in a few hours. They'll explain everything."

"I'll write down any questions I have."

"You can write whatever you want, but you have to sign *this* contract. I can't go back and start renegotiating anything. It'll just delay things and piss people off. If I fucked something up, you'll have to live with it. I did the best I could."

"Thank you again." My voice was still quiet. "Chris?"

"What?"

"Why didn't you ever remarry?"

He regarded me as if I were an alien. "I've got a vault filled with cash, I've got the best business in the world, I've got pussy and ass whenever I want and however I want, I've got all the toys and shit. Why would I marry some whiny-ass bitch who'll take my money and give me headaches?"

I said, "There are a lot of nice women out there."

"I'm sure there are. I'm not interested in nice." A pause. "No put-down to you. You're very nice." He furrowed his brow. Then he said, "I think you're asking me if I could ever love another woman. The answer is no. One love of my life is enough, thank you very much." He looked at me pointedly. "With you, I don't have to explain myself. Which makes you easy." Another pause. "You're also . . . I shouldn't tell you this. It'll swell your head. But you're good in bed."

That was a first. Never heard that from him before. Not that he ever complained.

His eyes got far away. "I've been with a *lot* of women."

I raised my eyebrows. "I'm aware of that."

His eyes came back to my face. "I love what I do, Terry, but believe it or not, it's still a business. When I'm with a newbie—after I pay her, of course—I'm always thinking, *Is she good enough, is she enthusiastic enough, is she compliant enough, does she have enough spunk, what are her facial expressions, what noises does she make?* It's the difference between a sex worker and a good sex worker. A thousand things rush through my mind. Even when I pay for it with one of my workers, I'm cognizant that I'm with my own employees and I don't want to damage the merchandise. I never fully leave my brain behind.

"When I'm with you, baby doll, I feel this out-of-body experience more potent than any drug I've ever taken, because I can finally let myself *go*." His eyes met mine. "I don't mean to hurt you. I really don't want to cause you pain. Forcing you is a terrible tactic and it always comes back to bite me in the ass. But sometimes, I get so worked up, I just can't *help* it."

I didn't say anything. Challenging him wouldn't help get my son back.

He said, "Which is why no matter how mad you get at me, no matter how you keep fucking me over, I'll keep coming back. And I'm not the only one, you know. Devek's still madly in love with you. I know he's hurting. He's as much an idiot as I was. He would take you back in a heartbeat. But Pramod would never allow it."

I was confused. "You've talked to Pramod?"

He paused. "Again, I don't know if I should tell you this, but here goes. No judgment, okay?"

"Okay."

"I work with casinos all the time. I get a lot of my workers from them. When certain people accrue gambling debts, I buy the debt from the casinos at a discount for quick cash—usually sixty to seventy percent—and then the people come to my place and work off the full amount of the obligation plus ten percent. I pocket the difference. Most are sex workers, but a few, like Karen in the commissary, do regular jobs—cleaning, serving, bartending. Anyway, while they're working off the money, they still get their tips, but I keep their percentages until we're even. It usually takes anywhere from three to nine months. After that, the workers are free to continue or get the hell out. About thirty percent stay on.

"Now, the vast majority of people who owe money to casinos

don't become sex workers, obviously. They pay off their debts by getting loans from their families or hocking valuables or working in the kitchen, or something like that. And the vast majority of people who think they can do sex work are unsuitable. In an initial interview, I can tell in five minutes if it'll work or not. But, when I do get someone, he or she has never, *ever* owed the amount of money that Devek had accrued, because casinos cut you off when the losses pile up. When Devek first told me how much his obligation was, I was astounded. No casino I've ever worked with will let you get that far unless the gambler is filthy rich—which Devek wasn't—or has a guarantor. Guess who your husband's guarantor was?"

"Pramod. He controls the purse strings. But he already told Devek that he wouldn't cover his debt."

"Apparently that bastard told *management* that he'd cover Devek's debt, knowing full well that he was going to let Devek drown."

"Sounds like him," I said under my breath. "He is a bastard."

"It was Pramod who sent Devek to Goa in the first place. He owns the hospital where Devek works. Did you know that?"

"Actually, I did. He hates Devek. He's jealous of him because Devek is better educated and is smarter. Pramod is a slimeball."

"I'm sure that's true," Chris said. "Pramod has lots of businesses in Goa."

"He has businesses everywhere," I said. "I don't know if he's a billionaire, but it's close."

"He has more money than I do, that's for sure."

"Chris, how do you *know* all this?"

Silence.

"Did Pramod *call* you?"

Chris shrugged. "He was very unhappy about you moving away."

"And?"

"What do you think? He made me an offer. If I send Juleen and you to him—back *home* was how he put it—he'd take care of his brother's debt, you'd get your son back, and I'd walk away an even richer man."

I was in utter shock. "I don't know whether to believe you or not."

"Doesn't matter to me, but in this case, it's the truth." Chris stopped talking.

"What?"

He said, "There's this archaic law in Goa—just in Goa because it was a Portuguese state—I don't know if it's ever been implemented or not, but it's on the books. A Hindu man can take on a second wife if his first wife doesn't produce sons. Pramod only has daughters. Maybe he wanted you as number two . . . to get some sons out of you."

"He told you *that*?" When Chris didn't answer, I said, "That's ridiculous. I'm forty-two years old."

"You can still have babies. How old is Pramod?"

"There are three sisters in between Devek and him. He's around sixty."

"To him, you're still a young woman. The law is a good excuse to get you in his bed."

"I'd never have sex with that goat!"

"You would if he threatened to take away your kids. That's why Juleen had to be part of his bargain."

I was stunned silent.

Chris said, "It didn't matter what he offered me. I'd never let you go for all the money in the world. Think about that the next time you get mad at me." He stretched his long frame. "I'm getting some coffee. Do you want anything?"

I still couldn't speak

He patted my shoulder. "You need to relax. Take a Jacuzzi or something."

I didn't answer.

"Terry?"

I said, "I'm not taking a Jacuzzi with all those yucky men that you call clients. As a matter of fact, if I never see another male in my life, it'll still be too soon."

"Yeah, we're dogs." Chris smiled. "I've got a private hot tub on my patio. Go there."

I got up and pulled the curtains back. I thought the fabric hid a window. In fact, it was a sliding glass door to a patio where, indeed, there was a hot tub. I had been in this office about a half dozen times and I had never bothered to look around. I said, "I've been dying for a bath. You're just telling me this now?"

"I wasn't hiding it from you," he said. "You never asked."

"Who's been in there?"

"You mean like people? In the last six years, no one except me." He held up his left hand and wiggled his fingers. "Well, sometimes I come with Mary and her four sisters, but I think you can handle that." When I didn't answer, he said, "TMI?"

"Y'think?" I shook my head. "I'm sorry, Christopher. I'm still in shock. I can't believe what you just told me about Pramod."

"I'm a great liar, but I don't have the imagination to make that up." When I remained silent, he tapped the papers. "This is your future, Teresa. *Our* future. Together. Now forget about what I told you. Relax and take a Jacuzzi."

Finally, I said, "I don't have a swimsuit."

"Why would you need a swimsuit? No one will see you except me." He looked at his watch. "If you go in now, I can join you for about fifteen minutes." He came over and pulled me to my feet. "C'mon. Let's have a nice hot soak together, okay?"

He disrobed and so did I, and we both got in. He sat me on his lap and turned me around so my back was to his chest. He was hard underneath, but he didn't make an attempt. He began to massage my shoulders. "Relax, relax. You're very tight." I said nothing. "Feel good?"

"Heavenly."

"Good." He ran his fingers down my spine, pressing his thumbs into my back muscles.

"Where'd you learn to do this?" I asked.

"From getting massages. I get them at least three times a week. I'll set you up if you want. I just didn't think you'd want my workers touching you."

"If they're good, send them over."

"Sure." More rubbing. That lasted a few minutes. Then he kissed the back of my neck. "I have about five minutes before I have to get out." He wrapped his hands around my breasts and played with my nipples. "The way I feel right now, it's enough time. Is it okay?"

And what could I do after what he told me. I owed him a debt I'd never be able to pay off. "Yeah, it's okay. Thanks for asking."

"I'm trying," he said. "I'm not used to it, I don't like it, but I'm trying."

Five minutes later, he got out of the tub, dried off, and began to dress. "Water and drinks are in the bar. Help yourself. I'll be back before you meet with the lawyers. I'll bring something to tide you over before dinner. Take as long as you want in the tub, but don't get dizzy, okay?" He bent down and kissed the top of my head. "See you later."

After he left, I sat in the hot bubbling water and luxuriated, thinking about going from one doomed marriage to another. I didn't know if Chris was lying or not, but his story had the ring of veracity. Pramod had mistresses—a lot of them. What did he need me for? But then I thought: maybe he just wanted what his younger brother had. That I could see.

Pramod had always dominated Devek. The constant competition wore my husband down emotionally—and sexually. Devek was a decent lover in New York, but once we got to Mumbai, he turned tepid. As the years crept along, we didn't engage much. When he took on another woman in Goa, we were nearing the end. I certainly didn't care. Perhaps he disengaged because he knew what Pramod had in mind. Or maybe he just didn't like me that much. Whatever the reason, sex became nonexistent.

Chris was another story. No matter what he'd done on his trips away from me, he was always interested when he came back. He liked me and he liked sex with me. And he liked excitement in sex. He liked different rooms and different positions. He liked doing it with people in the house or when Gabe was watching TV in the next room. He liked doing it in his cars and on his motorbikes. He really liked doing it outside at night. Sometimes he'd take me to public places like parks and alleys, albeit they were deserted in the wee hours of the morning. He liked to dress me up and playact. He liked to call me dirty names. He liked it when I called him dirty names. He liked doing it while watching porn and munching on popcorn and giving me a play-by-play of what was happening in the video, often narrating things I didn't want to hear. If it was new and different, he was game. For him, it was all about the hunt for novelty.

With me, sex was all about relaxation. Just push the right buttons and let me go into my head to drift to my favorite scenes in my favorite places. The more relaxed I am, the better the orgasm.

He had climaxed, but I hadn't.

I sat back in the warm water, put my fingers between my legs, and closed my eyes. It took about a minute. Chris would have done me. He would have even been late for his appointment in order to get me off. In that one regard, he had always been unselfish. My excitement got him excited. But sometimes, when you really want to climax without taking a lot of time, it's just better to lie back and DIY.

HE CAME INTO the bedroom a few minutes before five in the morning. I scooted over and he scooped me into his arms. I didn't even wait for him to ask. He was quick and, for a man of his size, light on my body, his long, strong arms carrying most of his weight. Afterward, I went to wash up, and when I returned, he was hanging up from a call.

"Everything okay?" I asked.

"Fine." We went back to our original spooned position. He nuzzled my neck. "You interested in anything, babe?"

"I'm going to have to take a rain check. It was a tiring day. My head is still spinning from all the legal mumbo jumbo."

"Yeah, lawyers speak their own language."

"So, what happens now that I signed the document?" I asked.

"I just got off the phone with the lawyer in Mumbai. It'll take about a week to register the documents and then you get your final papers."

"Then what?"

"Then we get married." A long pause. "After that, I go to India and get your son."

"Are you nervous?"

"Not about getting married. Not at all. Are you nervous?"

"No," I lied. "What about India?"

"I'm not thinking about that yet. I don't get nervous or anxious when I'm on a mission. I sort of get this heightened awareness, this focus. It's actually exciting."

"Just please be careful."

"Always." He drew me closer. "How do you want to get married?"

"You mean like a ceremony?"

"Yeah, like a ceremony. Gabe's coming in at the end of next week. We can have something small with just Juleen and him, if you'd like."

I thought a moment. "I really don't want Juleen to see us getting married. I've only been separated from Devek for months."

"She knows what's going on, but she's your kid. Do what makes you feel comfortable."

"Thank you."

"If you don't want to go intimate, then how about this? You've been here almost three months. You're a resident, but even if you weren't it wouldn't matter. How about if Gabe comes here and watches Juleen while you and I have a blowout in Vegas?"

"What do you mean by blowout?"

"Shows, dinners, shopping, massages, gambling, and lots of sex, which will happen regardless of where we are."

"I don't gamble." I paused. "Do you?"

"No. It's a waste of money and I have an addictive personality. But I'll give you like five grand to play the slots. Fuck-it money. Pack some nice clothes and let's cut loose."

I hesitated. "Will you be doing business there?"

"I've got some housekeeping, sure. I have a list of possibilities that I've let slide since I've been with you. I'll just be interviewing, Terry. And even if you don't believe in my sterling character—which is very dubious—I wouldn't do anything that would get me in trouble with the law. Prostitution is illegal there. If I'm interested in anyone, I'll buy a plane ticket and finish up the interview in my territory."

"When I'm gone?"

"Yes, when you're gone. Nothing while you're here." I was quiet. Finally, he said, "Terry, if you want me to sell the place, I'll do it. Badger would buy it in a heartbeat."

"Why would you do that?" I was stunned. "You love what you do, right?"

"Absolutely. I've got the best job in the world. The question is do you love what I do?"

I thought about that for a long time. "No, I don't love what you do. And yes, I do get jealous when I think about it. But I think we're both beyond a reset of who we are. Let's keep the status quo for now."

I felt tears in my eyes. I was so emotional lately. "Thanks for the offer, handsome. I appreciate it. Vegas sounds fun. Let's do it."

"Great. I'll arrange everything."

I waited a beat. "I've been looking online at houses in Vegas—in and around the city."

"I thought we decided on Reno."

"I know, but Vegas is more international. My children are used to India—it's not only crowded, but it's also a hot climate. I think they'd do well in the desert." I paused. "Also, they're not white. Sanjay is really dark. I think they'd be more comfortable in a bigger city."

Silence. Then Chris said, "You want to look for houses together while we're there?"

"Yes."

"Then I think two, three days there would do the trick."

I turned around and kissed his lips. "Thank you for everything, Christopher—for saving me, for saving Juleen, for getting Sanjay back, for helping me heal, for doing all my divorce work, for all your financial support, not only this time but over the years. You have always been there for me. Always."

"That's truer than true."

"Chris, I really *want* you to be happy. Do whatever you want—as long as it's legal. You have my unwavering support." I kissed him again. "There will never be another man in my life. I swear. I take you as is. Thank you again."

"You're welcome." A pause. "Let's get some sleep."

"Okay." I turned over and closed my eyes.

A minute passed. Then he said, "When you were with Devek, did you ever think about me?"

"All the time." I sighed. "I missed you in bed. I missed your excitement. I missed your craziness. I missed you."

"So why didn't you contact me? I reached out about a hundred times."

"I know. I was afraid. And I had Juleen to think about. As time passed, Gabe said you had a girlfriend. I thought you'd moved on."

"I tried everything to forget you. Nothing worked." He kissed my neck. "I don't think a day went by when I didn't think about you." A pause. "Mostly not good thoughts."

I smiled although he couldn't see it. "I'm sure."

"Anger kept me going. It motivated me to take control of my life, to do what I wanted and fuck the rest. This is my place! This is me!" Pause. "But in a way, you were the catalyst behind my success."

"Then you should be thanking me."

"I wouldn't say that," Chris said. "All I'm saying is that jealousy and misery can take you far. They can take you to some very strange places."

CHAPTER 26

McADAMS KEPT CHECKING his phone to make sure they were taking the right roads. The car was passing through rural countryside—miles of oaks, pines, and maples—as they wended through the Ozarks. Not a lot of civilization through these hillsides. The reception kept going in and out. He finally gave up and unfolded the paper map they'd picked up at the St. Louis airport. "I think we're on the right highway." A beat. "Where the hell is Kelbo?"

"Just follow the marker line that the woman at the rental place drew."

"The map doesn't give me the exit road."

"That's why she told us there were only two exits: Piedmont Avenue and Main Street. I'll take Main. You never can miss with a Main Street. If we get lost, I'll call Loretta Stoltz."

"If we ever get some reception. We should have gotten a car with navigation."

"This is what they had available," Decker said. "Besides, you kept saying you could do it on your phone."

"I didn't realize we'd be in the middle of the boonies."

"Harvard, I may not have gone to an Ivy League school, but I can follow a marker line on a paper map."

"Yeah, yeah." McAdams folded the map. He wore a white short-sleeved shirt and a pair of black linen pants that, after a long car ride, were sorely in need of ironing. "How long are they keeping Brock Baer behind bars?"

"Bail hearing is tomorrow. We couldn't have timed it better." Decker drove steadily. He was comfortable in a blue cotton shirt with long sleeves rolled up at the elbows and dark blue slacks. "Now let's see if he'll talk."

"He was arrested for burglary. Why would he talk to us about a murder case?"

"You're right. If I were him, I'd just deny it and immediately ask for a lawyer." Decker thought a moment. "What we have to do is approach this from a nonthreatening way."

"Ask him for his opinion."

"Exactly, Harvard," Decker answered. "You say something like, 'You were Pauline's husband. What do you think happened?'"

"He's been through the system," McAdams said. "He may be too savvy for that approach."

"Yep. But a lot of criminals are not only egotistical, they're dumb. They don't think things through. That's why they're criminals. Unless you get the rare breed like Donatti—who's taken his psychopathology and channeled it into a very profitable business." Decker checked his watch. They had flown into St. Louis last night and left the airport motel at seven a.m. It was close to nine in the morning. They still had time on the road to devise a strategy. "I'm open to any other ideas you may have. Here's your chance to get creative."

"I don't feel creative."

"A wing and a prayer are always good options," Decker said.

"Sure, we can roll with that," McAdams said. "You do the winging and I'll do the praying."

SERGEANT STOLTZ WAS over six feet with wide shoulders and long arms. She was leading Brock Baer into an interview room, a shuffling man in an orange jumpsuit. He was cuffed in front and was being kept in the station house jail until Kelbo finished processing the paperwork to transfer him to Springfield. His charges were multiple counts of breaking and entering and burglary. Baer was of average height and build, but even with his grizzled face, Decker could tell that a good-looking man lurked somewhere inside. His stubble was brown, as was his hair. His face looked to be around mid-forties, although his posture suggested an older age. He appeared not to have slept much, having red-rimmed, milky eyes framed by sagging eyelids and pronounced bags.

The small interview room was bare basics: a table crammed against a wall with seating for three. The felon sat jammed between the table and the wall with Decker sitting next to him and McAdams on the opposite side. McAdams had a notepad and his iPad. On the tabletop were three bottles of water and a station house tape recorder. McAdams was also recording the interview on his iPad.

Stoltz said, "You hungry, Baer? I've got some potato chips and corn chips."

"Both."

"No problem," Stoltz told him. "These two men have a few questions for you."

Baer rubbed his eyes with his right hand and his left hand came along for the ride. He stared at Decker, then at McAdams. He said, "You two from Springfield?"

Stoltz answered: "No, they're not from Springfield, but that's where you're headed. I'll be back with your chips. Try to be cooperative. It'll get you further than being a mule."

Baer remained silent, but there was hatred in his eyes.

To Decker and McAdams, Stoltz said, "Be right back."

"We'll still be here," Decker said. After she left, he said, "How are you feeling, Baer?"

"Me?" He took a bottle of water and opened the cap. He drank greedily. "This is good. The tap water here smells like shit. I think they get it from the toilet."

"There's been some flooding in the area. Gets into the pipes."

"A reason don't make it taste any better." He finished up the bottle. "I'll take yours if you're not drinking it."

"Help yourself." Decker pushed the bottle over to him.

Stoltz came back in and plunked around a half dozen bags of chips on the table. "Don't make a mess, Brock. I do the cleanup myself." To Decker and McAdams, she said, "Just give a holler when you're done."

"No problem," Decker said.

After she left, Baer said, "Bitch!" Silence. "Treats me like I'm three." He imitated her: "*Don't make a mess.* What the fuck does she think I'm going to do? Shit in the corner?" When Decker gave a small smile, Baer said, "Yeah, you get it."

Decker threw him a bag of chips. "How's the food here?"

"Not good, but not as shitty as prison. You ever been inside?"

"Me? No. I'm an honest cop. I keep my nose clean because I know what would happen if I went inside."

"You'd be hamburger, old man," Baer said.

"Maybe, but I'll never know."

"You . . ." He was looking at McAdams. "You're a pretty boy. You'd be very popular."

"I'm already popular," McAdams said. "And my friends don't expect me to spread my cheeks."

Baer opened the chips. "Why are you here?"

The question Decker had been waiting for. "Why do you think we're here?"

"No fucking idea. That's why I'm asking."

"Detective McAdams and I are from Greenbury, New York. Ever heard of it?"

"Nope."

"Doesn't ring any bells?"

"Not a one."

"It's a small town best known for its colleges. Its population consists of retirees and a lot of second-home owners. It's pretty because it's surrounded by dense woodlands and trees, and it's a great place to go camping and hiking in the summer. The forests are thick, and you can bury things there and no one will find them for years and years." A pause. "Ring any bells now?"

Baer was quiet and continued to eat his chips.

Decker said, "Our body has a name. Pauline Corbett. You two were married."

"And now we're not."

Silence.

McAdams said, "You show an amazing lack of curiosity about what happened to your ex-wife."

"That's because you're going to tell me, so why should I ask questions?" He opened a bag of corn chips.

"When was the last time you saw Pauline?" Decker asked.

"I don't have to say anything to you." Baer was munching happily.

"It's a simple question."

"And I don't have to answer it," Baer said.

"I'm just trying to get a timetable."

"No, you're trying to get something on me."

McAdams said, "We already have something on you, Brock."

Decker said, "We're just trying to give you a chance to explain the situation."

"What situation?"

"A DNA situation," Decker said. "Meaning we have yours in odd places."

Baer stopped eating momentarily.

"I'll explain that later," Decker told him. "Let's go back to the beginning, Brock. When was the last time you saw Pauline?"

"If there's a DNA situation, you probably know the answer." A pause. "I don't have to talk to you."

"We know what happened," Decker said. "We know when it happened. What we don't know are the circumstances . . . if there was a reason for what happened other than a drunken brawl. If you give us your explanation, you'd be helping yourself."

Baer was quiet.

"Okay," Decker said. "This is what we have. We have enough to arrest you for murder because we have your DNA mixed with Pauline's DNA. We know you stabbed her—"

"Nope," Baer said. "See? That's why I don't say anything. You morons jump to conclusions."

"Then enlighten us," McAdams said.

Baer threw down the bag of corn chips. He leaned back and exhaled salty breath. "I didn't stab anyone."

He seemed remarkably calm for someone accused of murder. Usually—unless you're a Chris Donatti—people give off some kind of tell. Decker said, "Then explain to me how your DNA got mixed with Pauline's."

"Why bother?" Baer looked at him. "You won't believe me."

"Try me."

"It was self-defense."

He was right. Decker didn't believe him. "Tell me about it."

"She was a fucking lunatic. When I tried to grab the knife from her, I cut myself."

Decker tried to keep his face flat. He said, "Are you telling me that she came after you. And you grabbed the knife in self-defense. And you cut yourself."

"Exactly." He shook his head. "See, you don't believe me."

"I just think there's more to the situation, Baer," Decker said. "Pauline was stabbed multiple times. How do you explain that?"

He stared at Decker. "She did it! Not me!"

"Pauline stabbed herself?"

"Not Pauline!" Baer sneered. "Elsie! She found us together, walking back to her house. Pauline was gonna leave her and go with me. Elsie found out and went fucking crazy! She went out looking for us. When she spotted us, she parked the car and charged us like a fucking bull. Swearing and cursing at me, but also at Pauline. She went after me at first, but I dodged her. Pauline got between us, and Elsie swiped her. I think it was an accident, but once she started, she wouldn't stop. That's why I grabbed the knife." He made a lunging motion. "And that's how I cut myself."

In an even voice, Decker said, "You're telling me that you took the knife from Elsie because she was stabbing Pauline?"

"Yeah. To get her off Pauline. When I did it, the blade sliced me open across my fingers." He held up his hand. "I still got the scars."

There was a jagged line across the insides of his fingers, between the first and second knuckles. McAdams said, "You took the knife away—from Elsie?"

"Yeah, I just said that."

"What did you do with it? The knife?"

"Tossed it on the ground, I think."

"You *think*?"

"My brain was a little fuzzy. I had a lot to drink. But I remember enough to know I'm telling the truth."

"What happened after you tossed the knife?" Decker asked.

"I gotta think." He started pantomiming, doing little things with his hands. Then he said, "I think at this point, the bitch must've realized what she did. She just folded. She started breathing hard and she dropped to the ground, screaming and crying . . . Crazy cunt!"

"And Pauline?" Decker asked.

"Dead."

"You took her pulse? You checked her breathing?"

"Didn't have to do anything like that because I know what dead looks like." He blew out air. "The bitch was in full panic mode. Kept on saying like, 'What do we do? What do we do?' What do *we* do, bitch? You mean what do *you* do!"

"What did she do?"

"She killed Pauline. That's what I've been telling you."

"Okay," Decker said. "Got it. What did Elsie do after she killed Pauline?"

"Put her in the trunk of the car." He shook his head. "I helped her. I'll cop to that. Elsie was going nuts, and I couldn't leave Pauline on the side of the road. I couldn't do that to her. Plus, everyone would suspect me. We'd been fighting that night." He rubbed his eyes again. "We brought her back to Elsie's place."

"SID went over the car, Baer," Decker said. "There wasn't a drop of blood in the trunk."

"That's because Elsie was driving Pauline's car. Elsie's was in the shop and she didn't get it until the next day. I don't know where she was having it fixed, but how many auto shops can there be in that area? Check it out."

Decker's thoughts were whirling. The story, however crazy, had a ring of truth. "What'd you do after you got Pauline back to Elsie's house?"

"Cleaned her up. Kept her in the kitchen while we figured out the best place to dump her. Elsie came up with the spot."

"It's a long way to drive to dump a body," McAdams said.

"I didn't know that at the time. All Elsie said was she knew a spot that was far away and wouldn't throw suspicion on either one of us. Besides, Pauline didn't work. It wasn't like someone was expecting her."

"Go on," Decker said.

"We both wanted to do it soon because . . . fuck, let's face it. Who wants a dead body in the house? The next night we left Baniff in separate cars. I took Pauline's body and Pauline's car. Elsie took her own car. I followed her. After we buried her, we went our separate ways. I never looked back and I never saw the bitch again."

"And when again did you bury her?"

"I dunno. After midnight."

"What day?"

"The next night after Elsie knifed her to death."

"You're taking a chance, Baer," Decker said. "You're riding with a body in the trunk of a car, going a long, long way."

"Didn't know it was so far at the time. Like I said, I didn't choose the spot." Baer thought a moment. "How long did it take you to find her? The body?"

"Why?"

"I'm just surprised that anyone found her," Baer said. "We were in the middle of nowhere."

McAdams said, "If you acted in self-defense, Brock, why not call the police?"

Baer rolled his eyes and cocked a thumb in McAdams's direction. "Is he a moron or is he just acting like one?"

"Shut up," Decker said. "You're in crap up to your eyeballs. If you keep acting nasty, things will get even more difficult for you. Now just answer the damn question. Why didn't you call the police?"

Again, Baer rolled his eyes. "I don't have much luck with officers of the law." Then he took a breath and let it out. "Like I said, we were arguing that night. People saw us, people heard us. I knew it didn't mean a fucking thing, but they didn't know it. Pauline and I used to fight all the time. We got drunk, we argued. We always got back together—until I beat her up. My bad. Totally admit that. But the truth was, I loved her and she loved me, and if Elsie hadn't killed her, we'd be together now, getting drunk and fighting and making up."

No one spoke.

Baer said, "We put each other through shit, but we were great together when it worked. We're just that kind of people. We party loud, we fuck loud, we fight loud."

Silence.

Baer said, "Elsie was fucking psycho. Couldn't get along with anyone."

McAdams followed Decker's lead and they both kept quiet. Keep the guy talking.

"Pauline *asked* me to come to Baniff so we could talk," Baer said. "She wanted to get back together. She was crazy about me. Crazy, too, but that's for another day."

They still didn't answer him.

Baer said, "Look, I didn't have to talk to you two. I could have lawyered up. I know this system. What I told you is the truth."

Decker waited for Baer to continue. When he didn't, he said, "We'll be back in a bit." He opened the door and called for Stoltz.

When she came, she asked, "Are you finished?"

"Can you get someone to watch him?"

"No problem." She came back a minute later with a uniformed officer. "What do you need?"

"Do you have an office?"

"Sure. Follow me."

To Baer, Decker said, "One minute."

"You tell her how cooperative I've been," Baer said.

"Right." He closed the door, and the three of them walked into Stoltz's office, leaving a police officer with Baer.

"Have a seat." She pointed to some empty chairs. "Man, he's a piece of work."

"I've seen worse." Decker sat down. He turned to McAdams. "What'd you think?"

"Part of it sounded plausible." McAdams shrugged. "I'm probably easily conned."

"I'm thinking about the scar across his fingers. It could be a slip while you're stabbing someone. But it looks like a grab-the-knife wound."

Stoltz said, "I wouldn't believe a word that comes out of that guy's mouth."

"He handed you some good lies?" Decker asked.

"Not even good ones," Stoltz said. "The stolen goods weren't his.

He was holding the goods for a friend. He bought the goods from strangers and didn't know the pieces were stolen. Not very original at all."

McAdams said, "The story he told us was pretty original. He admitted to helping Elsie bury Pauline, just not to the stabbing. But that, of course, could be a deflection."

"When is arraignment and bail?"

"Tomorrow afternoon," Stoltz said. "He isn't going anywhere."

"Good. That gives me some time to think about things." Decker paused. "Where is the car he was driving?"

"It's been impounded," Stoltz said.

"We need to get it processed. It should have a wealth of information."

"We'll get someone from Springfield. It'll be taken care of."

"Thank you." Decker stood up. "Once that's done, we'll have more than enough to hold him for murder."

"Once we're done, he's all yours." She stood up as well. "Where do you go from here?"

"I'm not sure," Decker said. "The only other witness we possibly have is Elsie Schulung. Trouble is, we can't find her. In the meantime, he's behind bars. Good luck to you."

"And you as well," Stoltz said. "Can I offer you two anything?"

"No, I think we'll be on our way," Decker said.

"We've got a long drive ahead," McAdams said. "Anywhere to grab coffee and a bagel?"

"The diner down the street has bagels in the morning, I don't know about now. They definitely have coffee."

"Thanks for the tip," McAdams said. "This was helpful, even if it wasn't what we expected to hear."

"Sometimes it works that way," Stoltz said. "Whatever the convictions and however temporary, at least for now, we got a bad guy off the streets."

CHAPTER 27

THEY STARTED BACK in the afternoon, equipped with six bagels, a pint of cream cheese, and a thermos of coffee. Decker took the first shift behind the wheel. Eyes focused on the road, he said, "Now that you've had a chance to play it out in your mind, what do you think?"

McAdams said, "Baer's story explains why his blood was there without admitting to murder. But why confess to anything? Why admit to all the after-the-fact crimes?"

"Maybe he's thinking that his blood might also be in Elsie's house. His confession would help explain why it's there."

"True," McAdams said. "Part of me believes the story even though it does sound a little fantastical."

"What don't you believe?"

"That Elsie went out looking for them specifically, that she just happened to see them across the road. What's more logical in my mind is that Baer and Pauline were arguing, and Pauline called Elsie to come pick her up."

"Go on."

"Maybe Elsie pulled out a knife. But it wasn't meant for Pauline, it was meant for Baer."

"Back off, dude," Decker said.

"Exactly," McAdams said. "But what if Elsie missed him and accidentally got her? Or maybe Pauline stepped in between the two of them to break something up." He took a bite of bagel. "Or maybe Baer killed Pauline. He's certainly had enough time to concoct a story."

"Yep." Decker exhaled. "Can you get me a bagel?"

"Sure." McAdams fished one out of the bag. "Here you go."

"Thanks." Decker took a bite and said, "Baer is trying to make us second-guess what we know. But I agree with you that it's a little strange for him to cop to all those after-the-fact charges."

"So where are you on his story?" McAdams asked.

"Parts of it ring true." Decker took another bite. "I do think Elsie Schulung had some kind of involvement. Murder? I'm not sure. But I'm thinking that she did something bad enough that she didn't feel safe calling the police."

"Protecting Bertram?" McAdams asked.

"I don't know, Tyler. No one at the home gave us any reason to believe that Bertram had been traumatized. Certainly, if he helped bury the body, he would have been traumatized. But I know what you're thinking. Why was Pauline buried so close to the diner?"

"Bertram has to fit in somewhere, Deck. He, Kathrine, and Elsie all disappeared around the same time."

"Right." A pause. "Is the coffee too hot for me to drink?"

"Let me check." McAdams filled a paper cup halfway. "I think it's okay."

Decker took the coffee, sipped, and gave it back to Tyler. "We've got to find Elsie. No one else can put the pieces together except her."

"From what we found out, she isn't with Bertram's family anymore," McAdams said. "She could be anywhere."

"And she's not a fugitive," Decker said. "She's just someone we suspect, and that's not good enough to involve any agency."

"We have Baer's story."

"Which is unsubstantiated right now." A pause. "At the moment, we are stuck."

"I would agree."

"I really don't want to leave for my sabbatical in Israel until I know what happened."

"Don't hold your life up for this, boss. Surely this isn't the only unsolved case you've ever had."

"No, it isn't. I left Los Angeles with several open files hanging over my head. But this is the only unsolved case that I have in Greenbury. It would be great to leave batting a thousand."

ELEVEN YEARS AGO, I left New York, a married woman seeking a divorce and a new life in India. Four months ago, I left India, a married woman seeking a divorce and a new life in the States. What was the takeaway? There is no such thing as a new life. There's only life.

Chris and I married on the outside deck of the top floor of the Lucky Seven casino, a four-story building in downtown Vegas with a view of the strip, sparkling multicolored gems illuminating the massive hotels. We exchanged our *I do*s in front of a justice of the peace provided by Guy Benedetto, the CEO of the consortium that owned the casino. Guy had decked the area with white roses, lilies, and mums and draped the railings in silver satin cloth. He had provided the champagne for the toast afterward, and all of it gratis: his wedding present to the "Beast," his name for Chris. He and his wife, Anna, also served as witnesses.

Like Chris, Guy was a charmer—around sixty years of age with an average height, a slender build, and a full head of pewter hair. He had an avian nose, thin lips, and sharp and focused brown eyes: all in all, not a bad-looking man. He was not only CEO of the Lucky

Seven, but he also presided over several other casinos in the area and two in Reno.

He was also Chris's ex-brother-in-law.

He was the oldest sibling of three, and, like Chris, he came from a crime family. But Guy had managed to keep his nose clean. He had set up several shadow companies that allowed him to squeak past the gaming commission's ever-watchful eye.

Decades ago, Chris had been married to Guy's sister, Maria. She was the middle child, and a woman whom Chris barely tolerated. The youngest of the three, Lorenza, had once been Chris's fiancée. Although she was more attractive and smarter than Maria, Chris really hated her. In our teenage years, he often described her as a Mafia princess, spoiled and entitled. The reason for their union had to do way more with the families than with the individuals. Their engagement dissolved once Chris went to prison. Marriage to much less attractive Maria was Chris's punishment for being in love with me.

Guy's wife, Anna, was around my age. She was taller than her husband and towered over me. She was lovely—blond hair and blue eyes, with a great body that included big breasts and shapely legs. How much of it was due to surgery was anyone's guess, but it looked great on her. When Guy and Chris had business to discuss, the two of us went shopping. Anna was anything but a ditz. She, like me, played it close to the vest, revealing little about herself and even less about Guy. Instead, we talked designer duds, diet fads, fashion trends, and we even touched on politics during lunch. Anything except the men in our lives. Together we picked out a cream-colored Chanel suit that I wore for my nuptials.

The trip to Vegas also included a gift from Chris from a pawnshop and a house hunt. Since I didn't know the different areas, I suggested that Chris set us up in a rental until I could decide what community was best suited for my family. He refused. No one would have a set of keys to my place except the two of us and an armed guard of his choosing. We compromised on a suburban three-bedroom house with a pool and a price tag that wouldn't dent his vault. It was late afternoon when we arrived back in our hotel suite. On tap for the evening was dinner at a chef-driven restaurant and the latest show by Cirque du Soleil. He had scheduled the plane to leave around midnight because he wanted to be back in Mountain Pass before the morning. I felt it best to pack up now rather than rush it later on.

The bed was covered with stuff. Chris had neatly laid out his clothes and accoutrements while I was, by nature, much less regimental. But during our years together, I had learned that order was very important to him. Everything that went into the suitcases had to be properly folded—even the dirty laundry.

He came into the bedroom from the living room, clicking off his phone and stowing it in his pocket. He said, "You're not my valet, Terry. I can pack my own clothes."

"It's fine," I told him. "I know how you like it."

He approached me from behind and put his hands around my waist. Then he turned me around. "I can look after myself. I've been doing it for eleven years."

He peered into my eyes. They started to water. It had been such an emotional time, and this was just the topper. I just couldn't seem to control my own life. He seemed to read my mind.

"I know this isn't what you wanted—"

"Chris—"

"What you wanted was an independent life without a man dragging you down. But a devil took your boy, and you made a deal with another devil to get him back. And although this devil really wants you to be happy, he can't let go. He did that once and it nearly killed him. But he's trying hard to give you some independence. It's not what he wants, but he's trying."

I stroked his face. "We've both been through so much, baby. Let's try to make this second act a fresh start, okay? We both deserve that." I stood on my tiptoes and kissed his lips. "Are you sure you don't want me to pack your clothes?"

"No, I'll do it. You never did it as well as I did anyway."

I picked up a pair of his black pants and swatted him with it.

He said, "How're your cuts?"

I looked down at the bandages on my knees. I scratched them while kneeling on the balcony floor, doing . . . I said, "They're fine."

"Good." He kissed the top of my head. "I'll push the house through escrow. I know you're going to want to move in as soon as you get Sanjay. I'm going to Mumbai in two weeks, so there may be a week or so that you and the kids will have to stay with me before escrow closes. I take it that'll be okay."

Again, my eyes became pools. "Do whatever you think is best." I stroked his cheek again. "Christopher, *please* be careful."

"I'm not worried."

"I am."

"You have more at stake."

I looked down. "I'm petrified that something will go terribly wrong. With Sanjay, of course, but also with you. I don't want you to get hurt either."

"That could happen. And that's what makes it so exciting. If it was a gimme, you wouldn't need my help." He drew me close, picked up my chin, and kissed me hard. "How did I get so lucky? To get a second chance with the only woman I have ever loved." Another kiss. "What angel was looking after me?" Another kiss. "Teresa, I'll do everything in my power to get your boy back. These last months have been worth all the pain of the last eleven years." He kissed my wedding band. "If I died tomorrow, I'd die happy."

I started to cry. How could such beauty and such cruelty occupy one body? I hugged him tightly. "Don't die tomorrow."

"I'll try my best." He looked into my eyes. "I want you very badly. Do you want me?"

I nodded. My eyes swept across the bed covered with clothing and then to his three pairs of exotic-hide boots resting on the floor.

The heels added two inches to his barefoot six-four-plus height. A slow smile spread across my lips.

He said, "What?"

"Nothing."

"Tell me."

I felt my face getting hot. I didn't know why I was embarrassed. My emotions had become so unpredictable. "No."

"I can't do what you want unless you tell." He stared at me. "Why are you blushing? Terry, we're married, for fuck's sake. *What?*"

My voice was soft. "Putting on your boots and riding the bull."

"*That's* your nasty?"

"Pretty tame, huh?"

"Y'think?" He kissed my forehead and laughed. Then he gave me a blinding smile. "I'm ready whenever you are."

I broke away and started to clear the clothes from the bed.

He said, "Just leave it."

"We'll mess up the clothes."

He picked up a pair of electric-blue ostrich-hide boots, took my hand, and led me into the suite's living room. "Baby, that's why God made sofas."

WITH NOWHERE TO go with the Pauline Corbett case and with Baer behind bars, Decker tried to concentrate on other things. Daylight became shorter and the feel of autumn permeated the air. Leaves were changing, painting the landscape in a multicolored patchwork of golds, burgundies, and oranges, and temperatures were dropping. Rosh Hashanah—the Jewish New Year—was just days away, and with it, a chance for renewal and change, for good health and happiness, and for God's love and mercy. After Simchat Torah, the culmination of the weeklong holiday of Sukkoth, Decker and Rina planned a trip to Israel to finalize real estate papers and the schematic drawings for the renovation of their little house. It might be a quick turnaround or it might be a lot longer. It all depended on how Decker was doing with the Corbett homicide.

Because the family was coming in for the holidays, Rina had been baking for weeks: breads, pies, cakes, rolls, muffins, and cookies. The kitchen had become sensory overload. The smells wafting through the house were diabolically enticing. Every time Decker came in, he couldn't help grabbing a cookie or a muffin fresh from the oven.

"You're going to kill my pancreas," Decker told her.

"Men, unlike angels, were born with free will."

"Not this man when it comes to your raisin buns."

Rina smiled. "It'll be lovely for everyone to get together for the holidays. Especially after the COVID years. You really appreciate intimacy."

"Let's see if you're still saying that in a couple of days." He took some walnuts from a bowl. "Good stuff."

"Peter, I needed those for my cookies. I just candied them."

"Make more." Decker took another handful. "A boy needs his nuts." Then he realized what he said and both of them broke into laughter. He put the walnuts down and drew Rina into a big embrace. "God, I love you."

"I love you, too." She regarded his eyes. He looked a little lost. "Are you okay?"

"Yes, I'm great. Why do you ask?"

"You seem a bit restless."

"I suppose that's true. Leaving one phase and going into another. Your mind is always filled with what-ifs and contingencies. But you can't plan for everything. I guess it's good to throw away the instruction sheet every once in a while."

"And you're okay with leaving Greenbury PD?"

He sighed. "I'd feel a little better if I could wrap up the two cases I'm still working on."

"I'm betting that you'll get solves on both." She looked down at her almost empty bowl. "Finish the nuts. I've got another bag in the pantry."

He thought a moment. "I thought you don't eat nuts on Rosh Hashanah. Doesn't it have the same gematria as *sin* or something like that?"

"Indeed, you are right. These are for the care packages I'm preparing for *after* the holidays. The kids will need something for the ride home."

"Always a step ahead, eh?" Decker said. The house phone rang. "I'll get it." He picked up the receiver. "Hel-lo."

It was Radar. He said, "Guess who just walked into the police station?"

"Give me a hint."

"Elsie Schulung."

"That's more than a hint." Decker's heart started beating harder. "Have you talked to her?"

"Not yet. I thought you'd want to be there. When are you coming down?"

"As soon as I hang up from you."

"See you in ten minutes."

"Do me a favor, Mike. Call the kid."

"Already done."

CHAPTER 28

DRESSED IN JEANS and a blue-and-white-striped shirt, Elsie Schulung sat in an interview room, head up and spine erect. She had a long, thin face with wrinkles around her sky-colored eyes and her mouth, short-cropped blond hair, and a complexion as white as powdered sugar. Her hands were long with spidery fingers, clasped together and resting on the tabletop. Mike Radar had provided her with a bottle of water and a cup of coffee. When Decker came in, she rose to her feet. She appeared to be around five eight or nine. Decker knew she was in her forties, but she could have been older. He extended his hand and she took it.

He said, "We've been looking for you."

"I've been out of the country." Her voice was high and chirpy. "With what's going on, I knew I had to come back."

Decker nodded. At that moment, McAdams entered the room. He wore tan slacks and a black polo shirt with Vans on his feet. After he introduced himself to Elsie, the three of them sat. "Ms. Schulung just told me that she knew she had to come back. And I'm glad you did. First things first, did you take Bertram Lanz and Kathrine Tay-lor out of the country when you left?"

"Everything was voluntarily. They wanted to leave. I just helped them along."

"People were worried about Bertram." Silence. "We spent a lot of police hours looking for him. And for Kathrine as well." When she didn't answer, Decker said, "I suppose past is past. Are they okay?"

"They are happy." She answered in a clipped voice with a slight German accent.

Decker said, "And you've been in contact with Kathrine Taylor's parents?"

"Kathrine called them to say that she is happy. Everyone is ac-cepting of the situation, including Kathrine's parents."

"I'd still like to talk to Bertram and Kathrine. Can you arrange that?"

"I will talk to Bertram, but no promises." She gave Decker a harsh look. "They were free to come and go as they pleased. They wanted to go overseas. I was their chaperone."

"I understand they were emancipated adults. But they had some issues. It might have been helpful if you had told their caretakers. Like I said, we spent a lot of time trying to find them."

"Their wishes, not mine."

It was clear that she wasn't going to take responsibility for their wasted time. Decker moved on to the more pressing case. "Why are you here?"

"I heard you talked to Brock Baer."

"We did," Decker said.

"How did you hear about that?" McAdams said.

"Brock called me. He's in jail and he wanted my help."

"When was this?"

"Two days ago."

"Did you help him?" Decker said.

"No. Why should I? He threatened me."

"That's not nice," Decker said.

"Not nice at all. I don't like threats."

"How did he threaten you?" McAdams asked.

"I'm sure he told you a ridiculous story. That's why I'm here. To clear up the facts."

"We'd love to hear what you have to say."

"What did he tell you?"

"Elsie, why don't you tell us what happened?" Decker said. "Can I call you Elsie?"

"I don't care."

"I'm thinking that you're here to tell us your side of the story," Decker said.

"It's not my side. It's the only side. Because it's the truth." Decker waited. She shook her head. "Pauline could be very stubborn. I told her not to meet him. I always knew that she was not as committed to our relationship as I was. But to go back to him?" She shrugged. "That's lunacy."

"When was this, Elsie?"

"When?"

"Do you remember the date?"

"No. I have to look it up in my calendar."

"How about the day?"

"Thursday or Friday. Baer called up Pauline. That's what Pauline said. It might be that she called him. Pauline was not trustworthy."

"Whoever called who, they got together," Decker said.

"Correct," Elsie answered. "Pauline said it was just a friendly hello." She made a dismissive sound. "I knew a lie, which didn't surprise me. Pauline had been a drug addict and alcoholic. Most of the time, when she was with me, I could keep her under control. But she'd get resentful of me. I told her it was a bad idea. I told her it was doomed to fail. But she was a grown woman. If she wanted to be stupid, what could I do?"

"Tell me about that night, Elsie. The night that Pauline died."

"I have to think." She sighed. "I believe she went out around seven. It was daylight, that much I know. I offered to drop her off, but she said she'd rather walk."

"Okay," Decker said. "She left the house at seven to walk into town?"

"Yes."

"When was the next time you saw her?"

"You're missing parts of the story," Elsie said. "It would be better if I told you what happened."

"Sorry. Go on."

"Pauline left at seven or a little after. I was worried. From everything that Pauline said, Brock was bad news. I know he used to abuse her. I know he beat her. He treated her like dirt. Why would she want to see him?"

For sex, Decker thought. Instead, he waited for her to continue. She wasn't about to cut to the chase. He'd just have to be patient. Right now, it was all about Elsie Schulung.

Elsie crossed her arms in front of her chest. "Pauline could be so pigheaded. 'You're not the boss over me.' She reminded me of some of the people I used to work with in the home. But they had an excuse. They were mentally compromised. What was Pauline's excuse? Why would she willingly go back and meet with that horrible man? Huh?"

"I don't know," Decker said.

"Does that make sense to you?"

"I don't know her frame of mind, so I couldn't tell you."

"Well, it doesn't make sense to me!" A snort. "Anyway, if she wants to be stupid, let her be stupid. I went about my evening. I read. I knitted while I watch a documentary on climate change. I wasn't going to wait around for her. I went to bed."

"What time?"

"About ten or eleven. I didn't even call her to check up on her. I'm not responsible for her goings and comings, right?"

"She was a grown woman," Decker said.

"Exactly." Elsie took a sip of water. She looked at the ceiling.

She was stalling. Decker prompted her. "You went to bed around eleven. Then what?"

"Between ten and eleven. I don't know the precise time."

"It's fine, Elsie. You're doing a great job."

"A great job of what?" she snapped back.

"You're giving me details that I didn't know about."

"Oh." She turned her eyes away and then looked back. "She called me . . . It was after twelve . . . Maybe it was one in the morning. Actually, she called me twice. I didn't hear the first time because I was asleep. I decided that I wasn't going to answer the call. You want to do something stupid, go ahead. I don't want to hear your sad story."

"At some point you must have answered the phone," McAdams said.

"I'll tell you in a minute. You need background first."

She was doing a dance around the crucial parts.

Decker said, "Whenever you're ready."

"Thank you," Elsie said. "Anyway, she called me a third time. I thought maybe she's in trouble. I did care about her."

"I'm sure you did," Decker said. "What happened after you picked up her call?"

Elsie thought a moment. "It was hard to make out what Pauline was saying. She was drunk. He was drunk too. In the background, I could hear him yelling, 'Hang up the phone, hang up the phone.' Eventually, the connection was lost."

"Did you call back?"

"No. I figured Brock took the phone. Pauline would have called me back if she had it."

Decker said, "You must have been panicked."

"I don't panic." A pause. "But I was concerned." She took in a breath and let it out slowly. "I didn't know where she was. But I figured she couldn't be far without the car."

"You're positive she didn't have a car?" McAdams said.

Elsie said, "I had the car—her car. Mine was in the shop."

"Maybe Baer had a car."

"Impossible." She dismissed the idea. "He didn't have money. How would he have a car? Are you going to let me continue?"

"Go ahead," Decker said.

"My car was in the shop, but I had a set of keys to her car. I took it and went out to look for her. My first mistake. I should have let her handle her terrible decisions."

She stopped talking and the men waited.

"I found her by the road. The bastard was pulling on her arm. She was screaming at him to let go. I parked the car and got out. They were both drunk. He wouldn't let her go. He just wouldn't do it!"

"Stubborn," Decker said.

"Like the jackass he was!" She shook her head. "When he tried to grab the knife, that's when it really got messy."

"Okay," Decker said. "Let's back it up, Elsie. What knife?"

"The knife I brought with me for protection. That man was evil. I had no idea what he was going to do. I had to protect myself."

"Got it," Decker said. "You took a knife with you for protection."

"I just said that."

"Yes, you did. Where'd you get it from? None of the knives were missing from your kitchen block."

"It was in a drawer. It was a knife I used for filleting fish. Not too big but very sharp."

"Okay. You had this knife with you. And you showed it to Brock Baer?"

"I didn't show it to him like a photograph. I held it up in the air and told him to let her go. I was not only defending myself but also Pauline."

"Right," Decker said. "You held the knife up and told Brock . . . what?"

"I told him that if he didn't let her go, I would stab him. And that's when he tried to take it from me."

"And you stabbed him?"

"I stabbed Pauline . . . accidentally. She got between us—Brock and me. He still was trying to take my knife, so I slashed his hand." She made a sweeping motion. "That's when Pauline made a grab for the knife." An errant tear trickled down her cheek. "She started screaming at me. Not at *him*! At *me*! I was trying to help her and she's angry with me? Such ingratitude!"

Decker said, "It's hard when you're trying to do the right thing and it backfires."

"Backfires?"

"You're trying to help and she's getting mad at you instead of him."

"Yes, exactly. She was the one that called me. I was sleeping soundly."

"When she yelled at you, you became angry at her," McAdams asked.

"Of course I was *angry* at her!" she barked. "I didn't want her to go with that asshole in the first place."

"And now you were involved in this mess because of her," Decker said.

"I wasn't involved. I was just trying to get him away from her. And then she has the nerve to yell at me and tries to take away my protection?"

Decker said, "That would make me mad."

"Yes, I was mad."

"And that's when you stabbed her again?"

Elsie shook her head. "I didn't stab her. I was protecting myself."

"I see," Decker said. "And Pauline kept trying to get the knife?"

"Yes. Stupid fool."

Decker said, "Elsie, she was stabbed three times."

"If you say so."

"Yes, I do, and so does the coroner." Decker waited. No response. Then he said, "Stabbed, Elsie. Not superficial scratches. Stabbed."

"She kept getting in the way. That was not my fault."

"Was Pauline alive when you got her to your house?"

"I'm not sure." A pause. "Perhaps."

"If she was, why didn't you just take her to a hospital?"

She looked upward and sighed. "I knew they'd ask questions about what happened. I knew they wouldn't understand. I didn't have time to explain it because of my other plans." Decker waited. She said, "I promised Bertram to take him home to Germany. It wasn't his fault that she messed up. But it wouldn't have mattered anyway. I knew she wasn't going to make it." A pause. "Now what?"

"I still have a few questions, Elsie."

She looked at her watch. "Go on then."

Decker said, "Pauline was stabbed—"

"It was her fault."

"Okay. It was her fault. But she was still stabbed. Injured. Or was she dead at that point?"

"I told you it was hard to tell."

"Right. You put her in your car."

"Her car," Elsie said. "Mine was in the shop."

"Right. You put her in her car and took her back to your house."

"Yes."

"What happened to Brock?"

"She was too heavy for me to carry, so he lifted her into the car."

"Who's 'he'? Brock Baer?"

"Of course. Who else was there?"

"It's just . . . well, one minute you're trying to stab him, and the next minute, you two are working together?"

"When we realized the seriousness of the situation, we had

no choice. Pauline was wounded badly, and we knew we had to help her."

Decker nodded.

"It was the right thing to do," Elsie said.

"Absolutely." A pause. "Let me make sure I have this correctly. Brock Baer and you decided to stop fighting and help Pauline."

"Yes."

"Then Baer helped you put Pauline into your car. Wait, her car. Yours was in the shop."

"Yes."

"After Baer did that, where did he go?"

"To my house, naturally."

"Naturally," McAdams echoed.

She turned to him. "Of course!"

"And then what?"

"He brought her into the kitchen to see the damages." She paused. "He was still stinking of alcohol, but he seemed more rational."

"What happened after he brought her into the kitchen?"

"Pauline was dripping blood. If she wasn't dead, she was barely breathing."

Decker nodded and waited for her to continue.

Elsie said, "It was clear she was not going to survive."

"And you didn't even consider taking her to the hospital?" Decker asked.

Elsie thought. "No."

Just like that.

No.

"All right," Decker said. "After she died in your kitchen, you cleaned up the blood?"

"Yes. With bleach."

"Did Baer help you clean it up?"

"Yes." Elsie thought a moment. "He was a terrible man. But I don't think he wanted her to die. I certainly didn't want her to die. But things happen."

"Things do happen," Decker said. "You cleaned up the kitchen. Then what did you do?"

"Brock and I sat down to think. It had been a crazy evening."

The mistress of the understatement. Decker said, "I'm sure."

McAdams said, "Where was Pauline while you were cleaning everything up?"

"In the trunk of her car, wrapped in plastic."

"Then you were *planning* on burying her."

"Of course," Elsie retorted. "I couldn't leave a body rotting in my house while I took Bertram and Kathrine to Germany."

Decker said, "You buried her quite a distance from your home."

"Yes."

"Who chose the spot?"

"I did." Elsie exhaled. "I wasn't thinking well. I should have buried her closer, but I knew that spot because I had been there before. It was where Bertram and I planned on meeting up a couple of days later. It was hidden and it was wooded. After we buried the body, I camped out in my car, walking to Pauline's grave and saying a prayer. It was only a couple of miles from the spot where I was going to retrieve Bertram at our appointed time."

"Once you got there, you never left?" asked McAdams.

"No, I did not."

"Elsie," Decker said, "we found your car in the woods."

"Yes, I left it there."

"How could your car be at the spot—in the woods next to the diner—if it was in the shop?"

"Because we didn't bury her until the next evening. By then, we had two cars. Hers and mine."

"What happened to Baer?"

"What do you mean?"

"I mean if you didn't bury her until the next day, did Baer stay with you the entire time? At your house?"

"Yes. I needed him to help me bury the body. I couldn't do it by myself. He got the shovels and the bags and everything."

"He just decided to stick around and help you bury her?" McAdams asked.

"I told him if he helped me, he could take Pauline's car—and he did." She shrugged. "I had to give him something. And maybe he wanted to help bury her. Together, I must say, we did a very nice job giving Pauline a proper resting place."

A proper resting place. Decker hoped his face was flat. He said, "So Baer and you drove to the spot near the diner the next day and the two of you buried her."

"Yes."

"You in your car, and Baer in Pauline's car with the body."

"Yes. We were very lucky that no one stopped him. It was summer. The body had started to decompose and smell a little. But only a little. We kept ice on it. That was my idea."

"Sounds like you planned for a lot of contingencies."

"I was as thorough as I could be. If I was thinking more clearly, I would have done it closer to home. But . . ." She shrugged.

"What happened to Baer after you two buried Pauline?"

"He left."

"In Pauline's car."

"Yes."

"Did you two keep in contact?"

"No—well, not until the other day. But right after, no contact. This whole mess was a distraction from what I had to do."

"Leaving with Bertram and Kathrine and taking them to Germany?" Decker asked.

"Yes."

"If you left your car in the woods, how did you get to the airport to take them to Germany?"

"I had arranged an Uber. We took the back roads. I didn't want any cameras picking us up. Then I rented a car and picked up Kathrine."

"It looked like your car."

"It did but it wasn't. It was a rental."

"Seems like you put a lot of energy into taking Bertram and Kathrine to Germany."

"I did." She paused. "They needed to be together. Anyone could see that. I just helped."

Decker said, "How much money did you get for it?"

"I didn't ask for anything," she said. "Just for the tickets, the rental, the hotel, and expenses."

"You didn't receive anything beyond your expenses?" McAdams asked.

"I didn't say that. I said I didn't ask for anything. Once we all got to Germany, Bertram insisted on giving me something for all my help."

"How much did he pay you for helping him?"

"None of your business!"

Decker said, "Bertram didn't have access to a lot of money while he was in the States."

"Well, maybe not in the States, but he has access to plenty of money in Germany. And how much compensation he gave me isn't your affair."

"Indeed, it's not," McAdams said. "Unless charges are brought against you for kidnapping."

"I didn't kidnap anyone. They were going to leave anyway. I just helped."

Decker said, "Right now, kidnapping is the least of your worries, Elsie."

"I know. I will go to prison. It was in self-defense, but I'm sure you don't see it that way. Nonetheless, I had to set the record straight. I refuse to hide and be a fugitive, because I did nothing wrong. It was an accident, and she had no chance of survival."

Decker said, "How do you know that? You said she was barely breathing."

"I was there. You were not. Now it will be up to my lawyer and a jury." She stood. "I have nothing more to say. I'm tired and hungry, and I'd like to rest in a jail cell."

"Okay," Decker said. "Elsie, I'm going to charge you with murder, among other things. I'm going to read you your rights." He turned to McAdams. "Do you have the card?"

Tyler sprang up. "I'll get one." He left.

"What card?"

"It's a card that tells you your rights. You sign it after I say them out loud to you."

"Okay. And what happens after that?"

"We have a holding cell here in the station house. You'll be booked on the charges—"

"What charges besides murder?"

"Murder, tampering with evidence, concealing a body, kidnapping—"

"I told you I didn't kidnap anyone."

"Sometimes not all the charges stick, okay?"

"Good." She shrugged. "What happens once I'm booked and in jail?"

"I'll get you some lunch and consult with my captain on the charges."

McAdams was back with the card. Decker Mirandized her, and once that was over and she signed the card, he said, "You'll be appointed a lawyer unless you have one."

"I don't have a lawyer."

"Okay, we'll get you one. You should be arraigned in the afternoon. Because you have a current passport and access to somewhere outside the country, you probably won't get bail. The prosecutor will deem you a flight risk. But your lawyer can try."

"Very good."

He looked at McAdams. "Let's go."

She offered her wrists. When Decker didn't do anything, she said, "No handcuffs?"

"Do I need them?"

"No. I just thought it's what the police do."

"We have discretion," Decker said. "Besides, there are two of us and only one of you." The two men flanked her, and the trio walked down the hallway. They took the elevator down one floor to the booking station. No one was there.

McAdams said, "I'll find someone. Hold on."

Decker waited with Elsie. She said, "Can't you just do this?"

"I can roll fingerprints and take a DNA swab, but I'm not good with a camera."

A minute later, Kay Arby, the booking officer, came back. "Sorry. I'll take it from here."

While Elsie was being photographed, Decker said, "Harvard, stay here until she's behind bars. Once that's done, get her some lunch. I'm going to talk to Radar, and we'll call the D.A."

The kid smiled. "No problem, boss, it's all good. And while you're making phone calls, ring up Rina and tell her to start packing. Have a good trip." Another smile, but this one was sad. "Have a good life."

Decker should have felt elated. Instead, he was weary and more than a little depressed. He gave a small smile and tried to muster enthusiasm. "You rock, Harvard." He mussed up the kid's hair. "Thanks for a wonderful ride."

Sincere words. But sad ones nonetheless.

CHAPTER 29

THE NIGHT BEFORE Chris was scheduled to leave for India, I went to sleep earlier than usual, not because I was tired but because I was a nervous wreck and didn't want my anxiety to rub off on him. He seemed completely normal when I left for the bedroom, absorbed in manning his Captain America video pod.

I was all set for his departure. Chris had finally entered me into his high-security system. I had total freedom. I could come and go from his room and from Juleen's room. I could use the private elevator. And in addition, he arranged for me to have access to a driver and his hot tub adjacent to his downstairs office. The final act of liberation included access to his vault, ergo his money. It was a tremendous act of trust, one that I didn't take lightly. It said to me the most horrific of statements.

I may not make it back with your son.

When he came to me at four-thirty in the morning, he didn't even have to wake me up. I had been up most of the night except for several catnaps from which I woke up startled and disoriented, in a cold sweat with my heart going a mile a second.

He usually slid under the sheets and scooped me to his chest. Instead he sat on the bedcovers. I rolled over and faced him.

"Everything all right?"

He stared at me. His white hair reflected the moonlight coming in through the window. "I'm in a mood, Teresa. Don't fight me. It won't end well."

Okay, I thought. *He's feeling mean.* Maybe that was what he needed to get the job done. To feel mean. If that was the case, it was okay with me. I wanted him to feel mean. I wanted him to be mean and cruel and merciless and the biggest son of a bitch imaginable. Because when working with amoral, conscienceless beings, nice guys were toast. If I had to bear the brunt of his cruelty in order for him to get the job done, so be it.

I turned around and supported myself on all fours, waiting for the pain. He hiked up my Manson girl dress, and then he growled out, "I hate this fucking thing." He ripped it in two along one of the seams. Once naked, I closed my eyes and felt my whole body go tense.

He did nothing for a moment. I could hear him breathe. I sensed his sweaty presence. I felt him grip the nape of my neck with his massive hand. But then he released his long, spindly fingers and I felt them travel down my spine, vertebra by vertebra, the tips dancing over each bone as if he were reading braille.

When the sex came, it was normal . . . assured but gentle—so much so that after it was over, I found myself aroused.

Afterward, he said, "Sit up against the headboard."

I did what he said. He came toward me. I waited for him to make a move, to loop his hand around my neck and bring me to him. When he didn't, I said, "What do you want, baby?"

"Don't close your eyes, Terry," he told me. "Look at me when you do it, angel. *Look* at me." Telling me: *I'm the one you're doing it to. I'm the one in control.*

Anything he wanted. When he climaxed, he leaned against the wall, breathing hard, his eyes closed, his head tilted toward the ceiling. I waited for him to disengage. He did a few moments later, then he nodded to me. My signal that I could get up and head to the bathroom. I brushed my teeth, rinsed my mouth, and stepped into a steamy shower.

He joined me a minute later, just as I was soaping up my hair. He dumped shampoo on his hair, and then took my face in his hands and kissed me hard and with desperation. He kissed me again. And then again. I felt him grow and I reached down, but he batted my hand away.

"Ignore it." He continued to kiss me, his tongue intertwined with mine.

"I don't want to ignore it," I said. "I want you."

He pulled his face from mine. "The sexiest words in the English language."

He carried me from the bathroom and tossed me on the bed, both of us wet and covered with shampoo. As he lowered his head between my legs, I stopped him. I said, "I don't need it." I flipped him on his back and climbed on top. The room was cold, I was dripping water, and I started to shiver. He sat up until we were chest to chest and brought my mouth to his. We kissed as we made love. He said, "You're cold." He rubbed my back. Then he flipped me around until my back was against his chest. With one hand between my legs, he pulled my head back by my hair with his other hand and kissed me hard. I brought one hand to his cheek and the other between his legs.

He sighed like a moonstruck teenager. It brought me back to years ago and made me feel like that hormonally driven sixteen-year-old girl who would have drunk poison for him. Two stupid kids in love. And twenty-six years later, I was having sex, tingling with electric shock as his hands trawled my body. I climaxed first, but only by a few moments. It was a long, hard orgasm that came in waves of hot blue fire.

After we both caught our respective breaths, he carried me back to the shower—still running and still mercifully hot. He took the handheld showerhead and washed off my soapy hair and then his own. He got out first and gave me one of his many black silk robes. He took a hand towel and dried my hair.

He said, "I'll blow-dry your hair."

"I can do it."

"I know you can, but I want to do it."

"Why?"

"Because I want to cut it. It's too long. Sit down on the bed. I'll be right back."

I sat. When he came back, I said, "Not too short."

"Stop worrying. I like you with long hair. Just not that long." He brushed out my hair and took scissors to my back. He drew a line about eight inches below my clavicles. "Right here."

I didn't answer. When the snipping was done, I felt the warm air going through my tresses as he brushed and curled. When he had finished, he took the dryer and passed it through his own shoulder-length white locks.

I looked in the mirror.

He said, "What do you think?"

"You're a man of many talents." I actually did like the length. It still made me feel feminine but a lot freer. "It's lovely."

"Glad you like it, angel." He took out his phone. "Now take off the robe and lie on the bed."

"What are you doing?"

"What does it look like I'm doing?" He aimed the phone and a bright light attacked my eyes. "Settling old scores."

"What old scores?"

"Last time we did this, you shut me down."

"Chris, I was sixteen."

"The statement still stands."

I sighed. "Nothing porno."

"To be determined." When I didn't answer, he said, "The pictures are just to get a feel for what I want . . ." Another shot. "Which is to draw you."

"Full circle, huh?"

"Full circle."

"Don't tie me up." I was serious. "I always hated when you did that."

"Yeah, I was really into bondage back then. Take off your robe. Have you ever seen Goya's naked Alba?"

"Yes, I have."

"Let's do a variation of that. Okay?"

"That's fine. What do you want?"

"Lie on your side with your head propped up with your hand." He positioned my hair so that my nipple played peekaboo with the tresses. He shot a few photos. "I must say that this is a pleasant surprise. I expected more resistance."

"If I did it at sixteen, I think I can handle it at forty-two with my husband."

He smiled. "Yes, you are indeed my wife."

"Happy about that?" I asked.

"Yes, I am. If you ever take that band off your finger, I'll put it around your neck."

"You say the most romantic things."

"Chalk it up to my charm."

"Remember the first pose I did for you?"

"Of course. I have the old sketch pads in my vault." He lowered the camera. "We should do a then and now."

"Okay." I sat up. Then I hunched over and folded my legs, bringing my chin to my knees. At sixteen, I was very embarrassed, and the pose was the most efficient way to cover my chest. "It was something like this, right?"

"Yeah, except you were wearing panties."

"Not the entire time."

"No." A wide smile. "You're right about that." A pause. "I'll get my sketch pad and my pencils. Just stay like that." He returned with a chair and his art supplies. He came over to me and made adjustments, pulling my hair over my shoulders, slightly parting my legs to allow a little visibility. He stood up and nodded with approval. "Beautiful. Don't move."

He put on a pair of rimless glasses and laid out his supplies. I heard his pencil going over the paper in quick movements. A sound etched in my brain from so long ago. After Gabe was born and we got back together, he rarely drew me. I felt he wasn't a fan of my postpartum body. After a few minutes of silence, I said, "The sex . . . tonight?" He waited. I said, "It was wonderful."

"Yes, it was."

"It wasn't what I expected."

"You and me both."

"What changed your mind?"

He scratched his cheek and stopped drawing. "I just got this overwhelming feeling of warmth. I didn't want what I thought I wanted." He started drawing again. "And I'm perverse. If you resist, I'll fight. If you give in, I'm flexible."

His pencil against the paper: *scratch, scratch.*

He said, "I can't stand to be told no. But I especially hate it from you. I feel it's a prelude to you leaving me. I don't trust you."

I sighed. "I'm not going to waste my breath defending myself."

"You left me three times."

"Two. You can't count high school."

"Yes, I can."

"We weren't even dating. You had another girlfriend. You screwed her on the night we were supposed to run away together. Or don't you remember that, Donatti?"

"I'm not senile yet. I not only fucked her, I fucked her twice. I was a fucking idiot. And it caused me a whole lot of grief, including half a year in a medium-security penitentiary, in order not to get you involved in my mess. It may not sound like a lot of time, but believe me, prison is the ultimate shit show."

I paused. "I stood by you."

"For a while."

"Christopher, I'm committed to you. I married you. You're my husband. And that's all I'm going to say."

He looked up. "Forgive me if I'm a bit insecure."

"That's an odd adjective to use."

"I'm human. I have my weaknesses." He yawned. "I could use a cup of coffee. Don't move. I'll do it. Is the machine set up?"

"Yes."

He got up and returned a moment later, took a sip, and started sketching again.

I said, "Are you okay doing this?"

"Doing what? Drawing you?"

"No, not that." A pause. "You know . . ."

"No, I don't know." His voice was gruff. "What?"

"Rescuing Sanjay?"

"Oh, that." He stretched. "Yeah, I'm fine. Shooting people isn't one of my weaknesses. But I don't think it'll come to that." He went back to his sketch pad.

I tried to remain calm. "Did you take something this morning?"

"What? Like drugs?" He looked at me. "No, I didn't take drugs. I need my wits about me for the next week."

"What about Viagra?"

"Of course I took Viagra. I won't see you for at least a week, maybe longer. I knew I wanted a lot of sex. You need a hard dick for that."

"It's not good for you, baby."

"I'll survive. Pick your chin up about an inch. A little more. Stop." He surveyed what he saw. "Spread your knees about two inches. Stop. Hold the pose."

He sketched furiously. About ten minutes later, he took off his glasses, waved me over, and showed me the pad. "What do you think?"

I smiled. "I think you made me look sixteen instead of forty-two."

"No, I drew the lines on the eyes and forehead." A pause. "Maybe I softened them a little, but it's what you look like, baby. You are that gorgeous."

I whispered a thank-you.

"You can put your robe on." He got up and came back five minutes later. "Okay. Here's what you looked like at sixteen." He showed me the sketches from twenty-six years ago. They were in a laminate plastic, but still roughed up at the edges and yellowed with age. He said, "Not that much difference between now and then."

"Yeah, right!" I stared at the picture. "I was so young. How did you talk me into doing that?"

"You loved me."

"I would have died for you." I took the sketches and laid them on the floor. I sat on his lap. "Please, please be careful." I kissed him. "Please."

He kissed me hard, then gave my butt cheek a slap. "I've got to pack." He got up and opened a cupboard and brought down the same leather bag that he had shoved in my chest just a few short months earlier. I felt tears coming. He turned to me. "None of that."

"Sorry." I sat on the bed and watched him start to pack.

He said, "You have total freedom now, Teresa. You're in the system. I even gave you the codes to my vault in case something happens to me. Theoretically, you can steal all my cash and run away anywhere. So, you be good, okay?"

"I'm not going anywhere, baby. You are stuck with me."

His smile wasn't cross, but it wasn't friendly. "I believe you." He blew out air. "That could be a deadly mistake."

Anything I'd say he would misinterpret. I said nothing.

He said, "Be a good girl and get me another cup of coffee."

"Of course." I took his mug, refilled it, and poured one for myself. I gave myself a pep talk and walked his mug back to the bedroom. When I got back, he had taken down a small duffel. He was quick and efficient in his packing. When he yawned, I said, "Do you want to rest a little before you go?"

"I don't have time. Besides, I can sleep on the plane."

"How are you going? To India?"

"My jet to Chicago. Chicago to London. London to Mumbai. That's where the event will be."

"You're not piloting your jet, are you?"

"Copiloting you mean. Not this time."

"Good." Silence. "Juleen wants to say good-bye."

"Really? Why?"

"Maybe she likes you. Maybe she just wants to get out of her studies. Just pop in and say good-bye."

"I can do that before I leave, which will be in about"—he checked his Rolex—"forty-five minutes."

Panic seized me. "I'll miss you."

He zipped up his duffel, then came over to the bed and sat down beside me. "How much will you miss me, angel?"

I smiled. "*Whatever you want* type of miss you."

He laid me down on my back. It was sweet, sweet lovemaking. Not the kind that you want when you're on fire, but the kind you want when you're sad, filled with wistfulness and longing.

When he was done, we both took a quick shower. We dressed, then we went to see my daughter.

Juleen looked up from her studies when we came in. Her lips turned upward into a grin.

Chris smiled back at her. "I'll see you in a little over a week. Take care of your mom."

"I think it's the other way around," I told him.

"I don't know about that, Terry. Sometimes I think she's stronger than you."

I smiled. "You're right."

Juleen walked over to him, and he knelt down until they were eye to eye. He said, "I expect you to practice while I'm gone."

"Of course."

"And work on your studies."

"Yes."

"And be good for your mother."

"Always." A pause. "Will you see my father?"

"Yes, I think I will."

"Say hi for me. Tell him I love him."

"You can tell him yourself. I'll have him call you."

"I can talk to my father now?"

"Once this is all over, of course you can. I'm sure you miss him."

"I do." She threw her skinny arms around Chris's neck. "Thank you for helping Mommy and me. You are not my father, but you are my friend. And I am very grateful."

"You're very welcome, Juleen."

"Please be careful, Chris."

"Yeah, your mother already warned me." He patted her back and pulled her off him. He gave her a warm smile. "You need anything, call that lazy brother of yours."

She nodded and he stood up. "See you soon with Sanjay. Relish your last minutes as Mommy's only kid."

"Bye, Chris."

"Bye." He grabbed his leather case and his duffel. Together we walked down to his waiting limo. He took me in his arms. I started to cry: deep sobs of sorrow and loneliness and longing.

He said, "I should go away more often."

I tried to smile but couldn't quite pull it off. I certainly couldn't answer him. I was too emotional.

"You're my girl?"

"Always and forever."

He kissed me, then broke off the hug. "I've got to go. You be good."

"You be careful, Christopher. Whatever happens, I want you to be safe."

"I'll do my best." He kissed the top of my head. To my bodyguard, he said, "You keep your eyes on her at all times."

"Certainly, sir." He opened the door to the rear passenger seat. Chris climbed in and the bodyguard shut the door. The windows were tinted, so once he closed the door, I couldn't see him. He rolled down the window and waved.

I waved back and watched the car drive off.

I inhaled deeply and exhaled with a whoosh. The uncertainty of the next week or two was so anxiety provoking that I knew that the only way I could cope was to bury any outcome deep within the recesses of my brain. I just couldn't deal with it. And when that happened, the safest thing for me was to ignore it until it was right in front of my face. Sanjay was now in Chris's hands, not mine.

"Ready to go back, Doc?"

I turned to my protector. Ben was on duty. "In a minute. Go get yourself some coffee. I'll meet you upstairs."

"I'll wait for you, Doctor."

"Ben, I know you're doing your job. But right now, I'm the boss. I won't be more than a minute or two. Get some breakfast. You'll work better with food in your stomach. I promise, I'll be there by the time you get back."

He didn't move. A Mexican standoff.

I smiled sweetly and winked. "Our little secret, okay?"

He shuffled his feet. "Just this once."

"Thank you."

I watched him head for the cafeteria. He was a soft touch. Within a day, I'd be able to do whatever I wanted.

I felt numb.

I felt alone.

But strangely enough, I breathed easier.

For the time being, I was free.

CHAPTER 30

I T TOOK UNTOLD man-hours, hunting for someone who had never been missing, but it was a happy ending. Three weeks after Elsie Schulung and Brock Baer were arrested and charged with second-degree murder of Pauline Corbett, Decker received an invitation to the wedding of Bertram Lanz and Kathrine Taylor.

"You should go," Rina told him. "It would be a lovely way to end the case and end your time here in Greenbury."

"I don't think so," Decker answered.

"Why not?"

"The wedding is in Germany, for one thing."

"But there's a reception in the Berkshires," Rina countered.

Decker said, "When I close the case, I close the case."

It was five in the afternoon and lunch had just ended. All the children and grandchildren were in the backyard getting the last bits of sunshine while Decker and Rina were debating whether or not to tackle the dishes. The family had come in for the last two days of the Jewish holidays—Shemini Atzeret/Simchat Torah—except for Gabe and Yasmine. Yasmine was with her parents in Los Angeles, and Gabe was out of the country. It had been a lively time—boisterous, with a lot of laughs: everyone bunking down in their small house, siblings catching up with one another, and cousins catching up with cousins, because who knew when they'd all meet again. There wasn't a square inch of floor to be seen; all of it was covered with toys, baby equipment, and sleeping bags.

Decker rolled up his sleeves. "Shall we?"

"No time like the present." Rina dug into the soapy water basin and began rinsing dishes. "Nice couple of days."

"Indeed."

"Will we miss this when we move to Israel?"

"Probably not, because they'll all come visit us for the holidays," Decker said. "I'm already putting away money for hotel bills."

Rina smiled and handed him a dish. "Do you think that's really going to happen?"

"Actually, yes, I do think they'll come and visit," Decker said. "But probably not all at the same time." He wiped a plate. "But children or no children, I'm ready to cut ties with Greenbury."

"I'm glad you reached that decision on your own." Rina put a pile of wet dishes on the counter.

"It was a great interlude between Los Angeles and our future, but it's over."

"Then we should seriously think about the offer we received for the house."

"It's a good one," Decker said. "What do you think?"

"If we sell, it's final," Rina said. "We are really cutting ties."

"Even if we decide to come back to the States, what's the likelihood that we come back to Greenbury?"

"If you are definitely quitting your job, we're not going to return here," Rina said. "If we buy anywhere, it'll be close to the kids."

"Do you want to take the money from the house and buy in Manhattan?" Decker said.

"Not really. What about you?"

"Your decision. Your trust fund."

"And it was your house that we sold in Los Angeles to buy a bigger house that we sold. Don't lay it on me, buster." Decker smiled. Rina said, "Honestly, I'd rather help all of them buy bigger apartments with a guest room. Let them do all the maintenance."

"I like it." Decker paused. "Let's counter the offer and see what happens."

"I'll call the agent right after Yom Tov." She looked at her watch. "About an hour and change from now."

Decker finished drying the holiday dinner plates and put them on the top shelf. "Last time we celebrate a holiday here, huh?"

Rina said, "I can finish this up. Go outside and be with the kids."

"I've been with them for the last two days. I'd rather have the quiet time with you."

"Thank you. That's a lovely thing to say."

"Heartfelt."

"I'm glad you finished off all your cases here."

"Took a while, but like I've always said, Missing Persons cases usually have happy endings."

There was a loud knock at the door. They looked at each other.

"Someone must have locked themselves out." Decker put down the dish towel. "I'll get it."

He managed to sidestep his way through the maze of toys, cribs, playpens, strollers, and bedding. He opened the door, and standing on the other side was a man looking at him at eye level. Or maybe Decker was looking upward an inch or two. What he saw were jumpy blue orbs darting from side to side. The man's mouth was downturned and his expression was frantic. Dressed in all black except for red boots, he was breathing hard, holding hands with two children: a boy around five and a girl around eleven. Decker stepped aside to let him in.

"What's wrong, Chris?"

"Is Gabe here?"

"No, he's out of town."

"That's probably a good thing." Donatti crossed the threshold, children in tow. "Right now, I don't want to deal with him."

"What's going on?"

Donatti let go of the children's hands. "Terry's missing." When Decker didn't answer, Donatti said, "The boy and I came back yesterday from India, and my wife was gone."

Tears were in the little girl's eyes. She whimpered, "I'm sorry."

Donatti looked down at her. "Juleen, stop apologizing. Your mom wasn't your responsibility."

Rina materialized. "Terry's gone?"

"Apparently," Decker said.

"I just *spoke* to her right before Sanjay and I left." Chris blew out air. "We all talked for about fifteen minutes. She was happy, right?"

"Yes." Tears were running down Juleen's face. "She was so happy."

"I can't believe this!" Chris started pacing. "Everything was going perfectly between us. And even if she did leave me, why wouldn't she take Juleen with her? It doesn't make any fucking sense! Except that it's Terry!"

Quietly, Decker said, "Why don't you start at the beginning?"

"There is no beginning, Decker. I told you everything I know."

Decker said, "It just might help me to get a little background."

"This is the background," Donatti said. "Sanjay and I came back from India, and she was gone. I've questioned everyone at my place. No one seems to know anything!"

The little girl said, "I tried to call Mommy, but her phone kept going to voice mail."

Donatti said, "I don't know if she took off on her own or if she was kidnapped by the motherfuckers I just dealt with. I thought I had a handle on that. I thought we had an understanding. But with people like that, I could have been conned."

"Are any of Terry's things missing?" Decker asked.

"All her clothes are in the closet, but her purse and phone are gone. If she left, it was with the clothes on her back." He wiped sweat from his face with his shirt. "I've got a vault filled with cash in my bedroom. Before she left, I told her all the codes in case something happened to me."

"Is money missing?" Rina asked.

"I did a brief check. It all appears to be there, but I haven't counted each and every stack. She could have easily grabbed a handful of bills at the bottom and left."

"Chris, is there a reason *why* she'd take off?" Decker asked.

"No! We were getting along fine." Donatti was still pacing. "Yeah, we fought. We always fight. But she wasn't pissed at me when I left. In fact, she was crying. She kept telling me to be careful." Back and forth and back and forth. "I used to be able to read her perfectly, but I can't anymore. Yes, it could have been an act. Yes, she might have been planning this from the start. But she married me. She swore she was committed."

No one spoke.

"Yes, I know what that is worth, idiot that I am." He stopped pacing for a moment. "If she took off on me, I'll find her. Believe me, I will find her."

Rina said, "Any idea how she slipped past everyone at your place and no one noticed?"

"No!" Donatti looked up at the ceiling. "Before I left, I put twenty-four-hour guards on her just to avoid anything happening to her. Apparently, she kept ditching them. It drove them crazy because she was always disappearing on them. They called me about it. I told them not to sweat it. As long as she came back, it was okay. And she always came back. They got used to the patterns. I'd be furious at them except they called me, and I was the one who pulled them off. I'm such a moron when it comes to her. Maybe she was trying out a couple of dry runs and had wanted to leave me all along.

Okay. I could understand that. But even if she wanted to leave me, she'd never leave without Julee—" He flashed to an earlier memory: her packing up after they had a knock-down, drag-out fight. He had beaned her with a pack of money. Her words sparking in his brain after he had accused her of abandoning her child—again.

I'm not abandoning her! I just want to be settled before I come get her.

"What?" Rina asked.

"Nothing." Donatti took in a deep breath and let it out. "Nothing at all. Look, I've got to get back to Nevada. She disappeared over there, not here. I've got to figure this out, and I can't do it while babysitting her kids. I can't get a hold of Gabe and I can't leave them alone at my place for obvious reasons."

Again, he looked upward.

"I'm really sorry to do this to you two—again—but can you look after them until I can get some answers? I can't search for her and be responsible for them at the same time."

Decker and Rina stared at him.

He said, "I swear it's only until I can figure out what's going on. They have a father. Devek will come for them, but I don't want to call him until I find out what happened to my wife. It's only for a few days. Maybe a week at the most. Please!"

Rina said, "Of course."

Decker said, "Excuse me?"

"Decker, I swear I'll take them off your hands. Just give me a week. This isn't a repeat of my son."

Rina turned to her husband. "He was there when we needed him."

"Yeah, because he owed us big time."

"Please!" Donatti said. "I'm desperate."

Rina said, "Peter, go back with him. It looks like he can use some help."

"I don't need help," Donatti said.

"Yes, you do, Chris."

Decker said, "Rina, I'm not leaving you alone with Terry's children."

"I think after all my family rearing, I can take care of them for a couple of weeks."

"It's not that," Decker told her. "What if Terry *was* kidnapped and someone is coming back for the children to extort more money? There is no way I'm going to leave you alone with a target on their backs."

"Then both of you stay here," Donatti said. "I don't need help."

"Why don't you both go with him and I'll watch the kids?" The three of them turned to the source of the voice. Cindy shrugged. "I've got children and the house has plenty of room."

Decker explained, "This is my daughter."

Donatti said, "I figured that out in a glance."

Decker said, "Cindy, I'm not involving you in his problem."

"You're not involving me, Daddy, I'm involving me." She looked at Donatti. She knew all about him, although she had always thought of him as older when in fact she knew that he was younger than she. He seemed older. Maybe it was the white hair. Maybe it was the panic on his face. Her eyes went to the children's faces. She walked over to them and knelt down. "I'm Cindy. I'm your brother's foster sister. As soon as Gabe comes back, I'll give him a call and we'll work this out together, okay?"

Rina said, "Don't you think you should ask Koby about this?"

"Koby will say yes." She stood up. "He knows what it's like to be a refugee."

At that moment, her two identical sons and her husband walked into the living room. They were dripping in sweat. Koby said, "It was a good game, Grandpa. You should have—" He stopped talking and looked at the two kids. The girl was a shade lighter than his own skin tone; the boy was darker, like him, both of them with straight black hair. They looked Indian. Thinking that, he realized that they were probably Gabe's siblings. "Hello there."

To her husband, Cindy said, "These are Gabe's brother and sister. Their mother is missing. I offered to watch them until Daddy and Gabe's father can figure out what is going on. Is that okay?"

"Do you mean Daddy me or Daddy your father?"

"Daddy my father."

"Sure, we can watch them." Koby turned to Decker. "Can someone tell me what's going on?"

"Their mother is gone . . . as in vanished," Decker answered. "We're trying to figure out whether it's a voluntary or involuntary disappearance."

Within moments, the other Decker children began to pile into the house: Sammy and Rachel with their two children, Hannah and Rafi with their baby, and Jacob and Ilana. They all stopped in their tracks and stared at the strangers in their parents' living room. Jacob felt the tension in the room and said, "What's going on?"

Koby said, "These are Gabe's siblings, and this is Gabe's father, as if you couldn't tell by looking at him."

Donatti introduced himself and the children by name. "Their mother is missing. I need someone to watch them until I know what happened to her. Gabe is out of the country. Furthermore, I don't want to tell him until I know where she is."

Koby turned to Donatti. "Don't they have a father?"

"He's in India," Decker said.

Donatti said, "I just brought the boy back from there to be reunited with his mom. I don't want to contact Devek just yet. And where I live . . . it's not appropriate for them to be there without their mother."

Cindy said, "We all know all about you."

"Good," Chris said. "Then I don't have to explain myself."

"Koby and Cindy offered to watch them," Rina said.

"When's Gabe coming back?" Sammy asked.

"In a week," Hannah said. "I can watch the kids. Gabe and I are close. We live within a few blocks from each other."

"That is not going to happen," Decker said. "You have your own baby to look after."

"Ilana and I can watch them," Jacob said. "We don't have children."

"No, you will not watch them either," Decker said. "There might be risk involved. It's possible that someone took their mother by force." He turned to Donatti. "You just redeemed the boy, right?"

"Right," Donatti said. "I thought we had a deal, but they're criminals."

"None of my children are going to watch them, Chris. I will not put them at risk."

"Daddy," Cindy said, "I'm just as much a cop as you are, and no offense, but my reflexes are probably faster than yours. And Koby certainly knows his way around a gun."

Donatti looked at Koby. "You're a cop?"

"I'm a doctor, but I was in the army."

"Israeli army," Cindy added. "He's just as good a shot as I am, and that's saying a lot."

Donatti said, "I know this is a big ask. I'll hire you whatever bodyguards you need for your protection. As many as you want."

"The answer is still no," Decker said.

Cindy said, "Daddy, that's not your decision to make."

"But I'm going to make it anyway," Decker said.

"Thank you, Abba, I know that you care," Koby said. "But Cindy is right. This is our decision. You and Rina have enough on your plate. And believe me, with my experiences, I know how to avoid an enemy. I promise we'll be careful." Koby turned to the children. "We'll all sit down and make a plan, right?"

"A guard may be helpful," Cindy said. "Have a pair of eyes on the kids."

"Whatever you need," Donatti told her. "And I'll give you whatever money you need, as well."

"One thing at a time," Koby said. "Let's first make a plan and then we'll go from there."

"I agree," Cindy said. "We can give Sanjay and Juleen the spare room."

One of Cindy's sons looked at the kids and said, "I'm Aaron, he's Akiva. Gabe is our uncle. And since you guys are Gabe's sister and brother, that makes you our aunt and uncle."

Sanjay was confused, but Juleen gave a small smile. The boys looked around her age, but they were *way* taller than her.

Akiva said, "Actually, Mom, Aaron, and I can bunk together so they can each have their own room."

Aaron said, "Yeah, we sleep in the same room a lot of the time anyway."

"Thank you, boys," Koby said. "That's very mature of you."

Juleen whispered a thank-you. Then she nudged her stunned brother, who also whispered a thank-you.

"Thank you, Mrs. . . ." Donatti paused. "I'm sorry. I don't know your last name."

She said, "It's Kutiel, but you can call us Cindy and Koby."

"Thank you for your help," Donatti repeated. "Thank you, thank you, thank you. All of you. I'll make it up to you."

"Not necessary," Cindy said. "Gabe's our brother."

"I see that," Donatti said. "No wonder Gabe turned out so well." He took out a piece of paper and gave it to Cindy. "My phone number, my office phone, my secretary's phone. Call if you have any problems." He turned to Decker. "Thank you. I'll leave you all to it now."

"Peter, go with him."

"I don't need help, Rina." When she didn't answer, Donatti said, "But if you're offering, I suppose I could use some fresh insight. I certainly have no answers."

Rina said, "We'd be happy to come, but you have to wait an hour, Chris. The holiday isn't over yet."

"My jet is waiting. If I don't leave by a certain hour, I'll get fined."

"Up to you," Rina said.

Donatti shook his head. "Of course I'll wait. Give me a little time to settle my brain."

"We'll start packing, then." Before Decker could talk, Rina took his hand and led him into the bedroom. She shut the door.

"This is a terrible idea," Decker said.

"Probably." Rina took down a carry-on with rollers.

"She's left him before," Decker said. "And she had no problem abandoning Gabe. What makes you think this is different?"

"It may not be different," Rina said. "It could be that she's abandoning her children again. But *if* something bad happened to her, I want to look Gabe in the eye and tell him that we did everything we could to help his mother."

"That's not up to us, Rina. That's up to Donatti to figure this mess out."

"You are as much a father to Gabe as Chris is."

"That's below the belt."

"Maybe so, but it's still true."

"Fuck!" Decker whispered to himself. "If I could get away with it, I'd kill both of them." He took down a suitcase. He was angry. "You should have at least consulted with me before you made a unilateral decision."

A pause. "You're right." Rina took out some clothes. "I'm sorry."

Decker retrieved several pairs of pants, several sets of sweats, and four polos. For footwear, he decided on two pairs of tennis shoes. He said nothing.

"I really am sorry, Peter. It was out of line."

"You told Cindy to consult Koby. What about me?"

"Again, you're right. I've apologized, and I'll apologize in front of the children if you want."

"It's fine." Decker shook his head. "You're just a nicer person than I am."

"I'm sure you've had it up to your neck with the both of them. You've had the relationship. I've just been a bystander."

"That's not true. Chris feels closer to you than to me. He's always calling you. That's probably why he came to us. He knows you're a soft touch."

"It's not him, it's the kids."

"Whatever."

"Please don't be mad at me even if you have cause."

Decker exhaled. "Well, it was my suggestion for Gabe to call Chris, so in a way, I guess this is my fault."

Rina stopped packing. She came over to him and threw her arms around his neck. "You didn't do anything wrong. We didn't do anything wrong. They are both crazy. We know that. But . . ."

"The kids."

"They look so lost and so scared. Not to mention Chris. I've never ever seen him like that. He's a wreck."

"He is frantic," Decker said. "Know how I know that?"

"He said please and thank you," Rina said.

Decker gave her an eye roll. "You ruin all my punch lines."

Rina kissed him. "I am sorry about bulldozing over you."

"Oh, forget it," Decker said. "I bought a house without asking you."

"You didn't *buy* it without me. You just put in an offer."

"You're nitpicking."

"I'm giving you an out."

"Yes, you are." Decker kissed his wife. "Thank you."

Rina smiled. "I've never flown on a private jet."

"That makes two of us." Decker checked his watch. "I hope he hired a good pilot. This would be a bad way to end it all."

"Stop being morbid."

"I want to shower before we leave," Decker said. "That way when we crash, I'll have on clean underwear."

She pushed him away. "I have no intention of dying, so if that happens, you're on your own." They finished packing in silence. She checked her watch. "We still have some time before the Chag goes out. I'm going to start cleaning up."

Decker said, "Let the kids do it. It's their mess."

"I'm sure they'll help."

"I don't want them to *help* you, I want them to *do* it for you. They're adults. They'll be happy to do their fair share. But you have to ask them."

"You're right. I'll just check on Sanjay and Juleen."

"No need for that either. Let Cindy and Koby deal with them. They're going to be with them anyway."

"I can see you just want me to sit here and watch you be angry."

"No, that's not what I want. While everyone else is cleaning up, I want you to talk to Chris alone. He's probably holding back, and you can get more out of him than I can."

"Okay, I can do that." A pause. "And what will you be doing?"

"I'll be here in my bedroom, in private, stewing in my juices after being roped into yet another fiasco."

Rina gave out a small laugh. "Would you like a little wine with your stew?"

Decker thought about it. "Anything left over from lunch?"

"We've still got a half bottle of Herzog Special Reserve."

"Bring it on," Decker said. "And don't bother with a glass. I'll just swig it from the bottle."

CHAPTER 31

THE TAKEOFF WAS delayed because of fog. Since Donatti was co-piloting the plane, Decker didn't have a chance to question him on the flight from Greenbury to his place in Mountain Pass. The ride was bumpy and tense. The space was small. Decker had to stoop to walk to the bathroom, which barely had enough space for a hamster. But seated, it was fine, and he could stretch out his legs. Both he and Rina had downed enough coffee to wake up a small city. Finally, at 4:30 a.m. PDT, the six-seater jet touched down, everyone exhausted. After being chauffeured from the airstrip to Donatti's place, they all got out. It felt good to stretch.

Chris spoke to his bodyguard. "Go home and get some rest. I can take it from here."

"Are you sure, Mr. Donatti?"

"I'm sure. Go." Donatti watched the limo leave, then he turned to the building that housed his office, his bedroom, and his son's bedroom. He opened the door to a sally port. Once inside, he opened the interior door, turned on the lights, and stepped aside to allow

Decker and Rina to go in first. He said, "I'm sorry, but I need to close my eyes for twenty minutes or so. Right now, I'm so tired, I can't think."

"We're fine," Decker said. "Go rest."

"I'll be in my office. There's a bedroom to the right of the bar if anyone wants to sleep."

"I'm not tired," Rina said. "We napped during the day yesterday, and I've had too much coffee." A pause. "It's a little cold in here."

Donatti adjusted the thermostat. "It should warm up soon. Help yourself to anything in the fridge and anything at the bar." He went into his office and closed the door.

Rina rubbed her arms. She said, "You can go rest, Peter. I'm fine."

"Too wired right now." Decker opened the refrigerator. "There's orange juice if you're interested."

"Yes, please. I'd love some juice."

He took out the container and retrieved a couple of cut crystal glasses from behind the bar. "He's got a real setup here."

"The surrounding area looks vast."

"How long has he been in Nevada?"

"I don't know for sure. I think around ten years."

"And he moved after Terry left him?"

"No idea." Rina looked around the office. "I always figured brothels to be like western ranch style. This appears to be more like a Vegas resort. It's got a bank and a casino right near the airstrip."

"And a pawnshop," Decker said. "No wonder the kid has piles of cash in a vault."

"The kid? You mean Chris?"

"I do," Decker said. "Every time I see him, I keep expecting that eighteen-year-old boy who went toe-to-toe with me. Sometimes it's hard to reconcile that image with the white-haired psycho." He drank juice. "Although he was probably a psycho at eighteen. Did you get anything out of him when you talked to him alone?"

"Not really."

"What'd you ask him?"

"I asked about his relationship with Terry. If there were things that he did that would make her leave him again."

"And?"

"He admitted being sexually aggressive. Sometimes too aggressive. But he claims she was used to that. And he said when he left to redeem her son, they parted on good terms. She was crying. She said for him to be careful. She seemed genuinely concerned about him. And she put up with him all this time to get her son back. Why would she leave just before that happened? He's really worried that maybe the same people who kidnapped Sanjay and tried to kidnap Juleen took her while he was gone. He thinks there's a possibility that maybe those men are going to try to extort more money out of him. In the back of his head, he thinks he might be getting a phone call about a ransom."

"So, he doesn't think she left voluntarily."

"He's also considering that because she's done it before."

"What about the people around here?" Decker asked. "What do they have to say?"

"Apparently no one knows a thing. Terry had full access to come and go as she pleased. Yes, he put guards on her, but she was constantly evading them. They told Chris that it was almost like a game with her . . . what she'd have to do to get them off her tail. But she always came back, and when she did, she always made a point to check in with them. Chris is wondering if she was doing a number of dry runs to get them used to the fact that she's out of their control."

"Bizarre," Decker said. "Not that she would leave him, but that she would stick with him long enough to get her son back and then leave before she could see him. And it's also odd that she left Juleen here. Is she that bad of a mother?"

"She left Gabe."

Decker said, "There were exigencies with that. None this time. I don't understand her."

"It seems that no one does."

"I think I'm more exhausted than I realized." Decker leaned back on the couch. "I'm gonna close my eyes. Is that all right?"

"It's fine, darling."

"You should rest, too, Rina. We probably have a busy day ahead."

"I'm fine for the moment." She rubbed her arms again. "At least it's not so cold in here."

But despite herself, Rina felt her eyes close. She was in a light sleep when she heard the door open. Her eyelids bolted open and she stood. A curly-headed woman who appeared to be in her thirties was on the other side. She was wearing a bright red jumpsuit and sneakers. A Gucci belt bag was around her waist. Her eyes grew wide, and her expression was shocked.

"I'm sorry," she said. "I didn't think anyone would be here."

Decker woke up. Rina smiled at her. "I'm Rina Decker. My husband and I came back with Mr. Donatti after he dropped off the children."

"Oh." She seemed stunned. "Okay. I'm Talia."

"Nice to meet you, although not under these circumstances," Rina said.

"Right."

A moment later, Donatti entered the room. He stretched and yawned, then sprawled out on one of his many leather office couches. To Talia, he said, "You're here early."

"I just wanted to get some work done before you arrived." She was still standing at the doorway. "I thought you were coming back later."

Donatti said, "This is my assistant, Talia." To her: "These are Gabe's foster parents."

"Isn't he the police detective who sent you to jail?" Talia said.

"To prison," Donatti corrected. "Good memory. But I don't hold it against him."

Decker rolled his eyes. "You conveniently forgot that I also got you out of prison."

"Selective memory is a good thing," Donatti told him.

Talia smiled as she carefully started toward her desk, inching forward instead of walking. Rina regarded her face—pretty and pale. Something about her was off. And then Rina realized what was twanging her antennae.

Who dressed like that for work? Especially in this kind of hyper-masculine environment. Especially as Christopher Donatti's right-hand person. She knew Chris well enough to know that he liked being around beautiful women who were dressed to please men.

Rina blurted out, "Could you make me a cup of coffee, Talia?"

The woman turned to her.

If looks could kill.

Rina was taken aback.

Donatti said, "Yeah, good idea. Make a pot."

Talia's lips were smiling, but her eyes were furious. "Of course."

"Why are you dressed so casually?" Donatti asked.

"I didn't think you'd be here."

"Even so, you know better." He gave his head a shake. "You look ridiculous."

She put down the coffee bag. "I'll go change."

"Yeah, do that, but make the coffee first," Donatti told her.

"Of course." She looked down like a chastened child. "Sorry, sir."

Donatti waved her off. "I'm in a foul mood."

"I understand."

Rina looked at Talia, who was carefully measuring out the coffee beans. The assistant put them in a grinder and said, "While you were gone, I got your favorite coffee, Chris. It's that time of the season."

Lost in thought, Donatti didn't answer. Rina caught her husband's eye. She jerked her head toward Talia's desk.

Decker regarded his wife and shrugged.

Rina repeated the gesture.

Slowly, Decker ambled over to Talia's desk. He tried the top drawer, but it was locked.

Talia turned. She saw Decker at her desk and turned white. "What are you doing?"

Decker looked up. "Do you have the key to the drawer?"

"I beg your pardon?" Talia answered.

Donatti had come to life. His eyes darted between Decker and his assistant. He said, "What's going on?"

Decker said, "Just like a quick look inside, if that's okay, Chris."

Donatti paused. Then he said, "Give him the key, Talia."

The woman put down the coffee bag and began to rummage through her belt bag. She pulled out a ring of keys and studied them one by one. She looked up and said, "I'm so sorry, but I must have put it on a different chain. It's not here."

"It's fine, I can get it open." Decker pulled out a pocketknife. "But it is odd that you came to work without it."

Donatti was on full alert. "What are you thinking, Decker?"

"Not sure, Donatti. Give me a second." Decker played with the blade, wedging it between the bolt and the desk drawer. It finally popped. He opened the drawer: pencils, pads, paper, paper clips, a lipstick, a packet of tissues, a pair of sunglasses. Nothing weird.

He looked up at his wife and shrugged.

Rina marched over. She stuck her slender fingers all the way to the back. She wasn't even sure what she hoped to find—maybe a key or something—but instinct told her something was there. She kept at it until, lodged in the corner, she felt something small, round, and metallic. Two things. She inched her fingers forward until she was able to grab them, then she dumped what was in her hand on the desktop.

A gold ring featuring two round diamonds, and a gold wedding band.

Donatti stood, his eyes wide and jumpy, in total disbelief. The orbs went from the rings and landed on Talia's face. She put down the coffee and crossed her arms over her chest.

"What gives her the right to come barging in here after eleven years . . . being the little princess after she cheated on you and dumped you . . . when I was the one who nursed you and got you off heroin, and stayed up nights with you during your shakes and your shivers, and cleaned your vomit and shit, and loved you unconditionally without *any* thought of getting anything in return! When I was the one who planned every single one of your parties and events and sat in the background to make sure everything ran smoothly. When I was the one who remembered the birthday gifts and the Christmas gifts to your clients and to your own son, and bought him a piano when his mother abandoned him. Who gave that bitch the fucking right to come back and be wife and mother when she threw it away without a second thought to anyone but herself!"

Decker walked over to Donatti. "Give me your gun, Chris."

Donatti didn't move.

"Give me your gun."

"I'm okay," he whispered.

"I know you are, but give it to me anyway," Decker said.

Donatti looked at him, then unholstered his gun. He walked over to Rina, who was blocking the door, and gave it to her. He went up to Talia, who was still at the coffee machine. He put his hands on her shoulders. He whispered, "Where is she, Talia?"

"She's alive," Talia said.

Donatti closed and opened his eyes. "That's good, sweetheart. Where is she?"

"I would never really hurt her." Talia's face started to crumple. "I would never do that to you."

"I know you wouldn't."

"I just wanted her to feel what it was like." Tears started running down her cheeks. "To be isolated and passed over and feel like you're nothing after you put your heart and soul into a relationship. It isn't fair, Chris."

"I see what you're saying," Donatti answered. "I hurt you deeply. And I'm sorry. I know it wasn't fair."

"Exactly."

"Where is she, Talia?"

The woman wiped her eyes with her fingers. "She's alive. I swear she is."

"That's great," Donatti said. "Then no harm done."

"You're mad at me."

"Not at all, honey." He lifted her chin and looked her in the eyes. "I'm not mad. You know when I'm mad, right?"

"Right."

"No, I'm not mad. But I do have to know where she is. Tell me."

"You'll never find it on your own," Talia said. "I'll have to show you."

"Okay." Donatti licked his lips. "Where is she?"

"In the mountains. We could walk, but it'll be faster if we drive to the head of the trail and walk from there." A pause. "We should probably wait until it's lighter, Chris. It's hard to see right now."

"Phones have flashlights, honey," Donatti said. "And I know the area pretty well."

"O-kay. But it is pretty overgrown."

"Let's get to the trailhead and then we can decide."

She smiled. "Good idea, boss."

Donatti took in a breath and let it out slowly. He took out his phone and called for a car. Another smile. "Let's go." He nodded to Decker and Rina.

"They're coming?" Talia was indignant. "*Why?*"

"I brought them all the way out from New York." Donatti managed a grin. "Might as well let them be useful. Their phones' flashlights can help light the way. Let's go."

He took her arm, and as they left the office, Donatti pocketed the rings. Once the limo pulled up, he opened the door to the backseat. Talia started to go inside, but Donatti held her back. "Him first." Referring to Decker.

Donatti placed his assistant between Decker and himself. Rina took the front seat. When Talia pressed herself against Chris, Decker saw him stiffen.

To the driver, Donatti said, "Ride to the trailhead, please."

"Yes, sir."

Then no one said a word during the three-minute jaunt over. The car parked and everyone got out. It was still dark but no longer black. Gray was peeking over the horizon.

Talia said, "It's about a mile up." She looked at Rina's flats. "I don't think you'll make it in those shoes."

"I'll be fine, thank you."

Talia shrugged. "Don't say I didn't try to warn you." She turned to Donatti. "Are you sure you don't want to wait, boss?"

"It'll be light soon. We'll be okay if we stay on the trail." Donatti took her arm. "Let's go."

Decker and Rina walked about ten steps behind. He whispered, "How did you know?"

She shook her head and shrugged. She gave Decker the gun. "I think you'd better keep this."

Walking was slow because the sun wasn't up. But with the gray turning to orange, it became easier to see. They walked on the trail for about twenty minutes, then Talia veered to the left. Within seconds, they were walking between bare trees and overgrown shrubbery where everything was gray, shadowed, and looked the same.

Rina checked her phone. No reception. Decker pulled a compass from his pocket and showed it to her. "Pays to be a Boy Scout."

She nodded appreciatively.

Talia zigged and then she zagged, but she walked with purpose. It was another ten minutes before she stopped. She stretched out her arm and her index finger, pointing to a large shadow behind a grouping of trees.

Decker studied the blur: it was a dilapidated outbuilding, maybe an old mining shed. Nevada was well-known for the Comstock Lode, an area abundant in silver ore. Even today, mining was a primary industry in the region. The mountains around Elko were dotted with abandoned lean-tos once used by prospectors.

This shed had a padlock on it. Donatti dropped Talia's arm and ran to the building and started kicking in the rotted boards, screaming Terry's name as he attacked the wood with his feet.

Decker walked over to Talia. "Can I have the key, please?"

A strange smile spread across her face. "Golly, I must have forgotten that as well."

Decker gave the gun to Rina. "Watch her." Then he ran over and helped, the two of them kicking in the horizontal boards.

Bam! Bam! Bam! Bam!

Within a minute, the wood had splintered sufficiently to create a small hole. With bare hands, Decker and Donatti started pulling off the boards until there was crawl space. But the men were still too big. Rina grabbed Talia's arm and ran over to the men. She gave Decker the gun and said, "Your turn to watch her."

Being smaller, she managed to contort her body through the jagged hole, scratching herself on the raw edges. She barely felt the pain even though she knew she was bleeding. It was nearly pitch black inside. With her phone light, she surveyed the area. It was a space of about three hundred square feet. There were animal tracks and loads of scat. There were spiderwebs and wasp nests and lots of creepy-crawlies. She saw an old rusted stove, pots scattered over the floor. There was a cot with bare springs and a shredded mattress. Then, in the corner, there was a lump of something. Could be a dead animal, because there was a definite smell of excrement. Her heart was racing so much that she could barely breathe. She focused the illumination onto the heap and a pair of eyes blinked.

She ran over to the body, repeating over and over, "You're safe, you're safe, you're safe." Shouting to the men: "She's in here. She's alive."

Terry's complexion was blue. Her skin was ice. Eyes were vacant. She appeared unresponsive. Her hands and feet were bound with plastic ties. Rina took off her jacket and laid it over her body. At that moment, Chris finally broke through. She said, "I need your jacket. She's freezing."

He took off his jacket and scooped Terry up in his arms. "Baby, say something."

No answer.

Once outside, Donatti was shaking, his face covered in sweat as he held on to his wife. He turned to Talia. "Which way out? And don't you dare fuck around on me!"

"I told you she was alive."

"Which . . . fucking . . . *way*?"

When she didn't answer, Donatti moved toward her, feeling for his emptied holster. Decker took out his pocketknife and cut Terry's binds. He said, "I can get us back. I have a compass." He moved slowly, but within ten minutes they were back on the trail. Donatti ran down as fast as he could without losing his footing, while Decker led Talia down with Rina behind him with the gun. As soon as they got to the bottom, Donatti said, "She's not answering me."

"There's no reception here," Decker said. "Chris, you go down to the car with Rina and take Terry to the hospital. Call the police when you get some bars. I'll wait here with Talia."

Rina handed her husband the gun. "Be careful."

"Always."

Chris gently slid Terry inside the limo, then himself. Rina sat on the other side, and then the car sped away.

Talia shrugged and looked at Decker. "What now?"

"Now we wait for the police."

"I'm cold."

"Not as cold as Terry."

Talia shrugged again.

Decker said, "How'd you do it?"

"Do what?"

"Get her to come with you."

"It wasn't planned," Talia said. "I saw her walking on her own and it just came to me. I knew about the miner's shed from my own hiking. The next day I bought a padlock and waited. It took a few days, but I finally managed to waylay her. I put a gun to her head and that was that."

Decker said, "She was tied up, Talia. With plastic ties. That seems pretty planned."

"Well, once I decided to lock her up, I had to do it right. I didn't want her escaping and telling Chris until I had a chance to explain."

"Explain what?"

She turned and looked at him. "Why I did it, of course."

Decker had no answer.

She said, "She was classy. I'll give her that. She saw the determined look in my eye. She didn't beg for her life or freedom or anything. I think she knew I'd never hurt the kids. I dunno. Maybe she just had enough of life. She looked worn out. I think that's why I let her live instead of shooting her on the spot. I found out I just couldn't do it."

"But it was okay for her to be tied up and freeze to death?"

"Yeah, she was lucky. One more day out here in the cold and she wouldn't have made it. I don't know how your wife knew." She turned to Decker. "Maybe it was a woman thing."

That could be, because Decker sure as hell had had no idea that she was the guilty party. He said, "You were coming back to your office to get the rings?"

Talia nodded. "I picked them out. They should have been mine in the first place."

Decker said nothing.

"I was going to leave this place for good," Talia said. "With Terry here or even with Terry gone, I knew Chris was never going to come back to me. And I couldn't bear to watch him suffer over her." She started crying. "I really, really love him."

"I'm sure you do."

"You don't know how painful it is to see him love another woman with that intensity. Him looking at me like . . . like I'm just cardboard." She wiped her eyes. "I'd rather be dead than exist like that." Decker nodded. She regarded the gun in his hand. "You won't need that. I'm not going anywhere."

"Forgive my cynicism," Decker said, "but holding this fully loaded Glock and being a crack shot, I *know* you're not going anywhere."

CHAPTER 32

WITH THE HEAT going full blast and Rina rubbing her feet, Terry began to rouse. Her eyes drifted upward to Donatti's face. She moved her mouth.

"Don't talk, angel." Donatti cradled his wife, rubbing her cold arms. She was still icy to the touch. "You'll be fine, baby."

"Sanj . . ."

"Sanjay's fine. So is Juleen. They're with Decker's daughter. She's a cop, so they're safe." Donatti was still sweating. He was breathing hard. "I forgot her name."

"Cindy." Rina opened a bottle of water she found in the limo and put a capful to Terry's lips. When she didn't drink, Rina moistened her cracked lips.

"Gabe?" Terry asked.

Donatti said, "He's out of town. He doesn't know a thing. I don't think I'll tell him until you're better."

Terry whispered, "Tell . . . I love them."

"I don't need to tell them," Donatti said. "You can tell them your-self."

A puddle gushed from Terry's body, covering Donatti's pants and dripping to the floor. He looked down and put his fingers to the wetness. They came back sticky and red. He said, "Were you shot?" He started examining her body.

Rina said, "I think it's her period."

"Oh." Donatti was gasping. "Okay. That makes sense."

But deep inside, Rina knew that it wasn't her period. She knew it because she had been there. She took off her seat belt and leaned over to the driver. She whispered, "Can you go faster?"

"We're about five minutes away, ma'am."

Rina nodded and slapped her seat belt back on.

"What is it?" Donatti asked.

"Just wondering how much longer."

The answer satisfied him. He turned his eyes back to his wife.

A few moments later, Terry looked at Chris and said, "Thank..."

"No thanks necessary. I'd do it again in a heartbeat. I love you so much, baby."

Another gush of blood.

They pulled up to the entrance to the hospital, where a gurney was waiting. As they loaded her onto the stretcher, Terry managed to grasp Donatti's hand. He ran with her as they wheeled her down the hallway to the emergency room. As the double doors opened, she said, "I love you, Christopher."

"I love—" His hand was suddenly yanked from hers and the doors shut closed on him. "I love you, too, Teresa—"

He turned around. Rina was there. He said, "She'll be fine, right?"

"She's in the care of people who know what they're doing," Rina answered.

"That doesn't answer the question."

"Chris, I know as much as you do."

He sat down on a bench and covered his face with his hands. Then he looked up at Rina, who was still standing. "She was up when they took her in. That's a good sign."

"Yes."

"She was talking. She told me she loved me." A pause. "Or maybe I imagined it."

"No, you didn't imagine it. I heard it too."

"She said it, right?"

"Right."

He stood up and began to pace the full length of the hallway. Back and forth, back and forth, several times. He stopped. "How'd you know? About Talia?"

Rina shrugged. "A gut feeling, as Peter would say."

"Fucking cunt blindsided me." He sat, then he got up again. "I should have fired her as soon as Terry came back. I should have known! None of the girls liked her."

Rina was silent.

"I was an idiot. I was lazy. It was just easier to keep her on. She was with me from the beginning."

"Chris, this isn't your fault," Rina said.

He waved her off and began pacing again. "It is my fault. Totally my fault." A pause. "What the fuck is taking so long?"

Rina looked at her watch. It had only been around ten minutes.

He said, "Shit, I forgot to call the police."

"I did it."

"You did?"

"Yes," Rina said. "I called 911."

"Someone's thinking. Did you give them the location?"

"I just said at the trailhead in the mountains. Should I call them again?" At that moment, her phone sprang to life. "It's Peter. Hold on."

"Put it on speaker," Donatti said.

Rina complied. Into the receiver, she said, "You're on speaker. We're at the hospital."

"Is she okay?" Decker asked.

"We don't know anything yet. Where are you?"

"At the police station. It has two jail cells, but they don't have a facility to book her or keep her. A guy named Saverhall called in Nevada State Police. I'm waiting here until I know she's in the proper hands."

Donatti took the phone from Rina. "Saverhall's a good guy."

Decker said, "Yes, he is, but he seems a little out of his element."

"We don't get murders around here." Donatti paced as he talked. "Or attempted murders. You should have left Talia out there to freeze. Feel what the fuck it's like. Just wait with her until the bitch is taken away."

"That's exactly what I'm doing, Chris." A pause. "You're going in and out of reception."

Donatti handed the phone back to Rina. She took it off speaker and said, "When are you coming here?"

"When the proper authorities get here. Am I still on speaker?"

"No."

Decker said, "I need to explain everything. She's just as much a psycho as he is, and I don't want her talking her way into bail."

"Do you need anything?" Rina asked.

"No, I'm fine. I even got fresh coffee. What about you?"

"We're just waiting."

"You seem to be holding back on me. Is that true?"

"Maybe." She looked at Donatti. "I'll call you when I know something."

"I love you, Rina."

"Love you too." She hung up.

Donatti was still walking back and forth. "What do you think?"

"What do you mean?" Rina asked.

"What are they doing?"

"I'm not a doctor, Chris."

"Yeah, but you once worked as a medic or something in Israel. You told me that when you fixed my bullet wound, remember?"

He had a good memory, although getting shot was probably one of those things that was forever etched in the brain. They had been walking in the streets of New York when gunfire broke out. He had taken a bullet in the chest protecting her.

"It was a long time ago," Rina said.

"I won't hold you to it," he answered. "What do you *think*?"

Rina sighed. There was no way she was going to tell him what she was *really* thinking. "She was dehydrated and hypothermic. They're probably getting her body temperature up with warm fluids."

He stopped pacing and turned to her. "That's no big deal, right?"

"I think she was in shock."

"She recognized me."

"Not shock as in surprise," Rina said. "It's a medical term when you lose a lot of liquid in your body. It throws everything off."

"Like your kidneys?"

Rina sighed again. "Yes . . . mainly you worry about low blood pressure."

"So, if they give her fluids, she should be okay, right?"

"Sometimes. But sometimes, it's not that simple."

"Jesus!" He sat down and clamped his hands over his face. "When will they know if she's okay?"

"I can't answer that because I don't know." She checked her watch. It had been about twenty-five minutes. "Can I get you anything?"

"How about getting me out of this hell?"

"I'm so sorry, Chris."

"If this ends badly . . . God, I don't want to think about it."

She nodded.

"Probably better to keep positive," he said.

She nodded again. But she had her doubts. She tried to sweep them from her mind. Her phone rang again. Rina said, "It's Cindy. What do you want me to tell her?"

Donatti gave her a wave.

Rina pressed the button. "Hi, honey."

"What's going on?" Cindy asked.

"Terry's in the hospital."

"In the hospital?" Cindy shrieked. "Is she okay?"

"We're waiting to hear."

"What *happened*?" A pause. "Or can't you talk now?"

"Exactly. I'll call you when I have an update. Don't say anything to the kids until we know exactly what the status is."

"Of course."

"How are the kids?"

"They're not saying much . . . to be expected."

"Did they sleep?"

"They said they did. They ate breakfast. Now they're watching TV. Sanjay is. Juleen is in the room with the door closed. When I checked on her, she was lying on the bed reading. I don't want to bother them too much right now."

"I agree." Rina paused. "Thanks, honey. I'll call you later."

"Where's Daddy? He's not answering his phone."

"He's with the police. I'll explain later."

"Oh my God. Someone hurt her?"

"Yes."

"It's serious?"

"Yes. I'll call you later."

When she hung up, Chris said, "Kids okay?"

"Probably disoriented, but physically they're fine."

About ten minutes later, Donatti's phone rang. "Shit, that's Gabe. Can you talk to him?"

She took his phone. "Hi, honey."

"Juleen called me. She said Mom is missing. She said that she and Sanjay are at Cindy's house. What the *hell* is going on?"

Rina waited a moment to catch her breath. "Your mom is in the hospital, Gabe. Please don't say anything to Juleen and Sanjay just yet."

"Where's my father? Did he *hurt* her?"

"No, nothing like that. Your dad's right here with me in the corridor, waiting to hear from the doctors."

"Can I talk to him?"

"He's not in much of a state to talk."

Donatti held out his hand, and Rina gave him the phone. "What?"

"You tell me, Dad," Gabe said.

"I can't tell you a fucking thing because I don't know anything."

"Is it serious?"

"I just said I don't know." A pause. "Where are you?"

"Budapest. I booked a ticket to come back as soon as I heard."

"How'd you hear?"

"Juleen just called me. She said that Mom was missing."

Donatti let out a gush of air. "Don't come home yet. Wait until I have news, okay? Can you do that for me?"

"Dad, I can't perform with this level of anxiety."

"Just wait, okay?" Donatti said. "I'll call you when I know something. Or maybe Rina will call you. Just don't tell Juleen anything about this until I have something definite."

"Of course not." A pause. "When you see Mom, tell her I love her."

"Yeah, I will. It goes both ways. Before she went into the emergency room, she asked me to tell you that she loved you."

"She was conscious then?"

"She was. I'm going to hang up. Talking to you is making me more nervous."

"I love you, Dad."

"Same." Donatti hung up and stowed his phone. He checked the time. "Why is it taking so fucking long?"

Rina didn't answer. It had been well over an hour and that usually wasn't a good sign. A minute later, Decker was walking down the hallway. She jogged over to meet him. She kept him there for a moment—away from Chris.

"Anything?" he whispered.

"No," Rina whispered back

"She looked like she was in low-volume shock."

"Probably." Rina took a breath. "I think she's pre—"

At that moment, she saw the two doctors emerge.

She knew instantly.

She said, *"Baruch atah Adonai Eloheinu melech ha'olam dayan ha'emet."*

Blessed are You, our God, King of the Universe, the True Judge.

She took Decker's hand, and they went over to Donatti. He looked at them and they at him.

One of the doctors said, "I'm so sorry, Mr. Donatti. I'm so sorry."

Donatti just stared back.

Nothing was sinking in.

The doctor lowered his head. His name tag said DR. DREW JAMISON. "She was very compromised to begin with. And we just couldn't stop the bleeding—"

"Bleeding?" Donatti said. "Was she shot?"

"No, sir, she was hemorrhaging from a miscarriage."

His face went white. "She was *pregnant*?"

Jamison scratched his face. "You didn't know?"

"No, I didn't *know*!" Donatti snapped back. "How many *months*?"

Jamison said, "Around eight to ten weeks."

"Could it have been longer than that?"

"Maybe."

Donatti said, "I want a paternity test."

The doctor was surprised. "We can probably do that—"

"Good, because I want it."

Decker said, "Chris, what difference does it make?"

Donatti ordered, "I want a paternity test."

"Let me go back in there and see . . ." Jamison said. "Hold on for a little bit and I'll see what I can do."

"Yeah, do that!" Donatti barked. "Fuck!" he said. "Fuck, fuck, *fuck*! If she came to me pregnant and didn't tell me . . . if she fucked around on me . . ."

"I'm sure she didn't," Rina said.

"You don't fucking know that, do you?"

Rina said, "Even so, Chris, Peter's right. What difference does it make?"

He turned to her with wild eyes. "What difference does it make? What *difference* does it make? It's the difference between giving my wife a proper burial and burning the bitch!"

CHAPTER 33

"HERE'S NO REASON why you should stick around," Decker said. It was eight in the evening, and he and Rina were in Chris's outer office. Where Donatti went was anyone's guess. "You gave your statement to the police. If they need anything, they can call you."

"The same could be said about you," Rina said.

"I'm a cop," Decker said. "It's different. I know these kinds of psychos . . . how they manipulate people. I just want to make sure it doesn't happen."

Rina said, "But Talia confessed."

"Not quite," Decker said. "She confessed to me but not to the cops. No one was around. I had a gun. She could say it was coerced. Of course, that's not going to happen. But I want to make sure it doesn't happen. I'll wait until after the funeral."

"I'm not leaving you alone with Chris," Rina told him. "He's too unstable right now."

"He's not going to shoot me." Decker smiled. "Besides, I have his gun."

"I'm not worried about that. I'm worried he's going to find a way to shoot her."

"Yeah, don't think I haven't thought about it."

"What was she booked with?"

"Two counts of first-degree homicide. They may reduce the charges for the fetus."

"That would be a pity," Rina said. "I'm also not leaving until after the funeral, Peter. Neither Chris nor Gabe is in any shape to plan it. Someone has to take the reins."

"If he doesn't burn the bitch," Decker said.

"Of course the baby was his."

"He doesn't seem convinced."

"He didn't think Gabe was his either," Rina said. "Honestly, I think he's just finding an excuse to be furious at Terry because anger is easier than devastation. The man lost his wife and child in one swoop. I can't even imagine what that feels like."

Decker lay down on the couch. "It was a horrific day, and the next few days aren't going to be any better."

"But the sun will come up in the east and set in the west," Rina said. "That's what's so crazy about death. Your life is forever changed, but the world goes on." She stretched out on her couch. "Let's talk about it in the morning. Neither one of us has had any sleep for over twenty-four hours. Nothing looks hopeful when you're exhausted."

Decker turned around and tried to get comfortable. The leather couch was tufted with buttons. It was hard. He had no pillow or cover. But Rina wasn't complaining, so why should he? A half hour later, Donatti returned to his office and flipped on the lights. Decker rubbed his eyes and sat up.

Donatti looked at him and Rina. "I'll get you some pillows and covers from the bedroom."

"We're fine," Decker said. "Where have you been?"

"Walking." His voice was completely flat.

"For ten hours?"

Donatti didn't answer. His phone rang. "It's Gabe—again."

"Have you talked to him?"

"Not since I told him," Donatti said. "I don't want to talk to him . . . I don't want to talk to anyone. And I really don't want anyone to come here and console me." He tossed the phone to Decker. "Tell him that for me, please."

He disappeared inside his office.

Decker answered the call and said, "Hi, it's me."

Gabe's voice was shaky. "He doesn't want to talk to me."

"He's in no state to talk to anyone."

"Which is why I should be there even if he doesn't want me."

"Gabe, give it a day. By then we'll have funeral arrangements."

"Who's arranging the funeral? Not him."

"Rina will handle it. Chris says that he isn't doing anything with your mom until he gets the paternity results back. But both Rina and I feel he's just blowing steam. The sooner we take care of your mom, the better."

"He's an idiot. Of course it's his baby. I saw my mom when she first got there—to his place. She was in the hospital. She was as thin as a razor blade."

"Like I said, he's in no state to be rational. Where are you?"

"I'm in London Heathrow. I should be in New York by six a.m. tomorrow. Then I'll figure out how to get to his place. He's always sent a private plane, but I can't ask him to do that now."

"Gabe, if you really want to do some good, go to Philadelphia and be with your brother and sister. They need you more than Chris does. He's in a very labile state. I don't want him screaming at you."

"I'm used to it." Gabe sighed. "You're probably right. We'll just fight, and that's not good for either one of us. I'll go visit my siblings. I'm sure he hasn't said much to them."

"He hasn't said anything to them beyond the call to Cindy. Juleen calls him, but he's not answering."

"Typical. I'll go to Philadelphia. Tell my dad I'm ready whenever he wants to talk to me."

"I will."

"Thanks, Peter."

"Gabe, I am so sorry. What can I do for you?"

"What Rina and you have always done for me. Be my support. Be a shoulder to cry on." Gabe hung up.

Decker sighed. He went over and turned off the lights. In the dark, Rina said, "How's he doing?"

"Gabe? He sounds thrashed, beyond the usual fatigue you get when traveling for long hours. I don't think he's processed anything yet." Decker took in a breath and let it out. "Let me give the phone back to Donatti."

"Where is he?"

"In his office. Hold on. Let me see if I can walk in the dark without killing myself."

"Turn on the light."

"No, I'm . . ." Decker reached the door and knocked. "It's me. You want your phone back?"

From behind the door, Donatti told him no.

"What about your gun?"

A moment passed and then the door opened. Chris stared at him with an open palm. Decker retrieved the gun and gave it and the phone to him. Donatti put the gun in his holster. He said, "I'll get you some bedding."

"It's not necessary—"

But Donatti was already out the door.

Rina said, "Are you okay?"

"Me?" Decker asked. "Sad for the kids and Gabe, but otherwise okay." He paused. "How do we plan a funeral?"

"I can do it," Rina told him. "I've done enough of them in my time."

"They've all been Jewish."

"I don't suppose there's that much difference."

"She was Catholic. It's usually open casket. And then there's a wake."

"I can do a wake," Rina said. "But I'll try to talk him out of open casket. It's a horrible thing to do to the kids. To see their mother like that . . ."

"Unless he burns the bitch."

"He's just ranting because the alternative is too dark for him to face. Whatever he does, it'll be solemn."

Donatti came in later with bedding. He turned on the lights. "When are you two going back?"

"Peter wants to make sure that Talia's properly charged." No comment from him. Rina sat up and rubbed her eyes. "I think we'll stay until after the funeral."

Donatti dropped the bedding on the couch. "Suit yourself." He headed toward his office. He stopped and turned to Rina. "You'll take care of it for me?"

Rina said, "Of course I will, Chris."

"Can you take care of Devek also? He wants to come. I think he wants to say his good-byes, but he also has to pick up the kids."

"I'll call him. Do you have his phone number?"

"I do." Chris sighed. "He asked about cremation. It's part of his culture. I told him it's a possibility, but I don't know yet. Terry's Catholic. I'm Catholic. I don't know if that would be respectful of her wishes."

"What do you want?" Rina asked.

"I want to go to sleep and never wake up again."

Decker said, "Maybe you should give me the gun back."

Donatti said, "I have more than thirty pistols, semiautomatics, rifles, and shotguns in a safe in my bedroom. One Glock is not going to make a difference if I wanted to blow my brains out." A pause. "I'll see you in the morning. You want lights off?"

"Please," Rina said. Once shrouded in darkness, she said, "I guess I'd better get to it tomorrow. I'll start calling around to funeral homes."

"What do you need from me?"

"I can do everything," Rina said. "I'll get the arrangements, get the flowers, make the calls to everyone including Devek, find a cemetery plot, and organize the entire affair. What you can do is take care of Chris. Make sure he doesn't do anything dumb—at least until after the funeral."

"I think I have the harder part," Decker said.

Rina said, "I do not envy you at all."

AFTER THE FUNERAL, after the speeches and the tears and the pomp, the crowd gathered for the wake, held in the lounge because so many people had shown up. Besides all the women and men who turned out for the boss, there was the Decker clan, who came in support of Gabe. Devek came to say his good-byes and to pick up his children. Terry's half sister, Melissa, was there, as dazed and confused as the rest of the crowd. She was now thirty-five, and it was the first time she had ever met her niece, Juleen, and her nephew Sanjay.

Wakes were not the solemn shivas of Rina's culture. Wakes were parties, celebrations of the lives of those who had passed. And Rina made sure that this was a grand one. She had ordered trays upon trays of foods from all cultures, she had stocked the bars with the best brands of spirits, and she had decorated the lounge with pictures of Terry from all parts of her life, from childhood to her recent wedding with Donatti. It included not only dozens of snapshots of Chris and her but also photographs of her with her children, even a few of her and Devek, at Chris's behest. He wanted everyone who had been involved in her life to be represented.

As Rina observed the crowds, she saw that Chris was in his element. The popular kid. He was talking, smiling, eating, and drinking, probably more drink than what was wise. His employees gathered around him, never leaving him alone for a minute. They were his paid admirers, but they seemed genuinely concerned for their boss. Some of the women were even crying. Every so often, Chris would find Gabe and pull him to his side, looping his arm around his son's shoulders and squeezing his neck. Then just as quickly, he'd drop his arm to his side, a sign that Gabe should beg off and return to the shelter of his fiancée and his foster family.

Rina kept a watchful eye, making sure that things ran smoothly. Gabe came up to her and introduced his aunt, Melissa. The woman had short blond hair and was stick thin. Devek came up to Rina, his children in tow, and introduced himself as Dr. Sharma. His height was around five eight, and he had dark skin, dark brown eyes, and straight black hair. His build was stocky. Terry had married two men whose physical appearances couldn't have been any more opposite. The children looked stunned. The boy clutched his father's hand, looking down at the floor and then at the crowds. Juleen seemed more remote—in her own world without a thought to her surroundings. Both of them were dry-eyed.

As the time crept on, women began to come up to Rina, thanking her for the wake. They had tears in their eyes. They had known Terry. She was great—funny, friendly, and not at all snobby. Most important, she was a good influence on the boss. She seemed to calm him down.

The hours dragged on and the hours raced by at the same time. That was how it was with funerals. Everything was crystal clear, but at the same time, everything was a blur. The wake kept going and going and going. The one good thing about the entire evening was that Rina got a chance to see the kids before she and Decker headed off to Israel for six months. Cindy and Koby were there but without the boys. Sammy and Hannah had also come without their respective families. Jacob had come with Ilana, who spent most of her time talking to Yasmine, trying to figure out what to do with the upcoming wedding now that Gabe's mother was gone.

Things finally started to taper off around five, and by six in the evening, the immediate family had retired to Chris's office. Donatti had chartered several planes to take everyone back: one bigger jet for the New Yorkers, and a separate one to take Cindy and Koby back to Philadelphia.

When it was time to say good-bye, Juleen cracked. She broke into sobs. She looked plaintively at Chris and said, "Why can't I stay here?"

Devek bristled. "Juleen, don't be ridiculous. You can't stay at a place like this. Furthermore, you're my daughter, not his."

"I don't want to go back to Mumbai. I don't like it there."

"Well, you have no choice."

She looked at Gabe. "Why can't I stay with you?"

Devek said, "Because you can't!"

"She can stay with me," Gabe insisted. "I'm her brother."

"But I'm her father!" Devek was getting angry. "You're going home, Juleen. No more nonsense."

"Why can't I stay with Chris?" Juleen said. "He's my stepfather."

"He doesn't want you here!"

Donatti said, "Don't tell her that!"

"Then you tell her!" Devek said.

"Don't you dare mouth off to me," Donatti shot back. "Not after what I've done for you. You owe me."

"You did it for her," Devek said.

"Of course I did it for *her*," Donatti said. "But Sanjay and you benefited. Just mind your manners, or Sanjay and I are going to have a long talk one day about what his father did and didn't do for him when he was taken for ransom."

Devek turned quiet. Then he said, "Sorry, Chris."

"It's been a long day. S'right." Donatti went over to Juleen and knelt down to her so they were eye level. "Your father is right. You can't stay here, Juleen. You know that."

"You're my stepfather."

"I am," Chris told her. "But he's your father. And you do what he says. You work hard, you study hard, you practice hard, and you can be anything you want to be. Make your mom proud, okay?"

"I don't want to go to Mumbai," she wailed. "I hate it there, Father. You're never home. I don't like Uncle Pramod. I don't have Mommy to take care of me. I don't want an ayah or a nanny. I want to stay here in the United States. That's what Mommy wanted."

"Well, Mommy's not here," Devek snapped back. "What's wrong with Pramod?"

"He's creepy!"

"Don't talk that way!" Devek said. "Pramod has been very good to us."

"I hate him. I don't want to go back! I want to stay here."

Devek lost his temper. "Juleen, no one here will take care of you."

"I just said she can live with me!" Gabe said.

Devek turned to him. "And that's okay with your girlfriend? That she tends to an eleven-year-old when you're away on your tours all over the world?"

"I can do it," Yasmine said. "It's no problem."

"Devek is right," Donatti said. "Gabriel, you're never home, and Yasmine is in medical school. How are you going to take care of her?"

Melissa said, "She can come live with me. I am her aunt."

Gabe said, "I love you, Melissa, but your lifestyle isn't child-centered."

Melissa started to cry. "I can change."

Gabe put his arms around his aunt. "Mom wouldn't want you to change. She loved you just the way you are."

"I'll take her," Cindy said. Then she looked at Devek. "I'm not trying to undermine your authority, Doctor, but I'm married to a physician. You boys do great work—and I'm sure you try your best—but physicians are busy people." She turned to Koby. "True?"

"You're busy as well," Koby said. "But you are home more than I am."

Cindy paused. "There are two of us, Devek. You're only one man."

"This is ridiculous," Devek muttered. "She is my daughter, and you're not her mother."

"You're right," Cindy said. "I'm not her mother, I never will be her mother, but I am a stable female with children around the same age. And Gabe is part of my family, so she's family as well. Even if it's just for a few months, just until Juleen can absorb the enormity of what happened, I'm happy to help. You need to settle back into your own life, Devek. You need time to think. Why don't you let Juleen stay with Koby and me for . . . maybe six months, and then you'll reevaluate?"

"I'll help out," Gabe said.

"I know you will, but this takes the responsibility off your shoulders." Cindy turned to Juleen. "I guess we should ask what you want."

"I would like to stay with you, Cindy, if it's no bother."

"Bother?" Cindy laughed. "You and Sanjay are the quietest kids I've ever met. You did nothing but read, which is great. Could you rub some of that diligence off on my sons? And maybe they can rub some of their boisterousness off on you."

With tear-stained cheeks, Juleen managed a small smile.

Sanjay said, "I want to go home with Father."

Juleen said, "I know, Sanjay. And he wants you to go home with him. But I want to stay here."

Devek was furious. "You don't even know what it's like to live here."

"Maybe I don't, Father, but let me try. I'm smarter than you think."

"Smart isn't the issue." He shook his head. "Who's going to pay for your support, Juleen?"

Donatti said, "I can do that." He turned to Cindy. "Whatever she needs."

"Thank you," Cindy said.

"I didn't agree to anything," Devek said.

"Yeah, but you will," Donatti retorted. "I'm not a great father, Dev, but neither are you. We're very different. But we're men and in one way we're similar. If I'd been a better husband, Terry would have never left me. And ditto for you. If Juleen wants to stay here in the United States, let her do it. Don't fight her. She'll resent you for the rest of your life."

Devek said, "Like you know so much about human nature."

Donatti sighed. "Obviously I don't, or Terry would still be alive."

Devek said nothing.

Juleen walked over and took her father's hands in hers. She talked through tears. "Please, Father. I will write every day. I will call you every day. I will work hard, and I will make you proud of me. Please, can I stay here for a while? I promise I'll be good."

"You don't have to promise to be good." Devek's eyes filled with tears. "You are good. You are actually *too* good." He wiped his eyes. "To stay here. Is this what you really, really want?"

"Yes, it is, Father." Tears falling from her eyes. "Please?"

Devek threw up his hands. He waved her off and looked away. The girl went over to Cindy and Koby. "I promise I won't be a bother."

Cindy mussed up her hair. "We've already had this conversation."

"The cars just arrived to take everyone to the airstrip." Donatti surveyed the crowd. "I'm going into my office and I don't want to be disturbed. So please leave. All of you."

Gabe said, "I'm staying, Dad."

Donatti walked over to his son and placed his hands on Gabe's shoulders. "Go back with Yasmine. You belong with your fiancée. That's what I want."

"I'm not leaving you alone," Gabe said.

"He won't be alone," Decker said. "I'm staying for at least another day. The police need further statements, and I want to be sure that it's all done correctly."

"There you go," Donatti said. "The old man will be with me. He's been dogging my ass for the last twenty-six years. Why should he stop now?"

Gabe's eyes filled with tears. "I could have been nicer to her, you know."

"You forgave her long before I did. She loved you very much."

"I don't want to leave you alone, Dad."

Donatti hugged him. "I loved your mother, but I lived eleven years without her. I was fine then. I'll be fine now. Go home. We both need a little quiet right now. We'll talk later in the week, okay?"

Reluctantly, Gabe nodded. "Okay."

Donatti tapped his son's cheek. He turned to Yasmine. "Take care of him. Without you women, we men would wind up eating each other."

"I'll look after him," she said. "God knows he's looked after me." She kissed Donatti's cheek. "Thank you, Chris."

Donatti opened the door to the office and sally port. It took around ten minutes of tearful good-byes, but he finally managed to get everyone into the cars and off to the airstrip. After the limos had left, he led Decker back into his office. He stood against the wall and looked up at the ceiling. "I'm the walking dead."

"Go sleep," Decker said. "I'm fine."

"I forgot to thank Rina," Donatti said. "She did a terrific job. If she ever wants a job as my assistant—"

"Over my dead body," Decker said.

"That just might happen sooner than you think."

"I'll watch my back," Decker said.

Donatti blew out air. He felt like an old man. He said, "Wait here for a minute." He disappeared into his office.

"Where would I go?" Decker said out loud.

No answer. A moment later, Donatti reappeared with an envelope. "This came today . . . before the funeral. I couldn't deal with it." He handed it to Decker. "Let me know what it says."

Decker looked at the envelope.

It was from a DNA lab.

It had been three days since Terry had passed. Enough time to do a comprehensive paternity test even on a fetus. He slit open the flap with his finger. He skimmed the results and gave the letter back to Donatti.

Chris took the letter with shaking hands. He read the report. If he had had any doubts, they were now torn to shreds. Which only made him feel worse. Anger was easier than heartache. The fetus had been nine weeks of age. He thought backward. Right around the time they first had sex. Did it happen with the quickie in the shower? Was it when he raped her? Maybe it was later on, when she came to him that night, while he was working, to thank him for his help and they made love for real. Sweet, sweet love. He decided that was the time. When they had joined as one in total harmony and bliss. He reread the contents. "It was a girl." A pause. "Why didn't this happen years ago? *Why now?*" A shake of the head. "God is one sick bastard."

Decker laid a hand on Chris's shoulder. "I am so sorry."

Donatti didn't respond. He put the letter in his pocket. Then he took out a vial of medicine. "Sleeping pills. You want one?"

"I'm okay." Decker paused, then said, "You shouldn't be taking meds, Donatti. You drank a lot."

"That was nothing. Right now, you'd need an elephant tranquilizer to knock me out." Donatti shook out two tablets and swallowed them dry. "These should kick in within a couple of hours. I'm going upstairs to sleep . . . to Gabe's room. I just can't . . . There's still too much of her in my bedroom."

"You can use the bedroom down here," Decker said.

"No. Gabe's room is comfortable. I'll be fine." He pointed to the office bedroom. "You should sleep there. It's way more comfortable than a couch."

"I may take you up on it."

"There's coffee and juice here. Will that hold you until I wake up?"

"As long as I can get to the police station by two."

"I'll be up before then." Donatti paused. "How's she doing? Talia."

"She's behind bars. I want to keep her that way."

He exhaled. "You know . . . it pains me to say this . . . but . . . if I was in her position, I would have done exactly the same thing."

"She's a nasty one," Decker said.

Donatti said, "She learned from the best."

CHAPTER 34

THEY TOUCHED DOWN at Ben Gurion Airport at two in the afternoon. By four-thirty, they had dragged four suitcases and two carry-ons up three flights of stairs. The sun was low in the sky, and they were exhausted. The last thing they wanted to do was unpack, but since this apartment was going to be their home in Israel for the next several months, they figured they should settle in. Decker had a slew of appointments with craftsmen and building supply companies next week, and he couldn't wait to start the remodeling. The weather had turned cool, and the days were shorter. The progression of the seasons never stopped.

He put the key into the lock and turned the bolt. He flicked on the lights.

The apartment was stone gorgeous. Two stories with high ceilings and marble floors. It was open plan with a front terrace that spanned the length of the living space. Since the unit was on the fourth floor, there was a view of beautiful old stone buildings to the north and a hint of city center. Electric lights were beginning to twinkle as the sun dipped below the horizon. The entire experience was magical.

Rina said, "Not bad, huh?"

"How did you *find* this?"

"I told you it belongs to one of my best friends, Rosie, and her husband, Ben. He went to yeshiva with Yitzchak. We haven't seen each other in decades, but we've always kept in touch. Rosie was delighted that we bought in Jerusalem. Lovely people. They won't be here until Pesach, so we've got around five months before we have to vacate."

"I don't know about that, Rina." Decker looked around. The furnishings were posh, the carpets were brilliant in color and texture, and the artwork was fabulous. "Squatter's rights."

She smiled. "I could get used to this."

Decker dragged the suitcases into the bedroom, which was actually a suite. "My goodness. We each have our own bathroom and closet!"

Rina joined him. The bedroom had hardwood floors, a king-size bed, and a big desk situated under a stone arched window. All the windows in the bedroom were arched. "This is palatial."

Decker said, "What's this costing again?"

"They're giving it to us at cost—utilities and maintenance. I'm going to hire a cleaning service once a week. I want to return this in pristine condition."

"I would say so. What does he do to be able to afford this?"

"Hedge fund."

"Ah." He walked back out to the living space and opened the double doors to the terrace. He stepped out and tightened his jacket. He looked east. "Good Lord. There's a view of the Old City!"

Rina joined him. She had taken off her coat and was shivering. Decker held her in his arms, and together they regarded the crenellations of the Old City's walls. Inside the stone confines was the mount where the holy temple had once stood. The rock barriers were lit from below, casting shades in yellows and gold. "Wow, that's beautiful." Tears formed in her eyes.

Decker took off his jacket and laid it over her shoulders. "So here we are."

"And I couldn't be happier," Rina said. "We need a little breathing room after all that's happened."

"I'll say."

"Think he'll be okay? Our boy?"

"Gabe?" Decker said. "It won't be easy, but he does have our family's support and Yasmine has a big family as well. I think they'll both be busy planning the wedding for this upcoming summer."

"It'll be hard for him," Rina said.

"It will be. He hadn't much contact with Terry in the past eleven years, but she was still his mother. It'll be painful. But lucky for Gabe that he's used to having another wonderful mother in his life."

"It's not the same." Rina sighed. "But I do my best." A pause. "What about Chris?"

"He's a survivor," Decker said. "He'll be fine."

"He did love her."

"He did . . . Whatever that means to a guy like Donatti."

"Do you think he's capable of love?"

"In his capacity, yes. But I think his ability to self-preserve is much stronger."

"I hope you're right." Rina looked around, breathing in the fresh, crisp air of Jerusalem. She smiled. "Should we unpack?"

"It's so gorgeous out here. Let's wait a little bit longer."

"You're right," Rina said. "We'll start our new adventure by living in the moment."

"Darling, that's all we've got."

THE ANNUAL HALLOWEEN Spectacle was canceled this year, as was his birthday party. When Thanksgiving came, there wasn't much to be grateful for. But as November led to December and the holidays, Donatti felt . . . well, he felt okay. He hired on a new assistant—a man named James who'd been working at the place for two years. He was bisexual, which made him useful, but it turned out that he was even better behind a desk than in the rooms. James was efficient, had a great organizational mind, and got along well with both men and women. He did everything from brewing coffee to executing the payroll. Donatti wondered why it took him so long to find someone who was pleasant and friendly but professional.

Gabe flew in for his annual Christmas bash, which took their minds off the elephant in the room. Since his son was his only living relative, Donatti finally put him into the system, gave him all the keys to the locks and the code numbers to his vault. Gabe was reluctant, but Donatti insisted. After his son left, Donatti didn't have much time to mope because the New Year's all-night rave needed to be planned. And there were also slews of new girls to hire on.

Since Donatti hadn't been with a woman except his late wife in the last five months, he forgot how exciting it was to have sex with different people. Some were good, some not so much, but the novelty was uplifting and pushed him back into a routine. He was no longer a "I/we/you" or even an "I/we." He was just an "I," and he enjoyed getting his kingdom back. The sole monarch. No one else to please, no one else to consider, just him and whatever he wanted.

January came and went, usually a slow time for business as everyone was winding down from the festivities of December. February was cold and cruel, but business began to resurge as word went out for his post–Valentine's Day party. While the actual date was reserved for the wives and girlfriends, the postdate was reserved for the real fun. After that came the St. Pat's gastropub extravaganza. Then it was quiet until after Easter. He took advantage of the lull to do what he needed to do but dreaded doing.

He hadn't slept in his bed since she died. But he was ready to take his room back, to rid himself of the last painful reminders and move on.

First on the list was getting rid of the gym equipment he had bought for her. He took it into the hallway and told the movers to take it to the gym used by his workers. Next, he took a big empty box and filled it with the decorative pillows and blankets she had purchased to soften the room. After he was done with that, he went to the vault and took out all his drawings and sketches of her. Dry-eyed, he sorted through them one by one. The ones that she had posed for when she was sixteen, clothed and naked, hunched over and protected. The ones he had done when he had tied her to his bed. Staring at them, he reached for the recent ones that he had sketched around six months ago. With his finger, he traced the out-line of her body and then her face.

With an exhale, he dumped them into the box with the pillows and blankets. He'd store them for another time, when he could remember without so much pain. On to the last and hardest chore. From the upper cabinet of his closet, he took down a large duf-fel. First, he took the framed portrait he had done off the wall and placed it on the bottom of the bag. Then he threw her clothes on the bed and began to fold them neatly.

Here was the black dress he had given her when they went to the lounge to meet Mike Badger and company. Her body had been smoking hot, but her face was still bruised. He had done her makeup to soften the impact of the beating she had taken. She had cried tears of joy when she saw how beautiful she looked, had kissed him like she meant it.

Here was the black dress she had worn for his Labor Day party, when he had raped her and sodomized her in one of the brothel rooms. He knew it was an idiotic thing to do, but he couldn't stop himself. She was so gorgeous—a magnet for the men at the affair—and he was burning with lust and jealousy. Afterward, when they went back to the bedroom, he was drunk and said horrible things to her. Still, she had helped him through his DTs, but not without looking at him with contempt. She felt sorry for him, but equally she despised him. It killed him, almost as bad as when she turned down his advances. All he wanted was to make up, but he wouldn't apologize. Not that she would have forgiven him right away. That kind of sadistic thing wasn't immediately forgivable.

Here was the red dress he'd bought for her for his end-of-summer party in his office. It took a while, but finally, she did forgive him. The makeup sex was mind-blowing. He was so turned on and in love with her, his body filled with coursing hormones and phero-mones. He had wanted to *consume* her.

Here was the cream-colored Chanel suit that she had worn for their wedding ceremony. She had bought the outfit with Guy's wife while he and his ex-brother-in-law had done business that had taken up the entire afternoon. Then the four of them had gone out for din-ner and a show. By the time Terry and he had returned to the hotel suite, it was after eleven. She was tired, but he was wired. She had taken one look at his face and had asked him what he wanted.

He had taken her outside onto the balcony. And when she ob-jected because the terrace light was on and there was no switch to turn it off, he had taken out his gun and pistol-whipped the fixture. Glass flew everywhere. In the dark, he brought her to her knees. He stood and gripped the balcony railing, staring out at the lights of the strip while she brought him to climax. She had cut her knees while doing it—not badly, but enough to warrant a few bandages. He didn't like her in serious pain, but the scratches she had sustained for him were kind of sexy.

Afterward, he said it was her turn. Whatever she wanted.

"Why does it have to be you and then me?" She placed a bandage over a cut on her knee. Her voice wasn't hostile, just curious. "Why can't it be a we? Why can't we compromise?"

"Sometimes we compromise," he had told her. "Sometimes it's a we. But I find it better if it's a me and then you, because each one of us gets exactly what we want." He looked at her. "There's a twenty-four-hour pawnshop a couple of blocks away. It's huge and has nice stuff. Let's get you some bling to wear for the ceremony tomorrow."

She was tired, but she agreed to go. The emporium was brightly lit and surprisingly busy even at midnight. The jewelry section was enormous. There were dozens upon dozens of diamond necklaces, bracelets, earrings—not the crown jewels, but good quality. She looked into the glass cases, and each time he suggested a piece, she shook her head. Finally, she announced that she didn't want jewelry. Instead, she pointed to his wrist and said, "But I'll take something like that."

Meaning his Rolex.

He raised his eyebrows. Then he laughed. He wound up getting her a pre-owned, certified Tourneau Rolex Lady-Datejust automatic in yellow gold with diamond numbers. It set him back around twenty grand, which was cheap compared with his eighteen-karat gold, black-face Sky-Dweller, but it still qualified as the most expensive blow job he had ever received.

Into the duffel went the Chanel suit, along with her heels, shoes, ordinary street clothes, toothbrush, hairbrush, hair dryer, makeup, perfume, and any other sundry items. He worked until the closet, dresser, and bathroom had been purged of her belongings. Then it was the home stretch.

Her nightstand.

On the top were around two dozen paperbacks, books that she had read to pass the time when she had been alone. They went into the garbage. Below were two drawers. In the top, she had kept her panties and bras. He thought about keeping a set, but decided that it would be a little weird. Not that he minded being pervy, but it was better to make a clean break. He started folding the underwear, then decided to dump it all into the garbage. Underneath all that cotton and lace were several jewelry boxes, including one with the diamond necklace he had given her. She had never worn it. Still, she had accepted it as combat pay for being raped and sodomized.

Donatti fished it from the drawer and opened the hinged top. Talia had picked it out. The woman had good taste. Then he reached in his pocket and took out Terry's engagement ring—also picked out by his former assistant. He had buried Terry with her wedding band, but for some reason he had wanted to keep the diamond ring. No more. He put the ring inside the necklace box, shut the lid, and threw it in the duffel.

The watch box contained her Rolex, her diamond studs that she adored, the pearl earrings that he had bought her when she was sixteen, and his mother's cross. Each piece was a slice of his life. But instead of dwelling on the past, he shooed the memories from his mind. He stared at the cross, then he took it out and put it around his neck. Some of the girls saw Terry wearing it at the end-of-summer party. They'd like that he kept it as a memento of her, wearing it like he wore his wedding ring. It made him a sympathetic figure. And when the ladies felt sorry for him, they worked harder. He closed the watch box with the Rolex and the two sets of earrings and dumped it into the duffel. He was almost there, just the bottom nightstand drawer left.

He opened it up.

It was empty except for one item stuffed inside: a jumbled mess of fabric.

It was her Manson girl dress.

Suddenly, he felt faint. Panting, he sat on his bed, and when he finally caught his breath, he took it out and unfolded it. It was now a single piece of cloth, since he had split it down an entire seam. He had ripped it the morning before he left for India. He had felt as mean as a hornet and had wanted her in an unhealthy way. Because of her, he was doing something dangerous. Because of her, he had forked over millions of dollars to redeem two people he didn't give a shit about. And what was his thanks? She had chosen to live in Las Vegas instead of Reno, putting her children's needs ahead of what he had wanted. Man, he was pissed. He wanted to hurt her in every way.

She complied, dropping to all fours without a whimper as he tore the dress off her body. But seeing her bent over, the bones of her spine sticking up through the thin skin of her back, and realizing what she had gone through in her life, knowing that he had been a big part of her misery, he felt his insides melt.

He took the dress, brought it to his nose, and inhaled deeply. She hadn't washed it. It still smelled of her. It smelled of her perfume, her sweat, and their sex. It evoked a thousand images and a longing so deep and wide that he felt eviscerated—a gutted fish.

This wasn't an interim.

She wasn't ever coming back.

He held the dress to his cheek and collapsed backward onto the newly laundered bedding, staring at the ceiling, eyes wide and wet, his heart racing and broken. He didn't move for a good while. Then, swallowing back lumps in his throat, he got up from the bed. He threw the duffel back into his closet, but took the dress downstairs to his office, folding it neatly and putting it in the drawer with his heroin kit.

Things you love but can't have.

But as time crawled by, the rip in his heart grew bigger and bigger, until it turned into a gaping hole. And at that point, he knew he needed help. He'd take out the dress every day and smell it. And when he did that, he took out his kit. A small shot in his veins and he'd sit back, clutching her dress and letting the warmth wash over him.

He could see her face.

He could feel her touch.

He could hear her sexy, throaty voice.

Her breath on his neck . . . she would talk to him.

You wouldn't like it here, baby. It's all souls and no bodies. There's no sex.

He'd smile and tell her, *Where I'm going, there's going to be lots of ass fucking by little red men with horns. Your ultimate revenge, angel.*

Then he'd hear her laugh. And he'd laugh too.

Her last words to him played over and over in his head.

I love you, Christopher.

Whispering back, *I love you, too, Teresa. Forever and ever, baby doll. For all eternity.*

And then nothing.

Time passed and the days grew longer and warmer. He realized that her aromas were fading from the material, until one day, all he could detect was the faint odor of old cloth. And on that day, he knew there was nothing left.

Sitting at his office desk, he took out his kit, warming the usual dose of powder with an extra couple of doses thrown in for good measure. He took out the rubber hose and made a tourniquet on his arm. He took the syringe and sucked up the liquid.

He paused.

He took off the tourniquet and pulled a piece of paper and a pen from his desk drawer.

He wrote:

Call up Mike Badger.

He neatly wrote down the phone number, then two high eight-digit figures.

The place is worth the top amount. If you can get the bottom amount, you gave him a good deal. Anything less is highway robbery.

He paused. Then he wrote:

There's a duffel of Mom's things in my bedroom closet. It includes her personal items and some valuable jewelry. Please give it to

Juleen when she turns eighteen. I expect you to support her in whatever way she needs. She's a good kid. Also, you take care of Peter and Rina. They stepped in when your mom and I failed you. They became the parents that you should have had all along.

He put down the pen.
Another pause.
Then he picked up the pen again.
He wrote:

Mom loved you with every fiber in her body. She was so proud of you. And so was I, although I never said much to your face. Go out there and be the man I never could be.
   Live because that's what Mom would have wanted.
   Live because I don't have the courage to do it anymore.
   Live your best life, Gabriel.
   Live.

He put the pen down, picked up the tourniquet, and wrapped it around his right arm. Then the prick of the needle, fluid in his vein, the warm flush flowing through his body. Just a few more minutes and he'd be there.
   Curtain down.
   House lights dimmed.
   Fade to black.